GUNFIRE LULLABIES

NORE I HOOGSTAD

ISBN: 978-0-6451289-3-2

ABOUT THE AUTHOR

Nore Hoogstad is a former Australian and UN diplomat, political advisor and press secretary to a shadow foreign minister, and communications consultant.

During her diplomatic posting to Jakarta and Dili, Nore covered the fall of Indonesian dictator President Suharto and East Timor's 1999 independence ballot. She also worked for the United Nations Transitional Administration in East Timor (UNTAET) in 2000.

Nore's formal qualifications include a Bachelor of Arts in Asian Studies and Comparative Literature, a Masters Degree in International Relations, as well as book editing and nutrition qualifications. She currently works as a Nutritional Therapist and is writing her second novel. Nore lives by the sea in Sydney with her partner and their fur babies. Her two children are grown up.

https://writingnore.com

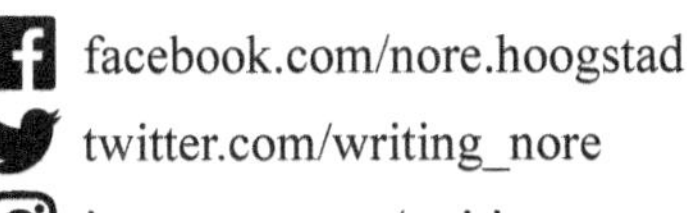

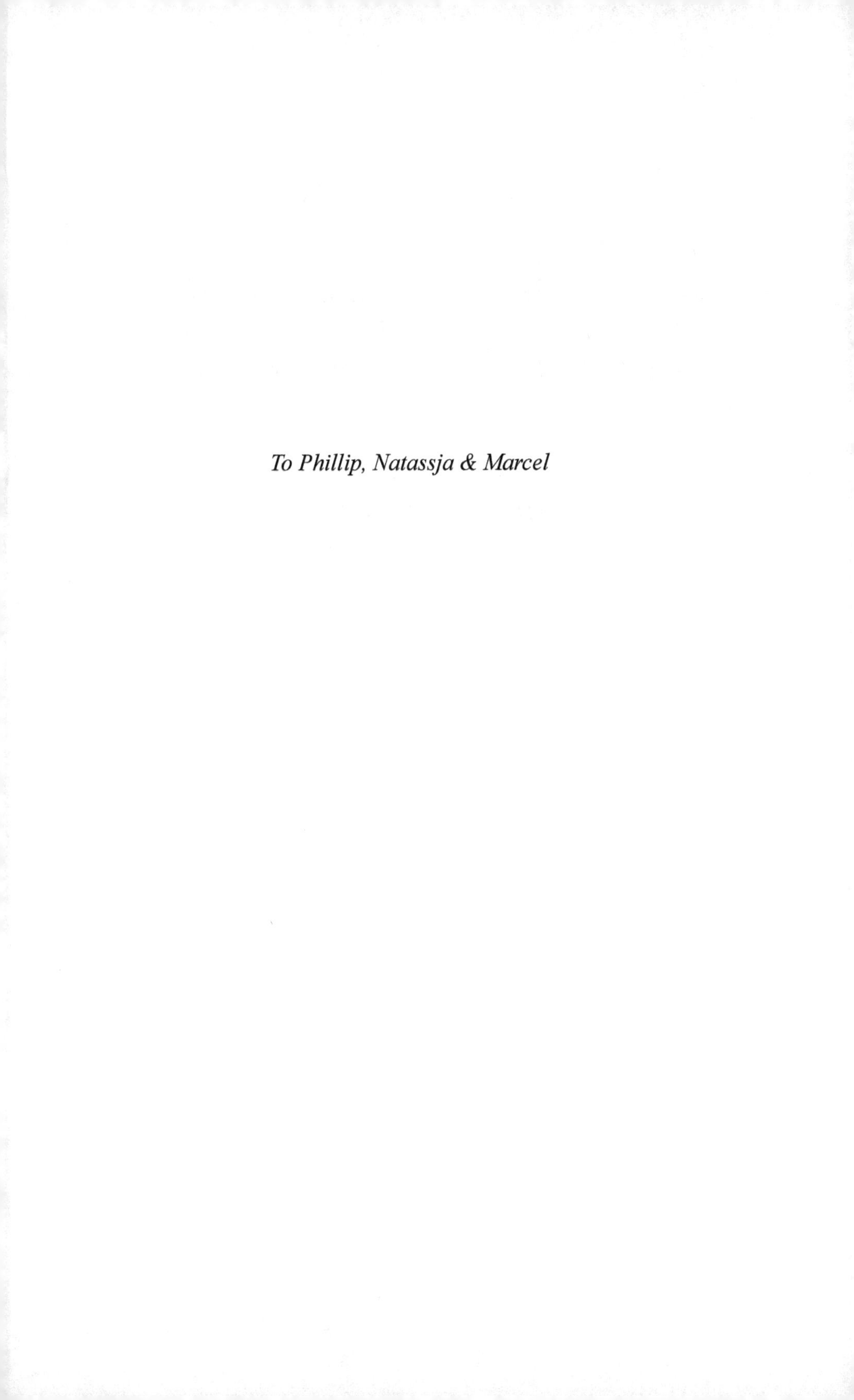

To Phillip, Natassja & Marcel

AUTHOR'S NOTE

In keeping with this story, some of the characters use words, phrases and acronyms in their local languages of Indonesian or Tetun (the local language in East Timor). While most are explained as you read, you will find a glossary at the back of the book.

Please note that the names of the two parts of the Indonesian island of Timor are west Timor (Timor barat in Indonesian) and East Timor (Timor Timur in Indonesian). The term west Timor is not a proper noun (name), but rather a description of the western part of Timor, so it is not capitalised. The western part of Timor is in fact part of the province Nusa Tengarra Timor (NTT). The province of East Timor is now known as the country of Timor Leste.

JAKARTA, INDONESIA, MAY 1998

Ava sat in her Ford Escort, idling in the middle of a near-deserted six-lane highway. She had a decision to make. After working late again she should be at home in bed, but instead was wracking her brain over the commotion a hundred metres ahead. Her long, rust-coloured hair fell across her face. She pushed it back and rubbed her eyes. Sleep hadn't featured much since the Indonesian crisis began two weeks ago. Everything had taken on a surreal hue, a blanket of low-hanging smoke from the smouldering build-ings amplifying the effect. Why hadn't she just driven by? It wasn't in her job description to rescue locals.

She refocused. Two middle-aged Chinese men, naked except for their old-man underpants, cowered on the bitumen, their arms clutched over their balding heads. God, they must have been dragged from their beds. A dozen Indonesians surrounded them, thin men, poor men, clutching long wooden sticks and machetes. The Indonesians closed the circle tighter around the Chinese and prodded their wobbling bellies as though they were dangerous animals. The Indonesians began laughing now, nervous, hungry.

Ava wanted to help the Chinese, but part of her wanted to leave too, to put her car in gear and go back as fast as possible to the nearby embassy.

Many of her colleagues would have done so by now, probably wouldn't have stopped in the first place. She could hear the ambassador's voice: *It's not your damn political crisis. Not your job to rescue foreign nationals.*

But during the last few weeks she'd seen enough to recognise the choices a person made in situations like these revealed their grit. For all her insecurities, she knew right from wrong, and what she could live with or not. It was she, after all, who'd insisted on writing a report to Canberra on the mass rape of Chinese women by government provocateurs. The same men who'd set fire to Chinese businesses, murdering their owners in the process while deflecting the blame for the hardships of the East Asian Economic Crisis away from their corrupt President, Sujati, onto the Chinese.

One of the Chinese men sobbed now as he begged for mercy. Ava wouldn't allow these men to join the toll.

As she ran through her options, smoke choked her lungs and she coughed. How could she help, a thirty-year-old white woman on her first posting, a junior Australian diplomat? She couldn't interfere in local matters any more than an Indonesian diplomat could tell an Australian what to do at home. Their countries were close, if only through the happenstance of geography, but in everyday talk this meant relations were sensitive. All she could hope for was that her presence alone would be enough to stop the Indonesians from harming the Chinese.

But what if it wasn't? What if they turned on her and her diplomatic number plates? She shuddered. Maybe she should leave.

Unease closed in around her. The streets were too empty, the atmosphere too oppressive and the city too silent, even for these fickle times. Sujati barely clung to power and everyone knew the crisis wasn't over. Perhaps that was why Jakarta's eight million residents had gone to ground. Did they fear the president's exit would be like 1965 when he came to power? Ava had seen the pictures of Indonesian rivers running red with the blood of supposed communists. Now the city held its breath— waiting, dreading, remembering.

She dialled up her car's air conditioning and redirected it onto her face. The engine ticked over louder and for the first time the Indonesians looked her way. They threw her warning looks with their fierce eyes. A chill colder than the air conditioning crawled down her arms and legs.

She took out her phone and pressed direct dial.

'Yearp,' said the sleepy voice of Bruce, a Colonel and the embassy's army attaché.

'Sorry to wake you.' She explained what was going on. 'Can you ask your police and army contacts to send someone? They're more likely to listen to you than if I cold-call them.'

'Not so sure about that.'

'Things are about to get nasty. They could be killed. We have to try something.'

Bruce sighed, probably at being appointed her co-conspirator. 'This is all very admirable, Ava, but is this really your job?'

She stayed silent. He knew her well enough to know the answer.

'I'll see what I can do.' As he hung up, Ava thought she heard him mutter the words *bleeding heart*.

She knew he didn't mean it. They'd bonded like soldiers, bearing witness to brutality as she'd followed the students, protesters and rioters in the streets for her updates to Canberra. He'd shown her where to watch protests safely when surrounded by the army and riot police, how to protect yourself when set upon by water cannons, and told her not to rub your eyes but wash them after being bombed with tear-gas. He'd taught her to be calm in the midst of terror.

The Indonesians glanced at her again, cautioning her to stay back. A second wave of goose bumps shimmied across her skin. Still, they hadn't hurt the Chinese men, yet. Time grew slow and heavy.

Out of nowhere a white van sped past and stopped, brakes screeching and rubber burning. Ava jumped. *What now?* Two Indonesian men flew out, the larger one wielding a TV camera on his shoulder and the slight one a long, fuzzy microphone on a stick—most likely freelancers capturing footage to sell to the news agencies. The cameraman thrust his lens into the Indonesian men's faces as the soundman raised his microphone above their heads.

Ava abhorred the media, opportunistic bystanders disguised as purveyors of truth. But perhaps their arrival was a good thing. The presence of their camera might prevent the Indonesians from turning more violent, or at the least buy time for the police or soldiers to arrive. On the other hand, if they were anti-Chinese like many locals, they might whip the men up further for the sake of some juicy footage. She watched, biting a broken nail she hadn't had time to file.

The camera continued to roll, the Chinese men hunched into kneeling balls, the Indonesians looking muddled. Some of them redirected their attention towards the film crew, pushing the journalists away, and waving their sticks and knives in their faces. The cameras loved this and moved in even closer. Manipulators.

But Ava couldn't sit here in her car forever. How long before the men directed their attention towards her? She called Bruce again.

'What did they say?'

'Who?'

Bruce had gone back to sleep. How did defence staff manage to go home early and get eight hours' sleep no matter what?

He cleared the sleep from his throat again. 'Oh, yeah. The police said they'd look into it.'

Ava hesitated. They both knew the police rarely took action. It was the army who maintained order here. 'Did you call the army?'

'I'll do it now.'

'Thanks,' she said, this time hanging up first.

Her car began to shake and a loud rumble fragmented the atmosphere as though heralding a violent storm. Ava spun her head around, her hazel eyes widening as she saw a column of a dozen army tanks—APCs according to Bruce—hurtling towards them. She'd seen them during the political crisis, cavalcades rushing up and down the main roads, tossing cars and people aside as they went from one trouble spot to another, and leaving trails of symmetrically churned bitumen and chaos behind them as though they were ploughing the fallow streets for a new future. But on a highway at midnight—Ava in her tiny car, the men now standing agog, the Chinese daring to hope and the journalists filming it all—the tanks loomed over them like apocalyptic locusts. What crisis were they heading to now?

Ava gasped. She couldn't move her car closer to the men, neither could she drive towards the APCs or outrun them. It'd be safer to stay in place. She put her hands over her ears as the tanks coursed around her.

In a few moments they were gone, her heart pounding loudly in the cavernous silence they left behind.

She checked the Chinese men one last time. 'There's nothing more I can do', she mumbled and took off. But rather than drive home, she headed back in the direction of the embassy. Her boss said she could stay in a nearby hotel if she ever felt overly tired or it was too dangerous to drive. She'd order a meal, not the cans of cold baked beans, instant noodles and bananas she'd been surviving on, but a thick steak with buttery mashed potatoes and plenty of steamed greens. She'd have a hot bath too, if she could stay awake long enough, and sleep for at least seven hours. A deep weariness swept over her, and she strained for air. She must get to the hotel.

Driving along the smoggy vacant roads, she fretted over the APCs. Why were there so many and where were they heading with such purpose? The palace was nearby, as was Sujati's home. A coup? A third forewarning of goose bumps crept across her skin. Perhaps it was '65 all over again. She grimaced at the thought of more killing.

Last night she'd gone home, which was empty apart from her security guard and live-in cook who stayed out the back. Her husband and nine-year-old daughter had been evacuated over a week ago along with some embassy staff, their families and thousands of expat Australians. She hadn't been allowed to leave. *You're essential staff*, her boss had told her. She'd felt too wired to sleep and had locked the doors and gates for privacy, stripped off and plunged into her pool, returning underwater laps until her lungs almost burst. It was peaceful down there, silent and free of the acrid smoke. The soft, amniotic water drew away her exhaustion and the scenes of human depravity receded from her mind—student protesters lying lifeless on the road while the soldiers who'd shot them stepped over their bodies like they were rubbish; the greedy faces of the looters carrying white goods on their backs; the terrified Chinese huddled together in corners; and the blazing buildings that spread to entire streets and suburbs so that Jakarta might soon be surrounded by a wall of flames. All as Sujati's soldiers stood by and did nothing.

The hotel's entrance neared, and Ava drove past military guards who noted her diplomatic number plates and allowed her through to reception. The army protected tourist interests but not those of the Chinese—perhaps the hotel owners had paid them larger bribes. A valet in full uniform stood waiting. Surprised this service was available, Ava handed him her car keys along with a tip. She reached for the giant glass door but an elfish, white-gloved porter beat her to it, smiling widely. Ava smiled back, before lowering her head courteously so as not to appear too much taller, even though she was.

The serene, majestic grey marble lobby seemed even more incongruous than usual against the ruins outside. It reeked of opulence with giant sparkling chandeliers, oversized stone carvings of stylised animals and a solid wood reception desk spanning six metres. She passed a small gamelan orchestra playing sweet haunting music and inhaled the luscious scent of frangipanis from the cornucopia of flower arrangements. Everything about this place was excessive, which made her feel bad, yet she relished the reprieve.

It was nearly midnight by the time she'd checked in and stood waiting for the elevator to arrive.

Her mobile rang. One of her student contacts. She clenched her jaw. *Surely not.* Perhaps she should ignore the call, but there must be a good reason for him to phone her this late.

'Iwan, *ada apa*?' she said, asking him what was happening.

'*Ibu* Ava,' he replied and took a deep breath. 'There's a rumour going around that Sujati's going to resign tomorrow morning and that Vice President Hidayat's going to be sworn in. Have you heard anything?'

'*Belum*,' she replied. Not yet.

She loved that word and what it represented. In Indonesia, things were viewed in infinite shades of grey, anything was possible even if in a roundabout way, and equally nothing was necessarily possible either. The word *no* sounded too coarse, too absolute and limiting. Replying *not yet* also came in handy when you wanted to cover up a mistake or an embarrassment, as she hoped to do now. How was it she hadn't heard the rumour yet? She remembered the APCs and rebuked herself.

'I'll make some calls and get back to you,' she replied, pushing away thoughts of food and sleep.

'*Bu* Ava,' Iwan said before she could hang up. 'We Catholics are concerned. Hidayat is more of a fundamentalist Muslim than Sujati. We don't know how this will play out for us.'

'I understand,' she said, and she did. She'd met the eccentric Hidayat more than once. While he was no fundamentalist, he had a vision of Islam transforming Indonesia into a great modern nation. But others with extreme views might take advantage.

'We have a proud tradition of secular government,' he continued 'but the separation between government and religion could erode if the extremists gain power. They'll oust non-Muslims from positions of power and violence against the Christians and Catholics will grow.'

'I'll get back to you,' Ava said.

She woke her boss, Donald, and filled him in on the night's events.

'Get back to the embassy and start phoning around,' he said. 'The Ambassador or I will be in soon.'

Ava's stomach rumbled as she strode back towards the front door where the nice porter ushered her back into the madness that was her beloved, exasperating Jakarta.

2

JAKARTA, FIVE MINUTES LATER

Ava arrived at the embassy, a plain stand-alone brick building that didn't look old but wasn't modern either. From her fourth-floor office, she looked down on the embassy's fence. The spiky green metal bars that surrounded her reminded her of an oversized bamboo jail like the ones the Viet Cong built to hold prisoners. But its main purpose was just the opposite—to keep East Timorese asylum seekers out. A year ago, a group of them had attempted to scale the much lower wall to draw Australia's attention to their independence struggle, an issue that had festered some twenty-three years since Indonesia's invasion of East Timor in 1975.

She sat down and pulled her tattered contact list from her handbag. The photo on her desk of her daughter, Juliette, caught her eye. It was one of those awkward school pictures and Juliette looked defiant, which made Ava smile. Yet it made her sad too that her husband, Pete, was missing from her small gallery. Their marriage had been shaky for a while. Jakarta would make or break them.

Struggling to read the names and phone numbers she'd scrawled on her list, Ava put her glasses on, lifted her long legs and placed her feet on her desk, a luxury she took when she worked late alone. These days she usually wore pants and flat shoes, having learnt the hard way she might find herself on the streets at any time and need to run from danger. Her office was nothing special with its corporate blue carpet, grey inbuilt desk and safe for secret papers. But having an office to herself after the open space desks in Canberra made her feel legitimate, as though she wasn't playing at being a diplomat any more.

Finding the confidence to apply to join the Department of Foreign Affairs and Trade or DFAT had been a huge challenge, not to mention competing against thousands of graduate applicants. In a fit of teenage nihilism she'd pulled out of high school halfway through her final year, trying a multitude of careers but struggling to find her calling. It took her six years to complete school and get a degree in Asian Studies, driven in the end by a belief that a job with travel was her only way to a better life. And here she was a few years later, on her first posting, successfully blooded by the greatest Indonesian crisis since 1965, making her the envy of her DFAT colleagues who craved the spotlight.

She lowered her legs and ran her finger across her jumbled list of phone numbers. Who to contact first? Journalists working for the Australian media. She punched in Denise's phone number, a friend from the *Sydney Morning Herald*. It rang out.

'Argh!' she growled. How could Denise ignore her phone at such a critical time?

She tried another friend, Sharon, from the *Australian Associated Press*. Again, no answer. Maybe Ian from *The Australian*?

'Yes,' he said. 'I heard the same rumour.'

'Did you see any military or police activity tonight?' Ava asked.

'No.'

'What about tanks?'

'All I saw was lots of ministers' cars parked outside the palace.'

'Interesting. Thanks.'

She moved on to Australians working for other news agencies. The *Reuters* correspondent's phone was off. After four years in Indonesia, he was counting the days before leaving. She was about to call another contact when she heard a noise outside her office door. She sat tall in her chair and the receiver slipped from her hand, clattering noisily onto her desk.

Quentin James, the Australian Ambassador to Indonesia, placed his hand on the door jam and leaned into her office. Ava grimaced, though it was ridiculous that at her age and almost a year into her posting she should feel this awkward around him when she was normally graceful and calm. His stern expression emphasised his chiselled jaw and high cheekbones. Many women found him attractive in that distinguished, grey-haired, fifty-five-year-old man way.

'So, what have you got?' he said in his deepest voice, half scowling.

Ava placed the phone receiver back wondering why her immediate boss, the gawky but harmless Donald, hadn't turned up. The matter must have been too senior.

She filtered her response to remove emotion and character—diplomatic speak. 'One of the Australian correspondents also heard the rumour about Sujati resigning. He also saw a significant number of ministerial cars parked outside the palace about two hours ago. I saw a dozen tanks hurtling in that direction at around midnight.'

Quentin's brow creased. He strode in, picked up her phone receiver and dialled a number. Ava slowly pushed her chair back.

'Bruce, Quentin here. Wake your *ABRI* contacts. Generals, whoever. We need to find out if this rumour about Sujati resigning is true. If it is, it's big. We may have to evacuate more Australians if it leads to further unrest.'

He put the phone back in its cradle. 'Let me know the moment you hear something. I'll be in my office.'

'Of course,' she said, hoping she didn't sound obsequious.

With no more time for self-doubt, she refocused. It was time to confer with her colleagues. She called the Brits first.

'Yes. We heard the same thing,' her counterpart said. 'We couldn't get confirmation.'

The Canadians hadn't heard the rumour at all. She didn't bother with the New Zealanders. Their mission was so small they relied on Australia for most of their information. She had little choice but to call the Americans. Australia was meant to be the specialist, *the* authority on Indonesia within their Five Eyes, English-speaking alliance that meant in exchange for Australia's expertise on Indonesia, America provided theirs on all other countries. Ava took a breath and dialled Trent, who answered almost immediately.

'Sorry to wake you,' she said.

'Not a problem,' he replied in that affable American way. 'I only just made it to bed.'

Ava asked him her questions.

'I heard the same rumour. But nothing that could be considered to be, let's say, definitive confirmation.'

Time to report to Quentin. Ava pulled her clothes straight, adopted what she hoped was a neutral face, knocked on his open door and entered a long room with a plain, modern desk at one end, wooden bookcase to the side and beige settee set placed around a glass coffee table. A few faded prints of famous Australian landscapes hung on the walls. There were no family photos or personal touches.

Quentin looked up from his desk and said, 'We got nothing from Bruce's *ABRI* contacts. They denied anything's going on.'

'Odd,' she said, her eyebrows raised. 'How senior were they?'

'A brigadier and two others below him.'

Not Bruce's best contacts. Yet again he wasn't pulling out all stops.

'But they were awake when you called,' she noted, an indication something was going on.

Ava filled Quentin in, and he rubbed his chin with his hand.

'Have the Americans informed Washington, and the Brits London?'

She paused, knowing how he'd interpret her answer. 'No, they haven't.'

'Surely if they thought there was any substance to the rumour they'd have advised their HQs.'

London. Washington. The most important and prestigious of postings for an Australian diplomat, and Quentin uttered these names with such familiarity. Yet Ava also detected bitterness. He was supposed to have been sent to a major Western post, but had been pulled at the last minute so politicians could serve there instead. Jakarta was a poor consolation prize.

Ava waited for him to decide. Why didn't he just call his senior contacts? Was it because the source was her contact and only a student?

He leant across his desk, his dark grey eyes piercing hers. 'Write it up as an email. The key conclusions—we've been unable to confirm the rumour and we can't act on it 'til we know for certain. Send it to the usual suspects. I'll call The Minister's chief of staff and let him know it's coming. That's all we can do.'

Ava fought to keep her exasperation off her face.

'And let them know the Americans have heard the rumour and haven't told Washington,' he added.

She bit her lip, looked down at the floor, then back up at him. DFAT's records were going to be denied this history-making moment because Quentin was a… yankophile?

'Could this go as a cable, for the record I mean?' Cables were the only formal communication they had with Canberra, the prime minister and ministers. 'What if one of the Catholic generals or that Catholic minister told Iwan about the handover because they're worried about the implications? He's tight with them, played a key role in what's been happening from the outset. He's their student proxy.'

Quentin glowered. 'If we had confirmation, I'd say yes. But we don't. You simply can't send something like that without presenting a view on its authenticity.'

'I'll sign the email *EMBASSY* then.'

Quentin's eyes narrowed, a hint of disdain across his face. 'Premjid is leaving soon and I was thinking of giving you the East Timor job—a promotion of sorts—given how you've handled the political crisis…so far.'

Ava wasn't sure whether he was serious or trying to buy her compliance. He'd never complimented her before. Of course she wanted a promotion. But East Timor, no thanks!

She about-faced and walked along the long and lonely corridor back to her office. If she was right, the record wouldn't show that Australia knew about this historic event before it took place because emails didn't make it into the archives. In years to come, when they were made public, no one would ever realise the embassy knew, Australia knew, or that she knew, first. All because a student had reported the rumour, and to her, and an American and Brit couldn't confirm it.

3

____

JAKARTA, LATER THAT MORNING

After only three hours' sleep, Ava stepped out of the embassy lift, punched in her access code and entered the embassy's fourth floor, home to the political and economic policy sections, and the ambassador's office. She rubbed her eyes and ran her fingers through her hair, which did nothing to make her feel more alert. Catching sight of her reflection she was shocked by how anaemic she looked, making the dark rings under her eyes and sprinkling of normally tame freckles across her cheeks and nose stand out. She was normally proud of her European looks, but right now she appeared anything but chic.

Donald had woken her not long ago with a phone call. 'You were right. Sujati's resigning and Hidayat's going to be sworn in. Hurry up and get to the embassy.'

In the ambassador's office, people were milling around Quentin's TV sipping cups of tea and coffee and munching on biscuits. It looked like a birthday morning tea, except they never had them. Far too busy.

'Come on in, Ava,' Donald smiled, exposing more of his chaotic yellow teeth than usual. 'This is your big moment.'

Donald's appearance was appalling, a few bits of lanky, dark hair failing to cover his balding head, dandruff dusting his shoulders, and his belly bulging above his skinny legs. And that mouth. But she liked him and the proud grin he often gave her, which extended all the way to his grey eyes.

It didn't feel like her moment. The atmosphere was casual, as though Sujati's resignation was an everyday thing they'd known about for weeks. Apart from Donald's private comment, none of her colleagues acknowledged her scoop. Were they envious? Had she made them look bad for not knowing themselves? Or was this just the default position of well-mastered diplomatic detachment? Sujati's resignation was the biggest thing that had happened in Indonesia, in the region really, since the Vietnam War. History was materialising in front of them, everything Ava knew from behind the scenes culminating here on TV. She wouldn't let them reduce her awe.

As she waited, she tallied the sum of revolutionary changes she'd witnessed in Indonesia since her arrival recalling the first cable she'd ever signed. What had she titled it? Something bold. Ah yes, *East Asian Economic Crisis - The End of Sujati*? She lifted her head and whispered, 'Ha.' She'd foreseen the possibility of today from the outset. She might actually be doing all right at this job.

'It's about to begin,' someone said, and they faced the TV.

The geriatric president, dressed entirely in black, entered the large palace hall and shuffled past red and gold curtains along a matching carpet. The audience was silent by the time he stopped in front of a lonely microphone directly underneath an elaborate chandelier. Normally Sujati preached from a podium, but there wasn't one today. He was no longer their god leader of the last three decades and was down now at everyone else's level. Yet he looked at odds among the generals, aides, heads of the two parliamentary chambers and his loyal sidekick Hidayat who'd put him in power and served him for years, but were now forcing him to step down. Ava almost felt sorry for him, the grand old man of modern Indonesia reduced to this remnant. How expendable everyone was in the end.

At last Sujati looked up through the large crowd of journalists and cameras, whose lights and flashes illuminated the room. With little emotion, he raised a piece of paper and read in that clever Indonesian way of saying little so poetically:

I have decided to resign as the President of the Republic of Indonesia, effective from now on this day, Thursday 12 May 1998.

For the help and support of the people while I led the nation and state of Indonesia, I express my thanks and seek forgiveness if there were any mistakes and shortcomings. [1]

Ava grimaced at the awkward language, no doubt insisted on by lawyers to distance him from an admission of guilt. Lights flashed again and a murmur broke out, both on TV and in Quentin's office. Ava felt outrage. How dare he distance himself from—even justify—the violence he'd instigated against his own people in the name of prosperity. It was common knowledge his family had squirrelled away billions, benefitting immensely from his unrestrained power.

She swallowed back the bitter taste in her mouth as a vivid image came to her of a student who, only days ago, had been shot by Sujati's snipers at a demonstration. She and Bruce had stood only metres away. At the time neither of them heard or saw anything. It was only when Ava nearly bumped into his two friends dragging his limp body through the crowd that she realised what had happened. His throat gaped open and his face was white, his blood already spent down his clothes and onto the asphalt. She watched with horrified deference as his feet skidded lifelessly on the road behind him, the crowd parting silently to let them through. This sort of political expediency was what she'd most remember Sujati for.

The disgraced ex-president was now shunted off to the side as Hidayat came forward. He'd be Indonesia's transitional president until general elections could be held the next year. Looking more impish and tubbier than usual under the bright lights, Hidayat read solemnly from a Batik-covered folder while a religious official held the Koran above his head. Ava checked her watch. Years of dictatorship had ended in less than seven minutes.

The dozen or so people in Quentin's office began to speak at once. Ava took the opportunity to approach a more senior political section colleague, Premjid, who currently covered East Timor. He'd arrived back yesterday from his holiday in the US having missed the entire crisis.

'This is the end of Indonesia as we know it,' she smiled cheekily, bolstered by her information coup last night and lack of sleep. 'Without Sujati to keep a lid on things, East Timor will get independence first, then Aceh and maybe even Irian Jaya, Sulawesi and Maluku.'

Premjid shook his head in the all-knowing habit of diplomats, though he came across as more self-assured than most. 'None of this will happen in our lifetime. Not unless the separatists get support from the international community, and it's not in any of our interests to back anything that threatens Indonesia's transition to democracy.'

Ava laughed before Quentin cleared the room, asking her, Donald, Premjid and Bradley from the economic section to stay behind.

'Right everyone,' he frowned. 'This is big for us. The build-up to today has taken more than a year and, while many of you are tired, don't be mistaken, we're only at the beginning.

'Canberra will be watching Indonesia carefully over the next year and our reporting will be scrutinised more closely than ever. In addition, there are plans for the prime minister and a number of ministers to visit, so we'll have our work cut out on that front too. *Ex nihilo nihil fit*. Nothing comes from nothing.'

There was a unanimous groan at the prospect of the visits. They created a tonne of work and took policy staff away from their core work reporting on developments and delivering messages.

'By the end of tomorrow,' Quentin continued, 'I want to see two solid draft cables by midday tomorrow. The first, an assessment of what Sujati's resignation means for internal stability and economic recovery—will Hidayat rule in his own right, is he capable of leading vital economic reform, and how will he deal with the ever-powerful armed forces?

'The second needs to look at what this means for Australia–Indonesia relations. What are the implications for bilateral and regional security? Could this be an opportunity to resolve the East Timor problem? Canberra would love to finally put that to bed.

'We'll probably raise more questions than answers at this point, but we need to lead Canberra in the right direction.'

Everyone nodded, their brows furrowed as they left for their offices. Ava went to her desk to send a quick cable on Sujati's speech for the record before beginning the more daunting task of writing her parts of Quentin's cables.

Donald knocked on her door. He clasped a brass elephant about the size of his palm.

'If they had big gold elephant stamps,' he said, 'And if I could find one in this riot-mad place, you'd be getting one now. This is the next best thing.'

Donald placed the elephant on her desk, continuing to hold it as he looked at her more closely. It smelled metallic in his sweaty hand.

'I'm sorry you didn't get your moment of glory.'

Ava gave him a questioning look.

'Last night I advised Quentin not to send your tip off as a cable.'

Ava shifted in her seat. She was hurt he hadn't trusted her source or her judgement, but worse, she felt disappointed he'd turned out to be an arse-coverer. Part of her wanted to tell him where to shove his second-hand elephant. Yet she also understood he was being honest. An apology from a more senior officer was unheard of.

'Just so you know, the Ambassador thinks highly of you getting that tip. He's seriously thinking about giving you the East Timor job. It'd be a real step-up.'

She could think of nothing worse. A human rights disaster with years of deadlock. Australia's great shame for its failure to condemn the invasion and stop the subsequent human rights abuses.

'Thanks Donald,' she said, nodding at his grinning face. 'It's all right.' It wasn't really, but what else could she do?

$$4$$

VILLAGE OF LIQUICA, EAST TIMOR, JULY 1998

Isabel Cardoso stood back in the waning July sun to inspect her efforts. She removed her straw hat and wiped the sweat off her forehead. Her parents would be pleased. She'd weeded their entire vegetable plot in readiness for planting off-season maize, something her family often did before the rains came later in the year when they could grow the more profitable *padi*, rice. Her satisfaction gave way to irritation at her chapped hands, aching back from bending over and sunburn on the nape of her neck. She didn't normally dwell on these things—after all, farming provided the food her family ate and the clothes they wore—but today the drudgery and toil of it gnawed at her like rats at a sack of rice.

She picked up her tools and navigated her way along the maze of narrow dirt embankments that retained water and demarcated one small plot from another. Stepping lightly onto the zig-zag path that led to the roadside, she was almost dancing, relieved to be moving freely again. Isabel was neither girl nor woman, pretty or ugly, but her strong brow, wide mouth and plain face hinted at something deeper, and her small, skinny body with its swan-like neck was grace itself. As she performed this accidental ballet, she seemed greater than her diminutive self. At seventeen, unmarried and a devout Catholic, Isabel was finally emerging.

She acknowledged villagers along the way home up the dry dirt road, past more vegetable and rice fields and small clusters of wild green vegetation. Thin old women with skin darker than hers carried loads on their heads, and men wizened beyond their years pushed carts of building materials and tools. Younger women went about their daily duties too, often with a child hoisted on one hip, another attached to their free hand and one growing in their belly. As ever, there were groups of young and older men wandering and loitering with nothing better to do than chain-smoke cigarettes.

'*Botardi,*' Isabel greeted each of them, attempting a smile with the women.

In Liquica, everyone knew everyone else and their business, so it paid to be polite. It also paid to remember that even when you thought you were alone, you were being watched. Not just by the usual nosy neighbours and meddling priests, but by the Indonesian authorities and their local Timorese cohorts because Liquica was a resistance stronghold.

The locals were most cautious about the mayor, a round little man when everyone else was thin. Supposedly their democratically elected representative, in reality he'd been appointed by the Indonesians. What the villagers despised most about him wasn't that he was an Indonesian flunky —somebody had to do it—but that he never did anything for them. Not even the Indonesians respected someone that servile.

But why did no one smile back? Was it because the women were so much busier than the men?

She sighed. Like them, chores were the mainstay of her life. As the oldest girl in the family, this was expected of her. Her mother, wed at fourteen, said it was good practice for when she got married, which everyone believed would surely happen over the next year. But Isabel wasn't sure how she felt about this. She knew marriage was her path, but she'd never experienced love. She'd had crushes on boys—*cinta monyet*, monkey love —but nothing serious or lasting. Sometimes as she lay in bed at night, she fantasised about a man pursuing her and her alone. She wished love would hurry up and happen. She was ready.

A couple of years ago she'd wondered about other possibilities. Daydreams had found their way into her head as she worked or sat in the classroom learning her lessons. She knew about different ways of living from the TV shows she watched on the communal village television. One soap opera featured a naive young man from outer Indonesia who yearned to go to university in the big city and build a good life to make his family proud. Only when he got there, he fell in love with a rich, unhappily married woman and turned to a life of crime to win her over.

But Isabel didn't find her true spark from television, rather from the local nuns who joined forces with her schoolteachers to encourage her to continue her education after the mandatory age of fifteen.

'Isabel is bright,' Sister Maria had said to her mother after school one day. 'She could go to university.' Her mother, a petite woman with a neat bun of greying black hair, turned away without acknowledging their plea with so much as a nod or look.

Inspired by the nuns' encouragement, Isabel had imagined a greater life for herself. She would finish school and get a job, like the bank tellers or secretaries she'd seen on TV. Dressed in a smart uniform, her hair pulled back in a neat roll, wearing bright lipstick and closed shoes with heels— not her usual thongs—she'd smile at grateful customers. When her bosses asked her to do something important, she'd beam with excitement.

In truth, the only office Isabel had ever been inside was the local mayor's, which was partially outdoors on his balcony. The nearest bank was in Dili, which she'd visited only twice. That was the problem with imagination. Once you let it grow, it carried you away until, before you knew it, you had dreams. Dreams were sneaky and unstoppable, like the trickle of a creek joining streams that merged into a great, raging river. The possibilities for Isabel soon multiplied into something grander again.

What if she became a teacher?

Such fantasies grew to be ever more possible for Isabel until one day, just before her fifteenth birthday, she approached her mother.

'*Mama?*'

'Yes *oan-feto.*'

Her mother was in an affectionate mood and Isabel hesitated for fear of spoiling things. 'Do you think I could stay at school? The nuns and my teachers think I could do well.'

Her mother dropped what she was doing and looked at her with a mix of disbelief and betrayal. 'How can you ask me this? Where will we get the money? Who will help me with the crops and the children? And what about Gil? He didn't get to stay at school and he's a boy.'

Isabel's heart dropped into her stomach and she flushed bright red with shame. How thoughtless of her to even ask. She could hear Father Ribeiro's voice in her head. *Discontent and dissatisfaction are the signs of a vain and selfish person. They are as much a sin as any other.* Isabel hung her head low, her hands fidgeting like those of a naughty child.

A more mature Isabel might have suspected her mother was saddened by her inability to give her what she wanted. Possibly, too, Isabel's request reminded her of the choices she'd been denied as a young woman coming from an equally poor family.

Isabel shuffled off, her head hanging low as she gathered her dreams and disappointments and pushed them somewhere inaccessible. From that day on she immersed herself in her routine, never daring to let her imagination run free, even when the hoe broke in her hands, the weeds refused to be pulled from the dry earth and the sun burnt through her hat until her head throbbed. Was this all there was to life—following someone else's bidding and never your own?

She stepped through the front gate of her family's home and past a simple shack made of thatched sides sitting atop a half-metre tall brick wall with a corrugated iron roof that leaked rain every wet season onto the dirt floor and beds no matter how many repairs her father made. To her right chickens pecked for food and pigs foraged, and beyond them, several dogs escaped the heat in the shade of palm trees. The familiar odour of palm oil frying on wood and kerosene stoves signalled mealtime was nearing. But the smell Isabel most welcomed was the wind sweeping up the hills from the nearby ocean, flushing away the ever present stench of motorbike fumes until there was only a tang of the sea air and the tacky feel of salt it left behind.

As she neared the backyard, Isabel heard men's voices. Her mother was still at the market with the babies, her father was out working and the older children were at school, so it had to be her brother, Gil. But who was with him? She listened more intently.

Aleixo, she heard, then *Independencia* and something like *CRT*.

Her breath quickened. This was political talk. Like all Timorese, she'd felt disquiet since President Hidayat's announcement he was going to give East Timor special status. They were told this meant having more of a say in how their province was run. But without further detail, people grew either fearful or expectant.

Outlandish rumours spread like wind rose at the change of seasons. Some claimed a Timorese military would replace *ABRI*, others that the public service would close and that many jobs—which were more like a type of social welfare than serious work—would be lost. Isabel's own sense was of an unstoppable cavalcade called change coming their way. Long before its arrival, the ground rumbled beneath their feet, and now it had landed at her family home.

She needed to bathe and prepare dinner. Although she had no desire to show herself to the men, she lifted her head and stepped around the corner. A dozen young men, all wannabe students like her brother, sat in a circle under the shade of the large Jackfruit tree. She bowed her head and averted her eyes as she clasped her hands in front. The men immediately fell silent.

'Oh. It's only you', Gil said, and the group dropped their shoulders in unison.

Isabel wanted to go inside the house, but her feet wouldn't move.

'Gil,' she said quietly, biting her bottom lip as she looked down.

'I'll see you tomorrow,' he said to the men, sending them away with a nod of his head.

They filtered past her, some bobbing their heads in acknowledgement.

At last she was free to move. '*Maun* Gil?' she said affectionately. 'What's this CRT?'

Gil got up from the plastic mat on the ground, the cloves of his *kretek* cigarette crackling at his mouth, and scoffed. 'It's C. N. R. T., the National Council for Timorese Resistance. It's the new name for the resistance's political wing.'

Isabel frowned. Under Indonesian rule people voted the way they were told. If they didn't, it meant suffering.

'Aleixo's clever,' Gil continued, speaking more to himself than to her. 'The *CNRT* includes all sides from the '75 civil war in the new independence group, but excludes the *Falintil* guerrillas. Now no one can accuse the resistance of being associated with violence, making us more acceptable to the Indonesians as well as outsiders. And they can't say we're fighting each other either given the *CNRT* includes all past Timorese sides.'

Isabel had suspected for a while that her brother was a member of the resistance. She'd heard him talk about their leader, Aleixo, the poet and political thinker who'd been locked up in a Jakarta prison for the past six years. Isabel had seen him once wandering in the hills when she was little. He was skinny and dirty, half Portuguese looking with tanned skin and a scruffy beard. Yet there was something that made her trust him. He'd given her a fatherly smile and waved as he'd continued on his way with his fellow *Falintil*, strange-looking accomplices clad in Indonesian military attire mismatched with traditional holsters and colourful, hand-woven belts and bags. Until now, Isabel had believed Aleixo's time was over, but it seemed jail couldn't contain him.

'So, you're a member of this *CNRT*?' she asked.

'Yes.' Gil's chest broadened. 'I'm a local leader.'

Isabel's heart beat faster and sweat broke out on her face. 'But Gil…it's not safe.'

It was one thing to hear about other people's secret activities, but another entirely to discover your own brother plotting openly at your family home. Neighbours would see what was going on, which would lead to talk, and talk would find its way to Indonesian ears. This was everything their father had warned them about. Their family motto to avoid politics meant they'd stayed safe. When *ABRI* conducted one of their sweeping operations in search of guerrillas, hidden weapons or independence propaganda, they sometimes even skipped her family's house or gave it the briefest of examinations. But now, Gil was risking not just his own safety, but that of her parents and five siblings.

'Safe, *alin-feto*?' Gil said, reminding her she was only his little sister.

'Father will be furious when he finds out.'

'No, he won't,' he snapped, his eyes flashing. 'Because you won't tell him.'

Isabel stepped back, shocked by his ferocity. Gil had never treated her this way before. They'd been close until the last three months when he'd grown angry and secretive. She struggled to see this new young man in front of her as her loving brother.

'But *maun,* you know how the Timorese love to talk. And Liquica is full of spies.'

Gil kicked the mat at his feet. 'Everything has changed, Isabel. Sujati's gone and at last we have a chance. The time has come for us to stand up and be counted. This is bigger than you and me and our family. This is our —this is Timor Leste's future.'

Isabel gripped her upper arms with opposite hands to steady herself. Gil knew exactly what he was doing but didn't care. Simply holding anti-government thoughts was punishable by execution under Indonesian rule, let alone if you acted on them.

'People are talking about rivers of blood,' she spluttered.

'You mean like the civil war in '75? That's just the Indonesians pitting us against each other as usual. It's fear mongering, Isabel, all you seem to listen to, you and *papa*.' He lit a new cigarette from the stub of another.

She shook her head. 'You know as well as anyone how good we Timorese are at fighting each other.' Family feuds, disputes among neighbours and clashes between whole villages were a regular part of their life. 'And father said the waters really did run red with the blood of the socialists and moderates killing each other in the name of independence. I'm scared, Gil, for you.'

Gil looked at her and for a moment Isabel recognised her childhood playmate, but he quickly changed back. 'You're not scared for me.' He frowned as he threw his cigarette down and ground it into the dirt. 'You're scared for yourself.'

Isabel's eyes watered. What her brother said was not only untrue but unfair. How could he think so little of her? If anyone was being selfish it was he.

She rushed out of the yard and ran through the streets, following a small dirt path rarely used by others. Unsure where she was heading, she just had to get away.

A man appeared in her way and she skidded to a stop centimetres from him.

'Going somewhere?' asked the retired *Kopassus* officer. 'Must be important if you're in such a hurry.'

Isabel stood rigid, almost too scared to breathe, her eyes fixed on the ground. The officer was a local resident, the kind Gil sneered at because he was drawn to the genteel holiday feel of Liquica with its white sandy beaches and crumbling stone baths, a remnant of the Portuguese weekend retreats. Should she answer him, or should she run? She wished she could dissolve into the dirt beneath her feet. Perhaps if she pretended she wasn't there, he'd disappear.

'What are you up to, girl?'

Isabel's eyes remained down.

'Just going to church, sir,' she blurted and took off in the opposite direction to the church. She didn't want him to find her there because today it felt like menace would follow her. This, she was beginning to understand, was the new and unsettled Liquica.

5

JAKARTA, JULY 1998

Judy Cameron, Quentin's PA, looked up from her computer at Ava, and barked her usual, 'Yes?'

A middle-aged woman with always-perfect hair, Judy often complained that as an administrative officer she was *unseen, undervalued and looked down on*, unlike the policy officers, the *real* diplomats, like Ava. Yet Judy had been cross-posted for twelve years, unimaginable for policy officers who normally sojourned in Canberra between postings, competing to be gifted the next one. Ava wondered if Judy's real problem was loneliness. Plenty of DFAT women—policy and admin—were single. Apparently unlike Ava's own husband, Pete, a lot of men weren't willing to be shunted around the world as the support act. Did these women also not like their men in a dependent role? Was that part of her problem with Pete?

'Hi Judy,' Ava said. 'Quentin asked to see me.'

'Go in.'

Ava knocked on his door. Only twice before had she been summonsed into his office for a one-on-one meeting. The first time was soon after she'd arrived when he'd given her *the welcome talk* and lectured her on the need to protect her territory. The second was over Sujati's resignation.

'You wanted to see me?'

Quentin looked up and pointed to the couch, exuding his powerful older man aura. He made full use of it at diplomatic functions, discretely tucking the phone numbers of attractive embassy contacts, female diplomats and journalists in his pockets. Ava had no desire to join that lot. As she lowered herself down, she folded in her skirt.

Quentin moved into his seat and casually rested his arms on the chair, splaying his legs out in front of him.

'Congratulations on your promotion to second secretary,' he said.

'Thank you.'

Ava applied before the riots and was interviewed not long afterwards. She was still exhausted and one of her responses was vague, but she managed to get through on her first attempt. It meant she was no longer at the bottom of the policy ladder. If she did well during the rest of her time in Jakarta she might end up a first secretary, or even a counsellor like Donald. Then she could be an ambassador at a small sized post. One step further and she'd be an ambassador at a medium-sized post, but that was a good way off.

'I wanted to talk to you about your work,' Quentin said. 'I saw what you did during the May riots, the way you handled our recent human rights visit to Aceh and how you managed to get the new cabinet list before anyone else. You're resourceful. People open up to you.'

Ava could hardly believe he was praising her, but didn't dare relax.

'As you know,' he said stroking his chin, 'Premjid's time here is up soon and the East Timor file will be opening up. That chap who's coming in September to replace him—English, Inglis?—none of us were terribly impressed with him when he helped out during the riots. I know Premjid was a first secretary, but you're nearly there now so I want you to cover East Timor. We're entering a new phase and believe you me, you could do well out of this. Very well indeed.'

Quentin's voice faded into the background. Donald had given her no warning this threatened change was real. She'd been covering Indonesian politics for a year now and it had taken this long to build her contact list and establish personal relationships. She'd studied Indonesia—its language, history, politics and culture—at university where its hidden complexities had fascinated her. Besides, Indonesia would always matter more to Australia than any other place in the region. Yet just like that she was supposed to give it up for the dirty, messy world of East Timor? Surely he hadn't ensured her promotion just so this could happen?

'You'll keep up with some of your key contacts,' he went on. 'Your close ones on domestic politics like the students and the speaker of the parliament.'

What? She'd have two jobs now? When would she ever see Juliette?

'And naturally you'll have to visit Timor regularly. But you can do a lot of your daily work from Jakarta once you've established contacts there.'

Ava nodded, not that Quentin seemed interested in her views. This was a transmit-only meeting.

She sensed her poker face slipping.

'Perhaps you can outline the key issues for Australia on East Timor,' she said, readying her pen at her notepad. She needed clear guidelines with written evidence for anyone who questioned her down the track, including Quentin himself.

'Donald can give you a more thorough briefing, but in short, the change in Indonesian leadership has provided an opening to resolve the East Timor problem. Australia's national interest is *not* to have all parties—East Timor, Indonesia and Portugal—walk away happy, you understand. What we need is to get the East Timor problem off our back, whether this means independence and peace, or not.'

Peace or not? Surely Australians would only be content once East Timor was peaceful. They'd followed the issue for years. But she wasn't naive enough to believe their government agreed. Covering East Timor would mean she'd have to uphold—represent even—a policy she opposed. How could she do that? She'd worked hard at separating her opinions and emotions from her job. But this went beyond professional compartmentalisation into the territory of ethics and who she was.

Quentin continued his briefing as Ava jotted down words with implications she barely understood—*rebel leader, Nobel Peace Prize-winning bishop, autonomy versus independence, UN special representative, roaming ambassador, ballots, diaspora.* She had so much to learn. Her second new job in a year.

Perhaps Quentin sensed her misgivings because he fixed his eyes on hers. 'Canberra is watching closely. We need to produce consistently good work at this end. You, in particular, have to perform. And let me tell you, you have a way to go with your writing. But if you work hard, you'll get there. It'll be the making of you.'

Ava nodded. He'd complimented her by giving her the East Timor job, and yet he had reservations. What if she was too slow in grasping the intricacies? What if her writing didn't improve fast enough? What if East Timor was simply too underhanded and gruesome?

Quentin paused again, only this time his face took on a smug look. 'Stretton is focused on the issue. Needed to give him something to do. They have to be made to feel important, you know, ministers. Otherwise they get bored, which is a dangerous thing. They begin interfering in who knows what.'

Adam Stretton, otherwise known as The Minister, had been a diplomat back in the days when you had to go to an elite male-only school to enter the old boys' network and get a job in DFAT. She'd heard from a witness about the day he became foreign affairs minister. He'd sat in the dingy DFAT café drinking cups of tea and glaring at people for an entire morning. Staff weren't sure whether he was trying to intimidate them or stake his claim. Was Quentin now competing with this man? Ava nodded at Quentin as though she understood—as though she was on his side, their side, the side of the bureaucrats versus the politicians.

'This will be a critical test of Australian diplomacy,' Quentin said, switching back to a professional tone. 'We haven't led on something like this for a long time. And don't be mistaken, this is our issue and we will lead on it in the UN. *Animis opibusque parati*: We must be prepared for anything. *Scisne Latine?* '

'Sorry?'

'Do you know Latin?' Quentin loved throwing Latin around, inserted it into cables even. It probably reminded him of his student days at—was it Harvard?

'Only the standard phrases.'

He fell silent and Ava realised this was her cue to leave. When she was far enough away from his office, she let out a rush of breath. She made her way to the toilet to gather her thoughts before facing Donald, who was no doubt waiting for her with his toothy grin. East Timor was a plum job, recognition of sorts, and he'd be happy for her. Perhaps he'd even put her forward. In any case, whether she agreed or not, Quentin's decision was final. The culture of diplomacy was militaristic, arcane and mostly male. There were no khaki uniforms, but you shut your mouth and did what you were told no matter your conscience or the impact on your family.

6

———————————————

JAKARTA, JULY 1998

It was too late for morning tea and too early for lunch when Ava stood alone under the canteen veranda sipping a hot drink. The sun glistened on the embassy's lap pool. Sunshine had never filtered through the smog before the economic crisis. But the lack of work and money meant Indonesians could no longer afford to run their cars, resulting in lower air pollution. There were still traffic jams at peak hour, but nothing like before. Ava could even see the tip of Puncak, the hill that stood behind Jakarta where tea was grown and, since colonial times, expats had escaped on weekends. Whenever she went to one of the embassy holiday houses there, she felt as though she was stepping back in time.

Bruce approached and held out a packet. 'Cigarette?' His chubby face, big nose and full lips reminded her of a toad, but in an affectionate way.

'I could use one.' She tried not to smoke, but every time she quit, a political crisis erupted and she took up it up again.

'What's up, mate?' he boomed, his great barrel of a chest and enthusiasm for life making it near impossible for him to talk quietly.

'You haven't heard?' she asked, pausing to let him light her cigarette.

He shook his head.

'I'm being given East Timor when Premjid leaves. It won't happen for a couple of months, but no more domestic politics, parliament, security, human rights, women…'

'News to me. But hey, congratulations. Quentin must think highly of you.'

Their smoke intertwined and curled upwards in the humid air.

'I know it's supposed to be a vote of confidence,' Ava said, 'but I don't agree with Australian policy on East Timor. We've been appeasing the Indonesians and ignoring their human rights abuses there for too long.' She drew hard on her cigarette and blew it out slowly as though painting a picture in the air. 'I don't know if I can do it, Bruce. Or if I want to.'

'That's exactly why you're the right person *to* do it.'

She looked at him, sceptical.

'You'll have a different mindset, a fresh way of looking at things. You have a conscience.'

'And that's a good thing?' She didn't mean to sound sarcastic. She genuinely wondered how she could do the East Timor job and sleep at night.

'It's a way off yet. Anything could happen now Sujati's gone. There could be a complete policy reversal.' Bruce pursed his lips and nodded. 'Yeah. You'll be great, Ava. It'll be good for everyone.'

Ava wanted to believe him after the danger they'd shared during the riots. Yet she knew he could be politically naive, particularly when it came to *ABRI*. Maybe he'd been on too many jaunts with Indonesian soldiers, travelling the country and drinking beer as they sung each other's national songs.

'I'm going to tell you something.' Bruce repositioned himself to avoid the sun's reflection from the water. 'The trip to Aceh you put together for the ambo a couple of weeks ago.' He took a long drag on his cigarette and locked his eyes on hers. 'It changed Australian policy.'

'What?'

'We stopped training the Indonesian special forces because of what you showed Quentin.' Bruce dropped his cigarette onto the paving stones and ground it out with his polished black shoes. 'It's true. After seeing first-hand what *ABRI* were doing to civilians in Aceh, there was no way Quentin could advise the government to go on training *Kopassus*.'

Ava's mouth dropped open.

'The thing is, I couldn't have proposed that kind of visit—meeting the victims of torture, the women's and human rights groups, the local victims. *ABRI* would've been really upset. Your predecessor tried too, but she handled it badly—so badly she was nearly thrown out of the country and made *persona non grata*. You, on the other hand, did it.'

Ava had organised a gathering in a remote Acehnese village in Pidie—a known trouble spot where *Kopassus* regularly conducted military sweeps that happened to stop just a few days before their arrival—so Quentin could hear firsthand from the locals.

In the village meeting hall, a raised, open-roofed platform made of palm leaves, several gaunt men with hollow eyes stepped forward and spoke about being beaten, tortured, and having their houses ransacked and burnt.

A mother then collapsed onto the floor, crying and prostrating herself at Quentin's feet as her young son clung to her skirt. 'Help me sir,' she wept. 'Please find my husband.'

Ava asked the woman for more details, carefully directing her questions and translating for Quentin. The woman told them that her husband and four-year-old son had been taken to the local *Kopassus* centre where the boy had been forced to watch his father being tortured. While the centre had also been shut down a few days ago and her son returned to her, her husband was still missing.

'Tell her I'll look into it,' Quentin said, nodding at the woman without expression. Was he so hardened, or simply good at hiding his feelings?

The woman thanked Quentin repeatedly, kissing his shoes as she wailed some more.

As Ava watched on, attempting to keep her face neutral and probably making her seem equally uncaring to outsiders, she doubted there was much they could do. It was unlikely her husband was still alive. She'd write a frank report to Canberra and contact Amnesty International requesting they look into the case, but this felt inadequate. She wanted to do something more practical. The embassy was looking to fund small programs from their discretionary fund. Maybe she could propose they train locals, who could train other locals in trauma counselling to help people like this woman and her son.

But now she'd learnt from Bruce that her efforts had amounted to something more. Perhaps the East Timor job would offer similar opportunities. Her stomach flipped.

'Thanks for telling me,' she smiled, picking picked up Bruce's cigarettes. 'May I?'

'You never have to ask, Ava. You and I, we've been on the front lines.'

Ava paused, looking him in the eyes. 'I hope you're right about East Timor. The political situation is changing rapidly. Guess I'll give it a go.'

7

JAKARTA, JULY 1998

Ava and Pete, who'd returned to Jakarta with Juliette not long after Sujati resigned, sat eating a late breakfast in their mausoleum of a house in the inner Jakarta middle-class suburb of Kebayoran Baru. The crunch of toast and muesli being chewed, and the clank of cutlery on their plates bounced off the marble floor and echoed around the open space. Ava pretended to read a two-week-old Australian newspaper, while Pete rested his dimpled chin on his hand. Juliette watched cartoons on the landing above.

Ava finished her mouthful and pushed her plate aside. 'So,' she said, attempting to sound casual. 'Have you found someone to invest in your latest invention? How much have you spent on this one? Two grand? Three?'

Pete with his large brown eyes came over all innocent. 'I'll find someone, Ava. Just chill.'

'It's July. We've been in Jakarta a year now.' Her neck and shoulders tightened. 'I thought you were going to find someone to help you to run your ideas past investors so you didn't have to spend so much money? And what happened to working part-time to buy materials? Why'd you even bother to do the English-as-a-second-language training?'

Pete sighed. 'Jakarta's a real opportunity for me to focus on my work.'

'Is that what you're doing? It looks to me like all you do is make stuff nobody's ever going to see, let alone buy or use. We had a plan. Remember?' A flicker of sadness, then anger crossed her face.

'Well, I didn't like the plan,' he said mockingly.

'You just forgot to tell me that?'

Pete shook his head. 'You never should've accepted this DFAT job, and now East Timor. Look what it's done to you.'

'What? Made me grow up and be responsible? Someone in this family had to.'

'So looking after Juliette's not being grown up and responsible?'

'Look after Juliette? We have a cook, cleaner-come-babysitter and security guards. I organise her school stuff and weekends. I buy her clothes and birthday presents. I go to the parent-teacher meetings. And before we had staff, I did all the cleaning and shopping and made her lunches. Every single day.'

'And I did the cooking and dishes.'

'You like cooking, Pete. Except on weekends, when I had to do it to give you a break.'

He looked wounded, the first honest emotion she'd seen from him in a long time. It took her by surprise and her anger dissipated into regret. Maybe they could have a reasonable conversation now. They could celebrate her career successes and she could praise him for being there for Juliette when she was working.

Pete leant back. 'Just look at how hard you've become, Ava.'

His words cut deep. Ava closed her eyes to steady herself. He'd made her out to be like the mean husband who complained about his stay-at-home wife's spending. A heartless career bitch.

When she'd first met him, going out with a brilliant, self-taught inventor seemed romantic, even though he was thirteen years her senior. He'd told her he'd love and support her forever at a time she found it hard to believe anyone could possibly feel that way about her. They'd married within a few months.

Back then he sold inventions, was featured in magazines and there were drinks and dinners with corporates courting him and his ideas. But she hadn't realised his career was at its apex. Juliette grew quickly, and so did their bills, just as Pete's success dried up, leaving them broke and her to support them through her cleaning work while she studied. Ava never wanted to be that poor or humiliated again. Their daughter was now nine and it had been more than six years since he'd sold anything substantial. Yet he refused to find regular paid work.

'We're meant to be a team, Pete. But I'm the only one on side.' Her eyes pleaded with him.

Instead he leered at her, a poor echo of his warm smile that had once delighted her. 'The only team you're on is Team Ava. You don't need me.'

Is that what was bothering him? Did he feel left out? Or was he trying to undermine her newfound confidence? Couldn't she be a career woman and happily married?

'I checked our Australian savings account yesterday,' she said more calmly than she felt. Pete's faced twitched and he averted his eyes.

'Where's the money gone?'

Pete put his hands over his face and rubbed them up and down. When he lowered them, he said, 'I invested it.'

'In what?'

'Online shares. I wanted to try something different, to find another source of income. I did it for us.'

Ava closed her eyes momentarily in an effort to keep calm. 'Without consulting me? Again? You promised you wouldn't. You promised no more get rich quick schemes.'

'You don't understand.'

'So it's gone? All fifteen grand?'

Pete looked directly at her, his eyes drooping.

'You've sent a total of twenty-three thousand down the drain now, which was meant for our house deposit. We hardly have any savings now. Are you happy?'

Spinning around, she stood and bolted into their bedroom—now her bedroom since they started sleeping separately—and locked the door. She fell onto her bed, hitting a pillow repeatedly before bursting into tears. It wasn't the money, but the betrayal that had knocked her for six, along with the heinous things he'd said. She buried her head in the pillow so Pete wouldn't know he'd got to her, that despite everything he could hurt her and she still cared. But not for much longer. Things had to change.

8

JAKARTA, A FEW WEEKS LATER

Sop ayam was Juliette's favourite Saturday lunch. She loved the ritual of putting cooked cabbage and bean sprouts in the bowl, followed by rice noodles, chicken and boiled egg, before pouring over chicken broth and finishing it off with a flourish of fresh shallots, crispy fried onions and a final squeeze of lime. But today she wasn't so enthusiastic. Like Ava, she was struggling to eat her food. Pete was leaving for a trial separation, and this was their last meal together as a family, perhaps forever. He'd decided to travel around Indonesia for a few months before returning to Australia.

Ava tried to make the occasion seem as normal as possible, but no one spoke with occasional slurping noises dominating the cavernous room. After they'd finished, Pete asked the maid to get the security guard to hail him a cab. The maid nodded as she carried the dishes back to the external kitchen where she preferred to work. Air conditioning, Indonesians believed, gave you *masuk angin*—a cold wind in your body that caused illness.

Ava stood and was hit with nausea. She rushed to the nearby toilet and brought up what little food she'd eaten. When it subsided, she splashed her face with cold water and checked herself in the mirror. She looked pale and drawn.

When she came out, Pete was hugging Juliette hard. He wasn't a tall man to begin with, but he appeared crushed and twice his age. He spoke softly to Juliette, then looked at Ava. 'Happy?'

She opened her mouth but found no words. She wanted to break down and sob, but also to scream at him for making so little effort. Instead she handed him a wad of cash, which was all he seemed to want. Not to discuss shared custody or be reassured about his future access to Juliette.

'I'll let you know where I am. In case you need me.'

'Yes, stay in touch for Juliette. Jakarta isn't exactly stable yet, and I start the Timor job soon.'

Pete nodded and paused before stepping through the front door into the dull humidity of the Jakarta afternoon.

As she watched him get into the taxi and drive away, Ava's stomach churned again. Next door, a gardener was hand-cutting the lawn. A *bakso* food cart announced its arrival with its ringing bell, and the family across the road pulled into their driveway with shopping. Yet after ten years, Ava's marriage had just died. How could life continue regardless of such a profound ending?

Her knees buckled as a deluge of emotion welled up inside her. She reached out to the wall to steady herself and attempted to swallow it down, but the lump in her throat made it difficult to breathe. She closed her eyes and took a slow deep breath in and out.

When she reopened them, she saw that Juliette hadn't moved from her spot. 'I don't understand,' Juliette said, shaking her head. 'Why is Daddy going? When will he be back?'

'I'm not sure. But I hope you know this isn't your fault. It's got nothing to do with you.'

She and Pete had tried to present a united front to Juliette. They'd sat her down and explained they were no longer making each other happy and needed a break.

Juliette was a sweet skinny girl with intelligent brown eyes who followed Ava everywhere. Oh to love and be loved like that—the recreation of oneself. Ava knew, had always known, there'd be nothing like it. If the truth be known, Juliette was her ballast, even after she joined DFAT and her confidence grew.

On the other hand, Juliette wasn't all light and ease. Complicated and insecure, her heart was so large and her needs so great she'd tested Ava from the moment she was born. She never stopped pushing the boundaries in search of proof she was both loved and loveable.

Taking the news of her parents' separation badly that day, Juliette had shut herself away in her room. But now, she directed her pain at Ava with daggers in her eyes. She ran up the grey marble stairs into Pete's workspace. Ava followed, stopping at the door to watch her examining her father's private space. Juliette touched his mechanical constructions, then ran her fingers over his drawings and the small maquettes arranged neatly on his worktable.

Ava gulped back tears. What was Juliette searching for? Evidence her father would still exist while they were apart, something to remember him by, or proof he'd come back? Maybe, like her, Juliette intuitively understood that Pete needed to invent things more than he needed Ava and Juliette, that he'd rather lock himself in this room making useless objects than help support his family?

With her dark muddy eyes and deeply creased brow, Juliette looked as though she was shouldering their collective burdens. Her grief felt even heavier than Ava's own.

'Oh darling,' Ava said. What had she done? What right did she have to break up their family? She was a selfish person, a bad mother. She crumpled onto a chair.

Juliette put her arms around Ava as though to comfort, and possibly forgive her. Ava placed her head against Juliette's small chest and burst into tears, collapsing momentarily into her daughter's tenderness. But she quickly grew uncomfortable. A child shouldn't be reassuring her mother. Ava wiped her face with the back of her hand and straightened up.

'I love you so much,' she said to Juliette, stroking her ashen face. 'And so does Daddy. Nothing will ever change that.' She pulled Juliette in close and held her tightly. Finally Juliette broke down, her sobs giving way to deep howls. 'It's okay to be sad, darling. It's normal.'

Juliette freed herself and rushed across the landing, slamming her bedroom door behind her.

'I'll wait out here in case you want me,' Ava said through the cracks as she sank into the landing couch.

Ava had tried to make things work with Pete for years. She'd gone to marriage counselling alone when Pete insisted there was no problem. She'd told the counsellor, a bearded man dressed in brown with unkempt hair, that she'd lost respect for Pete because he refused to earn money. No longer attracted to him, his smell even repelled her. The counsellor advised her to buy him aftershave. She never went back.

'One day, you'll understand,' she whispered, although she wasn't sure she believed that right now.

Her separation from Pete was meant to make the world lighter, easier, better. In reality it felt dimmer and less predictable. She rested her head in her hands. This too shall pass, she told herself. It must.

———

Two days later

Now that Ava was a single parent, her routine had to change. Usually she or Pete drove her into work by 9 am, which was late compared to admin and consular staff. But this worked with her late finishing time of 8 or 9 pm that matched Canberra's working day, which was three or four hours behind.

This morning she rose at 5.45 to get Juliette up and onto her school bus by 6.15, which used to be Pete's job. She planned to catch the 7 o'clock embassy van, hoping its early pick-up and drop-off times would limit her to ten work hours a day so she could spend more time with Juliette. She rushed to find her phone and lipstick as the driver beeped the horn a second time. As she let herself out the door, the call to prayer sounded around her, the combination of live and pre-recorded voices out of sync and jarring her nerves.

The driver stood by the van door. If he was annoyed at having to wait for her he didn't show it. He smiled with a show of politeness as he let her in, maintaining his *halus* face. She returned his gesture and thanked him, wondering how drivers' uniforms stayed so crisp and white in the heat, pollution and their cigarette smoke. As she moved to the back seat of the van, she greeted the other passengers, hoping they'd leave it at that. She wasn't up to conversation after the weekend.

'You're late,' Judy hissed from the middle of the van. 'The rule is the bus doesn't wait.'

Ava wanted to like Quentin's PA, but she didn't make it easy.

'And it won't next time. Not for anybody!'

Tears Ava hadn't realised were lurking beneath the surface rose up, stifling a response. Why was she this devastated when she'd initiated the separation with Pete? Other fears emerged now, like how the hell was she going to manage travelling to East Timor when she couldn't even catch a bus on time?

She gazed out the window at the tangle of traffic to distract herself. The mess of vehicles weaved around each other to the cacophony of horns and engines: brightly painted mini-buses overflowed with passengers, their conductors hanging out the side toting for business as they waved wads of notes around for change; armies of motorbikes with whole families balanced on their handlebars and pillions; multi-coloured *becaks* ridden by skinny men with muscly legs going at a pace oblivious to the Jakarta streets; and the ubiquitous *Kijangs*, cars similar in appearance to SUVs but with tame motors and no suspension. They moved together like an army of ants advancing in slow motion, each vehicle taking its turn to edge ahead before allowing others in, their drivers remaining calm as they navigated the chaos.

An awkward silence persisted for the rest of the trip. At the embassy gates, the guards checked under the van for bombs with mirrors on long poles. Ava couldn't help but wonder, had she swapped one prison for another, the jail of her marriage for another called independence?

9

LIQUICA, EAST TIMOR, SEPTEMBER 1998

As the light faded, fumes choked the air from food being cooked in open kitchens on wood and kerosene stoves. Isabel arrived home to find the little ones giggling and squirming every time their mother threw scoops of cold water over their soapy bodies. She smiled, forgetting for a moment what would be asked of her next.

'Take over,' her mother said, revealing her pink-stained teeth from chewing betel nut. 'Then you can help me with the fish and vegetables.'

'Yes, *Mama.*' Isabel placed her tools down, picked up a towel and glanced at the three small fish and bunch of greens and chilli they would share with their large bowl of rice each.

From the corner of her eye, she glimpsed Gil sauntering into the yard. His head hung low and he kicked the dirt in front of him as though it was to blame for his woes.

'Where have you been?' their father asked, leaving the woven cage he was repairing for his fighting cock. With his sinewy muscles and parchment face he looked older than his years, especially compared to his taller, plumper son.

Gil came alive. 'I've been in Dili, *papa*, demonstrating for independence. There were thousands of us. It was incredible!'

Isabel agreed, it was indeed incredible. Until now, protesting against the government would have got you bullets or prison.

Gil turned to Isabel. 'You should have joined us, *alin-feto*.'

Isabel knew that only young men attended such things. Women seldom had a taste for conflict, which was how it would end if the Indonesians followed their past ways.

'Don't be ridiculous,' their father said. 'Isabel is a sensible girl. She understands that selfish actions like yours will only cause our family problems.'

'Oh. I…' Isabel wasn't used to having a voice in these matters.

'The Indonesians are talking about giving us more autonomy,' Gil said. 'This is our chance to get something more. This is our chance at independence.'

Isabel knew what was coming next. She braced herself as she heard their usual argument play out in her head.

'I've told you before,' *papa* would say, 'you must stay away from anything political. You can't trust either side.'

'Either side?' Gil would reply with bitterness beyond his nineteen years. 'It's the Indonesian oppressors we can't trust. First they invade, then they integrate us using starvation, tyranny and oppression. Tens of thousands of Timorese died as a result of the famine they created, not to mention the murders and rapes. Most people would call this genocide, *papa*.'

Papa would become red-faced. 'You talk of genocide. The invasion only happened because of what we Timorese did to fellow Timorese, launching coup after countercoup, waging civil war and inflicting terrible cruelty on each other. And what for? Ideology. Socialism? Power? Always remember, my son, your *Falintil* guerrillas butchered many of their Timorese brothers, yet no one talks about that, do they?'

Gil would laugh furiously and trot out his usual socialist line. 'The

Indonesians bled us dry of sandalwood and coffee. They taxed us into poverty and still they reap the benefits of our gas and oil.'

'At least they invested in our roads and schools,' *papa* would retort, 'which is more than the Portuguese did in four hundred years of colonisation.'

Isabel readied herself for it to start.

'Gil, my son,' their father said, but in a calm voice that took Isabel by surprise. 'You may think you're immortal, beyond the reach of *ABRI* and the police and everyone else, but you're not. And neither, may I remind you, are your mother or your brothers and sisters and me. Your protesting will only bring us trouble. Heed my words, son. I don't exaggerate, I don't threaten. I know.'

Their father wrung his hands and Isabel saw how frail he appeared under the weight of worry. Gil looked away and opened his mouth to say something, but instead spun around and skulked towards the house.

'Wait,' Isabel blurted, but Gil didn't stop to listen or even look back at her. 'Gil, what father said…' she pleaded, but she might as well not have existed.

She wasn't even married and already she was invisible.

10

____

LIQUICA, THE NEXT DAY

In the middle of her family plot, Isabel measured the progress of the maize she'd planted nearly three months ago. Green stalks reached her chest, and the light wind of dusk rustled the leaves. She shook her head. By now they should be heavy with near-ripened cobs ready to be dried and eaten, but the crop's growth was stunted by the lack of rain. Would her family have enough to eat this year? Perhaps people were right when they said the seasons were all wrong—that the dry was drier, the wet later and the amount of rain in East Timor altogether less. Nothing was as it should be.

She picked up her bucket and headed to the large stream where she'd fill it with water, carry it back on a towel wrapped around her head and wet the plants' roots, repeating the process until every stem was watered. Although it wasn't as good as a downpour, she hoped it would get her maize through to next month when the rainy season was supposed to arrive. It needed to be out of the ground by December in time to plant her family's cash crop of rice.

A stream of sombre-looking local men ambled past. Still in their work clothes, they hadn't bathed even though everyone knew washing in the cold of night made you sick. And despite the workday being over, many of them clutched farming tools, wide-bladed knives and curved machetes. Her heart skipped a beat. The blades weren't tools—they were weapons. Something dangerous was afoot and she needed to know what it was.

She followed the men until they reached the village meeting place, an open platform with a roof for shelter used for community meetings, celebrations and to watch TV. She stopped well back, but not so far she couldn't see. Men of all ages crowded the stand and steps leading up to it, but barely anyone spoke a word.

Someone put the lights on and the men fidgeted, uneasily. Isabel noticed Rosario Nunes, the village head, standing in one corner of the platform in close conference with a small group of officials—a couple of *ABRI* and police officers, but also some outsiders, younger men whose heads were swathed in red and white bandanas, the colours of the Indonesian flag. Although they were East Timorese they looked bigger, tougher and more muscular than most. Isabel wondered if they were from one of those martial arts groups in Dili that people talked about in hushed voices.

Someone tapped her on the shoulder from behind and she gasped as she swung around.

'What are you doing here, *alin-feto*?' asked Gil.

Isabel relaxed a little, but on seeing the tension on his face, stiffened again.

Her eyes drilled into his. 'What's this about, *maun*?'

'It's a meeting.'

'What for?'

'All men aged between fourteen and sixty.'

'Who are those men Senor Rosario's talking to, the ones in bandanas?' Gil checked them out but said nothing.

'Gil?'

'They're from Dili. The big one with the dark sunglasses in fatigues is Gabriel Martinez. He's *preman*, runs cock fighting for *ABRI* at the markets and out in the villages. The Indonesian guy next to him in civvies looks like Intel. I have to go.'

'Be careful,' she said as he hurried off to catch up with his friends.

Isabel studied the stocky man called Gabriel. His skin was pale and he looked more full-blooded Portuguese than Timorese. Yet he carried himself like a local and seemed to fit in. His long, dark, slicked-back hair kept falling across on his face and he brushed it back repeatedly. In between, he sniffed and rubbed his nose while he shifted his weight from foot to foot. Isabel felt both repulsed and fascinated by his nervous toughness.

'Get on your way home girl!' an older villager said, scowling at her.

Isabel nodded and crept away, the unsettling image of the thug from Dili cemented in her mind.

11

JAKARTA, INDONESIA, SEPTEMBER 1998

Just after five on a cool October morning, the embassy car neared Jakarta's Soekarno-Hatta domestic airport. Ava sat inside and recalled her conversation with Juliette the previous night as they'd pulled up to Donald's place.

'I'll miss you, Mummy,' Juliette had said.

'Do you remember the piece of string that runs from my heart to yours?' Ava asked.

'Yes.'

'Whenever you miss me, or you feel sad or lonely, or you just want some love, think of that piece of string and you'll feel how much I love you. Even when we're apart, no matter what. I'll do the same. Okay?'

'Yes, Mummy.' She hugged her hard.

Ava took her suitcase from the driver, who'd insisted on hurrying around to open her door and pulling up its handle before passing it to her.

'Thank you,' she said.

She was one of a trickle of travellers beginning to fill the airport. As far as airports went, it wasn't bad. Simple and clean, the corridors radiated from a central hub and were decorated with occasional batik paintings and carved wooden sculptures. The place reeked of *kretek* cigarettes. Their clove scent took her back to her student days backpacking around Bali, Java and Lombok when these cheap local smokes were all she could afford.

As she wandered over to the check-in desk for East Timor, her eyes skipped over the life-insurance desk. She didn't need to be reminded of Indonesia's poor air safety record. The bright pink and orange sign begging her buy Dunkin' Donuts was equally unthinkable this early in the day.

It had only been a month since Ava had taken over the East Timor file from Premjid, but Donald insisted she visit. It posed a problem.

'I've wracked my brains and asked around,' she'd said to him, his back to her as he sat at his desk, 'but I don't know what to do with Juliette. I can't leave her with the maid. Juliette walks all over her and she can't help her with her homework.' Ava hoped he would let her postpone her trip.

'Pfft,' Donald had replied, waving his hand dismissively. 'She can stay with us. Alma will be happy to help. What's another child when you've already got four?'

Ava had little choice but to agree.

Flicking her long fringe off her face, she placed her bag down on the floor and waited for the man ahead of her to finish checking in. She was the only one in the queue. How coarse he looked, like a criminal, not because he was unshaven and unkempt with greasy hair and low-hanging jeans that revealed the crack of his bum, or even that he had a hacking cough and spat phlegm onto the linoleum floor between long drags on his cigarette. It was because of his face—rough, hard, mean.

Ava recognised his type from the Jakarta demonstrations—stocky middle-aged men who stood behind the student protesters, chain smoking and observing as they sneered into mobile phones. Bruce had warned her they were from one of the many Intel or intelligence services. Given this guy was probably going to Dili, she guessed he was *Kopassus*. She bit her bottom lip.

The Intel guy huddled closer to the airline clerk, joking around. He lifted his ancient vinyl carry-on bag branded with a now-defunct airline, and pulled out something silvery-grey and hard and placed it on the counter. A gun. A shiny toy-like pistol about the size of one of his chubby hands.

Ava's eyes widened. Why did he pull it out in plain sight? Guns could be carried in the hold, so he didn't need to sweet-talk the clerk. Maybe the weapon was personal, or he didn't have a permit, or couldn't be bothered checking it in because of the paperwork?

Or was this part of his Intel role—his presence and power ever visible to remind those who might be tempted to oppose the government that they were always being watched. But his arrogance was more than this. He was letting everyone know he was above the law. He could bend it to suit him because he *was* the law. Ava worked to keep the scorn from her face as the clerk picked up the pistol and fondled it. After more joking, he handed it back to the Intel guy, who stuffed it back in his carry bag. The clerk handed him his boarding pass and the two shook hands. Ava wasn't sure she wanted to share the flight with the Intel guy.

'Can I help you?' the clerk asked in English.

'*Selamat pagi,*' she said and handed him her ticket. She hadn't even arrived in East Timor and things were already grimy.

12

DILI, EAST TIMOR, OCTOBER 1998

The seemingly endless Indonesian archipelago spread beneath the plane, land turning to water turning to land again. Every now and then Ava glanced down to work out where they were. She'd lost track after looking through her background reading. She'd half intended to read the books when she was first given the new job but hadn't opened them, as though ignoring them might make the East Timor job go away. Spread across two portfolios, she hadn't had the time anyway. Yet here she was on the plane. She checked her watch. Only fifteen minutes to landing but all she saw below was water.

She finished scanning the second book and placed it on the empty chair beside her along with the other book, her glasses and a small makeup bag. The first one supported Indonesia's invasion of East Timor in 1975, arguing that in the context of the Cold War, the local socialists presented a genuine communist threat and that their civil war was causing instability that could spread. The second opposed it on the grounds that the invasion was illegal, the East Timorese should be given the right to govern themselves and they'd suffered much hardship under Indonesian rule. Ava understood both points of view, but regardless, Indonesia's human rights abuses in East Timor had to stop. At the same time, reducing the situation to goodies versus baddies was naive as both Timorese sides had slaughtered each other at some point.

Looking out the window again, she saw they were about to fly over a new island.

'*Permisi,*' she said to the hostess as she pointed. 'Is this the island of Timor?'

'*Ya, bu,*' the hostess smiled. 'We'll be flying over the border between west and East Timor soon.'

Ava felt a flutter of expectation. In a matter of minutes, she'd be standing on East Timor's bloodied soil, years of media reports coming to life in front of her eyes. But she was wary too. Talk of greater autonomy was creating uncertainty and instability. Did she have the stomach for further political turmoil, or the staying power for more late nights and time away from Juliette? And how would she deal with her moral dilemma?

The plane changed direction and headed north. Nothing indicated they'd crossed any hard border with west Timor—no great dividing fence, stations of troops or even roads, just dense vegetation and the glint of the odd metal roof in the sun. At last she noticed a landmark, East Timor's tallest and most revered mountain: Ramelau. Auspicious. She packed her things into her bag ready for landing and tightened her seat belt.

They were over the sea again. The plane's demented shadow ran across the rippling aqua water so its outline quivered next to fishermen in colourful traditional boats. In the distance, land at last and the outline of a town. Blocks of one, two and three-storey buildings sat lazily around a bay with a small harbour at the eastern end. Behind the buildings, to the north and west, were houses backed by hills. From the air, Dili looked like any other small Indonesian town.

They landed on the single runway and pulled up to the terminal, a glorified tin-roofed hut just like Ava had seen on other remote islands. She went inside and waited for her luggage.

The Intel guy passed her. As he approached the customs and police desk, they stood to shake his hand like they were welcoming an old friend. Ava couldn't hear what they said, but there was much laughter and back patting. The Intel guy walked straight past and outside without a single document check.

Ten minutes later her bag came. Ava pulled out her Indonesian identity card and a letter of entry from the Indonesian foreign affairs department, and fronted up to one of the two desks. She said good morning to the two men sitting behind it and handed her documents to the customs officer.

'It's already afternoon *bu*,' he chirped.

'Oh, *ya*,' she laughed.

'What's in your bags?' the policeman sitting next to him said as he peered suspiciously over the desk. 'Pornography?'

Ava raised her eyebrows at the pretence the men were creating to check her bag. She was a diplomat and her bag was Australian territory. In Jakarta they simply waved her through customs. But this was East Timor.

'Would you like to take a look?' she smiled and began to lift her suitcase onto the table, although she had no intention of showing them anything.

'No, no,' the official laughed, waving his hand to stop her.

She thanked them and manoeuvred herself between the two desks to find herself under a veranda. So this was East Timor.

A man with a welcoming look on his face approached her.

'Florencio?' she asked.

'*Ibu Ava*,' he replied, putting his hand out to take her bag.

'No need,' she said.

He led her to the car. Florencio wasn't really a driver. He was one of the local staff who worked on an Australian aid project delivering safe drinking water. But Ava was grateful someone was there to meet her. In other places, she was either left to her own devices or accompanied by a local official, often intelligence.

He navigated gaping potholes in the road as they headed towards a giant roundabout surrounded by grassland. In the centre, a large marble fountain with a cluster of fearsome bucking horses rose at least twelve metres out of a great empty pool. Did the Indonesians intend this monstrosity to represent themselves and their taming of the East Timorese people? Whether that was the case or not, the fountain looked abandoned, which perhaps said more about the situation here than anything else.

Florencio turned left onto a two-lane main road. After a while, they drove across a bridge spanning a wide river where old men hunched over flat woven baskets collecting pebbles. Ava looked more closely and realised the men weren't as old as they first appeared. They were simply worn.

The road got busier. There were no signs of the Indonesian occupation, just the occasional run-down van acting as public transport, stopping and starting at will, loud burned-out motorbikes weaving lazily in and around them, and trucks driving slowly. School children in neat uniforms ran across the road holding hands and a bus terminal buzzed with people buying food from women in sarongs squatting before produce displayed on blue plastic mats.

The first sign of Indonesia's presence came in the middle of more dry fields, a new housing complex with row after row of uniform, box-like residences sitting almost on top of each other in streets as narrow as the *kampungs* of Jakarta's poorer suburbs. How peculiar it looked in such barren, unwelcoming surroundings. Stranger again was the way the suburb appeared deserted, not *kampung*-like at all.

Now she saw a second sign of the occupation—an airport filled with army-green helicopters and men in uniform. It must belong to *ABRI*.

They passed through the shopping precinct and finally, to their left, lay the harbour surrounded by a beach with dirty, grey sand. On the right, some old stone Portuguese buildings and a white, two-storey structure were set back off the road. Ava recognised them from pictures as the governor's office. On the next corner was a church, and along the seashore, a derelict playground. Weren't children allowed to have fun here?

'Here it is, *bu*,' Florencio said as they made a right into a small car park edged by large European trees that formed a canopy of welcoming shade. 'Hotel Turismo.'

Ava got out and looked for reception but couldn't see a sign or anyone to ask. She peered into the courtyard, which had a lush but scrappy garden filled with coconut trees and old metal tables with tatty umbrellas. Flowers grew out of the back sections of World War Two bombshells whose wings acted as feet.

Florencio said, 'You'll hear stories from the older people about World War Two and how we hid your soldiers from the Japanese even though they were here illegally.'

Ava nodded, wondering if he really meant Australia shouldn't have abandoned the East Timorese to the Indonesians in the seventies given they owed them a debt of gratitude. He said goodbye and left.

Ava found an office and called out hello. No one answered, yet she felt she was being watched. She couldn't see a camera, but she could smell the ubiquitous aroma of *kreteks*. Somebody had to be close by. Was it the Intel guy, or was some other spy waiting around the corner?

She called out again and at last footsteps sounded on the stairs. An older Timorese man came down and stepped behind the counter. His face and nose were broader and more Melanesian than those of an Indonesian.

'Good afternoon. I am Augustino,' he said in stilted English.

'*Selamat siang*, Augustino,' Ava said.

He pushed a form in her direction, which she filled out.

'Your room. This way,' he said.

'I can speak Indonesian if that's easier.'

Augustino appeared relieved and indicated for her to follow him. 'Is this your first time here?'

'Yes.'

'I've been working at the Turismo for over forty years,' he smiled.

It clicked who he was. Premjid had told her about him. On the morning of the 1975 invasion he'd served breakfast—the last supper so-to-speak—to a left-wing Australian journalist who was then taken from the hotel by the Indonesians and summarily executed on the docks. Some speculated it was Augustino himself who'd snitched to the Indonesians. Surprisingly, no Australian government had ever demanded an explanation or apology for his death and the Indonesians had never offered one. No matter what the man might have been doing there—no matter whether he held communist sympathies, or even if he was a spy—Ava viewed this as a serious breach of justice. He was still an Australian who'd been murdered.

'Forty years is a long time,' she said to Augustino. 'I'm *Ibu* Ava by the way, from the Australian Embassy in Jakarta.'

'Oh,' Augustino said, his eyebrows lifting in surprise. 'The Ambassador was here a few months ago.' He lifted his chest with pride. 'I served him.'

Ava nodded. How different Augustino's accent sounded compared to the refined Indonesian spoken in the western islands of the archipelago. Thick and coarse, it made it challenging for her to understand. She'd have to work hard during her meetings here.

In one of the corridors upstairs, two men stood opposite each other, leaning against pillars and smoking silently. They glared at Ava with taut faces, and she wondered whether they were naturally suspicious or if they'd been posted there as watchdogs. She'd been watched like this in other Indonesian towns when she'd conducted security and human rights investigations, and wouldn't be intimidated so easily.

Augustino opened the door to her room and placed her bag inside before showing her around. It was plain but clean and had hot water and air conditioning—luxuries. She'd stayed in much worse places. In one *losmen* or hostel, cockroaches had crawled up her legs as she'd used the squat toilet in the middle of the night.

Once Augustino left, Ava opened the rickety French windows and stepped out onto the small balcony to take in the quaint, unspoiled bay. Small waves lapped nervously on the dirty beach, an imposing bronze statue crowned the hill to the right, and she could see an island that looked lonely in the middle of the sea—Auturo, where the Portuguese had fled after abandoning the colony to its coups and civil war.

She'd shared similar scenes with Juliette while travelling around the archipelago during their last holiday. Juliette hadn't enjoyed backpacking —too much grime and time spent on dodgy buses— and spent much of the holiday sulking. How was she going with Donald's family? She'd call her tonight as she usually did when she was away.

Ava had only two and a half days here to meet her new contacts and get to know the place well enough to write an update for Canberra. To provide a complete and balanced picture she'd need to meet all sides, beginning with Indonesian officials as protocol demanded, the independence lot including the guerrillas, and finally the pro-Indonesia East Timorese. At some point, she'd also visit the priests and nuns, Timorese journalists, and the human rights and women's groups who received Australian aid money. None of this would happen in any particular order. It wasn't the kind of place where you could plan meetings, Premjid had told her. You just turned up, made some calls and saw whoever was around.

There'd be a lot to take in if the history around her was any indication. Somewhere behind the hotel was the Santa Cruz Cemetery where hundreds of mourners were massacred by the Indonesian military in 1991. She'd forced herself to watch the footage of people falling whenever shots rang out, jumping with each loud crack. A boy died in another's arms and the living tried to drag their wounded and dead to safety behind graves and mausoleums. But the menacing sound of a siren, people screaming, groaning in pain and the desperate chant of the Lord's Prayer dominated the footage. Ava had bitten her lip hard to stave off her tears until afterwards.

Nearby too was the wharf of death where many were executed in 1975, and not two hundred metres away sat the infamous torture centre. Ava had seen photographs allegedly smuggled out that documented what went on there. One showed a bare-chested man with his hands tied behind his back sitting on a wooden chair with his head pulled back by a military officer.

He had ligature marks around his neck, what looked like cigarette or electrical burns on his chest and belly, and a chain that disappeared into the fly of his jeans. Sickening.

She rolled her shoulders one way then the other and checked up and down the street. East Timor reeked of fear and malevolence. There was an underlying bleakness no amount of natural beauty or quaintness could mask. She took in a deep breath of sea air, but it didn't expunge the sense of danger beneath the deceptive quiet. It lay in the menacing faces of the men who stood outside her room, the fearful expression of a mother who hurried by carrying children and shopping, the postures of men clustered in groups of two or three on the street, and in the silence where birds normally sang.

A knock rapped on her door and she jumped. 'Your car is waiting,' Augustino said.

She shouldn't have been alarmed he knew her business, or that a car had been sent for her when she'd said she would walk the three hundred metres.

Minutes later she was shaking the hand of Governor Fernandes, a bulky man with tattoos up his arms and a diamond earring in his left ear lobe. On his wall hung a photo of him wearing leathers sitting atop a Harley, and next to it a map outlining a road trip around the greater island of Timor.

'Do you ride, *bapak*?' Ava said, paying him full respect.

His eyes lit up. 'Yes. Do you?'

'No,' she laughed. 'But I always thought I'd like the freedom of it.'

After formally welcoming her to Dili, the governor licked his lips. 'I think you and I will get along well.'

Ava smiled.

'You seem to understand us better than the last one. For example, I think you know we Timorese are a violent lot who don't need more autonomy. Can you imagine the infighting if we have a UN ballot here, which some factions are pushing for? It will be just like in 1975.'

Ava listened and took mental notes, smiling inside at the way he seemed to believe he was convincing her with his political salesman talk.

———

JAKARTA, INDONESIA, THE DAY AFTER

Back in Jakarta, Ava waited at Donald's office door. She'd attended over twenty meetings in East Timor and in her hand held a draft cable of her first visit.

'Come on in,' Donald said, swivelling around in his chair. 'You've done it already?'

'Usually when I visit somewhere I take copious notes. But this time I decided to just listen and write my thoughts down later. I think it worked. It's short, just two pages.'

'Certainly is short for you,' he laughed. 'It'll be interesting to see if you came to the same conclusions as the Americans.'

'They were there recently?'

'A week before you.'

Ava's surprise turned into irritation. Had Donald insisted she visit East Timor now so he could compare her report with theirs? Was this a test?

'Give me a quick verbal summary.' He stretched and yawned so his shirt rode up and revealed his potbelly.

'Political tension is building. People don't want more autonomy under the Indonesians—they don't trust them. They want a UN ballot where they get to choose between complete independence or ongoing integration with Indonesia.'

Donald raised his eyebrows as if he found this moderately interesting.

'Since talk about autonomy began in July, human rights violations by all sides are up, but especially by *ABRI* against the independence side.' Ava paused. 'Perhaps most disturbing, though, are reports about the establishment of a new armed people's militia made up of Timorese locals, probably with *ABRI* or other Indonesian backing.' The people's militia were a kind of neighbourhood watch-cum-home guard *ABRI* had previously used in East Timor to do their dirty work.

Donald sat up straight. 'Are they reviving the old people's militia or forming new groups?'

'Both, I think. When you add that to the fact they seem to be deliberately pitting the pro-Indonesia and independence sides against each other, it's as though they're trying to create another civil war. Perhaps they want to claim the Timorese are incapable of peaceful self-rule and that Indonesia should therefore stay.'

'I agree. It's a worry. Emphasise it in your summary.'

Ava nodded, relieved he'd found her analysis useful.

'It sounds like you had a good visit. Your assessment is similar to the Americans' by the way.' Donald had a teasing smile and Ava wasn't sure how to respond. She usually got on well with him, but his smile supported her suspicion that he was assessing her. 'I'll read the rest and get back to you, but you certainly seem to have picked it up quickly.'

Ava stood and turned to leave. 'Donald, I meant to say... thanks for looking after Juliette.'

'Don't mention it,' he replied without looking up.

Ava scurried out, back to the safety of her own office.

13

___

JAKARTA, OCTOBER 1998

The Australian Ball was the highlight of the Jakarta expat social calendar. Other than attending obligatory work functions, Ava hadn't been out socially since her separation from Pete two months ago. The thought of spending more time away from Juliette made her cringe, especially when Juliette had told her she wished she could come. But tonight Ava deserved some fun.

The ball began with a three-course meal. Ava sat at a table of eight comprising some journalists and their partners, and two economic section colleagues around her age. Compared to many of the women around her who'd bought a new formal dress with matching, handmade shoes and handbag, and had spent the day getting their hair and makeup done, Ava's efforts were trivial. She couldn't remember the last time she'd shaved her legs properly or pumiced the callouses from her feet. It had been so long since she'd worn eye makeup she'd had to rummage around a drawer to find it. There'd been no time for shopping so her vintage Audrey Hepburn outfit would have to do, a royal blue off-the-shoulder sateen dress that flared into a full skirt at the waist reaching mid-calf, which she paired with pointy black suede shoes.

Yet even this effort felt like overkill. As she listened to the inane banter around her, it dawned on her that she was a thirty-year-old separated mother with slowly dimpling thighs, fine wrinkles around her eyes and emergent spider veins. What man was going to be interested in her? She'd be alone the rest of her life. Should she even bother staying tonight?

Between courses Quentin gave a speech from the podium. Lit from behind, his face appeared in profile. He was an accomplished speaker and handled the media with ease, but Ava wasn't sure what to expect of him tonight.

'An Englishman, an Irishman and an Australian go into a bar.' He chuckled and surveyed the room. 'The barman says, 'Is this some kind of bloody joke?''

Quentin laughed with the oblivion of a young child and a few people joined in, others following suit. Ava couldn't keep herself from giggling too.

He told a second joke with even greater enthusiasm. Ava watched him spray spittle at least thirty centimetres from his mouth. She swivelled around to see if her friend Denise from the *Sydney Morning Herald* had noticed.

Denise leaned in and whispered, 'Who does he remind you of?' Ava looked back at Quentin. 'Think Dame Edna's cultural attaché, Sir Les Patterson.'

Ava covered her mouth to silence her laughter.

The rest of the night she danced with colleagues and friends, steering clear of the married people who, since her separation, had lined up to tell her their marriage woes. When the ball ended, she wasn't ready to go home. The people from her table and some other embassy staff discussed going to a new jazz bar down the road.

'Come with us,' said Heather from the economic section.

Ava hesitated.

'I'll go with you,' said Denise.

Denise didn't normally party. She'd told Ava she'd got tipsy once and never wanted to be so out of control again. Her marriage was also on the rocks.

'Why not?' Ava agreed and the group hailed taxis.

They sat at the illuminated bar and ordered drinks, Ava in her old-fashioned dress and Denise in her childish floral print dress. The room was quiet, dull even. Apart from some tame background music there was nothing jazz about the place.

'So, this is single life?' she said to Denise, who was sipping lime and soda.

'I suppose so.' She had one of the warmest smiles Ava had seen.

A group of people burst in, laughing and talking loudly. Five middle-aged white men with Indonesian women half their age flopped down on the couches in front of Ava. The women had long loose hair and the men wore ubiquitous grey or black suit pants with long-sleeved white shirts. The shirt of the loudest and largest man escaped from his pants and his flaccid belly bulged over his belt. One of the giggling women collapsed onto his lap, draping her arms around him as she kicked her legs in the air. She and her friends ordered cocktails while the men chose beer and whiskey.

Another well-set man with more hair than the others moved aside from the young woman on his lap. He didn't seem to be enjoying himself, but the further away he moved, the more the young woman thrust her chest in his face. Had he taken his wedding ring off, or was he divorced and regretful? Maybe he had a daughter her age?

The man glanced up and his eyes met Ava's. Ava quickly looked away, but in that brief moment she witnessed embarrassment and humiliation, but most of all, sadness. The woman on his lap took her pink cocktail from the waiter and gulped it down in three sips.

Glancing at the group, Denise said, 'Pathetic, isn't it?'

Was this Denise's family values talking? 'I'm never going to meet a man here,' Ava replied.

'You want to meet someone?'

'One day. But what expat bloke is going to be interested in me with a child and mind of my own when they can have that?'

Denise scoffed. 'Who wants to be with someone who looks for love here because they can't deal with women from their own culture?'

'You're probably right,' Ava sighed. Not one man had so much as looked at her tonight.

'I'm going home. Want to share a taxi?' Denise asked.

'Thanks, but I'll stay a bit longer.' Ava ordered another champagne.

It wasn't long before Heather suggested they go to a nightclub in the port suburb of Kota. As they drove up in taxis, Ava saw that many burnt-out buildings from the riots hadn't been pulled down or renovated, yet their club hadn't suffered any damage. The owners must have been *TNI* or had the right connections.

Ava's group crammed into a small lift with walls covered in black velvet punctured by silver studs and a mirrored ceiling. The doors opened to an expansive room with a domed roof painted like a night sky. A throng of beautiful young Indonesians danced in unison to thumping techno music under coloured strobe lights.

They climbed some stairs onto a viewing balcony. Someone bought a round of shots and they downed them to get in the mood. The primal thumping of the bass carried Ava away, but also unsettled her. Everything about this place insinuated sex. Perhaps she could dance away her unease. No one wanted to join her, so she pushed her way through the crowd alone. As she reached the stairs, someone put their arm in her way.

'I saw you at the ball,' the owner of the arm said in an Australian accent. Curling blonde hair topped his white suit, matching Panama hat and mischievous face.

'Did you?'

'I'm Frank. Frank Leonard.'

Ava knew who he was. She'd been warned by the embassy's Federal

Police representative that Leonard was a suspected drug dealer. He put his hand out and she shook it.

'I'm Ava.'

'Ava. Are you admin or diplomatic?'

'Diplomatic.'

'Beautiful and smart.'

Inwardly she groaned and narrowed her eyes. 'And you? What do you do?'

'I own a restaurant not far from here. Cafe Banten. You might know it?'

'I do. It's a lovely place.' His restaurant and bar had wide teak floorboards, cowhide chairs, Baroque mirrors and soft-porn photos hanging in the toilets.

A waiter brought them champagne. 'I've ordered drinks for your friends too,' Frank said.

Ava realised she'd be obliged to talk with him until her glass was empty. Or perhaps not. She scoffed the bubbles down in two gulps.

'Thanks for the drink. I'm going to dance.'

She plunged into the pulsing crowd, almost swimming her way to the middle. The music vibrated deep inside her chest. Before Pete and Juliette came along, she'd lived to dance. The old feeling of surrender resurfaced and she lifted her arms above her head and closed her eyes. But as hard as she tried not to, she felt Frank's eyes on her and her moves felt forced. She didn't want him to think she was performing for him, yet there was no point in half dancing. She returned to the group. Perhaps if she'd taken some 'e' like the rest of the crowd…

Frank handed her a Cosmopolitan.

'Are you trying to get me drunk?' she frowned. 'I don't even like these.'

He laughed and leaned towards her ear. 'You can have something else if you like. A little blow?'

Diplomats should not do drugs, but she hadn't had this kind of fun since age nineteen. Lately, it had bothered her how much she'd missed by marrying and having a child so young.

'I need to go to the toilet,' she said.

'Take this with you.' He placed a small plastic bag in her hand.

Ava studied it. What if she got caught? She bit her top lip and closed her fingers around it. To hell with the rules.

In the bathroom, several young women burst out of a cubicle, their pupils dilated.

Ava finally got one to herself, jammed the door shut with her foot and lined up some coke on the cistern. She rolled up a ten-thousand rupiah note and snorted. A buzz of self-assurance rushed through her, pushing away her earlier unease. The drug had done for her what the alcohol and music couldn't. Finally she could dance.

She handed the plastic bag back to Frank and made her way to the dance floor, no longer caring whether he watched her. She writhed with the crowd, smiling. Everything fell away as she succumbed to the music.

'Good?' Frank asked when she eventually returned.

Before she had the chance to answer, Heather came over to her. 'We're going. Do you want a lift?'

Ava wasn't ready to face reality. 'I'll stay a bit.'

'You sure?' she urged, concern in her eyes.

'I'm good.'

As the group left, Frank moved closer. Ava didn't push him away. His lips kissed her neck before he nibbled her ears. If only Pete had done this. Frank pulled her to his body, which felt so much taller and leaner than Pete's. He kissed her on the lips, and she let him do that too. She kissed him back and thought how magnificent it was to be wanted. She hadn't felt this kind of desire for years. But was Frank the kind of man she wanted to attract? She pulled away.

Frank moved his hand lightly over her half bare back. She gave in to the sensation, everything heightened by the coke. He ran a finger slowly along the top of her dress, at the back first, then around to the front. Now he pushed his hand down inside until he found her nipple and she submitted to the deliciousness of it.

God, where was this going to end? Was she going to have sex with him right here and now?

Her flimsy hold on herself was faltering. What was she thinking? She was a diplomat in a Muslim country, and Juliette had a school concert early in the morning.

She moved away, this time taking several steps back. 'I have to go,' she said, rushing away to the sound of Frank's laughter.

Was this a trap? Perhaps she was being watched or filmed by the Indonesian police or some other nasty part of the Indonesian security apparatus. Were there cameras in the toilets? Were they going to use the information to make her their spy? Her thoughts ran off in a hundred directions. She'd be put in jail or thrown out of the country, a disgrace to the department. She'd lose her job.

She was such an idiot.

Outside the sun was already up as Ava hailed a cab. She checked if anyone was paying her special attention. As she got further away her fingers unclenched. Only the first-light joggers made her feel embarrassed now.

By the time she snuck into her bedroom, it was nearly 6 am. Juliette would be up soon. She caught sight of herself in her mirror. How ridiculous she looked in her ball outfit and eye makeup in the brash light of day. She got into the shower to wash it away.

'Hello Mummy,' Juliette shuffled in, rubbing her eyes.

'Good morning, darling,' Ava said in her best motherly voice. 'Get yourself a drink of water and I'll be out soon to make your breakfast.'

'Mummy. Did you just get home?'

Ava hesitated. 'Would you like pancakes today? I found maple syrup at Kem Chicks.'

'Yes please,' Juliette nodded before wandering away dragging Yello, her mustard-coloured teddy bear. She still slept with the eyeless near-bald toy Pete had given her when she was two. Ava's stomach wrung at the sight of it.

She dried herself, put on some day clothes and heavy concealer to hide the dark circles under her eyes. In the kitchen, she cooked for Juliette, pretending today was like any other Sunday, but vowing to never lose control like that again.

14

LIQUICA, EAST TIMOR, OCTOBER 1998

Isabel waited in the backyard for Gil to come home after the village meeting with the out-of-towners. A restless night breeze brought clean ocean air as the rest of her family slept to the buzz of chirping crickets. She wanted to know Gil was safe, but also what they discussed. When she'd asked her father earlier that evening, he'd refused to answer. From the worried glances he shared with her mother, she guessed it was something bad.

In the partial light of a kerosene lamp she passed the time reading the Old Testament. It lay open on the old table in front of her at the Battle of Jericho. She liked its story of spies, war and victory against all odds, although she knew Father Ribeiro would have preferred she focus on its message of obedience to God. But perhaps even more than the story's intrigue, she drew from it a sense of the past and her home. The great old battles—invocations of life and death—reminded her that here in Liquica clashes came and went as they'd always done, and probably always would, regardless of who held power. She looked up at the vast heavens, which reminded her about how meagre she was, and found her night anchor, the Southern Cross. But the bright stars that formed its diamond and usually made her feel rooted in Liquica, even when trouble rose up around her like in the Battle of Jericho, offered her no comfort tonight.

Her brother still hadn't returned, so she tiptoed into the bedroom where her younger siblings lay asleep on a mattress on the floor. The ammonia smell of urine stung her nostrils, but she found a dry space next to her youngest sister and lay down. She snuggled up against her in the hope her sleepy oblivion would be contagious, telling herself to forget Gil and the strangers from Dili. Slowly she drifted off.

Before long, voices woke her. She sat up in a fluster. Her little brothers and sisters were still asleep and there was no one else in the room. The voices came from outside. She tiptoed to the back door and peered around the doorpost to find her father and Gil arguing in whispers. She was relieved it wasn't *ABRI* or the police and slowed her breath to stop her heart from pounding in her head.

'No *papa*,' Gil said, his arms flailing as though making up for his muted voice. 'I will not join the militia! I don't believe in integration with Indonesia. I won't do the military's dirty work.'

'You don't believe?' her father hissed. 'Beliefs mean little when you've got no food or you're dead. Why can't you believe in your family? Why can't you do this for us?' Gil shook his head with contempt at his father.

'You could just pretend to be one of them,' their father begged. 'You wouldn't have to do anything. Just tag along.'

There was a moment when Gil seemed to be weighing things up, but a look of resolve settled on his face. 'Some things are greater than family, *papa*. What about the future of our people, of East Timor? What about my future? All your life you've been scared—scared of the Portuguese, scared of the Indonesians, scared of the neighbours, scared of starving, scared of everything. Well I'm not scared. I won't live in fear of them… Or you.'

Their father's shoulders shuddered as though weeping. Isabel swallowed back tears and stepped out of the darkness.

'*Papa*? Gil?'

Both men swung around to look at her.

'Go back to bed,' their father said. 'This doesn't concern you.'

Gil picked up his bag and stalked away.

'Wait,' their father begged, sorrow haunting his voice. 'I want to give you something.'

Gil stopped in his tracks. Their father pushed past Isabel into the house and back again with a tin in his hands. He pulled the lid off and took out some cash. Isabel let out a small cry. The money was intended for her confirmation. They'd been saving for two years.

'Take this,' their father said, holding the cash out for Gil. 'You may think I lack courage, son, but I've learnt nothing is as simple as it seems. The truth doesn't come easily in East Timor. You were born during the great famine, yet you're alive today. That didn't happen because of foolishness. Don't waste your life, *oan-mane*.'

Gil reached out and took the money. In the moment before their father fully let go of it, something passed between them—tenderness, sadness, and despite everything, mutual respect.

Isabel rushed up to hug Gil, but he thrust her aside.

'Gil,' she cried out softly.

'Where's he going, *papa*? When will he be back?'

'I don't know,' their father said, a tear sliding down his face. 'He wouldn't join the militia, even though they threatened...' He swallowed. 'Even though they threatened us with retribution.'

Isabel closed her eyes. The Battle of Jericho had this night come to them.

———

Days later

After attending mass with her family and teaching Sunday school, Isabel sat on a woven plastic mat under a tree in the back yard stringing beans for the family's evening meal. Her mother was crossed-legged next to her, peeling sweet potatoes and chewing betel nut leaves mixed with lime. Every now and then she spat a gob of bright red saliva, making lurid spatters on the dirt like eerie sea creatures. Isabel screwed up her face. The habit was disgusting and old-fashioned, but most of all she didn't like to think of her mother as being one of the village's wrinkled old biddies with their toothless pink holes of mouths.

One of the younger children napping beside them stirred and Isabel settled him back to sleep. Nearby her father stroked his fighting rooster to instil spirit into him. The older siblings out in the street squealed with delight at their game of soccer with the neighbourhood kids. Isabel loved the doziness of Sundays, the luxury of not having to do much and the village smells of vegetables and meat frying in palm oil for special Sunday meals. But today was tinged with anguish at Gil's departure. Even the rooster appeared to crow less.

'*Mama,*' Isabel said. 'When will Gil come home?'

Her mother stopped peeling her potato and gazed at her, tears gathering in her eyes. 'I can't answer that.'

Isabel swallowed. She didn't mean to upset her mother. She simply wanted to know.

A group of tattooed men in heavy boots and fatigue pants strode into the backyard, moving fast like a sudden storm. Isabel's breath quickened. They headed towards her father, who half-stood. Within moments they encircled him and pushed him back down. Isabel froze. Her bowl of beans spilling onto the mat beneath her.

'Where's your son, old man?' one of the men bellowed.

Isabel recognised him as the Portuguese gangster who ran cock fights for *ABRI*. What was his name? Gabriel. The Intel officer and the village head Rosario flanked him. Apart from a few locals, the rest of his gang were outsiders.

Her father continued stroking his rooster, refusing to look up at them.

'Gil was warned there'd be consequences if he didn't turn up yesterday,' said Senor Rosario.

What did he mean by consequences? Isabel slid back on the mat to manoeuvre herself behind the tree trunk, but her mother gripped her arm tight and shook her head. Isabel stayed put, silently praying. Help us Jesus, protect us.

Gabriel lifted his sunglasses and leant over her father, the veins in his neck bulging as he narrowed his dark eyes. 'Tell your son the leader of the Gardapaksi came to see him.' A spray of saliva fell over the old man. 'Tell him he needs to be at the village meeting place tomorrow morning at eight to join my militia group.'

Gabriel straightened up and Isabel's father looked up at him, giving little away. Gabriel signalled to the others it was time to leave, but his eyes fell on Isabel. Rather than leaving, he strode towards her. Should she run? She didn't dare.

'What's your name, *menina*?' Gabriel said in a softer voice as he stood over her.

She curled into herself.

'She's just a child,' her mother said, pulling Isabel in closer.

'She's Isabel Cardoso,' Senor Rosario said. 'A farmer.'

'Isabel Cardoso.' Gabriel paused and Isabel could feel his gaze roaming all over her. 'How old are you, Isabel?'

She hid now in her head in her mother's arms, hoping he'd go away.

'I asked how old you are, *menina?*' he shouted.

Isabel jumped. If she didn't answer things might worsen. 'Seventeen,' she croaked.

She heard Gabriel draw breath as though he was about to say something more. Instead he left, his entourage trailing close behind. Her mother let go of her, but rather than relief Isabel felt a chill crawl over her body. She didn't understand what had happened, yet she knew something had changed. One thing had ended, and another had begun.

15

JAKARTA, INDONESIA, NOVEMBER 1998

To say the traffic in Jakarta was congested prior to the economic crisis was like saying the sea was wet. It revealed nothing of the waves, rips and tsunamis—the perplexing chaos of Jakarta's roads where three orderly lanes turned into a six-lane gridlock as cars, buses and *becaks* pushed their way through the anarchic tangle, and horns bombarded the ears while drivers and passengers mingled with hawkers selling their wares, all united in a murky suffocation of exhaust fumes. Yet Ava preferred this organised madness to the stifling multitude of traffic rules in Australia.

Since the economic crisis—or *krismon* short for *krisis moneter* (Ava loved the way the Indonesians abbreviated just about everything)—her commute home had shortened from an hour and a half to twenty minutes. Juliette was pleased as she got to spend more time with her mother, but there was a downside for her too. Her much relished purple sunsets tainted by the thick layer of smog had returned to healthy oranges and reds. 'Boring', she scoffed whenever she saw one, making Ava laugh at the irony.

So it was unusual when Ava's embassy car became stuck in traffic on her way home after a meeting at the Indonesian parliament. Juliette's school had sent her home sick and Donald had agreed Ava could work from there and look after her when she wasn't attending meetings.

'*Macet*,' she said to Budi, the chubby driver with the constant grin who ate only Sumatran coconut curries.

How she adored the word. Its pronunciation, *mar-chet*, sounded exactly like a traffic jam—stuck—which was the word's literal meaning. But the fact that the congestion was so close to the parliament set off her radar. Déjà vu took her back six months when she'd watched students being shot in this exact area during the pro-democracy demonstrations.

'Have you heard anything about protests today?' she asked Budi, whose job it was to know about these things and get embassy staff to and from their destinations as safely and quickly as possible.

'No, *bu*. I'll check.' He radioed the embassy. '*Belum, bu.*' Not yet.

Everyone had hoped that after the political turbulence leading to Sujati's resignation, the violence was over. But parliament was sitting for the first time since Hidayat had taken over the presidency and Ava suspected the students were out demonstrating again. East Timor had become her main focus and she'd taken her eyes off them. She hadn't foreseen this recent development.

She took her phone out.

'Agus,' she said to one of her key contacts when he finally answered. She could hear a crowd shouting slogans in the background.

'*Ini Ibu* Ava,' she said louder. 'What's happening? Where are you?'

'We're protesting. Near the parliament.' His voice was shrill, breathless.

'What for?'

'For real democracy. We want *ABRI—maaf*, sorry *TNI*—out of politics and parliament. They may have changed their name, but they're the same corrupt lot. We're going to protest every day until parliament agrees to our changes.'

'I see. Thank you Agus.'

Ava smoothed her chipped thumbnail with her teeth. This meant on top of today's East Timor cable she'd have to send one on the protest, which would involve talking to all the student factions and their puppet masters who paid for their transport, food and daily allowances.

What if the protests escalated like last May? What if riots broke out again? Jakarta had that tinderbox feeling, like it might go up any moment. How was she supposed to look after Juliette and do justice to her job, especially given she was essential staff?

Ava sighed and looked at her watch. Juliette had been home with the maid for two hours and she needed to check on her. Usually by now the whiny half-hourly phone calls would have been in full swing: 'When are you coming home, Mummy? How do you do fractions? I'm lonely. Please can I get the maid to make Lamingtons? I can't find the glue. Please, Mum. Mum?' Then there was the ongoing guilt every time she had to attend a work function, at least three times a week. She'd arrive home at 10 o'clock to find Juliette still awake, making the next morning's 6'o clock wakeup even more challenging. Ava felt like a robot, and lately wished that Pete was still around. He'd done more than she'd given him credit for by simply being there.

'Is there a quicker way we can go?' she asked Budi.

'I'll do my best.'

In her notebook Ava listed the people she needed to contact and began making calls. If she was stuck in a tide of protest traffic, she might as well make the most of it. There was no going against the flow this time.

———

The next night

Ava sat on the couch at home with Juliette's head on her lap. Normally a self-contained child, she was still unwell. Ava placed a hand on her forehead to find Juliette even hotter and more clammy despite the two adult-sized paracetamol tablets she'd given her over an hour ago on the instructions of the embassy doctor. Ava took the thermometer from the table next to her and inserted it to her daughter's mouth. Juliette opened her eyes and winced. Thirty-nine and a half degrees. Shit.

'I'm sorry darling, but you're going to have to take a cold shower. The doctor said we need to do that if the tablets don't work. Have some water first.'

Ava held up Juliette's limp head so she could take a sip.

'Have some more. It'll help.' Juliette took some larger sips before laying her head back down.

'I don't want to have a cold shower, Mummy,' she cried.

'I know, my love. But I'll come in with you.'

Ava stroked her forehead. It was a pity she had to wait for her to be sick to enjoy this closeness. It was all Juliette wanted and yet most resisted. When she'd quietened down, Ava placed a cushion underneath her head before getting up to prepare the shower.

Her mobile rang. Of all the times. It was Agus.

'Oh God!' she heard him scream, his normal composure abandoned.

Her first instinct was to get out of range of her daughter. As she moved into the dining room, she listened carefully. Gunshots, an all too familiar sound.

'Are you okay? What's going on?'

'They've got guns. They're shooting at us.'

More shots rang out. Were they firing directly at Agus and his fellow students or into the sky? Were the bullets blank, rubber or live?

'Who's shooting? Where are you?'

'Near Atma Jaya. Have to go!'

'I'll see what—'

Ava stood as motionless as one of the room's marble pillars. Once again her thoughts moved to last May. She must prepare for all kinds of eventualities—more rioting, fires, chaos. Only this time she couldn't rely on Pete to evacuate Juliette to Australia.

She took a deep breath and reassured herself that the air wasn't filled with smoke from a ransacked city. Not yet anyway. She paced the shiny marble floor, which was cool under her bare feet. The swimming pool looked ludicrously serene. It was a strange life being a diplomat, luxury and destruction sitting so comfortably side by side. She decided to call her journo friends and get the facts.

Juliette. Bloody hell! How could she have forgotten her? She shouldn't have answered her phone. She wasn't supposed to put her work first.

Ava rushed back into the lounge and found Juliette sleeping peacefully on the couch, her face less flushed, and chest rising and falling evenly. When Ava felt her forehead, she sighed with relief. She put the thermometer back into Juliette's mouth. Thirty-eight and a half. The drugs had finally kicked in and her fever had broken.

'My girl,' Ava whispered, caressing her forehead.

But what if she'd walked back in and found her fitting, or worse? Guilt bore down on her. If she were a man, would she be having such thoughts?

Her journalist contacts told her the situation at the university had calmed down. 'There were some shots fired and a few students were carried away on stretchers, but no deaths reported. The traffic's moving again.'

Ava's shoulders relaxed, although she'd still have write it up tomorrow. But how would this be feasible while looking after Juliette, who was too sick to be left with the maid?

And there it was, her predicament laid bare. It was impossible for her to be a conscientious diplomat on posting as well as an acceptable mother without a partner to help. But she couldn't, and neither did she want to, cut her posting short to return to Canberra. It would be career suicide.

She picked up the piece of paper with Pete's hotel number from the telephone table. Before she could do anything, her mobile rang again.

'*Bu* Ava,' a breathy male voice blurted. Ava recognised it as Abel from Bishop Basso's human rights NGO in Dili. 'There's been a massacre in the village of Alas. You know, in the south of East Timor. We've confirmed nine dead but maybe up to forty-four, including some East Timorese soldiers in *TNI*.'

Ava paused to take in the news.

'I'm so sorry. What happened, Abel?'

'The killings took place days ago, but we just received confirmation tonight. It was sparked by some soldiers raping a local woman. *Falintil* responded by killing some *TNI*, who retaliated by killing some of them.'

'Has anyone made a formal statement?'

'*Belum*. I can email you more details.'

'Yes, please. As soon as possible would be great.'

Ava formulated a new plan of action. She'd call her Dili contacts to see what they knew and inform Donald before writing up that cable too. He might even want her to go into the embassy to send it tonight. *Damn.*

Pete's hotel number was still in her hand. She placed it back next to the phone, picked up Juliette and carried her dead weight body into her own bed where she could monitor her throughout the night. Her sleep would be disturbed as Juliette was a thrasher, but she would get even less for worry if she wasn't nearby.

After tucking Juliette in, Ava shook her head at the irony of the situation. Pete claimed he wanted to be needed, yet every time she did he was nowhere to be found, like when she came off a horse and injured her spine, but he refused to cut short his inventor's expo to look after her. Surely he knew Jakarta had turned volatile again. Why hadn't he called to check they were safe?

Ava's reflection in the wardrobe caught her by surprise. Dark rings hung under eyes, which drooped with sadness. Was she any better than Pete with her all-consuming career? She wasn't sure, except she'd supported his art whereas he'd undermined her posting despite her being the breadwinner. He was more than happy to let her pay the bills, but instead of acknowledging her, he tried to weaken her at every turn with the spiteful words of a man losing control.

16

____

JAKARTA, NOVEMBER 1998

A few days later, Ava and Bruce stood under the Semanggi overpass, an infamous tangle of clover-leaf shaped roads spreading in all directions near the Indonesian parliament, and observed a mass of students protesting below. Even though Juliette remained unwell, Donald insisted Ava attend the protest, promising that his wife would look after her again. She had little choice, agreeing only on the condition that Juliette stay in bed and his wife inform her if she worsened.

The highway before them was jammed with thousands of young men and women clad in bright university jackets trying to break through the security barrier into parliament where Hidayat presided. Back in May there'd been an air of expectancy and hope. They'd fought long and hard for democracy—risked their lives and futures even—but had been rewarded with only disappointment and disillusionment. While the Indonesian leadership had changed, the system had not. The military still held power, corruption was more rampant than ever and who you knew rather than what you knew mattered more than ever. The triptych of *KKN—korupsi, kolusi, nepotisme*, corruption, collusion, nepotism—was prospering now the lid had been lifted.

'It should be safer over here,' Bruce said, and they ducked behind the front lines near a large group of police taking a rest break.

'The police look agitated,' Ava said, watching one of them take a long drag of his cigarette before stubbing it out with excessive force, hate radiating from his face. 'I don't think they like being watched.'

'They're under-trained, under-resourced and inexperienced. They've never handled anything like this before. It's no wonder they don't want to be scrutinised.'

'They've been stitched up by *TNI* to fail in the hope of getting internal security back. Viva *dwifungsi*.' Ava referred to the army's dual responsibility to provide internal and external security, a practice that went back to the independence struggle but was now considered undemocratic.

Shouting broke out and the police surged forward, one of them pushing Ava to the ground.

'Careful,' Bruce said in Indonesian with a sternness she hadn't seen before. 'What do you think you're doing?'

The policeman ignored him, raised his long-barrelled rifle over Ava's head and fired into the crowd. Ava recoiled, covering her ears with her hands. She hoped she'd be safe if she stayed calm.

At last, the policeman stepped over her with his clumping black boots.

'There was no need for that,' Bruce yelled over the gunfire as Ava exhaled with relief.

'I'm fine,' she said, rubbing the bitumen from her bloody knee and hand. But perhaps Bruce was also talking about the police firing into an unarmed crowd.

Standing up, she examined the mayhem ahead of her. Intermittent gunfire continued as students ran in all directions, some trying to break through the police barrier for their own safety. Ava scanned the throng for bodies, but it was difficult in the chaos, until she glimpsed someone being carried off to the side. The student appeared lifeless.

'Bastards!'

She swallowed and picked up a spent cartridge from the ground. 'Is this from a rubber bullet?' she asked, knowing they could kill from this close.

Bruce nodded.

They hurried to an overpass where he thought they'd be safer. Ava made a few calls, but her journalist contacts had no fatality numbers yet. Her phone rang.

'Are you still at Semanggi?' Denise asked.

'Yes. I've been trying to get hold of you. Where are you?'

'We got chased away by the police. They aimed their weapons at us! In the end we had to climb over a high wall to get away. They're threatening foreign media now.' Denise's voice was filled with an outrage.

'Noted,' Ava said, thinking how *TNI*'s intimidation strategy seemed to be working. 'They don't want anyone reporting this botch up. Do you know how many are injured?'

'At least eight dead. There are reports of snipers too.'

'Christ.' If there were snipers it meant *TNI* was involved, and most likely *Kopassus*. They just couldn't keep away.

From their vantage point, Ava scrutinised a group of students in the forefront handing out Molotov cocktails. They'd told her they had a stock-pile of petrol bombs, but she hoped they wouldn't use them. They hadn't last May. But now, one by one, they set them alight and hurled them at the feet of the police. Long streaks of fire erupted along the road. At least they weren't aiming at the policemen's torsos and the flames were short lived. But what next?

The procession of Molotov cocktails continued as daylight faded into night. The police retreated with each round of petrol bombs before pushing back with their shields, and so they continued, taking turns at cat and mouse. As the night progressed, the crowd of protesters thinned out.

'It's pointless us being here. Let's go,' she said to Bruce. She needed to get back to Juliette.

They moved to safety and Ava dictated the salient points of a cable to a colleague at the embassy and found a cab to take them to Donald's place.

He lived in a rambling two-storey house, far shabbier than Ava's even though he was senior. Its garden was overgrown and his children's paraphernalia spread around the veranda and inside floors added to its ramshackle appearance.

'How's Juliette?'

'She's fine. She's asleep,' Donald said.

Ava and Bruce sat at the dinner table where a spot had been reserved for them. It was Donald's birthday dinner.

'Red wine?' Donald asked.

Violence followed by alcohol, their usual method of blunting the impact. Ava knocked it back.

'I'd better check on Juliette.'

Donald's oldest son bounded down the stairs. 'I can hear crying from Juliette's room.' His eyes darted between Ava and Donald.

Ava raced up the stairs two at a time and pushed the bedroom door open. The room was dark and Juliette wasn't crying, she was screaming. Ava turned on the light and rushed to her. Juliette was disoriented and faced the wall. Pink smears smudged her face, the front of her pyjama top and her pillow. Was it blood? Ava wrapped her arms around her and pulled her in tight. Her sweaty body smelled of sour vomit. No matter how much Juliette resisted, Ava knew this was the only way to calm her. Then could she work out where the blood came from.

'It's all right, darling. Mummy's here.'

Juliette's screams subsided into sobs as Donald walked in.

'Do you have a face washer?' Ava asked.

'Of course.'

She checked Juliette over but couldn't find any cuts. It was only logical she'd thrown up the blood. How alarming. Ava wiped Juliette's face and hands, put her in Donald's car with his driver and pulled out her phone to call the embassy doctor. Charlie was out to dinner and was none too pleased to be interrupted.

'It'll be from the screaming,' he said. 'A few small veins must have burst in her throat, hence the pink colour. Nothing to worry about. Call me if it happens again, but I doubt it will. Make sure she finishes those two courses of antibiotics and bring her in on Monday.'

Monday? Today was Friday. No, she'd bring Juliette in whenever she needed, but for now she'd take her home and monitor her through the night.

The streets were quiet, everyone barricaded inside their homes again. Ava took the phone number of Pete's latest hotel out of her purse and sighed. At least he called every now and then to give his contact details to the maid. Jakarta was on the brink of more violence and she was needed at work, but should she ask him to come back for Juliette's sake? The truth was that no matter how hard she tried, it was impossible for her to be a good parent and do her job well.

'This is a surprise,' Pete said, the satisfaction clear in his voice. 'What's up?'

Ava told him about Juliette and explained the city might go off again. She already sensed Pete saw this as a second chance for them, but there was no going back for her.

'I had no idea. I've been snorkelling on the islands.'

Ava held back a groan.

'I need to come back, don't I?'

'Yes, you do. For Juliette's sake. But Pete, this doesn't mean we're getting back together.'

'We can sort that out later.' He paused, then added, 'I never seem to be there when you need me, do I?'

Perhaps he had done some reflecting in Bali.

'I'll get on the next flight back. But,' Pete faltered, 'can you transfer some more money?'

Ava bit both lips to silence herself. Had he gone through three thousand dollars already, or was he hoarding some for later? She suspected he'd been doing so for a while. He'd already been amassing inventor supplies.

At home, Ava put Juliette to bed in what was once Pete's side. She lay next to her and petted her head. As Juliette drifted back to sleep, Ava touched her cheek and it felt familiar, as though she was touching her own face. Since birth, Juliette had been a reflection of the best and worst of her.

'Everything's all right now,' she whispered to Juliette. 'Daddy will be back soon and one of us will always be with you.'

Juliette opened her eyes to a slit, smiled faintly and rolled over. At last it seemed she might sleep the sleep of the contented.

17

LIQUICA, EAST TIMOR, NOVEMBER 1998

Isabel squatted on the ground as she washed rice for her family's evening meal. Two or three times a day she prepared this mainstay, the rice ritual of her life. Her family was poor, but not so poor they had to eat boiled root vegetables. *Falintil* called them the soul food of East Timor, but given a choice, she suspected they too preferred to eat rice. She rinsed the grains over again until the water ran clear.

Dusk was Isabel's favourite time of day, even if she spent it doing chores. The sudden cooling of the air and gentler light felt peaceful, and washing the sweat of the fields away signalled her work was nearly done. Best of all, she knew that soon she'd give herself over to sleep, her true escape.

Yet sometimes she fretted at night. After dark, hooded men in black took people from their homes, guerrillas clandestinely visited their families, and screams mixed with gunshots rang out. Husbands and wives moaned or argued too, and unsettled babies screeched for hours. In the darkness, unease festered in a way that wasn't possible in the glare of the day.

As if prompted by these thoughts, an unfamiliar noise came from the front yard. The hairs on Isabel's neck bristled. She heard her father arguing with someone, and now a group of ten men marched around the corner and headed in her direction. They wore signature red and white bandanas, and some carried guns—crudely carved wood with roughly welded metal pipes and trigger mechanisms adjoining a gunpowder chamber. Who were they coming for? She drew breath.

'You,' one of them said above the ruckus of her shouting father. 'Come with me. Now.'

This time Isabel recognised Gabriel. He couldn't be talking to her. Yet the only other person in the yard was her father, who the gang were blocking from getting near.

Gabriel towered over her, all puffed up like an engorged animal facing its enemy. He removed his sunglasses and in his other hand he held a military pistol. His breathing was laboured, sweat dripped off his forehead and he stank of body odour, alcohol and cigarettes. Isabel shut her eyes and told herself this couldn't be happening.

Moments later, her arm was wrenched so hard she found herself standing. The shock forced her to open her eyes, which met Gabriel's. At first she saw anger reflected in them, then fear, and now something she didn't recognise.

His men encircled them so Isabel was trapped.

But her father wasn't done yet. He launched himself at the gang and began yelling. 'You can't take her. I won't let you!' He took a run up, and just as he was about to plough into them, one of the gang raised his weapon and butted him on the head. He fell in a heap on the ground.

Isabel's mother was outside now. 'No!' she screamed, rushing up to the men and throwing herself down at their feet like a sinner begging forgiveness. 'Please don't take her,' she wailed and then kissed one of the men's shoes. 'Please. Please. Please.'

Gabriel's face went bright red and his neck stiffened. '*Diam!*' he screamed and everyone froze. Silence.

Gabriel looked down on her prostrate mother. 'I warned you that if your son didn't join Gardapaksi there'd be consequences. Where is he?'

Isabel's mother tilted her head up at him, her lower lip trembling, her eyes wide and pleading.

'Well?' he shouted and she flinched.

'I don't know.' She broke into gasping sobs.

Isabel looked away, unable to bear her mother's weeping. Words formed in her head as tears streamed down her face. 'Please don't hurt us, sir,' she heard herself say, some braver creature having taken control. 'I'll do what you want.'

'*Ayo*. Let's go then.' Gabriel pulled her arm as he marched her out of the yard. Isabel stumbled along, half willing and half resisting.

'If you bring Gil to me,' he shouted behind him, 'I might reconsider.'

The force of her mother's cries followed them and Isabel responded with loud, panicked yelps.

Villagers stared from their windows, probably relieved it wasn't them, their daughters or sisters being taken. Isabel's eyes pleaded with them. Will no one help?

Na'i maromak, Lord God, she silently beseeched the darkening sky. What have I done to deserve this?

But even God, it seemed, had turned his back on her.

18

LIQUICA, NOVEMBER 1998

Chafed and bruised from her journey along the rutted dirt roads, Isabel stood in an outdoor kitchen under a makeshift veranda. There were two buildings in the unkempt yard, a brick bathroom block and this small corrugated iron shed. They sat in Gabriel's militia post on the main road connecting Dili to the western part of East Timor. From here the militia guards who patrolled the perimeter could monitor and control the comings and goings of villagers and outsiders.

Gabriel asked Isabel to make tea and coffee. She set up one of the two kerosene burners but couldn't find what she needed among the basic cooking ingredients, utensils and crockery on the shelves. They must be inside. She gulped.

She opened the door to the shack where Gabriel and a close quorum of his militia men sat at the table. They didn't pay any attention to her so she snuck in and made her way to a cupboard, her head bowed in deference and to avoid making eye contact. She found what she needed and headed back out.

'You,' Gabriel said. '*Siapa namanya?*'

Isabel stopped. Was he talking to her? Was she so insignificant he'd forgotten her name? She turned around, still looking down.

'*Siapa namanya?*' he repeated louder.

'I'm Isabel, *pak*.'

'Oh yes. After our coffee and tea you'll make food for us tonight.' He tapped his fingers on the table and Isabel waited. 'Chicken saté and beef rendang. Enough for eight people. There'll be a special guest.'

She nodded.

'You *can* cook Indonesian dishes can't you? You're not one of those Timorese who only eat local food?' Gabriel's men sniggered.

'No *pak*. I can make them.'

'You know why I took you, don't you?' he said.

She froze, her hearing so acute she could almost detect the flapping of a butterfly's wings.

'A family like yours, not willing to support integration, not willing to give something back to Indonesia after everything it's done for *Timor Timur*. This is all you're good for.'

Gabriel's mocking words rung in her ears. She closed her eyes and wished herself away.

'Go!' he shouted.

Isabel rushed to the bathroom, the only place she had any privacy. Locking the door behind her, she leaned against it and let out a low muted cry as she doubled over and clutched her belly. She understood why she was here now, to be Gabriel's servant, a worthless slave. The urge to vomit came over her and she knelt down over the concreted toilet hole and retched, then wept some more.

When she was spent she moved to the bathing tub, scooped up a ladle of water and poured some into her mouth, spitting the acrid liquid into a drain on the floor. She wished she could trickle away down the pipes and into the ocean. The sea was only a few hundred metres away, but would she ever see it again? She cupped her hands and splashed her puffy eyes and swollen face.

Later that evening as she squatted stirring some saté sauce, a pair of polished boots came to a standstill in front of her. Isabel looked up. An Indonesian soldier loomed. Muscular and fit with a baby face that bore a long scar across one cheek, his leery smile made her skin crawl.

'Captain Sanadi,' she heard Gabriel say as he opened the door. She quickly got to her feet and stood back while the two men shook hands. 'How's Dili, *bapak*?'

Isabel fetched beer and food as they talked. Gabriel was grinning so hard he appeared foolish. From their conversation, she learnt that the captain was a *Kopassus* intelligence officer. Gabriel must either respect or fear him because he kept using the formal term *bapak* to address him.

'We have a problem,' Sanadi said as Isabel cleared the table. The men leaned in. 'We must convince Jakarta and the rest of the world there should never be a ballot here. They need to believe that if one is held, there'll be another civil war.'

Gabriel nodded and his men followed suit.

'The real question is, how we do that?' the captain continued.

By the smug look on his face Isabel suspected Sanadi already had an answer. Gabriel's brow creased.

'We're going to form new militia groups all over the western districts of East Timor.'

Why there? Most Timorese who supported integration with Indonesia already lived in the west. They often had family living across the border and welcomed unity, while most other Timorese did not.

'These *milisi* will play an important role in getting the message across to villagers that a ballot means violence,' Sanadi said. 'And you, *Pak* Gabriel, are going be a key part of this too. You're going to help *TNI* recruit, train and arm at least seven hundred militia men.'

Sanadi patted Gabriel on the back, who lifted his chin but his smile looked forced.

Isabel's stomach flipped. The news of seven hundred men with guns could only mean trouble.

'More beer,' Gabriel said to her, running his hand down his slick hair. 'And *Krakendang.*'

Isabel placed the bottles on the table. Gabriel took a long slug of a dark stout-like concoction and skulled a bottle of *Krakendang.* She hated the sickly sweet, pink coloured drink that was almost pure caffeine, and strained to stop herself cringing. Gabriel gasped for air as he wiped his mouth clean with the back of his hand and belched.

'Again,' he said, and she brought another round.

'You know,' the captain said leaning in towards Gabriel, 'this will mean a promotion for you, Gabriel. Once you've built up your Dili militia group, we'll make you the regional commander of all the western militia. Jorge will stay on as supreme commander—he helped us during the '75 invasion —but it's you who'll receive our orders, it's you who'll lead the militias. It's you who has the drive.'

Gabriel grinned, the insecurity of a few moments ago gone.

'A toast to you,' Sanadi said as he stood erect.

'Here's to us,' Gabriel replied. 'Because we're Timorese too. Because East Timor doesn't just belong to those *CNRT* sons of whores.'

Isabel shivered while the men cheered and the revelry began. She stayed busy serving drinks, but every now and then she caught Gabriel inspecting her. It was late when she walked over to him with her head cast down.

'Yes?' he said with a slur.

'Excuse me, *pak*. Is there anything else?'

A couple of the men snickered.

'Yes, there is. You can dance.'

She looked up at him with disbelief. 'Excuse me, sir?'

'Dance for me.'

'*Pak*,' I don't know how to dance and there's no music and—' She searched his face for a glimmer of humanity, but found none.

'Dance,' he yelled.

Isabel jumped. The men glared at her, some leaning forward, their mouths dropping open, while the captain sat back in his chair and folded his arms, bemusement on his face. She swallowed hard, closed her eyes and began to shuffle her feet along the ground and move her arms in the air.

'Not the Timorese way. Like those belly dancers. Your hips. Use your hips.'

She tried swinging her hips from side to side, but it felt awkward. She grimaced and squeezed her eyes tight. The humiliation.

'That's the way. Now backwards and forwards like this,' he said.

She opened her eyes to find him directing her with his hands. She did as he said, his eyes gliding up and down her body. Tears leaked down her face.

'Around more with the hips,' he gestured again. 'Yes. Now your arms. That's it.'

The men clapped and one grabbed his groin. Isabel swayed and rocked and swirled to Gabriel's commands.

After what felt like an age, he told her she could go. She snuck into the side room where she'd been told she could sleep and sat down on the thin mattress on the floor. As she waited for the room next door to go quiet, she leaned against the metal wall and hugged her knees. What would her family say of her shame? What would Father Ribeiro—what would God say?

'*Mama, papa*, Gil, where are you?' she whispered as she lay down on the mattress and curled into a ball. Closing her eyes she said a prayer, but it brought her no consolation. All she felt was absence. She listened hard for a voice, a message, something of comfort. But there wasn't so much as a whisper, not from God or anyone else.

19

———————————————————————

JAKARTA, INDONESIA, NOVEMBER 1998

The spiked steel gates of Jakarta's Cipinang Prison opened slowly for the ambassador's car, a shiny white BMW. The driver turned into the prison's entrance, inching the car forward so the ambassador had the least possible distance to walk. Quentin put his red, spill-proof cup down and Ava laughed to herself. Old and stained, shavings of plastic hanging off it, he took it everywhere, almost like a security blanket.

They stepped out into the rainy season humidity. It was November, the beginning of the wet, and for months daily afternoon rain preceded by intense heat would create an unbearable soupy atmosphere.

Ava was struck by how unlike any other Indonesian prison she'd visited this place was. Its grotty yellow walls were just three metres tall and topped with no more barbed wire than other Indonesian building. She couldn't see an observation tower either, though surely one must exist. She'd expected the infamous Cipinang to be more sinister.

Quentin led her into a white tiled waiting room housing a small table and chair in the centre. A guard sat on the seat smoking a *kretek*. He was fat and soft looking, as though he only stood or walked when absolutely necessary. Ava swallowed at the thought of entering a world of iron bars

100

and deprivation as she pulled a gold-crested letter of permission from the Indonesian justice minister from her handbag.

'*Selamat pagi, pak,*' she said, offering the letter to the guard. 'We're here to see Mr Aleixo Maestre.'

The guard glanced at her as he took the letter. He read through it slowly and picked up the telephone receiver on his table. After a brief call, he motioned them through the door behind him where they were told to follow another guard down a narrow corridor. It eventually opened up into a room with a wooden picnic table, bench seats and glassless barred windows. It wasn't private, but Ava suspected nothing here was.

She placed her basket of goods on the table and the guard made a cursory rifle through the red wine, chocolates, cigarettes and fresh fruit looking for contraband. They were asked to sit down and wait. Ava hoped Quentin hadn't noticed her excitement at meeting Aleixo, East Timor's legendary poet-leader.

A new guard entered along with a bearded man in smart casual clothes. Ava recognised Aleixo from photographs. About her height, slim and light-skinned, his face was long. Despite being in his fifties, he had a full head of only slightly greying hair. Ava thought he looked more Portuguese than Timorese.

'*Bondia*,' he said in a low, cigarette-fuelled voice, shaking Quentin's hand vigorously with both of his as he gazed into his eyes longer than others normally would. 'Welcome back, Ambassador. I am so pleased to be meeting you again.'

His English was slow and his accent thick, yet he treated Quentin like a long-lost friend.

He turned to Ava. '*Bondia.*'

'*Bondia.* I'm Ava Vuyk, second secretary. Pleased to meet you.'

She put her hand out to shake his, but he smiled, leaned forward and kissed her on both cheeks before quickly adding another on her lips. She was startled, but restrained herself from recoiling. Did he do this to all women?

Aleixo asked the guard to bring tea, who bustled away as though he was the great man's servant. You could buy anything in Indonesian prisons —food, cigarettes, drugs, guards too, but this was something more. He seemed to revere Aleixo.

'I'm responsible for covering East Timor in the embassy now,' Ava said to Aleixo in Indonesian, 'so I'll be interpreting for the Ambassador.'

Aleixo beamed at her. 'You will interpret for me?' he said in Indonesian. 'As you can hear, my Bahasa is terrible. My Portuguese and Tetum are another matter, but my Indonesian...'

'I'm sorry, but I don't speak either of those languages,' she said. How humble he appeared, or was it an act?

'Let's start.' Aleixo looked at Quentin with a new intensity as Ava began taking notes. 'First, thank you for the basket. Now, tell me your intentions.'

Aleixo's Indonesian was simplistic and coarse. It seemed heavily influenced by Portuguese, which gave him the wrong word choice. In the language of diplomacy, tones, absences and silences were almost as important as the words themselves. While being careful to convey the exact same meaning, Ava was glad she could finesse things a little.

'As you probably know, the issue of East Timor receives a lot of attention in Australia and my government follows developments very closely,' Quentin began. 'I'd like to get your views on recent events, including the UN negotiations, which seem to have stalled.'

Aleixo nodded, took out a cigarette, and as an afterthought offered one to Quentin and Ava. They both refused and he lit his up before inhaling deeply.

'Let me start with the recent UN negotiations.'

Aleixo took the ambassador through his side's frustrations with the Indonesians over the last meeting in New York. 'The international community must understand that we are willing to compromise but the Indonesians are blocking progress, as they've always done.'

Quentin nodded, his brow creased. 'Can you explain to me why a referendum is so important to you?'

Aleixo gave him a fatherly smile and leaned in. 'At the time of the 1975 invasion, we, the resistance, had thirty thousand weapons. By 1979, after the war against the Indonesians and their Timorese supporters, our bases were destroyed and we had only seven hundred weapons left.'

He was a born storyteller and dripped with charisma, Ava thought as she scribbled madly. Everything he said felt like an intimate tête à tête.

'Some years ago, I went to the people and asked them, 'Do you want to continue this struggle?' They told me, 'We want you to take these seven hundred weapons into the jungle and fight for independence'. You see, Ambassador, this is not *my* struggle, it comes from the people. I will accept a brief period of autonomy, which would be useful for ensuring a peaceful transition, but there has to be a referendum for all Timorese—the people must speak, no matter their views.'

Quentin stroked his chin. 'I understand.'

Ava thought she understood Aleixo's motivation better too. He claimed to speak for all Timorese, not just for those who wanted independence.

A guard approached and Ava glanced at her watch. They'd been talking for nearly an hour. The interpreting process slowed things down considerably.

'You will have learnt,' Aleixo said with gravity, 'that during the recent Alas killings, *TNI* used East Timorese militia, who they trained and armed, to lead the attack. This is a worrying development, pitting East Timorese against East Timorese. It's as though they're trying to create the impression of civil war.'

Quentin looked at Ava.

'Yes, that's what we understand happened too,' she said.

'I want peace in East Timor, Mr Ambassador. I want to bring about national reconciliation between the pro-Indonesia and independence sides. I want to reach an agreement that includes all Timorese. But with *TNI* manipulating the situation, how can anything we try be successful? All they want is to create conflict.'

Aleixo lit another cigarette and his face softened again. 'This is where we need you to step in. We require Australia and the rest of the international community to demand in the UN and international media, that Indonesia withdraws its troops from *Timor Leste*. At the very least, we need oversight by peacekeeping troops. Only then can reconciliation—can peace—have a chance. Only then can a political solution like a ballot or autonomy succeed.'

Quentin nodded. Ava felt sorry for Aleixo and the East Timorese. There was no chance the Indonesians would pull *TNI* out of East Timor. Neither would they allow foreign troops in to safeguard a political process as others had also suggested. Australia had asked, and more than once, but each time Hidayat had ruled it out, describing the idea as 'an affront to national integrity'.

'*Permisi*,' the guard said, politely lowering himself. 'It's time for Friday prayers.'

Aleixo shook Quentin's hand, almost bowing before he leant towards Ava and kissed her on the cheeks, again sneaking one on her lips.

As they entered the mad Jakarta traffic, Ava thought how strange it was that leaving Cipinang should feel like deserting an oasis.

'Do you think he's been strategising all this time for when Sujati left the presidency?' she asked Quentin.

'He's no fool,' Quentin said sipping cold coffee from his cup.

She agreed. While Aleixo's emotions were as passionate as any Latino's, his words were those of a wise old Buddhist. If only *TNI* had treated the Timorese like brothers and not as enemies at war.

'*Audaces fortuna iuvat*,' Quentin muttered. 'Fortune favours the brave.'

Ava was unsure if he was talking about Aleixo or the Indonesians.

'By the way,' he said. 'This Alas incident. I think we need to look into it further. Get yourself on a flight to Dili as soon as you can get clearance.

It's about time we got a fresh picture of what's happening on the ground anyway.'

'Okay,' Ava said. She'd be only too happy to escape Pete and Jakarta.

———

The balcony at the rear of Ava's house was her refuge. There she sought sanctuary from her estranged husband, the prying eyes of her domestic staff and the dank air conditioning in which she spent most of her days and nights. She was nearly done reading her pile of East Timor cables. Although she wasn't supposed to take them out of the embassy, everyone did. The alternative was spending even less time at home.

The last one done, she slammed it down and the pile back in a folder. East Timor was at a stalemate. Something had to happen to move things forward, but what?

She stared up at the high concrete walls crowned with jagged pieces of glass that surrounded her house. They protected her family from thieves and gave them privacy from the gawking eyes of neighbours. But lately, it felt as though the cost of this seclusion might be too great. The walls dimmed the natural light that might have eradicated the cloying mustiness, and stymied the cool summer breezes that could have brought relief. In moments like these, her home felt more like a prison than a sanctuary—a sad empty battleground in which her arguments with Pete echoed from wall to wall while Juliette hid in her bedroom. Perhaps she'd been wrong to ask him back.

Lately, work also brought her little gratification. She covered the two most important issues in Australian diplomacy for years—Indonesia's leadership change and the resolution of East Timor—and yet she felt more dissatisfied than ever. East Timor was going nowhere, just like the impasse of her marriage. They lingered in no man's land, the future beckoning but impossible to grasp.

Above her a cloud burst and a bright jack of lightening turned night into day. A thunderous clap followed, and rain pelted down so hard it sounded like hail.

Ava's heart skipped a beat. She walked to the edge of the balcony until she was centimetres from the downpour and put one arm into the deluge, then the other. She wanted to feel something again, a sense of reverence at being alive. Everything she'd buried deep inside, the moments of horror she'd witnessed as the dispassionate professional, now needed to be felt. But dare she let them surface? It wasn't that she didn't feel enough, it was more that sometimes she felt too much.

Stepping into the rain, she was instantly inundated. She tried to look up, but it was pelting down so hard it hurt her eyes. While the top of her head took the brunt of it, the pain still wasn't enough to spark any emotion.

She turned to go back and saw Pete standing in the doorway, hands on his hips and shaking his head.

'Your job, East Timor. I'm worried about you, Ava. Is it really worth—'

'Trying to undermine my confidence again, Pete?' She flashed him a hurt look. He'd caught her in a vulnerable moment, which he was attempting to exploit. She felt violated.

'You misunderstand me. They're hard bastards, but you're not. Do you really want to be like the—'

'I'm never who you want me to be, am I? Always too something. I can't win.' She stormed past him into her bedroom, leaving a trail of water.

She locked the door. Just because she had feelings, just because she cared, it didn't mean she couldn't hack it. And just because she couldn't cry right now, it didn't mean she was about to turn into them.

Did it?

20

—

LIQUICA, EAST TIMOR, NOVEMBER 1998

The drunk men had all gone to bed when Isabel allowed herself to drift off to sleep on her thin mattress, falling in and out of muddled dreams of drowning and nakedness and death threaded with memories and feelings of loss.

It wasn't long before she was woken by someone's touch. A hand grabbed her shoulder and another her hip, rolling her from her side onto her back. In her half-conscious state, and in the meagre light of the new moon outside, she believed her brother or *Falintil* had come to rescue her. But now the weight of a man's body descended on her, pinning her down with his legs. His hands grabbed both of hers and pulled her arms above her head.

'Argh,' she cried, choking on the sickly fumes of alcohol, cigarettes and sweat that percolated down from above. But rather than slowing him down, her whimpering egged him on. The man groaned as he reached his hand underneath her top and onto her breasts, hungrily squeezing one and then the other hard so they throbbed.

'Please, no,' she pleaded, never having been touched there before, never having been touched anywhere by a man before. She panicked and tried to pull away, but could barely move between the firm grasp of his thighs.

The man lurched his head towards hers and thrust a tongue into her mouth, a segment of his hair falling into her eyes. The tongue wriggled frantically as it chased hers so that she almost choked, the skin around her mouth burning from the rasp of his unshaven face.

Now he pulled his hand away from her breasts and reached between her legs and inside her underpants.

'No!' she screamed.

'Remember your family,' the man said in the hard voice of Gabriel.

Isabel stopped cold.

Gabriel sat up and used both hands to rip off her underpants. She struggled to keep them on, pulling at their remnants while kicking and squirming to get away. He smacked her hard on the face and she fell back onto the mattress. No match for him physically, she turned floppy, retreating behind her now-closed eyes.

Gabriel unzipped his pants and pulled them down. He clambered back on top of her and pushed himself into her, quick and hard. For Isabel it was as though she was being cleaved apart, burning and stabbing pains stealing her breath away. She stifled her cries as he thrust himself in and out of her. He sped up, riding her without mercy until he spasmed, calling out *Isabel*. He sighed and collapsed, his full mass bearing down on her so she could hardly breathe.

'You're my wife now. What are you, Isabel?'

'Your wife, Gabriel,' she said, only able to utter his name because she wasn't really there.

The real Isabel was running away to the safety of the dark forested hills where no one could catch her. The real Isabel had eluded Gabriel and his militiamen, his *TNI* friends and the villagers who'd betrayed her by doing nothing. Not even her brother who'd abandoned her for his ideals could find her there, or her absent parents or the guerrillas who hadn't rescued her. Not even God, not any more.

Gabriel rolled onto his side, draping an arm around her waist and a leg over hers. When he began twitching, she knew he was asleep.

As she lay awake, blood and semen slowly leaked from her insides and created a sticky wetness on the sheet below. If only she could find a cold river to cleanse her body of his grime, but she dared not. His grip on her was too tight.

'Hold me,' Gabriel pleaded in a childlike voice, his feet kicking. Was he fighting off his enemies in his dreams, or was he running too, only towards her and not away?

21

LIQUICA, DECEMBER 1998

Weeks later, Isabel stood under a tree at the edge of the militia post. She wore a girlish pink and white dress that Gabriel had bought her. It hung off her gaunt body making her look several years younger than she was.

She looked up at the sky and frowned. It was a typical wet season day nearing Christmas. Sunny and dry in the morning with clouds building until they dumped their contents onto the earth, usually in the middle of the afternoon. Isabel knew this cycle well from her farming days. Back then it had reassured her about the way of things, past and future. But the seasons, the seeding and growing and harvesting of crops she used to busy herself with, could no longer comfort her. These days, household chores and the duties of a militia slave filled her time, although unlike growing food they brought her no contentment. As monotonous and predictable as farming had once seemed, she now longed for its variability.

But what Isabel yearned for most was her family. Every night she listened for them and every day she hoped for a message or glimpse of them. It had been more than two months and nothing. Did they miss her? When would they rescue her? Were they injured, or worse, dead? Had they been forced out of the village? She tried to push her worries aside during daylight hours when she had work to occupy her, but during the long nights it impossible to contain her melancholy.

She looked down from the sky and gathered her shopping bags.

'Are you ready?' she asked the militia guard who usually escorted her to the markets.

'Not today.'

'*Senor*, I need veg—'

'You can go alone, *senora*,' he sneered.

Isabel's mind raced in many directions. Was she free? She couldn't be. Did they trust her? It didn't feel like it. Was she being given a bit of freedom? Perhaps. Did this mean she could also visit her family?

The guard saw her confusion and laughed mockingly.

'Go,' he said. 'But just to the market. If you go anywhere else, or try to escape, we'll hear about it. Remember, we know where your family is.'

Isabel wasn't intimidated by his warning. Rather, she felt excited because it meant her family was alive and living in Liquica. She grinned at the memory of hope.

Walking up to the gate she stepped across the boundary. This was the most freedom she'd been given since arriving. With every step, her ties to Gabriel and the militia post fell away. Soon the urge to run overcame her. She imagined herself travelling up the road like the wind, along the lanes and pathways and into the arms of her mother and father who would take her somewhere safe where she'd never have to see another militiaman again.

But Liquica was a pro-Indonesia stronghold now. It had a *Kopassus* and *TNI* base and the militia were everywhere. What chance did she have of escaping, even if she found her family? She walked at a sensible pace, the sharp stones that almost penetrated her worn thongs and dirt collecting between her toes grounding her.

She stopped in her tracks. She had little chance of finding her family again unless she got help. But who could she turn to? She moved again, only this time in the way a woman does without a man by her side to control her pace. Perhaps she could ask for help from someone at the market like an old neighbour or Father Ribeiro, or she may even bump into her family. So far she hadn't seen them, but it was different now she was alone. Her heart thudded in her chest, and she quickened her step until it was ahead of her—her link to freedom.

With her eyes wide and the corners of her mouth curling in anticipation, Isabel scanned the market. She'd grown up with the people here and knew many of them, but she couldn't see her mother or any of her family, and neither could she see their neighbours. No matter, she'd talk to some of the other women. They'd help her get a message to her family, or at least to the church.

She recognised a hawker from the outer village selling tomatoes, onions and garlic.

'*Bondia, Senora Gomez,*' Isabel said as she tried to catch her eye. 'I'll take these four tomatoes.'

The senora acted as though she hadn't seen or heard her.

'It's me. Isabel Cardoso.'

The woman continued to ignore her.

'*Senora,* please. I need to buy food or I'll get into trouble.'

Still nothing.

'Can you help me find my family? Are they all right?'

Isabel waited, but she might as well have not existed. She turned and walked away.

'Militia whore,' the senora called behind her.

Isabel's chest tightened, but she moved on. She approached another stall where she picked up some green vegetables. She took a five hundred rupiah note out of her cloth purse and held it out to pay.

'Two thousand rupiah,' the seller said.

Isabel knew Senora Salves well. She'd taught her children at Sunday school.

'But *senora,* it's me. Isabel Cardoso. I—'

The woman turned to talk to her friend at the next stall.

'I'll pay you the money. Just help me get a message to my family. Are they still in Liquica?'

The senora went on talking to her friend. Isabel took another fifteen hundred rupiah out of her purse, placed it on the makeshift table and took the vegetables.

'I beg of you, tell Father Ribeiro I need to speak to him.'

Senora Salves flicked her head around and spat on her. Stunned, Isabel took a few steps back and pulled out a cloth shopping bag to wipe the slime off her dress. She hoped no one had seen, but the more she tried to wipe it away, the more she felt she stood out. Worst of all, she didn't understand why the women were treating her like she was the devil himself. Yes, she'd been accompanied by militia when she'd shopped here before, but surely they understood she was their prisoner?

Isabel wanted to run and hide, but remembered she still had to feed the men. The problem was, she was given just enough money and at these prices she wouldn't be able to buy nearly enough food. She could tell the militia what the women had done, but that would get them into trouble and she didn't want that. Or she could say she lost the money and maybe get away with it this once, but what was she supposed to do next time?

She bought more food, dawdled back to the militia post and lay down on her bed, curling herself up into a ball. It was all ruined, her first moments of liberty, her dreams of finding her family destroyed by the same people she thought would help her. *Everything happens for a reason,* she heard Father Ribeiro's voice say in her head. *You may not be able to see it now, but it's all part of God's perfect plan.* None of this felt perfect, not a moment or a single thing.

As she lay on the bed, she knew she should be doing her chores, but she didn't care. She'd been stripped of her future, a nobody, a nothing, just as Gabriel had said. She closed her eyes and, with nowhere else to escape, fell into the forlorn sleep of the forsaken.

22

JAKARTA, INDONESIA, DECEMBER 1998

Jakarta newspapers lay sprawled across Ava's desk as she circled East Timor stories for her daily press wrap. These were long days as she waited for permission to visit again, and it felt as though she was sending the same message to Canberra over again—East Timor was at an impasse. At this rate, twenty-three years of Indonesian occupation might easily turn into twenty-four or twenty-five.

Judy appeared at her door. 'The Ambassador needs to see you. Now.'

Ava grabbed her notebook and pen and followed her into Quentin's office.

'Take a seat,' Quentin said, tidying the papers on his desk, then looking up at Judy. 'Close the door behind you please.'

'There's been a major policy shift on East Timor in Canberra,' he said, still not looking at her. 'Judy printed a copy of the cable for you but it's highly secure so it won't be on your system. Keep it to yourself.'

'Yes,' she said as she took it from him.

Was it an ultimatum, a proposal, an offer? She hadn't heard so much as a whisper about this. She wanted to read it there and then but didn't want to appear overly eager.

'I also have copies of a letter from the Prime Minister to Hidayat,' he continued. 'Directly after our meeting, take my car and personally deliver them to the palace and foreign ministry in that order. Tell them the original will follow later as per the usual protocol.'

The president. The foreign ministry. This must be big. But all this protocol was new to her, hand delivering copies of letters in certain order with the original to follow. She understood now why DFAT had a protocol section to advise on such processes.

'Also, I need you to accompany me on a call to the president tomorrow. We'll meet the foreign minister and others later this week.'

Ava stopped taking notes and looked up at Quentin.

He glanced out the window at the cloud-filled sky. 'The letter says we believe the Timorese are unlikely to accept anything less than a referendum as a solution. It urges Hidayat to come to an agreement with the Timorese. Something like the French have in New Caledonia—the Matignon Accords. It involves a long trial period of autonomy followed by a vote where the Timorese choose if they want to remain part of Indonesia or become independent. It's all coined very diplomatically, lots of flattery and so on.'

Ava worked hard to keep her surprise and concern from her face. She knew the Matignon accords well from past work and had even toured New Caledonia officially. This was a completely different situation. There was no way the Indonesians would support East Timor for years when they knew they would be voted out because it was way past them being able to win the Timorese over. What's more, supporting a referendum on independence was a complete reversal of Australian policy and the Indonesians would be furious at this betrayal. The Indonesians wouldn't like this suggestion one little bit.

'Make no mistake. This is huge', Quentin said, finally looking at her with narrowed eyes.

Ava nodded but needed more background so she could later explain it to the Indonesians.

'If I can ask, why are we sending this letter now? Where's it come from?'

Quentin began stroking his chin.

'The UN process has stalled and there's no sign of the Indonesians seriously engaging the Timorese in any other way. On top of that, *TNI* human rights violations are still rising… Plus…' He cleared his throat. 'I spoke to The Minister. He said the government's feeling the heat from the Australian public. Several ministers, including Stretton himself, nearly lost their seats over the matter in the last election. Beaumont lost votes too.'

Ava had read that several ministers had been in trouble, but she hadn't realised the prime minister had been at risk or that East Timor was the cause.

'How will we manage the bilateral relationship with Indonesia?' she asked.

'We'll focus on the constants. Our underlying position on Indonesian sovereignty over Timor remains the same—we hope the Timorese will vote to remain with Indonesia. We can also say this issue has been a burden on the Australia–Indonesia relationship and that it will be good to put it to bed, etcetera. In terms of the media, we'll play it down.'

Ava wasn't sure the government would be able to play it down. Since the murder of five journalists in Balibo during the 1975 invasion, the *Sydney Morning Herald* had been obsessed with East Timor and kept the issue alive for all those years. Their journalists would be onto this like bloodhounds.

'Was the embassy consulted about this policy change?' she asked, but what she meant was had he been consulted because she certainly hadn't.

He turned his head towards the window again.

Now she understood why he wasn't his normal self. He'd been left out of the process. The great ambassador's counsel had not been sought. Touché to The Minister.

23

JAKARTA, DECEMBER 1998

The palace, a single-storey, all-white building, looked plain compared to the ornate palaces of the old Javanese kingdoms built in the Hindu style. This was Ava's second visit, and she and the ambassador got out of the car at the main entrance and mounted the marble steps past the formally clad guards and giant pillars. They were shown into an anteroom, which had a lone bookshelf at one end, chairs for them to sit on at another and a wooden coffee table in the middle. The lack of grandeur didn't dampen Ava's excitement at meeting Hidayat again. The president. She pushed aside the pressure that her write up of the meeting would be closely read by the PM.

Ten minutes passed, a long time for an ambassador to be kept waiting. She pictured the photo in Quentin's office from less than two years ago when he stood in the palace's great hall, bowing slightly as he handed his letters of credence to old Sujati. Ava smiled at the realisation that this was about as obsequious as Quentin ever got.

At last Ayu came in, the president's foreign affairs advisor and part of his inner circle. Well known to them, Ava had always liked her modern Muslim voice of reason, and she was, of course, extremely intelligent.

'Ambassador. So sorry for being late.' Ayu smiled as she shook their hands vigorously.

Quentin's face lifted like an expectant child. 'I understand, Mrs Amari.'

Ava hadn't seen him like this before. Was he flirting? And was she flirting back?

'Ayu, please,' she said grinning back at him. 'You're too generous.'

She led them into a giant yet homely office. 'He trawls the Internet late at night,' Ayu said. 'He knows what the world thinks about Indonesia and East Timor.'

Minutes later the president entered and they stood.

Quentin said, 'Mr President. I'm so pleased you could see us at short notice.'

'Not at all Ambassador,' Hidayat replied as they shook hands.

It had been months since Ava had met with Hidayat, a short man with a small rounded stomach. As ever, his intelligent eyes bulged giving him a curious, mad professor demeanour.

'What can I say, but thank you for your interest in my country?' he added.

Ava was relieved by his excellent English meaning she didn't need to translate. But he didn't seem his usual effervescent self. And more interesting still, no representative from the Indonesian foreign affairs department was present. Hidayat and Ayu must have decreed this a political meeting, with no need for the technocrats.

'Sit down. Sit down,' Hidayat motioned to couches that in this country always felt too low.

A male servant entered, poured tea and coffee, and left.

'Please thank your Prime Minister Beaumont for his letter,' Hidayat gave a strained smile. 'You may tell him that I have read it through, many times.'

'I will,' Quentin said.

'You may also tell him that we have a meeting of the minds in terms of wanting the matter of East Timor resolved. As you know, the economic crisis hit my country hard and ongoing international support from the IMF and World Bank for our two hundred and twenty million citizens is critical for our future.'

Quentin listened carefully, his brow drawn. Ava frantically took notes, ensuring she captured every word.

'But there is a province to our east with a population of seven hundred thousand people called East Timor, and some of them have taken issue with us. Unless we resolve this matter, and soon, this much-needed foreign bail-out may disappear. Indonesia has, you see, become prisoner to a relative minority.'

Ava put an asterisk beside the word prisoner. Hidayat seemed to have little affection for the East Timorese.

'This letter,' Hidayat paused, looking away as he formulated his words, 'I want to explain why I don't like what it suggests. Basically it says that, like the French, we are colonialists and East Timor is our colony. Yet we struggled for independence against the Dutch, so how can this be true? We are not the French with New Caledonia and their...' He squinted and turned to Ayu. '*Apa namanya, kesepakatan itu?*'

'Matignon Accords,' Ava said quietly.

'Oh you speak Indonesian?' His face softened into a warm smile. 'You see, we have only ever welcomed East Timor into our nation to stand alongside us as an equal, unlike those Portuguese who did nothing but exploit the place. No, no, a simple solution for a small pacific nation will never work for us. Besides, if we offer such a thing in East Timor, where next—Aceh, Maluku, Irian Jaya? We don't want the Balkanisation of Indonesia.'

This was more like the Hidayat Ava had seen—unafraid to tell it how he saw it. Perhaps this directness was the influence of his years of study and work in Germany. That said, his Javanese side was evident in the way he openly criticised the letter and its message, but never than the man who'd signed it—George Beaumont.

'Second,' Hidayat continued, 'I don't like the idea of a deferred vote.

You see, Mr Ambassador, deferring a vote for ten years, or even a few years, would be too costly as Indonesia would have to continue funding the place. Why should we do that only for the Timorese to snub us by voting for independence? This is a matter of national pride, you understand.'

His reaction was just as Ava had feared. Quentin nodded, but said nothing.

'So, sir, I find myself in a difficult position. We've agreed with the Portuguese to find a solution to the Timor matter by April next year, and I would like very much for Indonesia to enter the new century with a clean slate. More than that, I would like to leave an enduring legacy. Yet, such a costly hegemonic solution as your prime minister suggests is just not workable. Frankly, I'm more inclined to grant the place independence right now than go down the path of this French imperialist solution.'

Ava was taken aback by Hidayat's idea of immediate independence and asterisked it several times. Surely he wouldn't do that. The push back from *TNI* and the nationalists would be too great.

'If I may,' said Quentin, and he took the president through the PM's proposal point by point, beginning by explaining that East Timor deserved special consideration because of three and half centuries of Portuguese influence.

Hidayat listened politely, but appeared no more inclined to change his mind than an Australian prime minister would had the positions been reversed.

In the car on the way out, Ava waited for Quentin to speak. She could practically hear his mind whirring.

'He doesn't appear to be exercised about this policy shift at all.'

'I agree,' Ava said, thinking that Quentin sounded surprised. Perhaps he'd expected, or wanted, Hidayat to be vexed. That way he could go back to The Minister and say, told you so. Quentin wasn't a petty man, but he demanded respect. He'd been bypassed and injured pride radiated from him. She understood how he felt. She was the East Timor subject-matter expert, yet he never asked her for an opinion.

'*Sui generis*,' Quentin said. 'He's one of a kind, President Hidayat. Include this comment in your cable to Canberra, will you, but let me have a look at it before you send it:

Hidayat accepted that East Timor had a different heritage from other regions in Indonesia and had to be treated accordingly. But he could not afford to focus all his attention on East Timor. There were competing demands from other provinces, including Irian Jaya, Maluku, Aceh and so on. If autonomy in the form the Indonesian government provided was not acceptable to the East Timorese, he was inclined simply to grant them independence. [2]

Ava closed her notebook and looked away. So this was how you informed your prime minister and minister that their proposal to a close neighbour had been rejected because it was unworkable, not to mention insulting. She'd have to write up the rest of the cable up just as diplomatically. Beaumont and Stretton may have thought their idea a masterstroke, a win-win solution that offered the best of both worlds to all parties, yet it was almost the opposite.

'Oh and Ava,' Quentin added. 'How about a bit of positive reporting on East Timor for a change? Surely it's not all bad news.'

24

JAKARTA, DECEMBER 1998

Occasionally Ava indulged in girls' nights—lunch or dinner out or a high tea before some pampering at a gym, hotel pool or spa. But tonight Denise had rented a suite in a five-star hotel in the city centre, just a few kilometres away from her house. Who exactly was she escaping? Ava wondered. The prying eyes of her domestic staff, her philandering husband and his three older children, or all of them?

Ava stood by the minibar opening a bottle of Australian wine she'd bought at the embassy commissary. In the next room, Denise was putting on a DVD for her twin daughters and Juliette to watch. Most women left their kids at home for girl's nights, but Ava and Denise enjoyed having theirs around for a change.

Denise closed the bedroom door and took a sip of wine, which Ava guessed would be the most she'd drink all night. Denise was a contradiction—a war-hardened journalist who'd covered everything from Tiananmen Square and Thailand's independence struggle to the first Iraq war, and at the same time relished her role as a Mosman mum of five with a gushing Sydney northern-suburbs accent and open mistrust of diplomats.

Ava felt the same way about journalists, but their friendship went beyond their work facades. They were Australian expats, mothers and women with failing marriages who worked in male-dominated arenas. Early in their friendship, Denise made things easier by assuring Ava that if she ever accidentally told her something she wouldn't find it splashed across the Sydney Morning Herald's pages. She'd learnt that lesson the hard way, she'd told Ava. It wasn't worth it. But still, Ava ensured there were no accidents.

'Did you hear the kids the other day when they were playing at my place?' Denise asked.

'No?' Ava said.

'They were playing evacuations. Other kids play doctors and nurses, but our kids play evacuations.'

'That makes me feel even worse after that business of Juliette being sick.' Ava buried her head in her hands.

'You were just doing your job, and not an easy one at that.'

Ava recalled what people had said when news of her posting had spread. 'What sort of parent would take a child to a hellhole like Jakarta?' a colleague ventured. 'Poor kid,' a family member declared, 'dragging her around the world like that.'

There was a knock on the hotel door and Denise let Sharon in, the *Australian Associated Press* correspondent. Her dyed blonde hair, permanently dark at the roots, was a tangled mess and she'd refreshed her red lipstick beyond the borders of her lips, which left Ava smiling sympathetically.

'Hello,' Sharon slurred, lurching at Denise with a hug before stumbling over to the couch. She bent down and kissed Ava on both cheeks before collapsing next to her.

Denise raised her eyebrows at Ava who was busy wiping lipstick away. Poor Sharon was often drunk these days. Despite being in her forties she'd never been in a serious relationship and reeked of loneliness. Sharon poured herself a full glass of wine, spilling some on the coffee table before taking several gulps.

'You okay?' Ava asked.

Denise shook her head, mouthing *no* but it was too late.

'I…' Sharon burst into tears.

Denise put an arm around her and patted her leg as though she was a child. Denise was of the opinion that Sharon hadn't quite grown up because she hadn't had children, who were her antidote to everything. Ava suspected Sharon's trauma from covering an Australian massacre had reappeared.

'What's going on?' Ava asked gently.

'Nothing. Everything,' Sharon replied. 'I can't get that Batak guy out of my head.'

'What Batak guy?'

Denise got up to open some dips and biscuits.

'You know how there was rioting in the Chinese area again after the students were shot a couple of weeks ago?'

'Yes,' Ava said.

'I was there with Jean, the *AP* photographer, when we came across a group of men in the middle of—'

She took a deep breath to stop herself from blubbering again.

'—in the middle of slowly murdering a retarded half-Chinese, half-Batak man.'

'Jesus,' Ava said, her skin crawling.

'He was lying on the ground in a pool of blood while a group of Indonesians stood around. We thought the Batak guy was dead at first, then we saw he was breathing. That's when we knew something was really wrong. We tried to convince them to let us take him away, but they refused. We called the police and ambulance services many times—I even went to the police station twice—but they never came. Then after a while, one of them took a knife out of his jacket pocket and, as though it was the most normal thing in the world, stabbed the Batak in the chest.'

Ava gasped.

'He writhed and struggled to breathe—he was half conscious I think—

and then lay still again. The man who stabbed him took out a cigarette, had a bit of chat with the others and that was that, until the next man took his knife out and stabbed him. It took four hours before the guy was dead. By that time they'd cut his hair off and some of his extremities—fingers and toes. It was one of the cruellest, most horrible, inhuman thing I've ever witnessed, and I can't get it out of my head.'

'You watched this for four hours? No wonder you're upset,' Ava said.

'We stayed in the hope we could rescue him, but...'

'The endless violence, it gets you down,' Ava sighed.

'What is it with that?' Sharon asked, looking between Ava and Denise.

Would Australians be any better in the same circumstances? Every country had its mindless thugs and deep prejudices.

'A senior Muslim cleric, who shall remain unnamed,' Ava said, 'told me he thought Javanese culture was at the heart of the problem. He confirmed what we've all heard before, and what I learned in anthropology, that people here are culturally conditioned to internalise their feelings because any outward demonstration of emotion is seen as being crass or disrespectful to those who demand respect. Feelings build and build until they—'

'Run amok,' Sharon said. 'Either rioting or taking it out on those weaker than them, like retarded Chinese-Christian Bataks.'

Ava nodded. 'He was ashamed that the term *amok* was the only Indonesian word to have made it into the English language.'

Sharon went to the bathroom to wash her face and Denise threw Ava a weary look. They'd witnessed so much brutality over the last year that if they allowed themselves to feel the full impact, they'd never get out of bed to do their jobs. Yet, Ava was aware of a repressed rage building inside her that wasn't dissimilar to what she'd just described about Indonesians. So far she'd directed it into writing cables in the hope they would influence policy. But how long before the department tried more aggressively to silence her from telling such unpalatable truths in favour of more agreeable ones that justified politicians' self-serving decisions?

Sharon rejoined them.

'I have a funny story,' Ava said.

'Yes please,' Denise sighed.

'This was a few weeks ago before Pete returned. I was in the car with Quentin when he asked me how I was going, you know, with the separation? I told him I was managing okay. But he must have decided I needed some fatherly advice because he told me he'd separated from his wife on posting and she'd taken the kids back to Australia.' Ava paused and chuckled. 'Then he said, I have to warn you, it'll take quite some time to get used to the house being so empty and quiet.'

'What?' Denise said. 'But you have Juliette.'

'That's not all,' Ava continued. 'He started giving me advice about single life and dating.'

Denise and Sharon burst into laughter.

'According to him there are two sorts of women. Those you can talk to —you know, the ones you're intellectually compatible with—and those you can have 'other kinds of relationships with'.'

'As in screw,' Sharon squealed.

'So a woman is either smart or attractive, but they can't be both,' Denise said. They laughed harder, this time at the absurdity of Quentin's attitudes until their humour petered out into whimpers of remorse.

'None of this surprises me,' Denise said. 'Sharon and I had some issues with Quentin when we first arrived.'

'You never told me that,' Ava said.

'As you know,' Denise continued, 'the last *SMH* correspondent was expelled a few years before I arrived for writing that story about Sujati's wife being corrupt. I was chosen specially to reopen the bureau and build bridges with the Indonesians. It was a big deal.

'Anyway, a couple of months into my posting, Quentin arrived. He decided to hold regular briefings with the Australian media and journalists to chew the fat on political and economic issues. He wanted to build a relationship with us.'

'He wanted to influence us,' Sharon said, and Ava smiled.

'So he held a couple of briefings. All good. The only problem was, Sharon and I weren't invited. We only found out about them afterwards.'

'Did he know you were in Jakarta?' Ava asked.

'Absolutely,' Denise replied. 'We'd each made calls on him to introduce ourselves and the embassy's media officer knew us well. There was only one conclusion we could come to—that he's sexist.'

Ava rolled her eyes and grimaced.

'So we wrote him a formal letter,' Sharon said, 'pointing out that we represented Australia's most read newspaper and only agency, and asked him why we hadn't been invited. He'd asked Australian male journalists who didn't even work for the Australian media, so why not us? We said we believed it was down to sexism.'

Ava nodded.

'The next thing we knew, he called us in for a meeting. He said he sincerely hoped we could sort this out, yada, yada, charm, charm. So we went along, and he admitted we should have been invited. He apologised profusely and said we'd be included in all future briefings.'

Denise took a breath. 'And then he asked us not to report any of this.'

'Ah. So that was his real motivation,' Ava said, Denise and Sharon nodding simultaneously.

'But seriously,' Sharon said. 'How could he not have invited us, even if we were women?'

'It's obvious, isn't it?' Ava said. 'Perhaps you confuse him with your sexy femininity and your brilliant minds.'

They laughed and Ava reached over for some dip.

'For that matter, perhaps you confuse him too,' Denise said.

———

January 1999

Late one January evening, Ava sat at her office desk eating a can of cold baked beans from the commissary for dinner as she wrote a cable on East Timor. So much for the glamorous diplomatic life. Since the fuss over the Beaumont letter, East Timor had been relatively quiet, although Ava had heard persistent rumours about a shift in Indonesian policy. Her mobile rang and she saw it was Denise. She answered.

'How are you, Ava?'

'I'm good, Denise. But it's late and I still have an hour of work to do. Can I call you back tomorrow?'

'There's something you need to know. It's important.'

'Okay,' Ava said, feeling bad about her assumption that the call was personal.

'I've just left a press conference given by the Indonesian foreign minister and information minister. They've announced some sort of choice for East Timor over their future.

'Choice. Do you have the exact wording?' Ava reached for a pen.

'I do, and I can send it to you, but the gist of it is:

A regional Autonomy Plus will be awarded to East Timor. If this isn't accepted, blah blah, we'll suggest that the Indonesian parliament release East Timor from Indonesia.' [3]

'Release East Timor from Indonesia. That's got to mean a vote, don't you think?'

'Yes, I do. They've also rejected Beaumont's idea for a period of autonomy followed by a referendum. Plus they seem to be indicating some-thing will happen sooner rather than later.'

'Wow.' Ava felt as though she'd awoken from a long sleep. This was radical and typical Hidayat. Perhaps he saw this as his chance to also put *TNI* in their place. Clever.

'Thanks Denise. I'll call you tomorrow.'

She phoned Donald before getting hold of the official press release and sending it, along with a cable to Canberra with an URGENT classification. This was big—a ballot. A giant leap out of the quicksand they'd been stuck in for months into an expectant new world.

25

LIQUICA, EAST TIMOR, JANUARY 1999

Gabriel stumbled into the militia post with Captain Sanadi by his side. He fell into his seat at the hut's main table where Isabel stood waiting.

'Get me a beer,' Gabriel slurred, his eyes reduced to drunken slits of suspicion. 'One for the captain too.' The captain shook his head at Isabel.

She never knew when Gabriel might return. He'd been spending a lot of time with *TNI* in Dili and most of it with the captain who she'd nicknamed *ne'e asu-hein*, the guard dog. Nevertheless, she had to be prepared for Gabriel to return at any moment with food and drink at the ready.

'The announcement of a ballot is a setback,' the captain said as Isabel poured beer and lemonade into glasses.

She too had heard the news about the president giving the Timorese people a choice over their future.

'But we must continue with our plan and put a stop to this vote. We have to convince Jakarta it will spark another civil war. We must grow militia numbers faster and show them it's not possible to hold a ballot without causing major instability.'

'They'll force us out of our own country, despite everything we've done for those fat Jakarta politicians,' Gabriel spat, his face askew with disgust. Isabel quivered at what this meant for her.

She had no idea if the men were hungry but went outside to prepare food. Gabriel pushed aside the plates of rice, shredded meat and coconut beans she placed in front of him. Nothing would please him tonight.

The captain soon left and Gabriel fell into bed beside her, which now had a base and thicker mattress.

'Hold me,' he commanded and she rolled over, putting an arm across his chest.

'No, *hold* me,' he said louder, and she moved her other arm underneath his neck and pulled his head towards her chest in the way a mother might comfort her child.

'What if I fail, Isabel?' he slurred. 'What if they blame me for the ballot announcement? What will happen to me?'

Isabel had learnt to say nothing. Gabriel didn't value her opinion, she was simply the vessel into which he emptied himself, as, when and how he pleased.

He took her face in one hand and kissed her softly on the lips. Until now she'd only known his force. She felt herself cracking open at the uncharacteristic tenderness. But just as quickly, his grip on her jaw tightened and he kissed her harder. Isabel's instinct was to pull away, but she feigned obedience and followed his lead. She only hoped it wasn't going to be one of those nights when he went too far.

He flipped her onto her stomach and she was almost winded at his strength. He began to manoeuvre himself into...where? No, he'd never done that before. With her hand she encouraged him into the usual place, but he was having none of it. He plunged himself into her rear and she shrieked at the searing, ripping pain like she was being torn open all over again. The shock made her draw breath, which had a choking effect that turned her cries into stifled, gurgling gasps.

'Please Gabriel. Not there,' she managed to say.

But the more she pleaded with him, the wilder he became and the deeper his pleasure. He enjoyed hurting her and she bit down hard on the sheet to silence herself.

When he was done, Gabriel pulled out. She cried in agony. It was almost as bad as his entrance.

'Isabel, my wife,' he said.

Wife? What sort of husband took pleasure from making his wife feel small and dirty?

'We're not married Gabriel,' she said, unable to stop herself.

Gabriel appeared too spent, too satisfied or too drunk to react. She crept out and went to the bathroom. She could smell her own faeces and grabbed the soap to wash herself. It stung and she saw blood and skin on the wash-cloth. She rushed to the toilet bowl but didn't get there in time. Her vomit merged with the soapy, brown muck from her body that pooled at her feet.

Utterly repulsed, she wondered if she should she give up, lie down in the mess beneath her and rot away to nothing? Instead she grabbed the water scoop and poured a scoopful after scoopful over the floor. Then she washed herself several times until she was soggy and cold.

When she crept back into bed Gabriel was awake. Was he waiting to punish her?

'I was four-years old when I found my parents hanging from a tree, dead,' he said.

The genuine sadness in his voice made him sound childlike. 'The police said *Falintil* killed them because they were pro-Indonesian.'

'That's awful.'

'I was taken in by an Indonesian who worked in Dili, a businessman who owned a chain of shops. He was good to me, but I dropped out of high school and got involved in the independence movement. Then one day I was caught trying to plant a small bomb to blow up a *TNI* outpost.'

Isabel was confused. Why would he side with the pro-independence lot after their guerrillas killed his parents?

'They didn't punish me, though. Instead *Kopassus* turned me, and that's how I became an agent.'

Gabriel began to weep and pulled Isabel towards him.

'Poor Gabriel,' she whispered, not just because he wanted to hear this, but because she pitied him. He was a mean man who lived off his temper and spite for others, but right now he was lost and alone. As hopeless and downtrodden as she was, she wasn't like him because she still had her family who loved her. All she had to do was find them and everything would go back to how it was.

26

LIQUICA, JANUARY 1999

Today was washing day and Isabel headed to the stream, the only place she was allowed to go by herself other than the market. She balanced the basket of dirty clothes on a rolled-up towel on top of her head, signalled to one of the guards and trod the narrow dirt path through the green scrub, tropical vines and trees to the water's edge. She relished this change of scenery, a small reprieve from her militia post prison.

Stepping over stones to get to the other side of the stream, she squatted at the water's edge. It was one of those still, overcast days, the low-lying clouds closing the gap between the sky and earth, restraining the light and heightening colour and detail. She could see every facet of the rocks, and the specks of dirt and moss that covered them, and the tree bark revealed a patchwork of colours rather than their usual plain browns. Sound travelled further too, and Isabel thought she could hear every drop of water as it flowed down the stream on its way to the sea. All else was quiet around her and she let out a long breath. For a moment, she could just be.

Taking a shirt, she soaped it up and scrubbed it on a rock. With one arm she raised then slapped the already washed surface against the rock's hard surface before scrubbing an unwashed area. The rhythmic motion of the raising, slapping and scrubbing sometimes lulled her into forgetting the drudgery, and at times, everything else.

When the clothes were finally washed, Isabel lay back and rested her legs in the stream. The delicious water rushed over her feet as they dangled in its sweet coolness. For a few greedy minutes she was at peace.

Bushes rustled behind her. Isabel stood and listened, slowing her breathing to hear better.

'Who's there?' She waited. Then louder, 'Who's there?'

A man stepped out.

'You,' she gulped.

He was one of Gabriel's militiamen, unusually tall and well fed with full lips and straight black hair, which probably meant he had Indonesian blood in him. They did that, the Indonesians, wooed and raped local women to get them pregnant and weaken the Timorese bloodline. Isabel had noticed him looking at her lately and suspected he was either spying for Gabriel, or had plans for her himself.

'I only want to talk,' he said wringing his hands. 'I promise I won't hurt you.'

Isabel eyed him with suspicion. Why would he want to talk to her? She picked up the scrubbing brush and raised it in readiness. 'Stay there or I'll scream. I'll tell Gabriel.'

The militiaman swallowed, appearing as nervous as her.

'My name is Sebastiao Santa. I'm a militiaman, but you won't have heard about me doing really bad things like the others. Is that correct, Isabel?'

His use of her name felt unreasonably personal.

'I've listened to you boast about hurting independence supporters. I've heard you brag about threatening their families.'

'I had to, to fit in. But I've never hurt anyone badly or killed them, have I?'

'What do you mean, fit in?'

'Will you keep this to yourself? Can I trust you?' His wide eyes implored her.

Trust? The only person she could tell was Gabriel and he'd either blame or take it out on her, like he did everything else. 'Why should I trust you?'

'Because I've taken a big risk coming here to talk to you.'

Isabel nodded. It was true that no one had talked to her for a long time.

Sebastiao took a deep breath. 'Bishop Basso asked me to join the militia to collect proof of militia violence for his human rights organisation.'

Isabel's mouth dropped open as she lowered the arm holding the brush.

'You've heard of the Peace and Justice Commission?'

She shook her head.

'The commission is trying to record what's happening so the international community will help us, maybe even bring UN peacekeepers here. We could save lives.'

'Save lives. By joining the militia and killing pro-independence supporters?'

Sebastiao shook his head vigorously. 'I will never kill anyone. The bishop said violence is acceptable, but I must not kill.'

She tried to take it in, a bishop agreeing to violence. This wasn't what she'd learnt in church. If it was true, what had East Timor come to?

'What about kidnapping? Does the bishop say that's all right too?'

Sebastiao peered directly into the eyes. 'Please, *mana*. I need your help. Bishop Basso needs your help. You must hear Gabriel say things, important things. Perhaps he brings home documents, ones that prove the militia are being controlled by *TNI*?'

He was asking her to spy on Gabriel. She'd been forced into doing many new things these last two months, but this was something else. 'I know nothing about these things.'

Sebastiao fumbled around in the back of his pants pocket. 'Here,' he held out a crumpled envelope. 'It explains everything.'

Isabel opened the seal and pulled out a letter addressed to her that was indeed from Bishop Basso. She'd never received a letter before, and it was such a formal and beautiful thing with its crest and neat typing. She read it through twice.

'How do I know this is real? How do I know you're not testing me, or working for Gabriel or the captain?'

Sebastiao looked hurt. 'How do I know you won't go to Gabriel and tell on me?'

She pondered his request. 'If I help you, perhaps you can help me? I need to find my family. I must rejoin them.'

Sebastiao chewed his lips. 'How about I tell you a story first. It might convince you about the bishop's request. It's about Aleixo.'

Isabel's hope remained static. Sebastiao hadn't said yes, but he hadn't said no either. She would listen to his story if that's what it took.

'Some years ago, Aleixo was in the eastern tip of East Timor. He was staying in a village when he heard *TNI* had entered the area and were about to conduct one of their sweeps. At the time, he was talking to as many people as he could to see if they wanted to continue the struggle for independence or lay down their arms. Things were at a critical point and he strongly believed it was their choice. Soldiers headed towards the house Aleixo was in. He knew what would happen to the family if they were caught hiding him, so he told them he was going to give himself up. They refused, insisting he hide under the bed.

'As soon as the soldiers entered the house, the little girl, who was five years old, chose the senior officer, climbed up on his lap and put on her best cute act. The soldiers fell for it and after a cup of coffee left without searching the place.'

'Phew,' Isabel said.

'As you can imagine, Aleixo was relieved. But he was also horrified that a five-year-old girl could even think about charming these soldiers let alone do it so well. The experience crystallised a few things for him. He couldn't let the East Timorese people go on living this way. There and then he resolved to continue the fight for independence. They say that when things get tough, he reminds himself about the little girl and why he's doing what he is.'

Sebastiao looked into Isabel's eyes. 'Perhaps you can think about helping that girl too.'

She nodded, possibly carried away by the emotion of the story, or willing to say anything to talk to another person again.

'I must go,' Sebastiao said. He took the letter from her hand before disappearing into the undergrowth.

Isabel felt his absence immediately. She hadn't realised how much she'd missed being noticed, and to be needed by someone was even more enticing. But could she trust him, and was it worth doing what he wanted for the sake of human contact? She heard her father's voice in her head, *The truth doesn't come out easily in East Timor, there are too many layers.*

She gathered her washing basket and chastised herself for feeling so lonely she'd risk her safety. A tear trickled down her face, partly because someone had found a new way to use her, partly because she was so desperate she was willing to do as asked, but mostly at the sad truth that her father might be right.

27

DILI, EAST TIMOR, JANUARY 1999

Ava sat at a long, wide table in the private room of a Chinese restaurant in central Dili. Opposite her sat Gabriel Martinez with Captain Sanadi beside him. A tacky print of a bare-breasted Javanese woman hung crooked on the grimy yellow walls. The room stank of stale cigarettes and cooking oil, and Ava blinked at the glaring fluoro lights above. A Chinese man, the owner perhaps, poured steaming jasmine tea from a giant aluminium teapot into small cups that he placed in front of each person next to bottles of irradiated water.

Ava thanked him and sipped her tea as she scrutinised the disreputable Gabriel. His arms were covered in tattoos of dragon-like monsters, skulls and scorpions, and he wore a clean t-shirt, jeans and sneakers rather than the usual army fatigues shown in the media. His long, lanky hair fell into his eyes, and the way he flicked it back made him look like a cross between a seventies porn star and bikie.

When *TNI* had offered to set up a meeting with him, she hadn't hesitated. It would give her the opportunity to determine whether Gabriel was a *TNI* mouthpiece or genuine leader. Besides, she needed to open the lines of communication if she ever hoped to influence him, though it was doubtful *TNI* would ever let that happen.

'Thank you for meeting me today, *Pak* Gabriel,' she began in Indonesian using the more colloquial term of address.

His brow was sweaty and the smell of alcohol mixed with body odour wafted her way even though it was only mid-morning. She sat back and waited, but he said nothing.

'Yesterday I held meetings with the *TNI* regional commander, the Governor and some pro-Indonesia supporters,' she continued. 'I thought it would be good to talk to you too given the militias are playing an increasingly important security role in East Timor. I'm interested to learn how you see things developing, *Pak* Gabriel.'

He turned to Captain Sanadi, flicking his hair again. The captain smiled, though not directly back at him. Was Gabriel looking for reassurance or permission?

'Security?' Gabriel swallowed, clasping the table in front of him as though for stability. 'There's been a lot of focus on East Timor—from Australia too—on things becoming more chaotic, supposedly because of us militias. But the facts of the last twenty-four years...being part of Indonesia and the militias, it's been good for the Timorese.'

Ava nodded, hoping her encouragement would help him to open up more.

'Another fact,' he said, appearing relieved to have gotten something out, 'We didn't kill Aleixo when we caught him. We're not evil. Aleixo murdered his enemies back in 1975, though he never admits it. That's why we pro-Indonesia supporters feel threatened. We're only trying to defend ourselves from his violence.'

Gabriel's spiel came out like a jumbled script of alleged facts, most likely drummed into him by *TNI*. He was no mastermind, just a malleable puppet. Yet there must be some reason *TNI* had chosen him as their nominal head of the militias. His readiness to resort to violence, his ability to instil fear? She knew the heinous things he'd done and swallowed back her distaste as he continued.

'The pro-independence side shout about wanting freedom, but I'm East Timorese and no one listens to my views. People talk about human rights, but mine aren't defended. Us pro-Indonesia supporters are forced to fight our own way out of this. If I kill the independence lot, they cry all the way to the UN, but if someone from my side is killed, no one cares.'

Ah the irony. Yesterday Ava had met with the independence side in a secret location after they'd received death threats from Gabriel. She'd caught a taxi to an unknown place where she'd been met by a car and driven to another and another, until finally she'd been delivered to a building where they awaited her, their faces strained with fear, their dark-ringed eyes darting from place to place. Despite such amateurish efforts at evasion, their anxiety seemed genuine. In comparison, Gabriel gave no indication of fearing for his life. He had the Indonesian armed forces on his side.

'Thank you for sharing your views,' she replied. 'My ambassador would wish me to point out that Australia has been, and remains, a good, long-term friend to Indonesia and East Timor. However, my government also believes that after twenty-four years of discord here the East Timorese people should have the right to choose a peaceful and stable future so that all the people here—no matter what their beliefs or background—can live well. Whether that happens by remaining part of Indonesia but with greater autonomy, or becoming an independent nation, Australia will continue to be a close friend.'

Gabriel's taut fingers fidgeted as though to restrain himself. 'Australia used to support us, and the East Timorese are generally grateful for your government's efforts.' He spoke quicker now, more from the heart Ava suspected. 'But we're confused. You seem to want everything—autonomy and independence. We have history together—we Timorese died protecting and defending your soldiers in World War Two. Some in your government seem to want to help us, but others want independence, and we're not ready for that. There'll be more chaos and violence until there's civil war here, just like before.'

Ava had heard variations of the civil war line from all the other pro-Indonesia interlocutors this visit. It was like they were reading from the same script. The Governor had used it to support the idea that autonomy should be imposed directly in East Timor, while *TNI* had claimed Hidayat hadn't thought the vote through properly so pro-Indonesians like Gabriel had no choice but to protect themselves with force.

But the most disturbing reason Ava had been given on why the ballot shouldn't proceed was by the police chief. 'The Timorese are physically and mentally substandard, possibly due to poor nutrition. How can we expect them to participate in a ballot when they can't possibly know what one is?' It had been a challenge to keep the disbelief from her face.

She looked directly now into Gabriel's eyes. 'One area my government believes will be important for the process ahead is reconciliation. What are your views on your side and the other coming together to discuss a way forward?'

'We're willing to talk to the other side, but only if *Falintil* lay down their weapons. But they never do, so how can we trust them when they say one thing and do another.'

Falintil-initiated clashes were indeed on the rise, but the situation was more complex, and insidious, than that. *TNI*, along with the militia they were training as well as arming, were drawing *Falintil* out of hiding by raping and killing their families along with other independence supporters. The inevitability of civil war was a fabrication.

'Thank you for meeting me today,' Ava said, standing and shaking Gabriel's sweaty hand. She wished to find the nearest basin to wash hers several times with soap, but instead smiled and said something about keeping the lines of communication open. One day, God forbid, if an Australian or key local contact was in trouble, she might actually need him.

28

LIQUICA, EAST TIMOR, FEBRUARY 1999

All was peaceful at the militia post. Gabriel was in Dili and only two of his men stood guard. Isabel headed to the market, shopping bags in tow and money in her pocket.

She took her usual route until she reached a pathway. Should she or shouldn't she?

She checked that no one was following her, and although her head told her no, she darted down a narrow, overgrown trail and ran to its end opposite the Liquica church.

Until recently the Church—Catholicism—had loomed large in her life. Mass twice a week since she could remember, choir practice, Sunday school and her forthcoming Confirmation. Yet now as she stared at the church, when it should have felt like coming home, all she felt was apprehension.

She crossed the road to the great white monolith of a building with its odd Spanish-styled bell tower and waited behind a tree in the dirt yard. After a while, a small man with a wispy beard shuffled in through the front door. Father Ribeiro. Although he was only in his mid-forties he looked like an old man, hunched over and tired inside his long, white robe.

Isabel decided it was safe to go in and hurried up the red concrete steps underneath the great metal cross before stepping inside and crossing herself with holy water. She crept up to Father Ribeiro who was off to one corner and stood waiting. He looked around with shock before quickly checking to see if anyone else had come in.

'Isabel,' he gasped.

'Father.' She bent over to kiss the ring on one finger, which he held out for her.

'What are you doing here?'

'*Senor Padre*, I need your help. I have to find my family.'

'Oh Isabel,' he mumbled, rubbing his face with one hand beginning at his mouth then up over his forehead and around his eyes. 'I'm not sure I can do that.'

'Why Father? Do you know where they are? Are they safe?'

He exhaled long and hard. 'I want to help you, Isabel, but what about Gabriel and—'

'You said in church you were on our side, Father, on the side of the Timorese poeple.'

He nodded. 'But you need to understand you're not the only one in Liquica who needs me. If I help you, I'll risk my position here, and where will that leave the others?'

Isabel didn't try to hide her hurt or disappointment. 'Has Gabriel threatened you or the nuns, *Senor Padre*?'

He shook his head, but Isabel wasn't convinced. He was hiding something. She dropped to her knees before him.

'Please help me, Father. I was kidnapped against my will because Gil wouldn't join the militias and we didn't know where he was, so they took—'

'Stop it Isabel.' Father Ribeiro's voice echoed in the empty hall. 'And for goodness sake, get up off the floor.'

Isabel stood, her head hanging low.

'There's nothing I can do to help you. Please leave.'

'Can you at least tell me if my family are all right, Father?'

The priest looked away and a heavy silence fell between them. No word from her family for months, not one rescue attempt, and now here in front of God, she felt more alone than ever. The Church had been her last hope, but it turned out to be her final betrayal.

'Why me, Father? What have I done to deserve this?'

'We can't know or understand everything that happens to us, Isabel. You must have faith, and you must resist the temptation to fall into self-pity. Somehow, this is all part of His plan. You will see in time that it is leading you—indeed all of us—to something greater. Pray on that, Isabel.'

'Can you give me Holy Communion then Father, so I can be—'

'You know I can't do that. The sins yo—'

'I'll confess my sins. Please.'

She moved towards the confession box, her last prospect of finding reassurance and consolation. But as she did, they heard footsteps coming from the front stairs.

'Leave now. That way,' he hissed, half pushing her in the direction of the back door. She stumbled but righted herself before turning to Father Ribeiro.

'I must know something. I got a letter from Bishop Basso asking me to get information for him. Was it real?'

'If it is, you should find great purpose in what the bishop has asked you to do.'

Her heart skipped a beat. So it was real. Did none of them care about the risk to her? And what did it mean for her family?

'Go!' he snapped.

Isabel's legs reluctantly transported her out of the church's back entrance. She felt more muddled than ever. Her confession unmade, her sins yet to be absolved and her faith more uncertain than ever. The body and blood of Christ were anywhere, it seemed, but in her.

29

DILI, EAST TIMOR, JANUARY 1999

At a table underneath a red umbrella in the palm-filled garden of the Turismo Hotel, Ava waited to order dinner. She usually ate elsewhere but was leaving in the morning and hadn't packed yet. She would be sad to leave East Timor. There was a sense of excitement and anticipation about the place, even if a feeling of foreboding was also building. Who knew when she'd be allowed to return next?

'A glass of red wine please,' she said to the waiter as she looked over the menu.

The chicken was good here. It came whole and barbequed flat, Portuguese style. The birds were small as they were raised locally in people's homes, but they were flavoursome and reminded her of the chickens her father had raised in their suburban backyard. She used to sit with them in their coop and talk. Quite the characters. But what Ava loved most about the food in East Timor was how the people here understood bread and wine. Indonesian bread was sweet and fluffy, often dyed lurid green, flashing pink or fake white, and while beer, local *arak* and rice wine were available throughout the archipelago as per the old customs, wine was foreign to those outside the wealthier classes of Jakarta and the tourist hubs.

'Do you mind if I join you?' said a familiar voice. It belonged to Aaron, an activist-cum-stringer she'd met at a dinner a couple of nights ago through Australians working on aid projects.

He looked younger than her and a little shy, but he was good looking in a James Dean way as he chain-smoked cigarettes beneath a curtain of thick black hair. She'd caught him looking at her several times that night and had returned his gaze, but their dance had led nowhere.

'Please,' she said, showing him a plastic chair. She was surprised he wanted to talk to her given his outspoken views against the Australian government.

Aaron ordered a large bottle of Bintang beer. He brushed a mosquito away and was about to say something when a couple came over to speak to him.

'Ava,' Aaron said after chatting to them. 'Meet Trish and Jeff from Melbourne. Trish is a teacher's aide and Jeff's a nurse. They volunteer here a few weeks every year. Ava works at the Australian Embassy in Jakarta.'

'We know who you are,' Trish said looking down her nose at her.

Ava had heard about them too. They visited every year to treat *Falintil* in the jungle. She admired their willingness to help in spite of the risk to their own safety, but she suspected that when it all went wrong and they were caught by *TNI*, or worse the militia, they'd demand she come running to extricate them. Ava stood and offered her hand to shake anyway, which they did reluctantly.

'Would you like to sit down?' Aaron asked them and Ava bit her bottom lip to hide her disappointment.

Aaron and the couple talked about life in Melbourne and the other things they did for East Timor such as fundraising. They threw the odd barb her way—all public servants were lazy and had no mind of their own, etcetera—which clung to her like the humidity. She finished her meal in silence, wishing they'd leave, but instead they ordered a third bottle of wine.

'So what *are* you doing here?' Trish said to Ava, her freckly, sun spotted skin luminous in the overhead lights. 'Attendingh cocktail parties?'

Ava sighed, tired of holding her tongue. 'Diplomats get to know what's really going on in a country so their government can make informed decisions about the relationship. We also pass important information on to other parties and negotiate things, from peace settlements and trade agree—'

'Informed decisions. Ha!' Jeff crowed, his pale, hollowed face looking ghostly. 'Is that what you call supporting autonomy for East Timor?'

Ava had copped it from all sides today. The Indonesians and their Timorese supporters had accused her of betraying them by supporting independence, the independence side had told her Australia wasn't doing enough to get *TNI* out of East Timor and UN troops in, and now these false allegations from home-grown activists. She should walk away but she couldn't bear the unjustness of their accusations.

She took a breath. 'The Australian government doesn't support either outcome, Jeff. The Beaumont letter to Hidayat talked about a period of autonomy leading up to an act of self-determination. The Indonesians have since said they'll offer autonomy to the East Timorese sooner rather than later, and if they reject it they'll free them. The details are yet to be agreed in—'

'Your kind,' Trish hissed, her face distorted and ugly with spite as she leaned in close and stuck a pointed finger hard into Ava's chest, 'with your bullshit words and your fancy terms. For twenty-four years people like you have twisted things to cover up the genocide of tens, no, hundreds of thousands of East Timorese.'

The people at the next table glanced at Trish and moved away. Ava moved her chair back, uncomfortable with her sudden aggression. Perhaps if she explained it differently.

'I understand what you're saying,' Ava said. 'But the Australian government has used the historical opportunity of regime change in Indonesia precisely *to* resolve things here peacefully. I'm here to find out what's happening on the ground, so they have the full picture.'

Part of her wanted to add that even though she hadn't wanted the East Timor job, she'd made it her mission to help the Australian and allied governments understand what was really going on here, despite the building resistance from Quentin and others over her so-called negative reporting.

'The full picture,' Trish screeched even louder so that people at other tables looked their way, spit hanging from her mouth.

Ava looked to Aaron and Jeff, but neither of them appeared concerned.

'You mean the truth. What's actually going on here?' Trish lifted her chest and chin, to match her righteous words. 'You wouldn't know the truth if you fell over it. And even if you did, you'd find some way of twisting it. Make no mistake, you—you personally are responsible for the last twenty-four years of genocide here. You're evil. If I had a gun, I'd force you down on your hands and knees like a dog, point it at your head and pull the trigger.'

Ava trembled inside and struggled to breathe. Her hearing and sight faded and her surroundings fell away. She tried to hide her shock. The woman was drunk, she rationalised, and surely her malice wasn't really intended for her. Yet Ava knew that if Trish had threatened her in Australia, she could have had her arrested. She looked to Aaron for acknowledgement that Trish had gone too far, but he looked to the ground. She was alone.

'You'd shoot me?' Ava managed to say in a low and deliberate voice to calm her. 'You don't see any hypocrisy in that?'

'Nope. You're scum,' Trish said as Jeff chuckled gleefully.

Ava stood and trekked across what felt like the never-ending courtyard, up the stairs to her room and unlocked her door without so much as a nervous fumble. To an outsider she might have appeared hard and unfeeling, but once she was inside she hunched over and deep sobs lurched up from inside. It was so unfair. She only wanted to stop the violence. How easy it must be for Trish and Jeff with their simplistic, black and white choices.

Someone knocked on her door. Ava stopped cold. Had those loony people found a gun?

Now came a second, louder knock.

'Who is it?' she said wiping her face with the back of her hand.

'It's Aaron.'

'What do you want?'

'Are you all right?'

He sounded concerned so Ava opened the door.

'Um,' he stood, shifting his weight from foot to foot. 'That was…out of control.'

Ava gave him a hurt look. 'Thanks for your support. Your silence made it seem like you agreed with them, that—' She burst into tears.

'Can I come in?'

She nodded and he stepped in and put his arms around her. Ava was still furious at him, but the comfort of his touch melted her resistance. It had been so long.

Aaron released his tight hug, found her lips and kissed them, and she kissed him back, this man who wasn't her husband, who of all things was a journalist of sorts and younger than her.

'Just a sec,' she said. 'I'm going to turn my phone off.'

'No don't,' he said, his eyes beseeching her. 'Someone might need you.'

She gasped. He was happy to see her be mocked, yet understood she helped Timorese when they were in real trouble.

They kissed a second time and made their way over to the bed. Ava had almost forgotten what this felt like—lust, sex. Yet here it was, amid all the madness of East Timor and her confused life, making something that felt like love. Glorious love.

———

Jakarta, INDONESIA

The fridge door stood ajar as Ava looked for her vegetable juice. She'd just got back from East Timor and it was late. She preferred not to eat directly before bed but needed something.

Pete came into the kitchen wearing a sarong and no shoes. He hadn't shaved for days.

'You're back,' he said, making himself some herbal tea.

'Yes. How are you? How's Juliette?'

'She's fine. We're fine.'

'Good,' Ava nodded, stirring her juice before taking a large sip.

'The Australia Day function. Am I invited?'

'No, sorry. No families. Just dippo schmoozing.'

Ava cleaned the juice from the corners of her mouth as Pete poured hot water into his cup, sighing loudly as Ava walked away. 'So I guess that confirms how irrelevant I am.'

Ava stopped and turned around. 'It's work, Pete, not a social event.'

'Riiiight,' he said, drawing the word out.

'I know this is unusual, being separated and living in the same house, but you agreed we'd do it for Juliette. You knew I didn't want to get back together.'

'Did I?' he huffed. 'I just thought if we talked maybe...'

Ava closed her eyes at the sadness of what he'd just said. For years she'd tried to talk to him, and he'd refused. Now, when it was too late, he finally understood the need.

'You know,' he said, a bitter edge to his voice, 'it's funny how despite all this travel and the shit work you do you look so...it's like you're revelling in it.' He half laughed. 'You look different. What have you been up to, Ava?'

She began walking away again, but instead of heading towards the TV room she traversed the cold marble floor towards her bedroom. Being made to feel bad about last night wasn't something she was up for.

'Juliette worries about you,' he said.

Ava stopped and turned around, her jaw tightening.

'She hears things about the shit fight in East Timor. She watches the news, sees you on TV. She's worked out it's dangerous and she's scared something's going to happen to you.'

'Juliette's never said anything to me.'

'She wouldn't,' said Pete, the corners of his mouth turning down. 'She thinks you're brave. Doesn't want to worry you—her courageous, absent mummy.'

How dare he use their child to get to her.

'I'm sure you did your best to reassure her, Pete? Told her I have special police protection or something like that?'

He glared at her.

'I'll try and be home in time to talk to her tomorrow. But what do you want me to do? Quit my job? I want to spend more time with Juliette but it's impossible. I'm on posting and lots of shit is happening and I get called in every single bloody weekend whether I like it or not. I haven't had a day off in months.'

Ava saw Pete searching her eyes, but failing to find the thing that had long been missing between them, he shook his head and made his way into the lounge room.

Ava went upstairs to check on Juliette who was a light sleeper, but tonight she'd risk it. She crept into her room, bent over and kissed her on her forehead.

'Goodnight my little one. I love you.'

Juliette partially opened her eyes and smiled. 'Mummy. Love you too.' Ava lay down next to her on the bed, draped an arm over her and smiled. How like Juliette it was to omit the *I*.

As Juliette went back to sleep, Ava listened carefully to her gentle breathing. Why didn't she check Juliette every night like this when she came home, even if it meant waking her? East Timor had taken over her life. Even when she had a couple of hours off, she spent it unwinding with colleagues rather than racing home. Her home and family felt increasingly remote.

'Mummy,' Juliette moaned. 'Can't breathe.'

'Okay,' Ava laughed, kissing her and getting up. Yet she hesitated to leave. Was it normal for a child to be so self-contained? It was a good thing, wasn't it?

30

LIQUICA, EAST TIMOR, JANUARY 1999

Isabel's long and lonely days were interrupted only by her shopping expeditions to the market and the humble pleasures of the stream. She often invented dirty washing as an excuse to go there. It wasn't just the time alone she enjoyed, or the calming sound of the water running over the rocks, but the possibility she might meet *him* there—Sebastiao. So far he'd turned up once since their first meeting a month ago, but he was her only real link to the outside world and maybe her future, so each time she went in anticipation. Yet there were days she grew tired of waiting too.

'Washing again?' said a familiar voice as she was elbow deep in suds.

'You think I like to wash, *maun*?' How quickly her objections fell away. She allowed herself a private smile.

'Sometimes *menina*, I think you invent washing just to come here and meet me.'

'I like the river. It's peaceful and it cools me down.'

'So that's why you've been here most days?'

She raised her brows, pleased he'd noticed, until she remembered why. She touched her chest above her heart and swallowed. Could she go through with it?

'Isabel,' he said in a serious tone.

'Before you ask. I have something for you.' She reached into her bra and pulled out a piece of folded paper. 'I copied this from a document in Gabriel's drawer.'

She handed it to Sebastiao who read it, his eyes bulging the further he went on. 'This is exactly what we need. It admits *TNI* have direct control of the militias all the way up to Jakarta. Can you get the original to me so I can take a copy? We need proof.'

Isabel's face dropped. She'd got up very early and smuggled the document into the bathroom to copy it. She thought Sebastiao would be impressed, grateful even, but it seemed she hadn't done enough.

'I'll try.'

She knew it wasn't that simple. First she'd have to steal it, and once Sebastiao had made a copy, return it again without Gabriel realising.

'The next time Gabriel's away, just get the document and put it in a container I'll hide in the crack of that tree.' He pointed to a half rotten tree trunk. 'I'll come by a twice a day to check it. Once I've taken a copy, I'll put it back in his drawer myself. Okay?'

Isabel nodded.

'This is important. Thank you for your help, Isabel.' Sebastiao parted the undergrowth and disappeared before she could say anything else.

She squatted down and grabbed a tea towel, soaping it up before beating and smacking it on the rock, harder and louder, on and on until the sound of the river fell away.

When she was finished, she sat back. Would he ever tell her about her family? Would her efforts ever be enough?

A new sense of hopelessness came over her. She looked down at her hands. The tea towel she gripped was threadbare and her hands red raw.

―――――

When Isabel returned to the post, Gabriel was sitting inside at the table, a cigarette in one hand and a soft drink in the other. He was without the captain for the first time in weeks. She stopped and waited for him to bark an order at her.

'For you,' he said, pointing to a whole fish, some tomatoes, onions and lettuce, and a bunch of flowers laid out on the table in front of him.

Isabel glanced between him and his gifts. Why was he being nice to her?

'Thank you,' she said.

She put the food away in the old fridge in the corner and sat the flowers in a jar. They were scraggly pink and white carnations, but they gave off a wonderful scent. No one had ever given her flowers before.

'Sit down,' Gabriel said, pointing to a chair.

Isabel sat and held her breath. Did he suspect her of spying? He didn't seem angry.

'I have to go to Bali for a few days. The general's asked me to attend a planning meeting.'

Isabel nodded as Gabriel sat taller, his chest seeming to expand.

'Things are ramping up, Isabel. My Dili militia group is operational, we've established other groups around East Timor and soon I'll be sworn in as the deputy commander of all the militias.'

None of this came as news to her.

'I'll be a powerful man and I…' his eyes pleaded with her. 'I want to…' He stood and walked to the door, locking it. 'I want you to be with me.' He undid his pants and lifted her onto the table.

Was this his clumsy way of telling her he had feelings for her? She balked. Him with his drunken temper, vile fists and wicked cock.

Over the next hour, he did things to her that were more punishing than ever before as though to punish her for igniting this need in him. But Isabel didn't care. She had long ago slipped into that distant place far away from his unending cruelty and her feeble, vulnerable body.

31

LIQUICA, 6 APRIL 1999

The sun rose on a panorama of red and white flags that hung from every flagpole, house and fence as far as Isabel could see. *TNI* had ordered the townspeople to display the Indonesian emblem as sign of their loyalty, yet without wind to give them life the flags hung as limply as the command itself. Most of the town's five thousand residents had either escaped to the jungle or were sheltering in Father Ribeiro's house nearby so there was no one to observe them anyway.

There'd been trouble the last few days and hundreds of militiamen from *Besi Merah Putih*—the Red and White Iron—from the nearby town of Maubara had gathered at Gabriel's post. They wore dark pants and t-shirts, the usual patriotic bandanas around their heads and army style boots or sneakers. Gabriel himself wasn't present—he was too senior to deal with local matters now—but his subordinate and the men's commander, Damiano da Silva, prepared to speak. From the sidelines, Isabel looked on as he stepped up onto a wooden box and cleared his throat. She detected an acrid odour in the air that she knew well—the smell of fear.

'Three days ago,' da Silva said in a voice that was loud for such a small man, '*Falintil* commander and Liquica village leader, Filipe Alberto and his men attacked our people in our home town. They picked a fight with us, they accused our families and friends of terrible things and they burnt down our houses.'

The men grumbled in low, angry tones. Da Silva's face was shiny with sweat.

'We've tried to negotiate Alberto's surrender, but Father Ribeiro and the pro-independence traitors refuse to hand him over.' He paused as though readying himself. 'Do we agree that Alberto must be made to pay for what he's done?'

'Yes,' the men said loudly.

'Do we agree that if he doesn't come out of Father Ribeiro's house voluntarily, we'll take him by force?' he said louder.

'Yes sir.'

'Let me hear that you want to defend our people, our families, our future!' da Silva shouted, thrusting a fist into the air.

'Yes, sir!' the men shouted back.

But Isabel wasn't convinced. Underneath their bravado she sensed doubt and reluctance. Like her, they knew it was the pro-independence side who'd been injured and killed, not the militia. The pro-independence side had also lost many more houses than the militia in the tit-for-tat burnings. The troubles also went back further than the last few days. Alberto and his people were only reacting to an attack by the da Silva and his men on their families earlier that week, who were reacting to an earlier one, and so it went back until she didn't know when. In truth, the families involved had been rivals for years. There'd been a bad marriage, an ongoing property dispute and an unpaid gambling debt. Yet it was only lately, with the mayor and *Kopassus* whispering in the ears of the commander and his militia—that a confrontation had spiralled into violence.

'Let's do it then!' da Silva screamed, red-faced and roused like an animal about to pounce.

He jumped the short distance to the ground and landed with a thud before leading the men away. They strutted with their conceited chests held high and fists clenched.

With the men soon gone, Isabel was left in eerie silence. A thought crossed her mind and she gasped. Could her family be in the house? She wished there was something she could do.

And then it occurred to her, perhaps there was.

————

In the local school across the road from the church where Father Ribeiro's house also sat, Isabel found a place to hide. If she stood between the side of the building and a bushy tree, she had a clear view yet was safely out of sight. She checked around her one more time, and certain she hadn't been followed, surveyed the scene.

The church to the left with its main door facing away, looked almost ghostly with its deathly white patina. Father Ribeiro's house, a pretty brick cottage with a rose-lined path that led to the front door, lay directly ahead of her and appeared lifeless. This made no sense given how many people were sheltering inside, although all the curtains were drawn. Isabel trembled.

Outside the churchyard, hundreds of men had gathered at the perimeter. Many were militia. They smoked and fidgeted with their weapons—home-made pistols, machetes, axes, knives, swords and even *TNI*-issued pistols and rifles. Policemen stood around too, ordinary ones as well as special riot police who carried long-barrelled guns, and there were soldiers, lots of them.

Isabel examined the faces of the militia to see who was there and whether Gabriel was among them. He'd been travelling to and from Dili a lot these last few days, dealing with Alberto's surrender or capture in between whatever he did in Dili. She recognised some of the men, but the others. The others...

She inhaled sharply. Those weren't real militia. They were soldiers dressed like militia. She knew their faces from their visits to the post and from seeing them around town. What did this mean? What were they doing?

At last Isabel spotted Gabriel stepping inside the churchyard alongside the mayor. Father Ribeiro came out of his house to join them. Gabriel quickly grew angry with Father Ribeiro, who was shaking his head, while the mayor planted his hands on his hips. Isabel hoped Father Ribeiro was refusing to hand Alberto over. Gabriel shouted something, threw his arms up in the air and stormed off. The mayor scurried away behind him as Father Ribeiro retreated into his house, stopping to glance behind him at the sea of armed men and crossing himself.

Gabriel joined the military commander and police chief at the outer boundary. The three huddled together closely, and Isabel could only imagine what they were plotting. When the military commander walked away, he spoke to several soldiers who began herding the militia into a group. One of the soldiers handed out plastic bags, which the men passed around. The real militias, not the *TNI* ones, took something small out and put it in their mouths. Sweets? she wondered. No, too small and too strange. Pills!

Gabriel shook hands with the military commander and police chief, got into his vehicle and drove away in the direction of the post. Isabel's heart thumped in her chest. She'd been so absorbed in what had been happening she hadn't considered the possibility of him returning home. What if he arrived to find her absent?

She took her thongs off and ran, her bare feet pounding the ground and her arms pumping. When she was almost there, she saw his car turning the corner. She was too late. She wouldn't be able to make it across to road without him seeing her. Her heart beat hard in her chest. What excuse could she possibly have? Nothing came to mind. She'd have no choice but to face him. As she was about to step across the road his car zoomed straight past her in the direction of Dili.

———

By the time Isabel returned to her hiding spot at the school, things had changed. The militia, *TNI* and police had entered the churchyard and surrounded Father Ribeiro's house. They stood in rows—lines of police at the front, the militia behind them and many *TNI* and police at the back. The militia gripped their weapons tight and fondled them, making the atmosphere tenser, stranger.

Damiano da Silva stepped forward. 'Father Ribeiro,' he yelled through a megaphone. 'Surrender Alberto and his accomplices now or we'll take him by force. This is your last chance.'

Isabel held her breath. No sound or movement came from inside the house as the lines of men outside stood silent.

Several police officers stepped forward. They tore the side door off its frame and threw something inside. Smoke billowed from the house and soon a pungent smell reached Isabel, making her cough and her eyes water. She wiped them with her handkerchief, her blurry vision slowly improving.

Now the men armed with long-barrelled guns in the rear rows raised their weapons and fired into the air. Even though she knew it was coming, Isabel jumped. The armed soldiers at the outer edge of the group dressed in either uniforms or as militia, yelled out an order, and the real Timorese militia in front of them ducked.

Villagers stumbled out of the house through the open door—women and children, old people and young ones too. Blinded by the smoke, they coughed, many of them crying out as they fell over each other. Isabel moved forward, searching for her family. She recognised some faces, but there was too much smoke and confusion to see everyone.

Her eyes were drawn now to the soldiers at the outer edge of the group. With no one in their way, they raised their guns and took aim.

'Please God, no,' she whispered.

'Fire!' came the order and the soldiers squeezed their triggers, loud cracks and screams tearing apart the surroundings as villagers dropped to the ground like dead insects.

Isabel sobbed in between choking on the air that reeked of hot metal, dirt, charcoal and something sour. She wanted to guide the people tripping over the dead and injured to safety, and to hold the hands of those writhing in pain. Instead she bit down hard on her knuckles and searched for her family as more captives attempted to flee.

On and on the gunfire went on until another order came and finally it stopped. This time the militia, who'd been squatting, stood up.

'Forward!' Isabel heard.

The militia launched themselves into the crowd of people, shouting like warriors. They raised their machetes and other weapons, and in a frenzy began hacking anyone who moved—men, women, children, babies even—like inhuman monsters. Like savages. Blood spouted everywhere and Isabel vomited onto the ground beside her.

A group of riot police made their way into Father Ribeiro's house, kicking the lifeless and writhing bodies out of their way with their hard boots. Isabel wiped her mouth with her handkerchief and refocused. Within moments several police carried Father Ribeiro out, who was resisting and crying.

As the militia continued their slashing, shooting started inside the house and more screams reverberated. Soon they came out again and half a dozen soldiers climbed up onto the rooftop. Once there, they began shooting downwards. Isabel gasped. Was Alberto hiding in the roof?

It was too much. She couldn't watch any more—the bodies piled lifelessly on top of each other near the ripped off door with others spread around the churchyard having been chased and macheted or shot. She slid down the school building wall into a squat, burying her face in her knees and covering her ears with her hands before rocking back and forth. She sang a children's nursery rhyme to block out the noise. Eventually her legs forced her up and carried her back through the empty streets to the post, barely caring any more who saw her, or if she lived or died.

32

LIQUICA, APRIL 1999

For hours military and police vehicles went back and forth along the road aside the militia post. Isabel sat at the table in the hut and listened, images of trucks filled with the bodies of her neighbours replaying over and over. A car stopped outside and Gabriel walked in. She should have prepared his dinner but hadn't been able to move from her chair. She looked up at him, her eyes glazed. She wanted to scream at him and hit him, and demand he tell her why this evil thing had happened, but what was the point? What was the point of anything?

Gabriel sat down in the chair opposite her.

'I went to the mayor's house,' he said, resting his forehead in his palms. What did she care?

'There were children there,' he gulped. 'They'd been shot.'

Isabel lowered her head too, and although she wasn't crying, tears flowed from her eyes. Gabriel leaned over the table, reached his hand out and placed it on her arm. She was uncertain what to think. His rare moments of tenderness never ended kindly.

'Were any of them my brothers or sisters? she asked.

'Some of them had bullet holes as large as my fist.' He looked blankly at her. 'The sisters tried to sew them up, but they... Their insides were just missing.'

Isabel tried not to picture the small bodies of the children with cavernous holes in their bellies and chests where there should have been life.

'Gabriel, were my family in Father Ribeiro's house today?' she asked louder.

'The whole time,' he continued, 'the mayor was telling people to go home and raise the Indonesian flag—to tie it to their right hand and show we're all prepared to die for our country.'

Isabel stood 'Gabriel!' she screamed, her body rigid, her hands clenched, and her face taught and red. 'Were my family there?'

He looked up at her, appearing confused.

'I'm scared, Isabel.'

She collapsed back onto her seat, rested her head in her arms and sobbed.

'I told you before that *Falintil* killed my parents.'

Isabel stopped sobbing.

'But really, it was *TNI*. I watched them do it. My parents were members of the resistance.'

Isabel raised her head and wiped her runny nose smudging snot and tears across her puffy face.

'I know I was lucky to be raised by an Indonesian. He was a good man and I was grateful. I was.'

She was visibly aghast now. How could he have sided with the people who'd murdered his parents?

Gabriel looked at her as though he'd just realised something. 'But what happens if I outlive my usefulness? Will they shoot me too? Will I die on a floor with great holes in me?'

33

ATAMBUA, WEST TIMOR, APRIL 1999

At the edge of a grassy clearing at the fringe of Atambua, Ava and Bruce waited for a *TNI* helicopter to fly them to Dili. Ava had always wanted to see Atambua, the infamous town on the west Timor side of the border that was ill-reputed for the cross-border forays launched from there targeting the East Timor independence side.

Despite the early hour, locals gathered on the outside of the fence. Ava smiled but they returned only steely gazes. Atambua was a well-known pro-Indonesia hub and the villagers had probably heard why she and Bruce were there. Their resentment might also explain why *TNI* had posted guards outside their hotel doors last night, although the fact that the Indonesian defence forces chief himself had granted them permission to investigate the Liquica massacre on the condition that *TNI* escort them might also explain it. This meant a longer, more circuitous route to Dili, which Ava suspected was deliberate to buy *TNI* more time to clean up their mess. They'd flown to Kupang first via a one-night stop off in Bali, before driving to Atambua and overnighting there too. Usually the trip took around six hours.

Ava searched the sky for the helicopter she could now hear.

'Why do you think they're letting us do this investigation?' she asked Bruce. She had her own theory but was interested to hear a military man's views.

'The international community have reacted strongly to the massacre reports and demanded an independent investigation,' he said. 'I guess if someone had to do it, the Indonesians would rather it be Australia than the UN, Amnesty International or Portugal.'

'I agree,' she said. 'Unlike that lot, we actually care about our long-term relationship.'

The helicopter's ageing metal carriage with its long, heavy steel rotors was soon hovering above them before beating its way to the ground. Ava and Bruce got the all clear and ran bent over towards the carriage before scrambling into the back seat.

'This is my first helicopter ride,' Ava shouted at Bruce as they strapped themselves in.

Bruce raised his eyebrows and laughed. 'Don't be alarmed if the master warning light comes on.' He pointed to a large red button in the front of the roof. 'It's common in these old beasts. Usually they just press that off button there.'

'So it doesn't mean anything?' Ava asked, frowning.

'Could do. Maintenance isn't the best in *TNI*. No money.'

Ava's eyes widened as the helicopter engine revved and rose into the air before crawling forward, defying all sorts of laws of physics. She tried to hide her excitement and pleasure, which felt all wrong given the reason for their trip. But the sun was shining and after the darkness of that grim, unwelcoming town where her thoughts had centred around the enormity of what she was about to do, she felt as though she'd seen daylight for the first time in weeks.

'Look,' Bruce said, pointing. The master warning light had lit up bright red.

One of the pilots pressed it several times. Finally it went off.

But within moments the light came back on. The other pilot pressed it repeatedly, only this time it didn't go off. The second pilot said something to the first, who reached for the light's cover, pulled it off and yanked out the diode along with the wire attached to it.

'If our time's up, it's up,' she shrugged at Bruce who was busy crossing himself and laughing so hard he almost choked.

Dili and Liquica, EAST TIMOR

TNI headquarters in Dili was a long, two-storey building with wide staircases that led to open corridors facing into several square courtyards. Every time Ava went there she was struck by the block-like conformity of each section and her inability to tell one from the other. Very military, she supposed.

She and Bruce sat waiting in the office of the East Timor military commander. Ava noticed two familiar rectangular areas on the wall where the paint was lighter—spots where photos of Sujati and his vice president had hung during their near twenty-three-year reign over East Timor. Their ongoing vacancy was a sign of what the Indonesian people coined *an absence of genuine political leadership*. She noted that most opted to have no pictures at all rather than put Hidayat up in the president's place, with many also removing his picture from its former vice-presidential position.

Colonel Tamala walked in with his deputy. Ava and Bruce stood as Tamala, a fit, handsome man in his late thirties who they knew reasonably well, greeted them warmly. Everything about him was archetypal Javanese, from his charming smile to his polished responses that were a mix of openness, subterfuge and fiction intended to confuse the truth while giving the impression of honesty. It was the Javanese way of keeping face. If he'd lost any sleep over what had happened in Liquica, it didn't show.

'Let us begin with a briefing by my deputy on events in Liquica that day,' Tamala said.

Ava nodded, turning her attention towards the lieutenant whose brow was glistening with sweat. He picked up a piece of paper with trembling hands and started reading in Indonesian, his voice croaky and wavering. Clearly he was no archetype:

'On the sixth of April, negotiations between the police and Father Ribeiro continued at his house. The police suspected the people inside had weapons but the priest insisted they did not. Out of the blue, a shot was fired from inside. It injured a solider. The police attempted to convince Father Ribeiro to let them process the shooting in accordance with the law, but he refused. When the militia, Besi Merah Putih *and the other civilians who had joined them heard the shot, they moved towards the house and ran amok.'*

This was the first Ava had heard about a shot being fired from inside the house. She underlined it in her notes and put a question mark by it, careful to maintain her deadpan face.

'There were two hundred and fifty other civilians outside. They had approximately one hundred and fifty homemade weapons. These guns are very loud and sound like grenades, but there were no grenades and no tear gas was used. TNI helped the police to control the situation so it did not turn into complete anarchy. We grouped the militia and their supporters so the Liquica people could run away. In total, five people were killed, including the main instigator, Filipe Alberto, and twenty-five were injured. It was very sadistic.'

Ava asterisked the contradictions and other points that stood out. Most disturbing of all was the number of deaths, which *TNI* had downgraded from twenty-five in their formal statement to the media on the day of the massacre, to five.

The deputy swallowed and put the document down on a coffee table and gulped.

'We need to look at the wider picture,' Colonel Tamala said, smiling. '*TNI* were able to contain the conflict between the two Timorese sides until Hidayat announced a referendum in January. Since then, *Falintil*, the *CNRT* and the communists have joined forces to run a campaign of propaganda and intimidation.'

Tamala looked at Ava and Bruce for understanding, sympathy even. He probably expected the mention of communism would invoke the heady days of the Cold War and get them onside. Ava maintained her deadpan face and Bruce followed her lead. Silence was sometimes the best space in which her interlocutors revealed themselves.

'Naturally,' Tamala continued, 'the pro-Indonesia side have formed paramilitary groups to protect themselves.' He paused and Ava saw his face go red and his eyes narrow. 'But really, what happened in Liquica a few days ago was the direct result of the central government's actions. The president simply doesn't understand or have faith in *TNI*. We know this place better than anyone. We are the tip of society—we *are* the Indonesian people—and we need to be respected. There were thousands of militia and pro-Indonesia Timorese alongside us in the Liquica churchyard that day, and we were made to look ridiculous—like we couldn't handle the situation—all because the president is *bodoh*, stupid.'

Ava looked up from her notebook. Clearly the colonel had lost his cool, verbally run amok. She debated in that short moment before looking down again whether to note his inflammatory comment about Hidayat in front of him or wait until afterwards. She decided to note it there and then. When she looked back up, his face was filled with regret.

She put her head back down again and asterisked another of his comments, the discrepancy between his report and his deputy's about the number of militia at the churchyard. In less than a minute it had escalated from two hundred and fifty to thousands.

Tamala poured some water for himself and drank the entire glass. When he put his glass back down he was newly composed.

'Of course, what we really want is peace. But if the UN process continues and independence wins, there'll be more of what *Besi Merah Putih* did in Liquica. There'll be much more running amok.' He leant in towards Ava and Bruce putting on his most charming smile while his eyes burrowed into Ava's. 'And be sure that if that happens, *TNI* will protect the pro-Indonesia East Timorese. We don't need peacekeeping forces, and if we're invaded, we *will* fight back.'

Ava refused to be intimidated by him, staying firm in her seat despite his close proximity. Instead she nodded to let him know she'd received his warning. Canberra wouldn't be pleased at his empty bravado. He knew only too well that if Australian peacekeepers went in, it would only be with the agreement of Jakarta. In any case, did Tamala really think his tin-pot army with their ageing, second-rate weaponry would win against Australian troops? Perhaps he did.

That night she lay in bed listening to warning shots being fired in front of their hotel at regular intervals, presumably by militias *TNI* had sent to back up Tamala's theory of looming anarchy. She didn't believe the militias would be allowed to harm them, but the close gunfire combined with the general atmosphere in Dili were unnerving. Just in case, she and Bruce had devised an escape plan.

'Sleep in your clothes,' he'd told her. 'And have your shoes and important stuff packed and ready to grab. We'll leave over the roof and the back fence together. But if something happens, go by yourself and we'll rendezvous at the AusAID office. If you have to use your phone, try and speak so they can't understand. Use colloquialisms.'

Bruce had also paid their plain-clothes guard wads of new US dollars from a large brown paper bag to look after them. But he was a disinterested man from Intel and Ava doubted it was possible to buy protection from anyone in East Timor, let alone his lot. Everything was a choreographed farce here. Nothing was as it seemed.

34

____

DILI AND LIQUICA, APRIL 1999

Early the next morning, Ava and Bruce sat silently in the back seat of a shiny, black SUV heading out of Dili for Liquica. An escort accompanied them, a large police truck with two benches fastened to the open back tray that were filled with riot police sitting back-to-back so they faced the edges of the road. Before they left, Ava heard them lock and load their rifles ready for use. She took a deep breath before stepping up into the car, remembering what Denise had said when she'd called her last night to wish her luck. 'I wouldn't want to be you right now for all the tea in China. Take care of yourself. Promise?'

She'd hesitated to respond. Until then the personal cost of the investigation hadn't occurred to her. It was simply something she felt compelled to do. Emotions rushed to the fore—horror, outrage and apprehension—but she pushed them aside. This wasn't the time.

The trip to Liquica took them past fields of rice and sugar cane before they hit the narrow winding coastal road and travelled through small fishing and salt-producing villages. The tense quiet of Dili felt even more pervasive out here. It was morning, yet no work was being done in the fields or along the shorelines, the schools were empty and they hadn't come across a single other vehicle. Everyone in the SUV was subdued the entire forty-minute journey.

At last they descended into a dense green valley where the Liquica town centre sat. Just beyond, the emerald blue water of the Ombai Strait glistened in the sun. As they pulled up to the local *TNI* headquarters, an old stone colonial house with wide front steps leading up to a grand veranda, Ava saw a group of forty or so militia milling in the yard. They seemed to be waiting, and on seeing her and Bruce, became agitated. Ava pursed her lips, annoyed they'd been told about their visit. But at least they had protection, she hoped.

As they got out of the car, a Javanese-looking man in *TNI* uniform came out to greet them. 'Welcome,' he grinned as he shook their hands with a little too much vigour. 'I'm Oscar Karisma, Liquica district military commander. Let's go inside.'

Karisma led the way, but half a dozen militia stepped in their path, blocking them.

'Stand aside,' Karisma said, shooing the men away with both hands as though they were dogs. '*Pergilah*!' Go!

For Ava, this was more proof that *TNI* controlled the militias.

Karisma took them into a room containing a carefully mounted display like in one of those quaint country museums she'd visited in Australia. But the objects were heinous.

'This is what we found in Father Ribeiro's house,' Karisma said, standing back so they could see the alleged booty. 'This is a *Falintil* flag and this is the gun that was used to shoot the policeman. There's some other paraphernalia too, knives and so on. It proves that *Falintil* were inside the house and that they were armed.'

Karisma left them alone while she and Bruce examined the items and took photos.

'These could've come from anywhere,' Bruce said.

'Do they really think we'll take their word for it?'

Karisma led them into the front room and asked them to wait. Before long a short, stout man crept in. In his hand was a handkerchief, which he used to wipe his sweaty hands. He stooped and bowed, unable to look them directly in the eyes.

'I'm the Mayor of Liquica, Gaspar Osorio,' he said, dabbing his forehead. 'I've been told I have to speak to you.'

Ava explained who they were, and that the Indonesian government had given them permission to investigate recent events in Liquica.

'Can you tell me what happened on the sixth of April?' she asked.

'The pro-independence side is responsible for this anarchy,' Gaspar said breathlessly, checking the window and behind him. Ava wondered who he was most afraid of—the militias who'd gathered outside or the pro-independence lot?

He told them that everyone blamed him personally for what had happened. 'On that day, negotiations between the police and Father Ribeiro continued at the priest's house. The police knew the people inside had weapons, but Father Ribeiro insisted they didn't...'

Bruce exchanged a look with Ava. It was apparent he'd rehearsed the same version of events that *TNI* had given them in Dili, reciting it almost word for word. Ava attempted to draw him out with some questions, but he sat there, wiping his brow and checking around him. The day was growing increasingly surreal.

'You can go,' she said, and Gaspar almost fell over himself trying to leave.

'Useless,' Bruce scoffed.

'They're deliberately wasting our time,' she said and they waited for the next character to be plonked in front of them.

A man in his twenties entered the room. Slight in build and a foot shorter than Ava, she recognised him as Damiano da Silva, the commander of *Besi Merah Putih*.

'Please sit down,' she said, attempting to look him in the eyes, which darted around appearing at once tired and alert. His pupils were miniscule.

'Is anybody home?' Bruce whispered as Damiano sniffed and wiped his nose with the back of his hand.

Ava had heard about the militia being fed drugs by *TNI*. Some men had apparently raped and killed their own mothers and sisters while under the influence, only to suicide once they'd come down and realised what they'd done. No one had told her about this formally so she hadn't been able to report it. Was Damiano on speed or something else?

'This society is too conflicted to compromise and find a solution so it's better if the UN consultation isn't held and the solution is *adat,*' he spurted, 'local customs, where we, the people's representatives, sit together and impose autonomy without a vote because UN democracy is not possible here and will create confusion like it did just days ago, so we had to kill *all Falintil* in the house.'

'Why did you have to kill them?' Ava demanded, but he ignored her question.

'*Falintil* incited the violence and refused to negotiate so they shot first and tried to kill us and there were more of them waiting for us on the outskirts of nearby Maubara yesterday, perhaps on Aleixo's orders, but we are ready for them, we are ready for war.'

'For war?' Bruce asked.

'Yes, war,' he said with spent saucer eyes.

———

Ava inhaled deeply and stepped inside Father Ribeiro's yard, walking along the front pathway lined with fragrant pink and red roses that led to a white front door. How odd that the flora would survive untouched when the people hadn't.

She stopped at the front door and suddenly something around her—or was it inside her—shifted. It was nothing tangible, more a disorientation, as though the earth had rotated a couple of degrees and she couldn't be sure exactly where she was. Was this an imprint left by the dying—a memory of their intense fear as their bodies took their last breaths? Goose bumps washed over her. Stay calm, she told herself.

Then as quickly as it had arrived, the feeling left and she was herself again, the smell of the nearby sea filling her nostrils and the crime scene fixed firmly in front of her awaiting her interrogation.

Only there wasn't much left of any crime. Men in military uniforms were putting the finishing touches on what appeared to be extensive repairs.

'Bishop Basso asked us to do this,' one of them said, and Ava kept her disdain hidden.

She and Bruce already knew from their helicopter ride over the house that *TNI* had put a new roof on, but now they could see the walls had been replastered and painted, the floors washed and resurfaced, and all the furniture and other household items removed. The inside of the house was a clean, naked shell.

'Put your nose up against the wall and smell for tear gas or grenade smoke,' Bruce said, not caring what anyone around them thought.

'I can't smell anything but paint,' Ava said after a time.

'Neither can I.'

'Would new paint cover it up?'

'Can't be sure. Perhaps they washed it down first.'

Bruce shook his head slightly and Ava wondered if it was out of disgust at *TNI* or scepticism over the teargas claim. She wanted to remain detached, but found the lack of proof frustrating.

She checked the other rooms. In a small toilet she found twenty bullet marks on the tiles that lined the bottom of the walls. That was a lot for such a small area. Her stomach turned. How many had they plastered over on the rest of the walls? She took photographs.

'Shall we go outside?' their *TNI* guide asked and led them to a tree.

'This is the tree that took the bullet fired by *Falintil*. It injured a soldier and triggered the violence. He pointed to a gash. 'As you can see, we cut a square chunk from the trunk for our investigation.'

Ava and Bruce nodded. Bruce moved away and Ava followed him.

'The trajectory's all wrong,' he whispered to her. 'Their claim that *Falintil* started shooting from inside is bullshit.'

She was secretly pleased, but they needed more proof. She drew a map and paced out the edges of the cottage as she considered the scenarios that had been put to them. This was her one opportunity to collect information and she must remain cool headed.

Next she checked the outside walls by the side door where tear gas had reportedly been thrown in and people had streamed out before being gunned down and knifed. She found at least fifty bullet marks. More evidence. It was plausible that people had been shot while trying to escape. She closed her eyes to contain her emotion.

She walked the perimeter and spied some Indonesian nuns up the road. She approached them and asked if they could talk. They looked anxiously at a nearby group of militia glaring at them.

'We can talk for a few minutes, but we must sit outside in plain view.'

The nuns told her that on the day of the massacre there was non-stop firing for an hour. This confirmed what Ava had heard.

'Later on, we went to the mayor's house to attend the wounded,' they added. 'There were at least twenty badly injured people there, children too, mostly with bullet wounds. We tried to sew them up with household needles and thread, but their wounds were too large, too serious.'

'They all died?' Ava asked.

'Yes,' the nuns nodded. She bowed her head momentarily in respect and to dispel the images from her mind.

The militia had moved closer and were staring at them menacingly.

'Come inside for a moment,' one of the nuns said before ushering Ava into a living room. On the walls hung pictures of Mary and sitting on a bench was a young, drawn-looking Timorese woman. She was thin and dressed in a ridiculous filly dress.

'This young woman witnessed the massacre,' said the nun and the girl glanced up at her.

Ava introduced herself and smiled but got no reaction. 'Can you tell me what you saw?' Ava asked.

The girl swallowed and looked up at the nuns with fear on her face. One of them smiled at her, yet she remained silent.

'Maybe you can nod if you saw *TNI* at the pastor's house that day?'

The girl looked at her, then nodded.

'Can you nod if you saw them shoot anyone, like the people sheltering in the house?'

The girl looked back at the same nun, tears running from her eyes. 'You can tell her,' the nun said.

The girl looked back at Ava, her eyes wider, and nodded again.

A nun who'd been on watch outside came in. 'You need to go now. They're getting close. We are women too.'

'Of course. What's your name?' Ava asked the girl as she stood.

The girl looked away.

'Her name is Isabel,' whispered the nun as she guided Ava out.

Outside, Ava couldn't find Bruce or their *TNI* escort. She'd have to go back to the *TNI* base alone. She fixed her eyes on the building up the road and walked past the militia, who mumbled unspeakable things about what they intended to do to her. It's just talk, she told herself, counting the length of her inhales and exhales to keep fear from her face. They followed just metres behind, but when she entered the base they backed off. Not so brave now.

'Time to leave,' their head police escort said.

'Can you get some photos of the militias' handmade weapons for Canberra first?' Bruce asked her. 'It's better if you do it.'

Ava was about to object, but the thought of taunting the militia, who were right now exposed and powerless, brought her some satisfaction. She took close-up pictures of them and their paraphernalia. They threw her angry looks, though their eyes spoke of fear. Who or what were they scared of? Surely not the now dead local resistance. Perhaps what they feared most was justice.

By the time they left the *TNI* base, Ava was grateful for the safety of their car. As they drove she noticed that every house had at least one *TNI* flag flying in it despite appearing abandoned. She glanced back at the town they were leaving, and there in the yard of a local militia post was the young woman, Isabel. Ava caught her eye and Isabel looked back at her. Ava couldn't help but feel she wanted something from her, but she knew that stopping would put her in danger. Instead she held young Isabel's gaze until they were too far apart to look at each other any more.

35

JAKARTA, INDONESIA, APRIL 1999

It was two in the morning as they sat around the large oval table in the fourth-floor meeting room. Ava still hadn't been home to see Juliette, nor had she eaten. She and Bruce had flown from Dili and come directly to the embassy to finalise the Liquica massacre report. After ten days of this crisis, she had little left to give.

'Is everyone happy with the conclusion?' Quentin said to the group that included Bruce, Donald and a couple of others.

Ava read it through one more time:

There is evidence that TNI assisted militia group Besih Merah Putih to take control of Liquica, creating a situation that led to the violence on 6 April.

There are credible reports that troops sided with militia group Besih Merah Putih in the clash with pro-independence supporters outside Liquica.

The evidence of TNI's direct involvement in the violence at the church is less persuasive.

However, it is clear that weapons used in the incident on 6 April are normally only in the hands of TNI.

At the minimum, TNI and the police forces personnel failed to stop a protracted attack by the pro-Indonesia militia on people taking refuge in the churchyard. [4]

Ava wasn't happy. Not at all. *TNI* were more culpable than this. True, it had been impossible to get a definitive account of what had happened in Liquica that day—she and Bruce were in East Timor for only five days, and at that time most eyewitnesses were either dead, in hiding or too scared to speak. Yet the case against them was stronger than this. Why couldn't the argument be turned on its head so that instead of casting doubt on *TNI's* direct involvement, the focus be placed on the possibility of it? Why couldn't they say something like:

There are indications that TNI were directly involved in the violence at the church.

First, the weapons used in the incident are normally only in the hands of TNI.

Second, we were given several accounts—including from Father Ribeiro himself—that TNI staged the incident, not just directing their own soldiers, but also the militia and riot police.

Third, reports of TNI dressing up as militia and donning weapons are a known TNI modus operandi, which has been captured on film.

Words, words, words. They could reveal or deceive, persuade or threaten, empower or destroy. Perhaps Stretton didn't want the report to damage relations with Indonesia any more than necessary and Quentin was giving him just that. But was that wise? Would Australia really hold more sway with Indonesia that way? Or would Indonesia believe they could get away with even more?

Alternatively, Quentin could have been instructed to tone down *TNI* and police violence for fear of the truth about the poor security situation in East Timor coming out and obliging the UN to cancel the vote altogether. Nobody except *TNI* wanted that, especially Australia whose goal it was to get East Timor off its back.

'No other changes?' Quentin asked.

Ava couldn't change the report's overall position, but one important detail had been left out that pointed to *TNI* and police involvement.

'We haven't added in the point that eighty per cent of injuries seen by the American doctor at his clinic in Dili were caused by high velocity, modern rifles. It backs up the claim that military and police-issued guns were used, and that *TNI* and the police might have been involved in an organised way.'

'Fine,' Quentin said. 'Put it in the body of the report. Nothing else anyone? You can hit the send button when you've done that, Ava. Just ensure all sources that need to be protected in the public version are taken out. See you tomorrow.'

In her office, Ava made the last change and peered down at the send button. At least they had done an investigation of sorts, and there was a public version the world would get to see. She took a breath, hovered her mouse over the button and clicked, this time glad the cable was signed EMBASSY and not with her name.

36

LIQUICA, EAST TIMOR, APRIL 1999

The sun was still rising as Isabel crept off to the stream. She found Sebastiao's hidden container in the nape of the tree and placed a sheet of folded paper inside. This was the third piece of information she'd left there, but doing so today was more dangerous because it was too early to wash clothes, yet the material couldn't wait. Tomorrow Gabriel would be proclaimed deputy commander of all the militias, and after the ceremony he was planning to conduct a cleansing operation in Dili. Having some small influence over the outcome made the risk worthwhile for Isabel.

'What have you got?' she heard a man's voice say and jumped with fright. 'I thought I'd check on my way to the post.'

'Sebastiao. You took me by surprise.' Isabel ran her hand through her hair, a mess of tangles, but quickly gave up. Her belly was upset too. She'd felt off since the massacre ten days ago.

'What's the document, *menina*?'

'You know the big militia parade tomorrow at the governor's office in Dili?'

'Yes.'

'And the sweeping operation after the rally?'

He nodded. 'In retaliation for Aleixo's war cry. We've all been ordered to attend.'

'Well… There's a blacklist.'

He frowned. 'Of targets?

Isabel nodded.

'Of what?' he asked, but Isabel could see by his distress that he understood. Gabriel planned to kill them.

'Who's on the list?'

She swallowed back tears. Since the massacre she cried easily and often. The simplest of things overwhelmed her, although there was nothing simple about more butchery.

'Activists *maun*. Low down ones. But I also heard them talking about the ex-governor's brother, the one with the refugees from Alas camping at his house.'

'Henriques?' Sebastiao asked and she nodded.

'You have to warn them, Sebastiao. They're going to get them straight after the rally.'

Sebastiao took the list from the container in the tree and read it, a look of quiet rage crossing his face.

'Thank you Isabel. This will be recorded and one day these people will be held to account.'

She gave him a half smile, wanting to believe him—that there'd be a future and it would be fair, just as she wanted to believe she was going to be rescued any day now.

'Are you all right?' he asked.

She looked to the ground. 'I'm just tired.'

'I understand. Many of us are exhausted. It won't always be like this.'

She looked up at him, her eyes watering. Perhaps he believed they were kindred spirits, and in some ways they were bound together by what went on at the stream. But their lives were not the same. Sebastiao wasn't forced to share the indignities she endured at Gabriel's hand, and he got to go back to his family every night.

He reached his hand to her face to touch her. There was tenderness in his eyes, but Isabel stepped back. She wasn't quick enough and his fingers brushed her cheek. She let out a small gasp. Being touched was what Gabriel did.

'I'm sorry. I didn't mean… Things will be better soon. I'll make it right.'

Better? Right? How? But before she could ask him, he disappeared through the bushes because, unlike her, he could do as he pleased. Unlike her, he was what they called free.

37

LIQUICA, APRIL 1999

Unseasonal rain battered the tin roof reminding Isabel as she lay next to Gabriel, of home. Memories of her family should have brought her comfort, but these days they only made her feel lonelier.

Where are you, mama? she often found herself asking the trees and sky. She needed her more than ever, to be enveloped in her protective arms while she took in the soothing words coming from her pink-stained mouth.

The rain grew louder, sounding as though stones were pelting down from the sky. She feared the roof might cave in and curled up into a ball, her chest tightening more and more until she was forced to sit up and gasp for air.

'What's the matter?' Gabriel grumbled.

She knew she mustn't give him reason to be angry and steadied her breath. It was her life's sole purpose to appease Gabriel, although there were days when nothing brought him peace.

'*Mana,*' he said in a demanding tone.

Isabel searched for courage. She had no choice but to tell him. 'Gabriel. I think… Please don't be angry with me. I couldn't help it. I think I'm pregnant.'

She lay back down, retreating once more into a ball. Gabriel stayed silent and she lingered in fear.

'This is a great thing,' he finally said, wrapping his arms and legs around her as though to reclaim her from her darkness. 'You and I will be tied together forever. This child will have parents, forever. He won't see the things we've seen. He won't be betrayed by his own people. Yes. When all this is over and we've won the ballot, I'll marry you and we'll become a real Indonesian family.'

Tears flowed down Isabel's face mirroring the wet outside. She thought Gabriel would be angry, that he'd beat her. She relaxed a little into his arms, allowing herself to feel for the first time the wonder of the life inside her, the tender thing they'd created from such barbarity. Until now, she'd alternated between fearing and hating it, the sinister way it had taken hold of her like a tumour, and yet it was so magical. Was it perhaps possible for her to love it given its father? If only Gabriel was always like this. Maybe if she changed, if she could please him like tonight, they could marry and live in a nice house and she'd be able to hold her head high among the villagers again.

'You're lucky to have me Isabel,' Gabriel said. 'No one else would take you, not like this. Since the first time I met you, I knew you wanted me.'

Any affection Isabel felt for him evaporated. 'Yes. Lucky.'

'When's the baby due?'

'October. November.'

'Good timing. We'll get married before then, after we win the vote. We'll get married in autonomous, Indonesian East Timor.'

Should she marry him? Could she, really? She imagined the alternative, her alone with a baby, Gabriel's baby. Who else would take her? Perhaps he was right. Maybe she had no choice but to make the best of things with him.

An alternative scenario popped into her head. 'But what if independence wins?'

She instantly felt her cheek sting from the smack of Gabriel's palm and coiled back up into a ball, stifling her sobs for fear of inciting more of his wrath, this father of her budding life.

38

JAKARTA, INDONESIA, APRIL 1999

Ava woke to a banging noise. Where was she? Should she throw on some clothes and run?

She listened for signs of danger as her eyes adjusted to the semi-dark. She was in her bed at home. The noise must be someone banging on her door. Her body relaxed a little. But what day was it? That's right, it was Saturday the seventeenth, the day of the Dili cleansing operation. This was her first chance since the Liquica massacre to get more than five hours sleep. She checked her clock. 6.25 am. So much for that.

'Phone,' Pete yelled from the other side of the door. 'It's urgent.'

So many things were urgent these days. Distress calls from her East Timorese contacts pleading with her to help them, reports of more disappearances and beatings and killings, and surprise media announcements about major political developments. But not many people had her home number. She put on her dressing gown and, clasping the collars so it didn't gape, poked her hand around her door, seizing the corded receiver from Pete, angry that he'd failed as her gatekeeper.

'Ava here,' she said drowsily to let the caller know they'd woken her.

'It's Donald. Sorry to wake you.'

188

He wasn't sorry otherwise he wouldn't have rung.

'I have to ask you something on direction from Canberra.' He hesitated. 'A version of the Liquica massacre report has shown up on the front page of today's *Australian*. Did you leak the report?'

'No, I didn't leak the report.' She sighed loudly to convey her irritation. Journalists had put her under immense pressure all week to slip them a copy. While she believed it should be made public, just as Stretton had initially promised but was now refusing to do, she'd urged them to lobby for its release instead. To be interrogated like this felt grossly unfair. 'Don't the defence department and ministers' offices usually do that sort of thing?'

Donald was silent, perhaps trying to decide whether to believe her or question her further.

'What would you say if I told you every conversation in and out of the embassy is taped?' he asked.

'I'd say I'm exhausted and today was my first chance in three weeks to get some sleep.'

Again he was silent.

'Okay. Sorry to disturb you. You can go back to sleep now.'

Yeah sure. As well as being overtired she was pissed off at his veiled accusations. She thought they were friends, but Donald was a company man all the way.

The real reason she couldn't escape back into slumber was Gabriel's threat to cleanse Dili of independence elements. A knot of tension twisted in her gut. Stretton had made multiple representations imploring the Indonesians to stop the operation. *This is an intra-Timorese problem over which we have no control*, they'd responded. In other words, this is what you get when Indonesia doesn't play referee—this is what East Timor will be like under independence. Yet it was, as ever, them who were *merekayasa* or manufacturing the chaos. Ava loved that often-used Indonesian word. It was perfect for this country of machinations.

She didn't like feeling this disempowered. Usually there was something she could try, or decide, or at least think that would constructively channel some of her frustration at the injustices piling up on East Timor. But right now she couldn't find anything. On top of that, she'd need to mentally prepare herself for news today that would take her understanding of human depravity to a new low. Expect to be shocked and she'd be unshockable, she told herself, knowing this was a lie. Each time she learned about another level of debauchery her heart retreated a little more, her view of humankind dimmed and her rage grew.

Australia didn't help the situation. Only yesterday Stretton repeated his claim that the violence in East Timor was down to *rogue elements* in *TNI*. Rogue elements! It was evident—logical really—that without high-level authorisation from *TNI* and the Indonesian government itself, the funding and organisation of the militias would be impossible. Stretton only ever made this assertion under parliamentary privilege to protect him from future lawsuits. This itself was another revealing factor.

For now, she put on her Walkman and hopped on her exercise bike. Cycling was as good a way as any to release her pent-up tension. Outside it was too polluted, busy and unsafe to walk or jog. She was pedalling fast when she heard a new barrage of door knocking.

'What now?' she yelled.

'Phone again,' Pete shouted.

She got off and took the handpiece from Pete.

'Your mobile's not on,' Donald said.

She'd deliberately left it off to get twenty minutes of peace before she faced more East Timor ravages.

'Dili. It's started. You need to come into the embassy.'

'Yep,' she said between gasps.

'Are you all right? You sound…emotional.'

'I was trying to get in a bit of exercise on my bike.'

'You knew this was coming. I'll drop by this afternoon to see how you're going. Don't send anything to Canberra until I've cleared it.'

Ava almost, but not quite, slammed the phone down.

———

In her office, Ava juggled phone calls that came in one on top of each other on her mobile and land line, with others on call waiting. Pro-independence Timorese contacts being attacked begging her for assistance, journalists in Dili beseeching her to get the Australian government to do something, and colleagues from other embassies sharing information and coordinating strategies. In between, Ava kept Quentin, Donald and Bruce updated.

Mid-afternoon a call came that she didn't expect.

'Ava?'

'Yes.'

'This is Tomas Henriques. I'm with the Irish foreign minister at the bishop's house in Dili. I'm calling because my son told me our house is being attacked. Is there anything you can do? I've called Colonel Tamala and he says *TNI* has to remain neutral. They've confined themselves to their barracks. The trouble is, so have the police.'

'I see.' Ava knew she had no time to waste. She'd hoped that because a foreign dignity was in Dili, the situation wouldn't become serious, but apparently the opinion of Ireland and the European Union was of no consequence to the Indonesians. 'Leave it with me. I'll call you back.'

She dialled Bruce and asked him to phone Tamala directly. By now news of the cleansing operation was on the wire services, which was good as it would put more pressure on governments to demand the Indonesians do something, now.

Bruce called her back. 'Tamala says there's nothing he can do. He claims the rally was peaceful until independence supporters sparked the violence. He also says, *He warned us foreigners what would happen.*'

'We have to keep trying. Call someone else in *TNI*. And the police chief.'

She phoned Quentin next and he called the Indonesian foreign minister, then Ayu, Hidayat's foreign affairs advisor.

'*Suggestio falsi*', he reported back to her. 'They said they'll do what they can, but this is between the Timorese. I'll inform the PM's office and The Minister. They won't be happy.'

Ava took a call from Sharon next. She was in Dili feeding her live accounts. Ava heard sobbing.

'Are you all right?

'It's too late. They're dead,' Sharon cried.

'Who's dead?

'Tonio—Henriques's son—and some others too.'

Ava had been at Henriques's house a few days ago during the massacre investigation and Tonio had served them coffee. He was just a kid, seventeen years old. 'Oh God.' Tears welled as she took it in.

'A group of us witnessed it. There was nothing we could do. They hacked him to death in front of us along with some others.'

A confusion of emotion stuck in Ava's throat—grief and sorrow followed by disgust, anger and dismay—but she had little use for it now, and Sharon was still a journalist.

'It's so fucking...pointless,' Ava said. Her call waiting and landline went off again. 'I have to go Sharon. But any details and proof you can get me on the attacks would help. How many were killed, photos, which militia were involved?' She hoped it would convince Stretton to stop publicly blaming rogue elements within *TNI*. He'd be pissed off that his and Beaumont's lobbying had amounted to nothing, and she could use that. She'd give them all the gory details so they'd have to speak out. The Indonesians were determined to make their point, but so was she.

39

JAKARTA, APRIL 1999

A week later on Saturday afternoon the Jakarta shopping mall was busy. Ava drove around with all the other drivers hunting for a parking spot. The busy shopping centre, traffic jams and the lack of parking meant the monetary crisis was over.

'There's one,' Juliette said from the back seat where she sat with her friend, Siti.

Ava indicated and drove up to the empty spot, but another car came from around the corner and gazumped her. She beeped her car horn and waved to the driver and his wife to let them know she'd seen the spot first, but they refused to move.

'Right,' she said, injustice pulsing through veins. She put her foot down and aimed the front of her car at the rear corner of the parked one, giving it a good bump, though hopefully not enough to cause any damage.

Juliette and her friend giggled nervously.

'Bastards. Two-faced, lying, compliant, murdering, fucking evil bastards!' she yelled, forgetting the girls were with her.

She hid her head in her hands and last Saturday came rushing back to her—the audacious cleansing operation, the intransigent Indonesian authorities and Tonio's senseless death. Today was her first day off from East Timor in months and she felt so very tired.

'Are you okay, Mummy?' Juliette asked.

Ava opened her eyes and saw Juliette's fear in the rear vision mirror. What had she done?

Two security guards approached her car, noticing the diplomatic number plates. Ava explained that the couple had taken her parking spot. The guards ordered the other car to leave before guiding her in.

'You don't have to worry about them again,' the guards smiled as she and the girls got out. 'We've noted their registration number and they'll never be allowed in here again.'

'Oh. There's no need for that.' Ava said, her face reddening.

'Of course there is. You're an important person.'

Ava covered her head with her hands. She was no better than *TNI* with her bare-faced hatred.

'I don't feel like shopping any more,' she said, bundling the children back into the car. 'Let's go somewhere else. How about seeing a movie? We can get ice cream.'

The girls were silent as Ava reversed out of the parking spot and muttered to the guards, 'Sorry. Sorry,' at the same time, resolving to hire a driver.

40

LIQUICA, EAST TIMOR, MAY 1999

The day after the Dili sweeping operation, Isabel squatted by a plastic bowl washing lunch dishes. The mood at the post was subdued with none of the usual militia swagger or camaraderie. Instead the men appeared sorry for themselves, which Isabel found as shameful as it was absurd.

Sebastiao stood guard at the gate. He was staring directly at her, which was unusual. Did he know about the baby? Did he want to meet? She couldn't tell.

When she'd finished the dishes, she took the dirty washing to the stream, sweat trickling down her back in the mid-morning heat. Lately she found no relief in routine tasks. Everything felt burdensome.

She was halfway through washing her pile of dirty clothes when she heard a tell-tale rustle.

'Who's there?'

Sebastiao emerged from the undergrowth, his face drawn and his eyes lined with dark circles. He squatted, lowered his head into his hands and wept quietly. Isabel placed her washing on the rock, rinsed her hands and sat nearby, though not close enough for him to touch her.

'What happened, *maun*?'

He shuddered and choked as Isabel waited.

'After the Dili ceremony, Gabriel ordered some of us to go to Henriques's house,' he said.

'Where the people from Alas were staying?'

Sebastiao nodded. 'He made me, Isabel. He told us we had to capture and kill.'

Isabel stared. Not him too?

'There were hundreds of refugees huddled inside. They were unarmed and begged us not to hurt them. But there were so many militia—no, so many *TNI* pretending to be militia—all armed with sticks and machetes or guns. Gabriel was watching me. I had to do something. I… I had to stab him.'

Isabel's mouth fell open and she looked away, feeling only numbness. She had no tears left to cry.

'The look in his eyes when I pushed the knife in. I tried not to go too deep, but he fell to the ground, and I don't know if…'

Isabel's breakfast rose up into her throat and she swallowed it back down. She knew Sebastiao sought comfort from her, but she couldn't give it to him.

'The blacklist I gave you. Did it save anyone?'

Sebastiao broke out in sobs again and she realised her efforts had been futile. She looked up at the sky. What was the point of any of it? Except that here, in front of her, was a chance to be kind, yet all she could do was pile cruelty on top of cruelty.

'Sebastiao,' she said. 'You were only doing what Bishop Basso told you to do.'

He gave her a grateful look, but what she'd told him had been a lie. No matter what, no man should stab another. Why hadn't he refused to do it? He could have run away. He could have sacrificed himself and saved others. Was the bishop's proof really more important than that man's life. Was Sebastiao simply weak?

'I have a question for you,' she said. 'What are you going to do after the ballot?'

The sound of trickling water filled the silence as he pondered his answer. Silent tears ran down his face.

'I don't know. What do people do in peacetime? Some people say everything will be different when we're independent. We'll all have good jobs, we'll never be short of food, we'll dress in beautiful clothes, drive big cars and live in two-storey mansions like on TV. But I can't imagine that. I can't imagine anything beyond…'

Isabel picked up a twig and snapped it into two, and those pieces again until the segments were so short she couldn't break them any further. She would speak her mind too.

'All I want is to run up Mt Ramelau and scream and never stop so the world can at last hear that I exist—that I'm me. I want to swim in the sea forever until I forget I'm a girl, until I become like a dolphin or a whale racing through the water. I want to run on the flat plains as fast as I can until I have no feet and no legs left like those African cats—until I become the air. And I want to—' She remembered the life inside her, the thing spreading from her womb and taking her over. It was hard to accept that even her own body had betrayed her. The villagers, *Falintil*, the *CNRT*, Father Ribeiro, God, her own family even, but her own body? At times she felt such intense loathing for the baby she wished she could reach inside her and tear it out.

Yet there were other moments when she was overcome with love for it and an intense awe at her body's ability to create life despite everything. She'd rub her belly and long to see what it looked like.

Sebastiao dried his face and Isabel wondered if she'd been foolish to open up to him this much.

'Perhaps I can climb and swim and run with you,' he said. Perhaps that will be my new purpose.'

Isabel looked away, confused by his softness after what he'd just revealed. She didn't know whether to like or loathe him.

He walked over to her, bent down and kissed her lightly on the cheek. Despite everything, Isabel allowed the smallest, shyest smile and an inkling of hope to break through onto her face.

———

A few days later

Gabriel threw his newspaper onto the table next to the black coffee and *pao* bread roll that Isabel had laid out for his breakfast, and flopped down on his chair.

'The UN's coming!' he growled at her, thumping the table with his fist.

She stopped what she was doing and peered at the newspaper's headline. Was it possible that foreigners were really coming to East Timor?

'There's going to be a secret vote on autonomy and independence on the eighth of August. That's barely two months away.'

Isabel was incredulous. Maybe Gabriel had gone too far in Dili? She had another thought. Perhaps the UN would help her find her family. She stifled a smile.

'Two hundred and eight civilian police officers. Fifty military liaison officers. Foreigners, here, telling us what to do!' Gabriel lashed out with his hand, knocking his breakfast to the ground.

Isabel began cleaning up his mess as he walked to the door.

'Do you want some more breakfast?' she asked quietly.

'Breakfast?' he hissed before kicking open the door and mumbling under his breath, 'Breakfast.'

41

DILI, EAST TIMOR, MAY 1999

Bishop Basso's garden was in full bloom. Ava walked through the yard and took in the sweet scents of ancient frangipani trees and a spreading Portuguese tree she didn't know the name of, and was momentarily transported away from the trials of East Timor. It was her rebellion, her way of not being shrouded by the bleak anxiety of the place, to relish these simple pleasures, even if she had to hide her joy for fear of appearing disrespectful.

She was also happy to be alone. Over the last few days, she'd accompanied the ambassador on one of his whirlwind trips and they'd had a disagreement. It had proven difficult to meet the *CNRT*, who kept cancelling or changing meeting times and venues for security reasons. Quentin wasn't one to accommodate others easily.

'Look if it's so damn difficult I won't bother seeing them,' he'd huffed as they'd waited for a taxi to take them to dinner.

Ava had witnessed these belligerent moods before. She understood he was tired, but he wasn't the only one. She'd worked day and night organising his meetings, transport and meals as well as writing up her meeting notes.

'With respect, how can you come here and not see the pro-independence side? Aleixo and the *CNRT* could accuse you of bias.'

'You can't say that to me,' he exploded. 'I'll see or not see who I damn well want.'

'Sorry. Sorry,' she said, regretting her child-like apology as soon as she'd blurted it out.

At dinner, Quentin shoved plate after plate of food in front of her, urging her to eat up. 'Have some more. You deserve it.' This was the closest she was going get to an apology, and she accepted the food even after she felt full. The next morning, they met the *CNRT* at the airport before Quentin's flight left for Jakarta.

The French windows to Bishop Basso's lounge room opened and he stepped out.

'*Bondia,* Your Eminence,' Ava said to him.

He greeted her with a nod of recognition as she continued on her way to the rear building where his human rights organisation was located. Despite being a Nobel Peace Prize winner, Bishop Basso was regarded as a grumpy, inaccessible man. He regularly shouted at foreign journalists when they sought his views on the latest developments. On other occasions, he made forthright public statements about Indonesia, which Ava found unproductive. Yet according to Abel, the head of the bishop's human rights organisation, he thought well of her, crediting her with the Australian government's change in East Timor policy last year which coincided with her taking over the job.

Out the back, Ava searched for Abel. She'd stayed behind in Dili to work with him on the reconciliation talks. Many hoped reconciliation would lower tensions between the pro-Indonesia and pro-independence sides, reduce *TNI's* authority over the militia and ensure the ballot's losing side wasn't victimised. Australia believed the only way the talks had a chance of succeeding was if they were held in neutral territory and offered to host the talks. This was why Quentin had ordered her to remain in East

Timor until the talks were in process, even though it meant weeks away from Jakarta and Juliette.

Abel was talking to a tall, well-dressed part-African man. They turned when they heard her coming and Abel wrung his hands.

Ava greeted Abel with a *bondia* and they kissed each other's cheeks.

'Ava,' Abel said, averting his eyes. 'Meet Thomas Quayle. Thomas Quayle, this is my friend Ava Vuyk from the Australian Embassy in Jakarta.'

Ava had no idea Abel spoke such good English, or that he considered her a friend. It was true there was a bond between them—a mutual respect grown out of their tacit agreement that he'd contact her about violence, arbitrary detentions and other abuses, and she'd do her best to stop or minimise them, even though Quentin and Donald told her such work was beyond her remit.

'Thomas is American but he's here representing the UN Assessment Mission,' Abel continued. 'He's going to be the top advisor to the head of UNAMET when he arrives. I asked him to join our meeting on the reconciliation talks.'

So that was why Abel was uneasy. He hadn't sought her agreement for Thomas to join them.

'Good to meet you, Thomas,' she said, reaching her hand out to shake his.

'Call me Tom,' he said with a General American accent.

'I'm glad you're here for this Tom,' she began as they sat down at the table. 'If the talks are going to work, we need the UN's endorsement.'

Tom hesitated, then said, 'The UN will support the talks being held in Australia so long as we believe it's in the interests of the Timorese to do so.'

'Tom,' Abel said. 'Both Bishop Basso and Aleixo agree that if the meeting is held in Indonesia it will fail because of *TNI* meddling. They believe Australia is the most logical venue.'

Tom nodded. 'But we'd want other countries involved. That way Australia couldn't be accused of hijacking the reconciliation process.'

Ava fixed her eyes on his. 'I can assure you that as a close neighbour of Indonesia and a country with a long-term interest in peace for East Timor, Australia genuinely wants reconciliation to succeed. We have no problem involving other countries. In fact, we encourage it.'

Tom held her gaze. 'While the UN is happy to participate as observers we wouldn't presume to play a key role, unless necessary.'

'I understand,' Ava countered, enjoying their exchange as Abel watched from the side. 'But Australia believes strong UN involvement is important to the success of the talks and to the UN mission here. The process of reconciliation is closely linked to a successful and peaceful ballot.'

Walking back through the bishop's lush garden, Ava recognised that nothing was resolved between her and Tom beyond an understanding that the UN would consider Australia's request. And yet, she felt invigorated. Yes, she was looking forward to her next argument with Tom Quayle from the UN.

42

DILI, MAY 1999

On the crest of a hill to the south of Dili, a giant bronze statue of Jesus stood atop a globe of the world. His outstretched arms, which either beckoned or pronounced, loomed over Ava, Tom and the rest of the rag-tag group she'd invited to dinner at her favourite outdoor fish restaurant on the harbour. Many East Timorese disliked the statue, a gift from the Indonesians commemorating East Timor's place as their twenty-seventh province. Its orientation towards Jakarta was not only a constant reminder of their colonisation, but an insult to Catholicism given that Jesus' gaze apparently landed in Mecca. As Ava peered up at the statue that glowed orange in the setting sun, she could only think how unconcerned Jesus seemed, content to look across the bay beyond their lesser lives.

She sat in the middle of the group, Tom on one side and the energetic, newly arrived UNAMET spokesperson, Stephen, on the other, with Abel and three young women from Amnesty International on their first ever sanctioned visit to East Timor sitting opposite. They shared barbequed fish with rice, salad and Ava's favourite local *sambal*, pillar-box red in colour, and sweet as well as hot. As they hypothesised and speculated over East Timor, Ava felt hope for the ballot process, hope for East Timor. Months of speculation and planning were at last gaining form and momentum in front of her. These people, their presence, was in itself movement and realisation, and Ava was excited.

'Can we go over there for a moment,' Stephen said in his London accent. He strode to another table with Ava and Tom following behind. Ava was pleased the UN recognised Australia's pivotal role.

'This is UNAMET's first press release,' he said, handing a folded sheet of paper to her. 'Tom's already seen it, but I'd love your views.'

Ava read it through. 'It's pretty forthright.' Did he have New York's backing to take such a critical approach? 'If you want to deliver a hard message to the Indonesians, this will do it. But they'll perceive this as hostile and combative. Is that what you're after?'

'The militias issued a warning to us today,' Tom said. 'They said UN personnel will *find themselves in danger* if we don't *remain neutral.*'

'I heard.'

'What they've been getting away with…it's outrageous,' Stephen said. 'We need to let them know it won't be like that any more.'

'Right.' Ava smiled, suddenly envious that she couldn't draft a frank press release like this. But that wasn't Australia's role.

Stephen raised his beer. 'The UN is here.'

'The UN is here,' Ava and Tom chimed in, clinking their glasses. Ava felt at once relieved and worried. For each step forward here, there was a doubly strong reaction back the other way.

A smell of smoke, stronger than the usual cooking fires, penetrated Ava's nostrils. She put her beer down and listened carefully, tuning into what sounded like gunfire clacking in the distance. Her stomach churned.

'Excuse me a minute,' she said, and strolled out of the restaurant, past her waiting taxi and onto the street.

Small groups of young men holding machetes high had banded together and anxiously checked around them. They had wild animal eyes, a look she knew well from Jakarta, but they didn't appear to be interested in her. Their gazes landed on the foothills to the right where she saw tall orange red flames.

'Bloody hell.'

Someone was burning houses and she was willing to bet it was the militias. Was this being done for their benefit? Tonight was a good opportunity for them to make a show of strength in front of Australia, UNAMET, Amnesty and Abel. They needed to leave.

She checked her phone. It barely registered one bar. The only vehicle between the seven of them was her small taxi. It had been a mistake holding the dinner at the edge of town.

'We're kind of trapped here,' she told the group. 'We have one car, which won't fit us all, and the only way back to Dili is through the armed groups. I think I should call my police contacts to get us out. If that doesn't work, I'll try *TNI*. Does everyone agree?'

They agreed, happy to let her take control.

'What about me?' Abel asked, his face turning ashen. 'I'm on the blacklist.'

'The blacklist is real?' asked one of the Amnesty women. Until now, the troubles in East Timor would have been academic to them.

'Let's hide you first, Abel.' Ava asked the restaurant owner to help. He was pro-Indonesian, and if it came down to it would unlikely defend Abel, but they had no other option. Ava assigned a couple of the Amnesty women to go with them.

'Does anyone have phone reception?' she asked. The group handed her their mobiles. She lined up all seven on the table in front of her and dialled the police from one phone after the other, willing one of them to work. After ten minutes she got through.

'They said they didn't know about the incident and will send some people soon.'

'Bullshit,' said Stephen. Ava was impressed he already understood how the Indonesians worked.

'Twenty minutes passed and still no police or military came. Ava didn't believe the group were the prime target, but all it took was one crazy man to commit one stupid act.

Next door was a small military post manned by a few soldiers. Why hadn't she noticed this earlier? Perhaps they could help.

'Excuse me, *pak*,' she said to a soldier. She explained who she and the group were in the hope he'd offer to help.

He didn't.

'Are you or anyone from *TNI* going to sort out the troubles over there?'

'This is a police matter,' he replied, lighting a *kretek*.

'I called the police half an hour ago. They said they didn't know anything about it and would come and get us out, but they haven't turned up. Maybe if you called too?'

The soldier continued smoking his cigarette, almost in slow motion. If he wasn't going to help, perhaps she could get some information from him.

'*Pak*, what's actually going on?'

'It's an operation by the *milisi* against the independence side. The militia just returned from a meeting with the generals and ministers in Bali. This might be a show of strength.'

Ava was intrigued by how well briefed such a low-level soldier was. She also knew about the Bali meeting. One of her contacts had told her that *TNI* had attempted to rein in the militias, but it hadn't gone down well. Was tonight about letting the Indonesians know the militia were more than lackeys?

'So the militia are conducting an operation against the independence side in an independence stronghold without *TNI*?' she asked.

'That's correct. This isn't a *TNI* operation. Not this time.'

Not this time. NOT THIS TIME! Everything went still as the soldier's words reverberated in Ava's head. He'd declared openly what no Indonesian, Australian or UN official had admitted publicly—that the violence in East Timor was being initiated and controlled by *TNI*. For a junior soldier on the ground to know and admit that *TNI* proper was behind these militia operations exposed Hidayat, *TNI* and Stretton's rebuttals for what they were—lies. Ava would certainly be reporting this to Canberra, pointing out that on the ground, *TNI's* involvement in the violence was common knowledge.

She thanked the soldier and returned to the phones. She got through to the police who again promised someone was on their way, and tried *TNI* but couldn't get through.

After another hour, two black SUVs pulled up. Inside each were two men, unshaven and groggy as though they'd just woken up. 'Intel. SGI I think,' she told the group, wondering if the police or the well-briefed soldier had directed them here.

'Get in,' the men in the cars motioned, and Ava waited for everyone to squeeze in.

'The clash is up there,' she told them, pointing to the fires. They laughed, one of them waving his hand at her. Her only consolation was that no matter *TNI's* dismissiveness, the UN had arrived. An independence vote was coming.

Up the road, groups of young men waving machetes grudgingly parted to let them through. They were probably pro-independence given their lack of red and white bandannas and the terror on the faces, but Ava couldn't be certain. As their SUVs crawled along, she stared back at them equally hard, glad that Abel was hiding at their feet.

'Phew,' one of the Amnesty women said quietly once they were out. The others nodded, perhaps subdued like Ava because they were all aware that while they were safe, plenty of locals were not.

———

Two days later

Ava stood in line at the airport café. It was a real pull to leave East Timor, especially given the emerging sense of optimism. Every day more UN staff and equipment arrived and the locals dared to look hopeful. But because the Indonesians had ruled out the possibility of the reconciliation talks being held in Australia, she no longer had a reason to stay. She was about to order when someone tapped her on the shoulder.

'Tom,' she said, giving him a quizzical look. 'I didn't expect to see you here.'

'I got your message about returning to Jakarta and came straight away.' He seemed anxious when before he'd been self-assured. 'I'm confused. Don't they need you here?'

Ava understood why he was here now. Perhaps he'd expected her to show him the ropes and pass him her contacts and information. Perhaps he'd assumed she'd be UNAMET's liaison point with Australia on the ground.

'The reconciliation talks are going to be run by the Indonesians in Jakarta now, so I've been ordered back.'

Tom still looked upset.

'Can I buy you a cup of tea?' she asked, giving him a small smile.

'Yes,' he breathed out loudly. With cups of streaming black tea in their hands, they moved to a couple of orange plastic chairs set away from everyone else.

'I hear our fish dinner was a headline in the Australian print media,' Tom said.

'Yes,' she groaned.

'Did you get into trouble?'

'The secretary of the department wasn't too happy. Apparently I'm not supposed to be here alone. No one told me that, yet it seems to be my fault and not my bosses'.' She sighed. 'What upset me most was the bloody journalist mentioning my name. I didn't get to warn my parents, so God knows what they're thinking.'

'That's tough,' Tom said.

After an appropriate wait he spoke again. 'So who's going to liaise with me—with UNAMET—now that you're leaving?'

'The Indonesians have agreed we can open a consulate here. Probably in the next month or two.'

'I see,' he said, his brow furrowed.

While Ava saw the logic of opening up a consulate in Dili, it had come as a surprise to her too. No one had clarified what it meant for her role either—whether she'd continue to work on East Timor, and if so, whether she'd still need to visit.

'But surely those new people won't know Timor like you do. They won't have your relationships or background. I was also hoping you'd give me some insights into the Indonesians. I know next to nothing about them.'

'I'd be happy to,' she said, trying not to let on she agreed with him. 'But some of what I, and the other Five Eyes embassies, have been doing here will be your responsibility now—the non-stop distress calls, the human rights investigations, liaising with *TNI* and the police.'

Tom placed his elbows on his knees and rested his head in his hands.

'It's a pity about the reconciliation meeting,' she said to fill the silence. 'The Indonesians blamed it on the deteriorating relationship between us and them. They also said we were colluding with the pro-independence side. But the truth is—as an Indonesian minister told my ambassador—there was never any chance the talks were going to take place outside Indonesia. You can report that if you like.'

Tom looked up and smiled.

'There's no way the UN will participate now.' He sat upright again. 'We don't want to be seen as condoning something that's clearly open to manipulation. We'll observe, but nothing more.'

'I'd better go. My plane's about to board.'

They stood and Tom stepped towards her and kissed her on both cheeks, the last one brushing the corner of her lip. Ava thought he might apologise or show some awkwardness, but he didn't. He stayed close to her. Although he was a colleague of sorts, she didn't mind. Then she looked down and saw his wedding ring. She must be mistaken.

'Will you be back?' Tom asked, staring at her.

'I never seem to stay away for more than a few weeks. I find it hard to sleep without the gunfire.'

Tom chuckled.

'You have my numbers and my email if you have any questions.'

'I'll be in touch,' Tom nodded, a wide-eyed expectant look on his face.

Ava picked up her bag, and as she walked away, couldn't help but feel she was leaving something behind—something indistinct, nascent, yet important. She queued patiently while Tom stood watching. As she walked onto the tarmac she waved at him. Goodbye, she thought. *To'o loron seluk.* Until we meet again.

43

LIQUICA, EAST TIMOR, MAY 1999

Isabel walked back to the militia post with her shopping bags half full. It was difficult to buy food at the market these days. Rice was impossible unless you signed a statement saying you were pro-Indonesian, and other food was increasingly scarce. After the massacre, many farming families left Liquica to live with relatives in safer towns. The remaining villagers had either given up growing or selling food because *TNI* and the militia simply took them without payment. The closer to ballot day, the hungrier the people of East Timor became.

'Isabel,' she heard her name being whispered urgently.

She covered her belly with her shopping bags as she checked the nearby scrub.

'It's me,' the voice said, and she was certain it belonged to Sebastiao. 'Meet me at the stream in an hour.'

Isabel bowed her head in a half nod and continued on her way, although she wasn't certain yet that she could, or even wanted to go. She'd only seen Sebastiao once at the stream since he'd told her about the stabbing, and their time together had been filled with prickly silences. She'd left more titbits of information for him hidden in the tree, but suspected they would make no impact, just like her previous warnings.

An hour later, she was dangling her feet in the clear stream water. She'd brought washing with her but decided it could wait. Sebastiao arrived and she pulled her legs in, leaning forward to conceal her small belly.

'Isabel.'

She began to smile, but on seeing the look on his face, stopped and looked away.

'So the rumours are true. You're pregnant,' he said as though accusing her.

She'd hoped that out of everyone, Sebastiao would understand. He knew she was forced to give herself to Gabriel or her family would die. But it seemed that just like the villagers, he'd judged her.

'Are you going to marry him?'

Isabel threw him a hurt look. 'I sought your help to find my family so I could escape, but you told me nothing. I begged Father Ribeiro for help, but he also refused. I don't know why I'm being punished, Sebastiao, I don't know what I've done. And I don't understand why no one will help me.'

'So you're going to marry him then?'

'If you really must know, he says we'll get married when autonomy wins.'

'Ha,' Sebastiao scoffed.

Isabel needed to stretch a little, but it was difficult to do so while concealing her bulge. Even though Sebastiao knew about the baby, the way it exposed her as Gabriel's slave was humiliating. Yet all Sebastiao seemed concerned about was marriage.

'The truth is,' she answered, 'I don't know what I'm going to do about marrying him. All I know is I want to be me again. The baby is taking me over. First it was the sickness, then I began to swell, and now it's through my blood so my head and heart are no longer my own. Sometimes, it makes me care for it. But I don't want any of this. I want things to be like they were before. I want to be home with my family.'

Isabel waited for Sebastiao to show her some understanding, but all he gave her was silence.

'Don't you see?' he said, his face lighting up. 'What Gabriel said, it's a trick. Everybody knows that if it comes to a vote, the people will reject autonomy under the Indonesians. What then of your wedding, Isabel? What then of your life with him? Will he still want you if independence wins?'

Isabel felt a chill grow between them despite the warm humidity of the day. She looked him in the eyes. 'I've asked you this before and you said you'd find out. Do you have any information about my family?'

Sebastiao held her gaze, his eyes narrowing as though he was calculating her mind and heart. 'You're joined with him forever now, aren't you? You've given yourself to him in a way you can never give yourself to any other man.'

Isabel gasped. He might as well have stabbed her in the heart. 'Why won't you help me find them? Is it because you want my information? Are my family your blackmail?'

Sebastiao didn't answer her because he was already disappearing into the bushes.

Alone again, she grabbed some washing, but she heard more rustling. Had he returned? She listened but the noise disappeared. Just like Sebastiao, just like her family. Just like everybody else.

———

Back at the militia post Isabel prepared lunch. Gabriel was about to say something to her when his phone rang. He answered, waving his hand at her and pointing to the door. She went outside to wash the rice and heard him finish on the phone. Within moments, he was standing in front of her.

'From now on you leave the room when I'm on the phone. Do you understand?' he snapped.

Isabel shrunk into herself. 'Yes Gabriel. But why?'

'Why?' he roared. 'How about the baby you don't want? How about not knowing whether to marry me? How about your treachery.'

The next thing she knew she was lying in the dirt, water and washed rice strewn over her and across the ground. She stayed where she was and watched as Gabriel climbed into his car mumbling something about a day and a reckoning.

44

JAKARTA, INDONESIA, MAY 1999

Ava and Tom sat on silk pillows on the floor of an Indian restaurant sipping cold beer straight from the bottle. See-through curtains billowed around them in the breeze of the fans. Two stone Ganesh statues sat prophesying atop wooden pillars, fringed umbrellas rested open in corners and the walls were busy with panels of ornately carved wood. They might have been in the middle of a Somerset Maugham book.

'Thanks for having dinner with me,' Tom said.

She smiled. They'd been talking by phone and email over the last couple of weeks. Yesterday, he'd called to say he was in Jakarta and invited her to a private dinner. The newly appointed head of UNAMET was arriving to meet the Indonesians and other key figures before taking up his post in Dili, but she hadn't realised Tom would be joining him. Why hadn't he organised the usual cocktail party or drinks for all the relevant embassies, she wondered, but nonetheless hadn't hesitated to accept his invitation.

'I know we'll see each other at your ambassador's lunch tomorrow,' Tom continued, 'but I thought it would be good to catch up beforehand.'

'Pre-meeting, mid-level talks.' She laughed.

The waiter placed pappadams and chutney on their table. They'd been too busy talking to look at the menu and happily went with his recommendations on the best dishes.

'Your Indonesian is impressive,' Tom said, smiling.

'Thank you. How long have you been with the UN?'

'A few months. They brought me in to draft the security annex for the 5 May Agreements.'

Ava wasn't sure what to say. The security annex was meant to guarantee the Indonesians would create a secure environment for a free and fair ballot. But it was non-binding, which amounted to an open invitation for the Indonesians to do whatever they wanted without consequence. The drafting was either exceptionally naive, or its real purpose was to free the UN of liability if things went wrong. The UN, Ava was discovering—and much to her disappointment—was not the magnanimous vehicle for world peace she'd imagined, but a toothless, giant beadledom of red tape and self-interest, only ever as strong or weak as its member nations permitted it to be. How could Tom be that innocent, or stupid?

'Are you a lawyer then?'

'No, an academic in international relations at Yale. By the time I finished my PhD I was too old to enter the diplomatic corps, so—'

'So now you're a UN diplomat.'

Tom looked pleased. 'So how did you get into the foreign service?' he asked.

'I wanted a secure job and to live overseas. Someone showed me an ad in the paper and I applied. Much to my amazement, I got in.'

'Of course you did,' he laughed, making Ava wonder if this was a form of flirtation? Her head contradicted her heart.

Tom leaned in and turned serious. 'How genuine do you think the UN is about running a free and fair ballot in East Timor?'

'That's what I wanted to ask you.'

Tom tore at the edges of his napkin. 'I have a couple of concerns. I'm not so worried any more about the ballot being rubber stamped like the UN did in Irian Jaya.' He paused, checking for her reaction. She remained poised. 'But I am worried about what might happen if, for example, a few international staff were killed in the lead-up to the vote. It's an unarmed mission. Member countries would withdraw their people and the UN could easily wash their hands of the whole problem and—'

'Blame the international community.'

'Precisely.'

Ava suppressed a smile. Not because what he'd said was humorous, but because Tom was no fool after all. He also appeared to care about what happened in Timor, meaning she wasn't the only one with a partiality for the truth.

'Is that really the mood in New York? I thought the UN needed a success story after their screw-ups in Africa and the Balkans.'

'They do. But why appoint Kaleem Malik, the former Pakistani diplomat—and a Muslim the Timorese distrust intensely—as the secretary general's personal representative on East Timor?'

'Perhaps the Secretary General thought a Muslim would have more chance of succeeding with the Indonesians. He was selected some time ago when Sujati was still in power.'

'Are you aware he's been trying to get our spokesman thrown out of East Timor for being too forthright in the media?'

Ava had been in regular contact with Stephen since the fish dinner debacle, but he hadn't mentioned this. He should have. Outside the three negotiating parties, Australia was the leading nation on East Timor in the UN, and it was funding much of the vote.

'I knew the Indonesians were trying to get rid of him, but your own people? Perhaps they should call it the dis-United Nations.'

Tom laughed and Ava knew now why he wanted to speak to her before tomorrow's meeting. He was telling her—or rather he was informing the Australian government—about the things that couldn't be said at the official lunch. Another Sunday sleep-in gone, she sighed. She'd have to write a cable on his comments before their lunch, and afterwards write up that meeting too.

Tom's hand moved closer towards hers along the tablecloth. Again she noticed the plain gold wedding band on his ring finger.

'How does your wife feel about you being here?' She looked directly at him, pulling her hand away. She thought she saw sadness cloud his eyes.

He took a deep breath in and let it out. 'She thinks it's fine if I stay for the ballot as a one off. But she wants to have a child, sooner rather than later.'

Tom held her gaze and she held his back. It was a deeply personal thing he'd just revealed. Was he trying to tell her his marriage was shaky?

'Is that what you want?' Perhaps she was pushing things too far.

'I thought I knew what I wanted. Only...it's a different world out here.' Their eyes became the only things to talk.

'And you? I don't see a wedding ring on your finger.'

'I lost it during my last house move. I'm married, but not really. We separated last year only I couldn't manage my job and our daughter by myself so my husband had to come back. We live separate lives though.' A lump rose in her throat. She was surprised at the burning feeling creeping across her face as she admitted her marriage was a failure.

'That must be tough.' Tom placed his hand on hers and squeezed it lightly. Normally she would consider this breach between colleagues as disrespectful, sleazy even. Instead she found it soothing. It gave her a sense of... was it inevitability? It had been years since she'd felt such a strong connection with someone.

'So you have a kid?' Tom said and they withdrew their hands.

'Juliette. She's nine.'

'You're a mother too. Wow.' Tom seemed to turn everything into a complement. Was this an American thing, his thing, or a Tom and her thing?

'To be fair, I'm more of a traditional father right now given the long work hours and travel.'

'You shouldn't have to make excuses for that. It's your job.'

Ava smiled, surprised that a man without children could have such empathy.

Brass bowls of curry, rice and more chutney along with beer arrived, and they ate and talked with gusto. When the restaurant closed and it was time to leave, neither was ready for the night to end. After they could no longer stand chatting in the street without appearing obvious, Tom hailed two taxis and kissed her goodbye on both cheeks.

'I'll see you at lunch tomorrow,' he said, remaining close to her.

'Yes.'

'Will you be visiting East Timor soon?' he almost whispered.

'Soon,' she almost whispered back.

Tom opened her taxi door and kissed her on the cheek. Tom was married, yet tonight felt like a promising first date.

45

JAKARTA, MAY 99

Diplomatic postings made for a transitory life. Every time Ava built a good working relationship with someone, they were replaced by another, and she'd have to begin anew as part of the endless system of rotations. Bruce was going to Generals' School in Canberra to learn to be a Brigadier and was being replaced by Neville, or Nev, a colonel who'd risen through the ranks of the Defence Intelligence Organisation, otherwise known as the spooks. According to Bruce, the spooks weren't regarded as being real army, nor were they trusted.

Tonight Bruce was being roasted as part of his send-off. Ava stood in the embassy's canteen that was air-conditioned to the point of freezing. She'd never been to one of these nights before where only Australian-based staff were allowed to attend.

The entire gamut of embassy staff were here, from a federal police officer to a couple of junior admin staff, an immigration officer to policy people like her. Even Quentin had turned up. He stood in the middle of the room with his lime and lemonade, which he drank from a wine glass so as not to set him apart. Ava wondered why a man like him didn't drink. Maybe it had once been a problem.

One of Bruce's junior staff, a captain and clerk called Simon, got everyone's attention. 'We're gathered here tonight to celebrate Bruce's posting to Jakarta,' he began and some in the crowd yelled out the obligatory yoo-hoos until there was silence.

'It's been two massive years. Bruce delivered the Irian Jaya aid project, went on countless beer-filled jaunts with *TNI*, and closely followed Sujati's demise and the fate of East Timor. But the thing Bruce will be particularly remembered for, is his strategic forecasting.'

The audience tittered.

'When he first arrived, he called his staff together to plot his two-year tenure. At the end of this one-day meeting he concluded, *There's no way Sujati will go, unless he dies of a heart attack.*'

Bruce looked to the ceiling, rolling his eyes before joining in the laughter.

'Still, you could say Bruce's time in Jakarta at least gave him the chance to expand his predictive capabilities. He also expanded something else during his time here—his waist, which we know for a fact grew by three inches.'

'Ooh,' the crowd said mockingly except for Nev, who stood at the back with a blank face drinking lemonade.

'Seriously though, the greatest highlight of Bruce's posting to Jakarta was last year's May riots. This was when Bruce, a senior colonel, was seen tramping around Jakarta acting as a bodyguard for a certain Political Affairs officer.' People sniggered. 'You know who I'm talking about. The rusty-haired bimbo from the fourth floor.'

The crowd broke into raucous laughter. Ava joined in to show she could be a good sport, even if she was at a loss to understand why she should be a focus of Bruce's roasting. Bruce, on the other hand, looked away as though he had something to be embarrassed about.

'His role as a bodyguard didn't end there, however,' Simon continued. 'When East Timor heated up, Bruce accompanied said rusty-haired-bimbo-from-the-fourth-floor on several visits.'

More merriment only louder, including from Bruce. He was relishing being linked to her as a dumb slut.

'But things got a little tough for Bruce. During the investigation into the Liquica massacre, the rusty-haired-bimbo-from-the-fourth-floor tried to talk one of the militia leaders—the infamous thug, Gabriel Martinez—into admitting that violence was wrong!'

Ava was no longer laughing even if the crowd lapped it up. She recalled the night in question, just days before the Dili cleansing operation. She'd shown Gabriel a press release in which Aleixo had retracted his earlier call for *Falintil* to rise up and protect the people against more massacres like the one in Liquica. This war cry, Gabriel had claimed, was proof the pro-independence lot were violent, murderous thugs. 'But now that you've seen that Aleixo wants peace,' she'd responded, 'wouldn't that make you and your militias violent, murderous thugs if you went ahead with your operation?' She was desperately trying to halt the cleansing operation.

But Simon wasn't done lynching her yet.

'Subsequently, Bruce was forced to pile the rusty-haired-bimbo-from-the-fourth-floor into their car and make a quick getaway to their hotel, where he stood by her door all night just in case Gabriel tried to seek *personal revenge.*'

The crowd roared, soaking up his lies. Ava saw that Quentin was having a good old belly laugh too. There was spite in Simon's words, malice. Disbelief and disgust rose in Ava. A man of lower rank putting a more senior woman down who was smarter than him and dared to not be ugly. Had nothing changed? And why hadn't Bruce told him he'd gone far enough. Of course, she realised, he liked it. Good for his ego. She felt hurt and angry but refused to let on.

Simon eventually talked about other aspects of Bruce's posting and the night came to an end. Ava made her way through the crowd, wishing she'd spent her precious night off with Juliette.

Judy sought her out and grabbed her arm. 'I think that name might stick,' she said with glee.

'Do you, Judy?' Ava replied, murmuring under her breath, 'Go the sisterhood.'

The walk to her car was awkward as she attempted to strike a balance holding her head up high and not appearing huffy, when all she wanted to do was hurry away.

'They didn't mean it,' she heard Bruce say from behind.

She turned around, weighing up whether to dignify him with a response. 'Fun's fun, Bruce. But that was nasty. And misogynistic. They have rules about that in the public service, though not in the military it seems.'

'Come on, Ava. It was just a bit of fun.'

She walked on and Bruce followed her.

'If I behave professionally, I'm accused of being hard and aloof,' she said. 'And if I'm warm, I'm accused of being a bleeding heart. I can't win.'

'They just wanna fuck you. Every man in that room wants to fuck you. I want to fuck you. Simon wants to fuck you. And the women, they're just jealous. They either wanna be you, or take you down because they aren't.'

Ava gasped, shaking her head as she got in her car. 'After everything we've been through, Bruce, all I am is a potential fuck? And way to go with your opinions about women.'

The corners of Bruce's mouth dropped. 'I've never met anyone like you, Ava. My wife gave up everything to be with me. She was an academic, had my children and never went back to work. I've never been on the front line with a woman before.'

She looked away, taken aback. 'You should've told Simon to stop. He went too far.'

'All of me,' he said placing his hands on his chest, 'my heart and mind and soul, are yours, Ava.'

He pulled a blue velvet box from his back pocket and gave it to her.

'Open it,' he said, then gently, 'please?'

She sighed, took the box from him and lifted the lid. Inside were two bullet casings set in Perspex. One was a live bullet and the other blank.

'This one's from the Trisakti student shootings and the other one's from the biggest day of protests when that guy next to us got shot.'

Ava closed her eyes. The gift was remarkable, and she felt a confusing mix of exasperation, hurt and appreciation. 'This is…' she looked at him smiling sadly. 'You're a royal prick, Bruce.'

'All of me, any time. Remember that.' His face was open and hopeful.

Ava closed her car door and locked it before reversing out. How dare he declare his supposed love for her just days before he was due to leave and give her this unforgettable gift that touched her soul.

46

LIQUICA, EAST TIMOR, JUNE 1999

Early one June morning, Isabel reached into her dress pocket and discovered a piece of paper. She waited until the bathroom was free, took out the note and saw that it was signed *S*. Sebastiao? It must be important to take such a risk. She read his messy scribble:

Must leave. Be careful. There will be a time for swimming and
running and flying. You will see.

Isabel broke into a sweat. What had happened to make him leave? Did Gabriel know she'd been passing information to him? She felt dizzy at the thought of what he'd do to her and slid down the bathroom wall into a squat, the baby kicking in protest.

When she could breathe again, another realisation hit her. Not only had she lost her family and the Church, but now him. While she doubted Sebastiao at times, he'd been her sole link to a world beyond this prison. He was also her last hope of reunification with her family. She reached her head back and uttered a silent cry of despair.

Someone knocked on the bathroom door.

'I need the bathroom,' said one of the guards.

She pushed herself up off the floor and splashed water over her face.

'Gabriel's back,' he told her as she stepped outside, squinting at the harsh morning light. 'He's looking for you.'

Rather than face him, she crept through the back fence and headed towards the market without shopping bags or money.

Wandering around the stalls, she searched for ever-diminishing fruit and vegetables as vendors fanned greying meat and rotting fish to fend off the swarms of flies. She checked each villager's face for gestures of kindness—the retired *Falintil* guerrillas, women whose children she'd taught at Sunday school and members of Gil's glorious *CNRT*—but as usual, there were none.

Lumbering along her usual route back to the post, an arm reached out and grabbed her before pulling her into the bushes. She was about to scream.

'It's me. Sebastiao.'

She gasped.

'I had to speak to you.' He was bleary-eyed and looked as though he hadn't slept for days. His clothes hung loosely on his body.

'What's going on?'

'He found out. About our meetings.'

'I know.'

'And he made me...' Sebastiao folded over and dry wretched. Isabel stepped back, knowing already what Gabriel had forced him to do.

'Why didn't you just run?'

'He held a gun to my head,' he sobbed. 'He said if I didn't do it, he'd shoot me.'

Sebastiao held his palms up to the sky as though this would bring him redemption, as though he had no power of his own. But those hands had taken at least one life, maybe two. By turning Sebastiao into a murderer,

Gabriel had not only destroyed his goodness and made a mockery of his human rights work, but he'd created an impenetrable gap between the two of them.

'Who was he, the victim?' she asked.

'An activist.'

Gabriel would have chosen him especially.

'It wasn't my brother, or father?'

'No. I would never—'

'Wouldn't you?' Isabel wondered what sort of man judged his own life to be worthier than another's.

'I have to go,' Sebastiao said, tears streaming down his face. 'The Church is going to hide me. When this is over, I'll be back for you.'

Her brows knit together, unsure about what he meant.

'Before you go,' she said, 'please, where's my family?'

'I can't Isabel. I can't.'

———

Gabriel, unshaven and stinking of sweat and alcohol, slumped over the table. Isabel stood opposite him, waiting.

'Where have you been?' he asked, his calmness unsettling her.

'Walking,'

'You were seen at the market.'

'Yes.' She dropped her eyes and waited for him to explode.

'I know, Isabel.' His face reddened and his body grew in size. 'I know all about you and that… peasant!'

Isabel focused her attention on a dead fly on the floor.

'There will come a time—and that time will be soon—when you'll have to choose which side you're on. But whatever you decide, that baby growing inside you—my baby, the one you don't want—is mine, and I want him.'

Isabel looked up at him. What did he mean by decision time?

'Do you understand me?'

'Yes,' she nodded, without understanding anything.

47

DILI, EAST TIMOR, JUNE 1999

In the bare, white-tiled waiting lounge at Dili airport, Ava glanced at a small gaggle of ragged, mostly Australian journalists. They chain-smoked and chatted as they waited for today's shared cargo.

'We need to keep them away from Craig, unless you think he'll want to say something?' Ava said to Dave, one of two DFAT colleagues who'd arrived from Australia a few days ago to help establish the new consulate. 'The last time we had a consul general here was in the seventies under Portuguese rule. Similarly turbulent times, really.'

'I'm confident Craig won't wanna say anything,' Dave said in his thick Australian accent. 'Up until four days ago he was high commissioner to Noumea. They pulled him out with three hours' notice, briefed him in Canberra and here he is.' Dave puckered his lips with confidence so they protruded through his thick beard.

'That would be tough. How well do you know him?'

'We were in Jakarta together. Probably why they posted me here.'

Ava sensed that Dave knew a lot about her when all she knew about him was that he was a second secretary. Since spending time with him he'd made his intentions clear, that the department's hottest issue would be all his now.

'When I had my briefings in Canberra,' Dave smirked, 'they told me you're the gloom and doom girl.'

Ava feigned a smile. 'Is that so? And who told you that?'

'People.'

'And did Simeon give you a reason?' Simeon was a recent addition to the East Timor section in Canberra. He was also ex-Jakarta and similarly desperate to make a name for himself over East Timor.

''Cause you only report bad news.'

Ava peered out to the runway. 'You've been in Timor a few days now, talked to a few people, heard the gunfire every night. What do you think? Am I holding back on the good news?'

'Err, so far there hasn't been a lot of good news. Bit of a surprise, really. Tension clouds the place. It's tangible.'

'So you thought all the reports—mine and the media's—were exaggerated?' Ava turned to look him square in the face.

'I thought maybe you were too close to the issue. And we all know how the media love to sensationalise.'

Stanley the admin officer, who seemed to only wear Hawaiian shirts, approached them. But on catching snippets of their conversation, veered away again.

'The Ambassador asked me to report more positively a couple of times. The last time was just before the Liquica and Dili massacres, not long after we'd doubled our troop numbers in northern Australia and put them on high alert.'

Dave stroked his beard. 'Right.'

'Wait til you meet the cast of characters here over the next few days. They'll be from all sides of the fence—*TNI*, the militia, local government reps, the guerrillas, pro-independence and pro-Indonesia leaders, the Church, students. I know them all and every one of them talks to me openly, which as you can imagine is a tricky balancing act.'

'Fair enough,' Dave said. 'Anyway, doom and gloom or not, Stretton said he wants it all now. No holding back.'

Ava closed her eyes and inhaled deeply. Suddenly it all made sense. Stretton was the one demanding more positive reporting. He'd blamed the spiralling Indonesian violence on rogue elements within *TNI* when he knew it was a lie and wanted her reporting to concur. The Minister was an answer looking for a conforming question. She shook her head. Countries usually responded better to quiet diplomacy, but after the Liquica massacre it was clear that not only were the Indonesian government and *TNI* responsible for most of the violence in Timor, but they weren't going to reign it in. Ever.

'I wonder what Canberra will be saying about you soon, Dave? It'll be something like you're too close to UNAMET and you lack objectivity, or your reports are overly detailed, a sign that you're going troppo under the pressure. Mind you, you should be under a lot less of that now the UN's here. They'll take care of the human rights nightmare I used to manage— the daily distress calls and pleas for help, the investigations into the violence and disappearances.'

'Point taken,' Dave nodded. 'Nah, you're all right, Ava. Who gives a stuff what they think anyway? I thought you'd be difficult over this handover. You know, possessive. I would be. But you're not—not very. And your reputation in Canberra's actually not too bad.'

So why test me? Ava thought. Yet in the end, Dave's poking and prodding told her more about him than it revealed about her. His world was a hostile, us-versus-them kind of place. Perhaps he needed to cut her down so he could build himself up. How exhausting.

'That's enough fishing, don't you think?' she said, looking him in the eyes.

'Agreed,' Dave nodded, as Craig's plane pulled up, the gaggle of journalists behind them ready to pounce with their cameras, tape recorders and note pads.

48

DILI, JUNE 1999

The moon rose from the horizon beyond Dili's bay. It was such a vibrant orange it might have been a new sun. Ava and Tom sat on the shoreline opposite the Turismo Hotel, staring at its reflection on the water. They hadn't seen each other since the official lunch in Jakarta, although there'd been phone calls and emails.

'Just look at that', Ava said, pointing to a long, streaky cloud moving across the moon.

'It's a broken moon now,' Tom said. 'A bit like this place. Strange, isn't it, East Timor?'

In the rare quiet under the fading light, Ava nodded. There was something unique about the place, but the word strange didn't capture it. For the locals, Timor Leste was a place of legends—a land imbued with ancient power, the people bred from the fierce reptilian blood of their ancient relative, the crocodile, whose rigid back became the mountains and scales the hills. To outsiders, it appeared restless, troubled and violent. Was this caused by four hundred and fifty years of foreign occupation, their twenty-four-year independence struggle in which a whole generation had been born into violence and suffering, or was there something else about the people and their history?

'How did your introductions of your new consul general go?' Tom asked.

'Interesting. One official refused to talk to Craig because he didn't believe he had proper accreditation. Luckily, he agreed to talk to me because of my Jakarta link.'

Tom laughed.

'But the best meeting was with Major General Zeze Endah. Do you know him? He used to head up *TNI* intelligence and covert operations. He's on the Indonesian task force for East Timor.'

'I know of him and his tactics, but I haven't had the pleasure yet.'

'I thought the East Timor commander, Tamala, was smooth,' she chuckled, 'but Zeze… Let's say I've never received such a charming death threat in my life.'

'Death threat?'

'Craig, Dave and I were told to sit down and wait for him in this pristine white room on a long wooden bench. The bench was so deep that when we sat back our feet dangled. It was like being a naughty little kid waiting outside the principal's office. When Zeze finally entered, he sat directly opposite us on this towering carved throne fit for a king. He paused for a while, then leant down to ask us his opening question about the ballot: *At what price freedom?* '

'Oh dear.'

'At that moment, I happened to catch something on a TV mounted in the corner of the room. Queues of penguins were plunging into the ocean where open-mouthed killer whales waited to devour them like lambs to the slaughter.

'The question is,' Tom said, 'who are the penguins and who are the whales? He'd have us believe the pro-independence side are the penguins, but it's his side that stands to lose everything if the ballot goes ahead.'

Ava grinned at the similitude between them. She only wished she could take off her shoes and shed her day properly, but beneath their feet clutches of prickly weeds poked through the dry soil. Pictures of colonial times flashed through her mind—Portuguese sunbakers on deck chairs scattered over the lush grass, well-dressed ladies with parasols hooking arms with hatted gentlemen in suits strolling along immaculate paths. Those East Timor days were long gone.

'Tell me more about this death threat,' Tom said.

'Zeze talked a lot about the consequences if independence won. How the Australia–Indonesia relationship might not survive, and that the independence side would seek revenge against the militia leading to spiraling violence, another civil war and regional instability. *TNI* would have no choice but to step in and protect the militias, of course. Then he leaned in and said, *We wouldn't want any Australians to lose their lives here such as yourselves, for example,* and that we needed to be *very careful.*'

'About what?'

'About how we align ourselves.'

Tom shook his head. 'It's sad more than anything. It doesn't have to be all or nothing like *TNI* are making out. Aleixo believes all Timorese can live here peacefully.'

'So do I.'

Tom looked to the ground, his expression turning wistful. 'I had a dream about this place last night.'

Ava sipped her red wine, which she'd brought from Jakarta to share with him.

'I told my wife I was staying in East Timor and never coming back.'

A twinge of excitement stirred in her belly. Was he telling her he was rethinking his marriage? Was it wrong that his sadness invoked her happiness? But what about his wife? How did she feel? The noise of the tiny waves lapping on the beach punctuated the silence.

'I had a dream too,' she said. 'My ocean dream where I'm in the sea being carried back and forth by huge waves, and no matter how hard I try, I can never reach the shore. Each time I almost reach safety at the top of the incredibly steep embankment, I'm pulled back by another wave.'

Tom moved so close to Ava she could almost feel his skin breathing. 'Tell me about your wife,' she said softly.

'Nancy? She's thirty-seven, a scientist and researcher. Really smart. Her skin is lighter than mine and she's shaved her hair off. She's very pretty.' Tom appeared to take pride in her appearance.

'Why did you get married?' she asked, refilling their glasses and shuffling away slightly.

'We'd been seeing each other on and off for years, then I thought we were over for good. I moved to Seattle and she to New York. Then she called and asked if I wanted to live with her. I said yes. After a while, we went on a long holiday to South America and got along. It was easy I guess, so we got married.'

'Did you love her?'

Tom hesitated. Had she pushed things too far or did his faltering indicate uncertainty.

'Yes, I loved her, and I still do. But our marriage is like a train. Every now and then we stop at a station and add another carriage or take one off, but we just keep meandering along the track like we've always done, not seeming to know where we're going.'

What an awful way to describe a marriage. The moon glowed through a cluster of clouds.

'So why did you marry Pete?' Tom asked.

She too hesitated. 'Pete was my best friend. One day he told me he'd love and support me forever. I was twenty-one and no one had said that to me before, and I thought no one else would. He made me laugh, though, and he seemed to understand me.'

'What went wrong then?'

Ava didn't want to discuss this, but Tom's kind voice coaxed her. 'I guess I thought I could change him, the things that concerned me early on. I thought love would conquer all.'

'Hmm. Once you're married, you just continue on, accepting things, until something happens, or someone comes along and you get a hint of what you've been missing out on. It dawns on you, that you might have made a mistake, that there's more out there.'

Chirping crickets grew louder and the sound of distant gunfire perforated the still air as though everything around them welled to reflect their emotions. Ava imagined Tom shifting his leg so that it touched hers, placing a hand on her face and tilting it towards him so he could kiss her. She wouldn't protest.

Argh. Should she even be having these thoughts, even if they weren't actually doing anything? And what about his wife?

'Did you see that shooting star? It's only the third one I've ever seen,' Ava said.

'No, I missed it.'

His face became stern. 'When your consulate staff ask to talk to me, I'm not going to tell them anything. As far as I'm concerned, you're the expert and you care about what happens here. You're the only one.'

Ava turned to face him. 'At least they still want me to come here and talk to my contacts.'

'I want you to keep coming here too,' Tom said, looking happy and relieved at her news. It wasn't a kiss, Ava thought, but it might as well have been.

49

LIQUICA, EAST TIMOR, JULY 1999

On her way back to the militia post, Isabel came across a group of foreigners greeting people in the street. They wore light blue caps with the letters *U* and *N* emblazoned on them. Proof at last that the United Nations had arrived. She stood aside and watched as villagers introduced themselves and shook their hands.

The foreigners' skin colour varied from white to darker than hers. Some were large and tall, others were small and petite like her, and surprisingly, there were women. The ones in police uniform had flags sewn on their shirt sleeves. Isabel counted six countries, including America and Malaysia. Memorising flags at school had finally paid off.

'Where are they staying?' someone in the swelling crowd asked.

'Father Ribeiro's cottage,' answered another. The group gasped and Isabel's skin crawled.

'Something's wrong,' an old woman gasped. 'The police don't have weapons.'

'What?' 'No!' 'How can they protect us?'

Isabel had imagined the arrival of the UN would be marked by thousands of marching soldiers accompanied by rows of tanks bearing terrifying weapons. *TNI* and the police would be struck with fear and retreat into their barracks for good. This small group was far from frightening. Gabriel's voice entered her head. *We'll cause so much havoc the UN will have to leave. If that fails, we'll make the people so scared they'll never vote.* Her heart dropped.

Then again, these people in blue UN caps strolling around her home town must mean something. She moved to the front of the crowd and fixed her eyes on a policewoman with sand-coloured hair. The woman saw her and smiled.

Isabel smiled back, a spark of hope causing her heart to skip a beat. Perhaps the vote would go ahead. Maybe a future was possible that hadn't been yesterday. And who knew, the UN might help her find her family and escape Gabriel.

Three days later

Hiding behind a tree at the militia post, Isabel stood and waited. Earlier she'd watched a convoy of vans and *Kijang*-looking vehicles drive past. They were loaded with goods and a mix of UN police, other foreigners and East Timorese. News soon reached the post that food, medicine and other basic items were being delivered to locals made homeless by the violence.

'How can the UN do that!' Isabel heard *Besi Merah Putih* commander, Damiano da Silva, yell into his phone. 'They're pro-independence, and so are the Timorese helping them. The UN is meant to be neutral.'

Da Silva left only to return not long after with dozens of militiamen, some soldiers and police. But they didn't come into the post. Instead they set up a roadblock. It was the perfect spot for an ambush because the convoy wouldn't see them until they rounded the corner. Once the forty militiamen dressed in bandannas and armed with handmade pistols, rifles and machetes had taken their places across the road, *TNI* and the police moved out of sight to the side, and they all waited.

When the convoy appeared, Isabel put her fist in her mouth and bit down on her knuckles. The militiamen stood firm, forcing the vehicles to stop. A few UN police got out, and using a translator, began talking to the militia. Isabel could see this was only making the militia angry, who began to push and hit out at them.

The rest of the militia surrounded the convoy to stop anyone from escaping. They began smashing the vehicles' windows and doors with their weapons and throwing rocks they'd gathered in rattan baskets. In the melee, Isabel wasn't sure who they were after, but it seemed to be the Timorese.

The crack of gunfire reverberated through the chaos, and Isabel jumped, but on it continued.

'Traitor. Traitor!' she heard someone shout as some militia pulled a Timorese man by the arms from the back of Kijang-like vehicle. But a large UN policeman inside the vehicle had hold of his feet and was dragging him back inside.

Isabel wanted to cover her eyes, but forced herself to watch the tug of war as the dozen soldiers and police on the sidelines laughed. She tasted blood in her mouth from biting her knuckles too hard.

The sound of a loud motor thudded nearby. Isabel looked up to see a white helicopter with a UN symbol on its belly hovering above. An angelic saviour? The militia took aim and fired up at it and the helicopter rapidly retreated.

When she could bear no more, she crept to her spot by the stream, the sound of the mayhem fading behind her. Was Gabriel right about the UN? Would East Timor be too difficult? She wouldn't blame them if they left. She probably would, if only she had somewhere to go.

By the time Isabel returned to the post, Gabriel's and the captain's cars were parked in the yard. They would most likely be celebrating, which meant cooking, alcohol and…

'*Bonoite*,' she greeted the men.

Gabriel didn't respond or even look at her, as was his way these days. Occasionally she caught him staring at her with a mix of feelings on his face she found too baffling to decipher.

She served them drinks and food and overheard their banter.

'We've managed to delay the vote by two weeks for security reasons,' smiled the captain. 'We must keep this up until October when it will be too wet for people to reach the polling stations. The UN will be forced to postpone the vote until the dry in April, by which time anything could happen.'

Gabriel's wicked snigger followed the captain's mocking giggle, sending shivers down Isabel's spine. How hard would they fight for them, these unarmed men and women of the UN, who had no real need to be here, and yet they still were?

50

JAKARTA, INDONESIA, JULY 1999

Ava flew down the embassy's fire stairs, nearly tripping over herself to receive a hand delivery. She whisked an envelope from the courier and ran back up to her office. Denise had sent her a leaked Indonesian government memo and wanted an expert opinion on whether it was genuine.

It bore a couple of government stamps, but the usual headers and footers were absent. Of questionable authenticity, Ava thought. Then again, if a public servant was going to leak something, they might cut such identifiers. The Indonesian was woeful too, which seemed odd, but the text wasn't as easy to dismiss:

The pro-Indonesia forces were dominant in the early months of this year, but since UNAMET was established the pro-independence forces got a second wind and now have the upper hand...

The recommendation is to develop a contingency plan in case autonomy loses that would include securing a route for retreat and, if possible, destroying vital facilities and objects before leaving East Timor. Signed, Major General Jasman, Deputy Chairman, Indonesian East Timor Task Force. [5]

Ava shivered and called Nev. As she waited for him to pick up, she ran through various scenarios in her head. It could be an Indonesian fake, created to scare the Timorese into accepting autonomy within Indonesia. The Indonesians had been pushing this option hard. It could also be an East Timorese fake, created to make the Indonesians look worse so the international community would pressure them into accepting peacekeeping troops. Unlikely. The Indonesians already looked bad, plus it didn't fit the independence movement's modus operandi, which to date had focused on negotiation and reconciliation mixed with some reactivity on the ground. It was also highly unlikely Indonesia would invite foreign troops in.

Nev answered.

'Can you get your experts in Canberra to check the document out?' Ava asked.

'Fine. Bring it down.'

A few days later, she called him back.

'My people would only say they can't confirm the Jasman document is genuine. At the same time, they wouldn't say it's a fake either.'

Ava sighed. Spoken like a true bureaucrat.

'And what do you think, Nev?'

'I couldn't say.'

Ava hung up, shaking her head. In a way, he'd done her a favour. His unwillingness to commit indicated they probably believed it was genuine. It seemed their government feared being accused of knowing what the Indonesians were planning yet failing to prevent it. She called Denise.

'That's what everyone says,' Denise said.

'Sorry I can't be of more help.'

'Can I just ask, what do you think, Ava?

Ava smiled and searched for the right words, wanting to say something meaningful without revealing too much or stirring things up. 'It could be genuine,' she answered. 'There was a story in the Indonesian press about camps being prepared in west Timor for a large influx of East Timorese refugees after the ballot. Also, Gabriel's been quoted several times as saying there'll be a sea of fire should independence win.'

Ava hoped Denise knew her well enough to read between the lines.

'Hmm. Perhaps they're trying to scare Aleixo into accepting autonomy without a ballot,' Denise said. 'I'm going to report it.'

'One more thing,' Ava said. 'I've been asked to request that you don't credit what I told you directly to the government. You can say your source was something like *a credible Australian expert*. Is that okay?'

'Sure. And thanks.'

As she put the phone down, Ava felt uneasy. Why hadn't Defence shared their views with her on the document's authenticity? Withholding their opinion from a journalist was one thing, but from her, and particularly given she'd handed it to them in the first place, was another entirely. What more did she need to do to earn their trust? What else were they keeping from her?

No more nice junior Ava, she thought as she strode down the corridor to get some lunch. Soon they'd learn that she too had a voice and opinions. They weren't going to like it, but being agreeable had only got her trampled.

———

Donald sat opposite Ava at the small meeting table in his office. He'd been promoted and was being cross-posted as deputy to the Australian UN mission in New York.

'I wanted to take this opportunity to say goodbye to you properly before I leave tomorrow. It's been a remarkable couple of years in Jakarta and it's been a true pleasure working with you, Ava.'

Ava saw tears welling in his eyes and was touched.

'We've worked closely on the economic crisis, the fall of Sujati, and now you've picked up East Timor and run with it better than anyone expected. It's been an incredible time for Australian foreign policy, and it's been special to share it with you.'

Donald took his stained handkerchief from his pocket and blew his nose, then smiled at Ava like a proud parent. He seemed a confusing mix of hard and ambitious, paternal and caring.

'Thank you, Donald,' she swallowed, 'for everything you've taught me. But most of all, for having confidence in me and giving me your trust along with the freedom I need. I'd work with you again any day.'

Donald beamed.

'There's something else I want to say to you.' Donald cleared his throat. 'I don't think you've been fully recognised for your work, which brings me to another point.'

Ava looked at him. Colleagues had told her he'd had more than one loud argument with Quentin over her performance appraisal. Twice in a row she'd been allocated the second to top rating when he believed she should have been in the top two per cent. In addition to her timely and in-depth reporting, she'd cultivated a wide range of contacts and obtained information critical for the Australian government, something no one else had accomplished. Donald also told her recently that she should have been promoted again since taking on East Timor. Her work was well above her pay level and she'd executed it extraordinarily well. This was something she hadn't realised.

'Whatever your future plans, you might like to think carefully about whether you want to continue to work in a big bureaucracy like DFAT,' he continued. 'It's a brutal environment and you may prefer somewhere less rigid. There comes a time when every DFAT officer needs to ask themself if they're willing to take on the values of the organisation. I'm not sure if you'd be better off working in a different, smaller place.'

Ava felt a confusion of praise and…was it criticism, or was she adding a layer of judgement Donald hadn't intended? He'd built her up only to put her down, insinuating she was a misfit, yet one he felt protective of.

'If you're ever in New York, please come and stay. We'd love to have you.'

Ava forced a smile, and using someone else's words in an effort not to be herself, because herself was now an outsider, said, 'You're on.'

51

———————————

JAKARTA, JULY 1999

By the time Ava arrived at Andy's birthday party, it was taking off. A colleague from another embassy, Andy was well known for throwing parties that featured dance music and chemical enhancements.

'Join us for *Krakendang* and vodka shots,' he said, kissing Ava on both cheeks.

'*Krakendang*,' she laughed. It reminded her of Gabriel, but why not? She welcomed a distraction from the frustrations at work and home. She downed a couple of rounds with a group of others and some dance music come on.

'Who's this?' she asked Andy.

'Fat Boy Slim. One guy and a machine.'

'I love it.'

Andy tipped an imaginary hat at her, grabbed her hand and led her into the lounge room where people were openly popping pills under a spinning mirror ball ablaze with strobing lights. They started to dance and Ava felt like a teenager again, until soon she was gasping for breath. She pushed through her weariness, allowing the music to take hold of her and drive her on. Andy left after a while, but she continued dancing, closing her eyes and

246

spinning to forget about East Timor and Pete, Donald and DFAT, and married Tom. When the music changed to something lower key, she rejoined the others.

'Awesome dancing,' Andy said. 'I had no idea you were…'

She raised her eyebrows. Had he pigeonholed her as a boring workhorse?

'…a party girl,' he finished, and Ava laughed.

She headed to the toilet. Within moments dizziness overtook her. She leaned on the passage wall, lowering her head until the faintness lessened.

'Bloody hell,' she mumbled. Instead of finding the toilet, she made her way to her car and got into the back seat, frightening her driver who was fast asleep.

'*Pulang*,' she said to him. Home please.

Resting her head against the rear quarter panel, she closed her eyes. After a couple of blocks she felt nauseous and opened the window for some fresh air. But there was no such thing in perennially hot and polluted Jakarta.

'Stop,' she said, opening the car door and throwing up in the gutter. But why was she ill when she hadn't drunk much?

'*Makanan busuk,*' she told her driver, pretending she'd eaten something bad. No doubt he'd tell her home staff and the embassy drivers that she'd got drunk. He held firm moral views, except when it came to being a gossip. Ava wiped her mouth and looked around, hoping no one had recognised her car's diplomatic number plates, which identified her as Australian.

They drove off as she rinsed her mouth with bottled water. This was the third time this month she'd vomited like this. She wasn't pregnant so maybe she was simply tired. She'd have to clean up her act—get some sleep, take a break, stop drinking, spend more time with Juliette and no more arguing with Pete. And she must clarify her situation with Tom. Yes. She must wrestle back control.

She sighed long and hard. She had a job people would kill for and it turned out she was decent at it, yet lately restlessness and dissatisfaction plagued her. The reality of relentless work on a grim subject matter without a proper break wasn't the diplomatic high life people imagined. Despite its importance, diplomacy was wearing thin on her and she hungered for something…more.

52

LIQUICA, EAST TIMOR, JULY 1999

Isabel stood at the back of a queue that snaked across a small field not far from the militia post. At the head of the line, foreigners wearing blue caps sat at makeshift desks in the shade of a tent. It was the sixteenth of July and the UN was registering locals to vote in the independence ballot just weeks away. Isabel had turned eighteen a few weeks ago and was eligible to vote, although she'd had to ask Gabriel for permission. He'd smirked and replied, 'Of course. We need as many people voting for autonomy as possible.'

It was hot and dry in the sun and Isabel was thirsty. She hadn't expected such a large turnout. Half the town was there. Perhaps they were also keen to register early in case something went wrong. She'd heard Gabriel saying that *TNI* and the militias had delayed the vote several times by weeks, yet they hadn't managed to stop it. Not yet.

The line moved forward in incremental shuffles and Isabel, now six-months pregnant, shifted her weight from foot to foot to ease her aching legs. She peered ahead to see why it was taking so long, but could see no special reason except the need to show various pieces of identification and fill in a long form.

She overheard the conversations of the unknown women around her about their families and neighbours, food shortages and other local issues. She listened longingly. How she missed talking to other women.

'Will our vote really be secret?' the woman in front of her asked her companion.

It was a good question. The UN had put banners up in the streets promising people their vote would be secret and safe. Isabel had also heard them say in information sessions that each person voted alone and put their ballot paper into a locked box. This was then taken by the UN police to Dili to be counted by UN officials and observed by representatives from around the world to ensure no corruption. But could Isabel trust these strangers? Were they open to bribery like the Timorese and Indonesians?

'The militia say they'll know if you vote for independence,' the woman's companion answered.

'But how?'

'How do they ever know?'

Isabel's head spun. She needed some water, but hadn't brought any with her. There were no sellers anywhere.

'Excuse me *Senora*,' she said to one of the women in front. 'Do you have any water?'

Both women peered around, but when they recognised her, looked away.

'Be careful what you say,' one of them whispered loudly to the other. 'She might tell *him*.'

Tears rushed to Isabel's eyes. She wanted to defend herself but couldn't catch her breath. She checked with the woman behind her.

'*Senora*,' she gasped. 'Wate—'

The woman pretended she hadn't heard and turned her back on her.

Isabel raised her hand to her face to fan herself but her arms grew heavy, her hearing faded, and her sight dimmed. She reached out to grab hold of someone or something, but finding nothing, fell to the ground as everything turned dark.

53

DILI, EAST TIMOR, JULY 1999

Driving one of the Consulate's new four-wheel drives, Ava pulled up in the parking lot of the Turismo. This time she was in East Timor to assist Dave and Craig with organising The Minister's visit, but also to do some reporting. A dozen red-faced journalists had gathered in the foyer and were gesticulating wildly. Ava caught snippets of conversation.

'Did you see them chasing us?' 'We were shot at.' 'They came at us with machetes.'

An Australian stringer Ava knew from university grabbed her by the arm. 'They bloody well attacked us. The fucking militia tried to shoot us! What are you gonna do about it?'

Ava was already aware of what had happened, but this information was news to her. 'Are you all right, Minh?' she said, easing her arm from his grip. 'Was anyone injur—'

'The Indonesian police did nothing to help us. We had to jump over a fence and hide in someone's backyard til the militia moved on. FUCKING outrageous!'

'But you and the others are okay?' This time Ava touched his forearm to calm him down.

'I think so.' Minh exhaled. 'Except for Sharon. She was hit in the back with a machete.'

'What?'

'She wasn't cut. He used the flat part. She was with a different group who were also being chased by the militia when she…' Minh gulped and looked down. 'She stopped running. Sort of gave up. The others had to go back and drag her along with them or I don't know what would have happened.'

Ava needed to find Sharon before writing up today's dose of violence for Canberra. 'How many Timorese casualties were there?'

'I don't know. One guy was macheted in front of us. It was brutal. A few others were injured.'

Ava imagining the cruel scene, her tummy backflipping. 'He was killed?'

Minh nodded.

'We'll take this up with the authorities,' she said, looking Minh in the eyes. The Indonesians had insisted on being solely responsible for security during the ballot process, refusing a peacekeeping force to assist them, but they were intentionally failing at their job. And now they appeared to be pressuring the international media to leave, probably to prevent the world from witnessing the final stages of their violent campaign. It was outrageous.

A large police truck pulled up. More journalists piled out of the back tray, Sharon among them. Pale and shaky, she attempted to climb over the tray's lip but her foot lost its grip and she fell half a metre to the ground. Ava raced to help her up.

'Are you okay?' she asked Sharon.

Sharon burst into tears and collapsed into her, the inquisitive eyes of her media colleagues upon them.

'Come to my room,' Ava said, leading her away.

'I'll make us a cup of tea,' she said, sitting Sharon down on her bed.

'Do you have anything stronger?' Sharon asked.

'No. But I can get something from downstairs.'

Sharon shook her head and sniffed. 'Tea's fine.'

'What's going on?'

'I just couldn't run any more. I tried but I...'

'You could have been hurt,' Ava frowned.

'I can't explain it. I was trying to escape but I felt heavy, like in a bad dream when you're running on the spot and going nowhere.'

Perhaps there were two types of people, Ava wondered. Those who fought and those who surrendered. Or was Sharon simply unfit or unwell? She checked Sharon's feet and she had running shoes on. They'd often lamented how they couldn't wear nice shoes on the job because they had to be ready to take off at any moment.

'We could train. Begin jogging,' Ava smiled.

Sharon grimaced and shook her head. 'I need a shower,' she said, standing and hugging Ava.

As she closed the door behind Sharon, Ava wondered if the day would come when she'd discover whether she was a fighter or yielder. The vote was just weeks away, the Indonesians' desperation was mounting, and militia intimidation and violence was ramping up along with threats to Australians.

She moved onto her balcony and took in the gentle sea ahead. She could call Juliette, but their chats were often difficult or fraught with silence as Juliette vacillated between anger and worry. Sometimes the aching of absence between them was unbearable. Speaking to Juliette would also remind her how distant Jakarta felt. East Timor, where the deadlock of her marriage was rendered trivial against the backdrop of life and death, felt more like home. She would call Juliette later, she decided, and undressed to take a shower.

54

DILI, JULY 1999

The international media crammed into a rectangular room that reminded Ava of a small Girl Guides hall. They filmed and photographed Adam Stretton, The Minister, a pudgy giant who towered over the East Timorese representing the pro-Indonesia side as they filed past to shake his hand.

Mr Pinto, Dili's mayor, stood to attention directly in front of him, handing Stretton a factory-woven traditional scarf with 'Autonomy' written on it as though it was a royal sceptre. The Minister accepted the scarf and held it up as they posed for the cameras. Ava tried to stay in the background, all too aware that any footage could be distorted. A tape of Bruce shaking hands with an Indonesian general at a formal ceremony was forever trotted out as proof of Australian appeasement of Indonesia. But she was called forward to accept a smaller, less impressive scarf, and did her best to keep her back to the cameras.

Once she'd ushered the media out, the atmosphere in the room became stiff and formal as each person took their seats on opposite sides of the long table. It was nothing like the *CNRT* welcome they'd just received at the other end of town. There an orchestra greeted them on the street playing traditional music with drums thrumming and poles thumping the ground. Men sang as smiling women wearing brightly coloured sarongs and feathered headdresses danced. How Melanesian and ancient their music sounded compared to the transitive, Hindu melodies of the Javanese gamelan.

Stretton had then ascended the red-carpeted stairs strewn with rose petals where he was met by a welcoming committee and a cheering crowd shouting, '*Viva merdeka! Long live freedom!*' It was impossible not to feel the warmth of it. While this was undoubtedly Aleixo's way of buttering up Stretton, it also felt like hope.

'Minister,' began Lando D'Souza, Indonesia's stern-faced Roaming Ambassador to East Timor. A lanky man, he'd been appointed by the Indonesians years ago, but seemed out of favour these days, and certainly out of date.

'For pro-Indonesia Timorese like us, the ballot scheduled for a few weeks' time after yet another UN-instigated delay is a negation of Indonesia's commitment to its people. We feel betrayed. That's why we consolidated our organisations into an umbrella group—the United Front for East Timorese Unity and Autonomy or *FPDK*—with the aim of supporting the Popular Consultation and creating a conducive environment for it to be held.'

Ava was amused by his twisted logic on the ballot delays, which had been caused by militia violence. But most of all, she wanted to laugh at the group's florid name. Without fail, the names given to Indonesian organisations were the inverse of what they stood for—the more positive the name, the more sinister the group's activities. The FPDK's true ambition was not about fostering harmony, but causing disunity and undermining the ballot.

'Thank you for your warm and welcoming words,' Stretton said. 'In response to your opening statement, might I say we welcome President Hidayat's bold decision to allow the East Timorese people to decide their future. Our judgement is that given East Timor's history, this is the best way of deciding the matter.'

The pro-Indonesia group listened carefully to Ava's translation, a process that slowed the discussion. The men made no attempt to hide their displeasure at his words.

'Let me make some other points that I also made to the pro-independence side,' The Minister continued. 'From Australia's point of view, we're not trying to guide your people on how to vote. We only want to ensure that should you want our help, we're ready to give it to you. You assisted us in World War II—hiding, feeding and protecting our soldiers—and now it's our turn.

'But of course in this ballot, one side will win and one will lose. It's important you hear from me personally that if you win, I strongly urge you to treat those who have campaigned against you with fairness. We, and the rest of the world, will be watching very closely to see that you respect human and property rights. There should be no retribution or payback.'

An uncomfortable silence descended on the room. A moth fluttered against a fluoro light above.

'I would like to make a comment,' said Mr Pinto, Dili's mayor. He was a tiny man who projected a big personality. 'East Timor's geographical location to Indonesia, and Indonesia's influence on us during the last twenty-four years with language, education and so on, should mean automatic recognition that we're part of Indonesia. We don't need a vote.'

Here we go, thought Ava.

'The second point I want to make to you minister is that we in the field agree with you that Australia is neutral. But there are groups of one-sided Australians working in the UN who are creating problems.'

'Yes, well,' Stretton replied swiftly. 'The Australian government is completely neutral on East Timor. After all, we supported integration with Indonesia for twenty-three years. I'm happy to look at evidence of bias within UNAMET, but the one or two stories I've heard so far are of no true significance.'

Pinto shifted in his seat.

'I want to add,' Stretton continued, 'that the Indonesian government and security forces have a responsibility to look after the safety of all foreigners here. Australia is a decent and reasonable country. But don't be mistaken, we don't like people who harm Australians. If that were to happen, it could have enormous implications. It would make the prime minister, the Australian people and me *very* angry indeed. So I'm happy to look at claims of bias, but it wouldn't help you one bit to harm any Australian.' Stretton leaned forward in his chair and looked the mayor closely in the eyes. 'Do not underestimate what I say.'

His haughtiness was working for him today, Ava saw, secretly relishing the moment.

'We interpret some of your government's recent moves as trying to mock the Indonesian government,' said Claudio Botelho, a local government employee closely involved in the militias. 'For example, in your Northern Territory you appointed an army officer as chief minister and moved two army brigades there. We interpret this as Australia telling Indonesia it would only take two brigades to defeat us.'

Stretton raised an eyebrow.

'Second, we know the acts of Australian citizens in UNAMET are those of individuals, but they're a guide to public opinion in your country that you're supporting one choice—independence. We know that army officer in UNAMET is a spy.'

Stretton showed no emotion.

'And third, I'd like to appeal to the Australian government to free the Aboriginal people from their concentration camps, or at least consider giving them autonomy or indepen—'

'That's a lie,' Stretton said. 'I'll respond to your points one by one.'

'Regarding the Northern Territory's chief minister. Do you even know how he's appointed? Never accuse someone before you have the facts, my man. It is not legal to be a member of any parliament in Australia if you're a government employee, from the armed forces or otherwise. It's unconstitutional. That man resigned from the Australian defence forces and was elected to the Liberal Party by his colleagues before being elected by the people to parliament. In any case, he has no responsibility for Australian foreign policy, which is entirely a federal government matter.

Ava translated for the group and some of their faces took on a forlorn appearance. Perhaps they'd expected to outsmart Stretton.

'On the brigades, there's one brigade in Darwin, so you're fifty per cent wrong. The Australian defence force has for many years concentrated our military in Darwin. This is nothing new and isn't because we're likely to take on a defensive role, but rather because we might need to evacuate Australians from Papua New Guinea or go to a hotspot such as Korea. We're part of this region too, you know, so we have more troops there because it's closer. We do not want to threaten Indonesia.'

Some of the men glanced down.

'Regarding Australians in UNAMET, this is no hanging offence. If you have concerns about this former army officer, take it up with UNAMET. As for Australia's Aboriginal citizens, you should have more respect for their wishes. They don't want independence because they don't want to lose the benefits of living in Australia.'

The Minister looked Claudio in the eyes, who drew back.

'Be wise. We supported integration here for a long time. Now there's a UN ballot and we'll do what we can to make autonomy work if it's chosen. But if the people really want independence, you can't stop that. You should be thankful for the good relations between Australia and Indonesia, and the support Australia provides. To show our neutrality, we even paid for you to visit Australia a few months ago and provided you with the necessary security.'

As she translated his words, Ava wished she could say such things to these men of deception and violence who all but quivered without their Indonesian masters and their weapons to hide behind.

55

LIQUICA, EAST TIMOR, AUGUST 1999

Isabel believed she was alone as she carried buckets of water atop her head from the stream to fill the bathroom's near-empty water tank. It was a job she'd been putting off for days. She'd recovered quickly from her fainting episode and had even registered to vote. Her sizeable belly swung from side to side making it difficult for her to avoid spillage and wetting her clothes.

As she shuffled back to the stream she sang out loud. Lately as she went about her chores, she found herself mumbling a tune that reflected her mood. When she felt lonely she might sing a soulful Timorese folk song, when she missed her family perhaps her mother's lullaby, or when she felt bold, as she did today, a song of protest.

She struggled to kneel down at the stream's edge singing:

Oh great land of the crocodile, you gave us the soil beneath our
feet, the food we eat and our home.
Oh great land of the crocodile, stolen from us, we sit by and watch,
lazy in the midday su—

She stopped. What if one of Gabriel's men overheard her singing a resistance song? She stilled herself and listened, but soon resumed her song.

Suddenly the sound of breaking dry twigs jolted her head up, her heart thudding noisily in her chest. Had Sebastiao come to see her? He'd been gone for more than two months. She stole a quarter smile in anticipation, but the bush around her went quiet again and she returned to her scooping. She finished the song:

It is time to waken great crocodile, so that we may lift our heads once more, and take back our land of promise.

The bucket was at last full and Isabel stood while lifting it onto her head. She used one hand to balance it and placed the other on her belly. The baby was moving and making her uncomfortable. She rubbed her belly and felt sharp something jutting out. Oh, she gasped. Was it a foot, or a knee, or an elbow? She felt it again. It was a foot. She rubbed it and the creature drew its limb back in. Tears of wonder but also sorrow collected in the corner of each eye. She understood, perhaps for the first time, that a human being was forming inside her. How was it possible to both love and hate something this much?

Gabriel had welcomed the baby since the beginning, often placing a hand on her stomach and waiting for it to move. His tenderness presumed all three of them had a future together. Yet no matter how hard she tried, Isabel couldn't picture them in a house like a real family—her trusting him with their child, his cruelty and anger gone, all of them thriving.

Overcome with claustrophobia, she faltered and the bucket tipped, drenching her as it tumbled to the ground. As she shook the water off, Isabel was hit with resolve. She knew she must fight, but for what? No alternative vision had yet appeared to her, but it would come. It would.

56

DILI, EAST TIMOR, AUGUST 1999

Day and night Ava observed UN staff working frantically to complete the preparations for the ballot, now just a few days away on the thirtieth of August. It seemed, much to her amazement, that the vote was going ahead despite the barrage of obstacles Indonesia had put in its way. UNAMET might pull this off.

She sat at a table in the Turismo garden waiting for her early breakfast of *pao* with boiled eggs, sliced tomato, butter and jam. She didn't normally eat breakfast, but in a few hours she'd be welcoming the Australian official observer delegation to Dili and would have little time for anything until they left in seven days' time.

Old Augustino, the hotel's long time bell boy come waiter, placed a tray in front of her as other tables filled. It seemed everyone was in Dili. The usual hard-nosed regional reporters had been joined by unknown journalists anxious to make a name for themselves and a surprising number of novice filmmakers. A host of groups with long-term interests, political and otherwise, had arrived alongside crusty Australian unionists, righteous Catholics, hopeful democracy advocates from Burma and Cambodia, zealous do-gooders and smug political activists. Gone were the days when a spontaneous dinner attended by all the expats in East Timor consisted of a close group of twelve.

As Ava chewed her *pao* she caught a glimpse of a bird, unusual in East Timor given birds and eggs were usually eaten by hungry locals or low-waged soldiers. Was it a pigeon perhaps with its glossy purple coat, emerald chest and impressive black-feathered headdress that shimmered in the sun?

'What sort of bird is that?' she asked Augustino.

'*Nggak bu*. Never seen one like it before.'

The bird flew onto a rooftop and searched the sky. What was it looking for? Soon another bird approached, a pigeon but with grey feathers and iridescent orange-lined eyes. It alighted in a tree, and within moments the purple bird began cooing and bobbing its head. Ava grinned, not just at the mating display, more because she'd seen two live birds in Dili in one morning, which gave her a sense of optimism.

Augustino returned with her pot of tea. 'My friend says the bird escaped from a cage. It's not from here. Our pigeons are grey.'

'So he's exotic.'

The grey female ignored the purple bird, but in response he flew down to her branch and danced more frenetically. The female sidled along the branch until she reached the end, glanced back at the purple bird's now frenzied display and flew away. The shiny bird searched for her, flicking his head this way and that, but she was nowhere to be found. He took to the sky, but after flying several loops returned to his rooftop perch where he began his wait all over again.

Ava sighed with a mix of pity and admiration for the glimmering outcast bird destined to wait in the hot tropical sun for a mate who'd probably never arrive. In some ways, he reflected her own life. The farce of her broken-down marriage, her unresolved relationship with married Tom and her penchant for the truth despite lies holding more currency. East Timor was poised, she was poised, but for greatness or disaster, for honesty or more lies? They waited, expectant, determined and anxious like the pitiful, steadfast glittering bird.

———

The day before the ballot, the opposition foreign affairs minister, Leigh Cornell, sat with a small group of fellow delegates on a bench. They'd just finished two days of meetings in Dili and Ava had brought them out to the regions.

They were inside one of *Falintil's* four cantonment sites atop a hill near the village of Gleno. Wild-looking men bearing old and new weapons stolen from *TNI* guarded the perimeter filled with primitive huts made of palm leaves and pieces of rusty corrugated iron. Emaciated and sombre villagers came and went carting water and other goods. It appeared to Ava like a children's holiday camp, yet the atmosphere was anything but playful. Aleixo had confined his men to these makeshift jails to prove to the world that the violence in East Timor was one-sided. It was a politically savvy move, and so far Falintil had resisted *TNI* and militia attempts to draw them out, even though they were being denied food and sympathetic locals were being terrorised around them.

Opposite the Australians sat a petite, clean but dishevelled looking Timorese man with matted black hair in a messy ponytail and a long bushy beard. He wore stolen *TNI* military fatigues with a maroon beret signifying the marines. As one of Aleixo's four *Falintil* field commanders his code-name, Bisa, meant venom.

'How long have you been in the jungle?' Cornell asked Bisa while Ava translated.

The delegation leaned forward, awaiting his answer.

'Twenty-four years,' he replied, his eyes darting around like an animal's.

The delegation leaned back when it became clear he wasn't going to elaborate.

'Commander Bisa,' another delegation member asked. 'Did you register to vote?'

'*Sin*,' he nodded. 'In a clandestine manner.'

'Who do you think is responsible for the violence in East Timor?' someone asked.

'The Indonesians,' he said without hesitation. 'Some of the police here are really *Kopassus*. I recognise them.'

'Are you going to disarm?'

'We haven't received instructions to disarm. The militias haven't disarmed, so why should we? But really, *TNI* are behind the violence and they'll never give up their weapons.'

'How many internally displaced people are in this area?' Ava asked.

'Two thousand three hundred and forty-six.'

The group gasped as Ava noted the number down and asked, 'Where are they, and do they—and you—have enough food and water?'

'Several hundred live here in the cantonment site. The community shares food as best it can, but many coffee crops were deliberately destroyed so they wouldn't have money to eat. Anybody who hasn't signed a form saying they're pro-Indonesian is considered pro-independence and banned from buying rice. Everything is manipulated by *TNI*.'

The delegation members nodded.

After more questions, Cornell asked if Bisa would pose with them for a photo. Bisa nodded and Cornell handed his camera to Ava.

'Watch this,' Cornell said to her, winking.

Ava lined the camera up and Cornell took a couple of cigars out of his shirt pocket, Cuban no doubt. Cornell, whose left politics were just like Bisa's, handed them to the commander. His face lit up with a guileless smile. Ava caught the Che Guevara moment as everyone broke into laughter, delighted that such an unsentimental man still had some child in him. It seemed cigars and not the two bottles of red wine she'd given him, were the way to his heart.

As they walked to their cars Lynne, the local government representative, asked Ava to come with her. She led Ava to a young mother cradling a small child in her arms and fiddling with its belly.

'Can you ask her if I can look at her child? Tell her I used to be a nurse,' Lynne said.

The woman nodded, pulling up her son's top and revealing an opening of skin in his abdomen.

'Thought so. It's a stoma,' Lynne said. 'The baby would have been born with a bowel problem. In our country it would have been fixed with a simple surgery, but in developing countries they create a hole so the child can defecate. Ask her how old he is?'

'She says two and a half.' Ava stopped herself from grimacing. 'He doesn't look older than eighteen months.'

'He's not absorbing enough nutrients. He'll live for a couple more years, til he's four or five maybe if he doesn't get an infection.'

The poor health standards in East Timor were not news to Ava. But the complete absence of simple life-saving surgery for a baby brought that reality home. She thought of Juliette and what she'd do in such a situation. But that was the point. The woman and her child had no other options.

'Tell her she's a good mother,' Lynne said. 'Tell her she's doing a fantastic job keeping his stoma clean.'

The mother beamed with pride, and Ava felt even more humbled by her luck of birth.

'I have something for her.' Lynne went to the car, returning with bandages and antiseptic.

'*Obrigada. Obrigada*,' the mother said, nodding her head with unwavering gratitude for the simple gift that Ava felt was beyond inadequate.

———

The convoy of cars carrying delegation members drove through hillside villages and down a narrow winding road towards the outskirts of Dili. Ava and the head police guard were in the front car, an open jeep, paced at least three hundred metres ahead. The quaint town of Dili lay below them, sparkling in the sun like that first day Ava saw it from the plane. East Timor was a contradiction—simple beauty taunted by a painful history. Yet from up here, there was no hint of tomorrow's vote.

'Looks like trouble,' Ava said as they descended into Dili's outer suburbs. Up ahead, groups of agitated young men lined the main road in. Some brandished knives and crossbows—probably the pro-independence side—while the Indonesian side were donned in red and white bandannas wielding homemade guns.

Lieutenant Ari, who'd spent much of the trip flirting with Ava and trying to convince her to have dinner with him, suddenly turned serious.

'Is there any other way into Dili?'

'Not without going all the way back and around, which would take hours.'

'We don't have enough petrol.'

'I'll radio the others and warn them.'

'Tell them to drive through it as fast as they can.'

Ari put his foot down and they soon reached the young men posturing in small groups along the edges of the road. The lieutenant wove around them but continued to accelerate. Ava could barely look, fearing they might hit someone, but felt compelled to anyway. Wild-eyed men feigned fearlessness, barely able to hide their terror. A bloodied body lay abandoned on the roadside. Anxious families peered out of their windows, possibly checking on their sons. How many people had died today? How many more would die before ballot day?

'Please don't lose the cars behind us,' Ava implored Ari as the gap between them widened. 'I'm responsible for the delegation.'

He nodded, but didn't slow down until they were through the trouble.

'Let's wait here for the others,' Ava said, looking behind her. 'Perhaps you could report this to police headquarters?'

'*Ya bu,*' he said, but the lieutenant didn't reach for his radio. Instead

Ava called Dave and the UNAMET joint operations centre, and asked them to report it to the Indonesian authorities.

The rest of the delegation and their police escorts made it through without incident. Back at the hotel they disgorged from their vehicles.

'That was thrilling,' said the delegation head and former Deputy Prime Minister, Wayne Holland.

Ava wouldn't have described the misfortune they'd witnessed that way. The federal senator scowled.

'That's a pro-independence area,' she told the group. 'There's been a lot of trouble there this year. A number of pro-independence supporters have been killed. I'll find out what happened and let you know at dinner.'

'That'd be great,' Wayne said. 'I must write up today's events for my book. See you all back here for dinner at six.'

Ava turned to find Lieutenant Ari waiting for further instructions. 'What time do you want me here for the delegation dinner tonight, *bu*?' he asked.

'Let's say 5.45pm.'

'And tomorrow morning?'

'We'll rendezvous here at 5.30 am.'

Ari smiled sweetly. 'And where shall we go for dinner?'

'Sorry Ari, but I already have a commit—'

'I only wanted to make your sad eyes shine again.' His face softened, yet Ava couldn't help but feel this was a line he'd used before.

'I can't. Sorry,' she said, careful to hide the anticipation she felt over her plans to see Tom.

57

LIQUICA, EAST TIMOR, 29 AUGUST 1999

Liquica was strangely quiet this night before the ballot. The streets were cloaked in a sea of red and white flags, but few people dared venture out. It didn't look like a celebration of democracy. Isabel turned on the radio for company as she ironed Gabriel's clothes. Earlier that day he'd rushed away to deal with another crisis and she'd been left alone with a guard. A local band came on and sang The Voting Song. Her feet tapped to its catchy beat. *Iha o-nia liafuan, Have your say*, had a happy melody and its upbeat words gave her optimism.

'You have a choice,' she sang, 'Listen, look and learn. UNAMET will show you how. On the day, have your say.'

When it ended the announcer introduced Mr Johnston, the head of UNAMET. Isabel had seen pictures of him in the local paper. He towered over the Timorese beside him, although he always appeared happy and friendly.

Mr Johnston spoke and a translator followed. He read something on behalf of the UN boss in America. Isabel put her iron down:

Tomorrow's Popular Consultation for the people of East Timor is a unique opportunity to settle a long-running dispute by peaceful means.

It is essential that the people of East Timor be able to vote in conditions free of intimidation and violence. I give all of you my solemn assurance that the United Nations will be present in East Timor in the coming months to work with you to implement whatever choice you make tomorrow. [6]

Isabel repeated the words in her head *we will be present in the coming months*. She'd seen posters saying the same thing and wanted to believe Mr Johnston, but hadn't he seen the Jasman plans for destruction if independence won? Did he think words alone would be enough to stop *TNI*, Gabriel and the others?

Besides, what had the UN really done for East Timor? While everyone had been able to register to vote, it hadn't stopped the killings. If things worsened, how could they respond without weapons?

Despite her fears, Isabel hoped that people would vote tomorrow for a whiff of a hope for a future that on this night felt an impossibly long way away.

58

DILI, EAST TIMOR, 29 AUGUST 1999
—THE DAY BEFORE THE BALLOT

By the time Ava and Tom met in the small rotunda at his house it was after 11pm. Ava put a tinned oyster on a cracker, handed it to Tom and made one for herself.

'This is to celebrate the eve of history,' she said. 'Tomorrow the people of East Timor get to vote. We hope.'

'Twenty-four years in the making,' Tom said.

'I thought Dili would be really tense. But there's more excitement tonight than trepidation.'

Ava savoured the taste of her oyster, a small luxury contrasting against the backdrop of the possible violence tomorrow. Like the Timorese, she had no idea what might happen in the coming days. This might be her and Tom's last supper. Ever.

'The UN's predicting a messy day tomorrow,' Tom said, wiping his hands on his handkerchief.

'Going by this week's violence, it will take incredible courage for the people to vote. If the Indonesians want things to go smoothly, they will of course. But if they don't…'

Ava looked past the rotunda's roof to the immensity of the star-filled sky. It was fitting to feel so insignificant against a people's future.

'Before I applied for this posting,' Ava said, 'I asked the powers that be —whatever or whoever that is—to give me a posting where history would be made. First there was Sujati's resignation and now East Timor.' She laughed. 'How self-important I must sound.'

'Not at all,' Tom smiled. 'I decided to work for the UN and come out here because I didn't want to end up another ageing academic stuck in the same institution forever.'

'Let's drink to that,' Ava said and they raised their glasses, looking to each other for reassurance.

'Were you ever religious?' Tom asked.

Ava shook her head. 'But that doesn't mean I'm not spiritual, which I am.'

'I was brought up Catholic.'

'I know.' Ava suspected his beliefs strongly tied him to his wife. 'Why are you still religious? Lots of people grow up in the Church but change their mind as adults.'

'It's hard to explain,' Tom said, looking down. 'It's part of who I am, my identity.'

'So it's more about identity than faith?'

'I suppose so.'

'What about the pressure from your family to go back to New York and have a baby. Is that religious or something else?'

Tom moved around in his seat. 'It's just...expected.'

'And yet, you don't sound happy in your marriage.'

Tom sighed.

'Is now the best time to have a child then?'

There was much that went unsaid but seemed understood between them. But tonight Ava wanted to learn the things about him she didn't comprehend. They hadn't kissed and yet Tom had alluded to a future together. Before tomorrow, she needed to know how serious he was.

'In terms of our marriages I think you're further down the track than I am,' Tom replied. 'Also, I think that your truth and mine are different.'

Truth? For Ava this wasn't about truth. It was about being brave enough to stand apart. Was his hesitation over them about his culture and belonging, or faith, or was American puritanism mixed up in this, which Australians couldn't fathom.

'Another question, this time about identity,' she continued. 'How important is being black to you as opposed to being human?'

'It's fundamental to who I am,' Tom replied without hesitation.

'Would you ever have considered marrying a white woman?'

'No. I don't have white friends, just like you won't find many white people in America have black friends. We work together, but interracial marriage is… It's still difficult. You'd face a lot of discrimination. You'd be ostracised by both sides.'

Ava's mouth dropped open. Tom hadn't just shattered her notion of American racial harmony, he'd closed off the possibility of a post-divorce future with her. Why had he pursued her these last months—the airport when they first met, the Jakarta date, his attempts to be physically close to her, his dream, his texts and calls and emails? Was he being dishonest then or now? No. She knew what Tom felt for her, just as he knew what she felt for him, and it was greater than this pretence. Her thoughts railed.

'So all that racial equality you Americans talk about is just rhetoric?'

'I had a white girlfriend once, with reddish-brown hair like yours.' He paused. 'She was smart and beautiful like you too. And we were very close, for a while. She got pregnant.'

Ava waited for him to finish but he looked away. It dawned on her what he wasn't prepared to say.

'So even though you're Catholic, you wanted her to have an abortion because she was white and you didn't want a coloured baby, despite you being somewhat coloured yourself?'

'It was her choice and I believe the right to choose ultimately rests with the woman.'

Ava looked away, a tense silence separating them.

'You asked me before, if I'd have considered marrying a white woman back then and I answered no,' Tom said.

Ava couldn't hide her bewilderment.

'But since meeting you, everything's different. If you asked me the same question now, I'm not sure how I'd answer.'

After some time, Ava gave him a forgiving smile, which he returned.

'What's really the matter with your marriage, Ava?' Tom asked.

'I'm sick of doing it alone, of having to be responsible for everything. I want to share things with someone, have someone I can lean on. I want to be with a man.'

'Ha,' Tom said. 'That's exactly what I'm expecting Nancy to say to me one day. Women want men to be everything.'

Ava couldn't imagine seeing Tom in the same way she saw Pete and the possibility shook her. Was it being with one person too long that did this to couples, or was it that Tom and his wife had always been mismatched like she and Pete? When she was with Tom she felt greater than the sum of their parts.

'You deserve to be happy, Ava.'

She closed her eyes, wishing it were so. She thought of Tom's wife, whose happiness she didn't want to steal, if indeed that was what they had together.

In the distance, gunfire rang out and Ava's heart pounded, in part due to the impossibility of tomorrow's vote, but also because regardless of their feelings for each other, a barrier of beliefs, cultures, race and his ever-present marriage had emerged between them. Yet Tom had left a door open for her. Should she wait for him to open it all the way? Would he?

'Do you hear that gunfire?'

'All night long,' he said.

'I always wonder what…who…if they're…'

'Me too.'

They shared a far-away look. In spite of themselves and the gunfire serenade, Tom edged his leg over until it touched Ava's. A current ran between them, which she imagined turning into a melting kiss that would numb the ache that was the millstone of their marriages and this damned place. This cursed, dogged, ever-hopeful East Timor.

59

DILI, EAST TIMOR, 30 AUGUST 1999
- BALLOT DAY

Ava accompanied the delegation convoy through the deserted streets of Dili to polling booth number twenty-one. Yesterday, the town had brimmed with more people and activity than Ava had ever seen. Hundreds if not thousands of outsiders had inundated the place—foreign officials, activists and NGOs alongside Indonesian officials, soldiers and police. But most striking were the large teams of media lugging their cameras and satellite equipment around as they interviewed for feature stories. *CNN*, the *BBC*, *AFP* and every other world services was there. Ava knew some of the regulars, but many were helicopter journalists flown in for a day or two especially for the vote. *Who's this Aleixo?* she heard one of them ask, making her chuckle.

Flanked by their police escort, the delegation approached the first of many polling booths on their list to formally scrutinise. Although it wasn't yet 7 am, there was a queue of voters, four deep and at least a kilometre long waiting for the gates to open. Perhaps this was why no one was walking around—they'd already arrived at their polling stations.

Delegation members showed their passes to UNAMET staff at the gate and entered the voting booth at the school, their protection team standing tactfully out of the way. Their first official duty was to sign off that the ballot boxes were empty and sealed.

'We have a problem,' one of the UN staff said to Ava and Wayne. 'Some local UN staff haven't turned up and we don't have enough people to begin. Someone said they've been threatened and are too afraid to come in.'

'Keep trying to get hold of them,' Ava said. 'They've endured a lot of intimidation so maybe they just need a little coaxing. Tell them everything's calm.'

Soon the missing staff trickled in and the gates opened. The men and women at the head of the queue walked up to the half a dozen UNAMET staff seated behind a long trestle table. Unsure what to do next the voters hesitated, gripping their identity cards tightly. UN staff took them through the voting process while those lining up noted every step. There was relief and clapping when the first lot came out and placed their ballots in the blue plastic boxes, their previously serious faces breaking into broad grins. The mood quickly improved as people understood they were being allowed to vote and weren't going to be killed for it. Not yet.

'It's like a miracle,' Ava said to Wayne.

'The lack of *TNI* and militia is so encouraging,' he agreed.

Ava walked over to a young couple and their baby waiting to vote and introduced herself. '*Bu. Pak,*' she said. 'May I ask, how you're feeling about today?'

'We're happy, nervous, excited,' said the father. 'But *bu*, this is really for our children. We know the coming days will be difficult, but we're willing to die for their future.'

'Otherwise, our children may die anyway,' the mother added.

This wasn't the first time Ava had heard such sentiments. She thanked them and moved up the line, asking two women with a toddler the same question. The older one looked at the younger, who nodded, grabbed Ava's arm and drew her in closer. 'I was raped in 1975 by *TNI*,' the older woman said. 'My daughter here was raped by the militia this year.'

Ava grimaced.

'I'd rather die than let my two-year-old grand-daughter suffer the same fate.'

Ava placed her free hand on top of the woman's dry and wrinkled hand. 'You're very brave, *Senora* and *Senora*,' she said looking at each woman in turn. 'Thank you for talking to me.'

As she walked away, Ava blinked back tears. The senator in the delegation, Maggie, an active campaigner on East Timor, saw her and came over. Ava told her the women's story.

'People are amazing, aren't they?' she said.

'Given half a chance they can be. But the day isn't over yet.'

———

Liquica, EAST TIMOR

On the outskirts of Liquica in a small building sat polling booth 42/43. Ava was uncertain why UNAMET had allocated it to them. Perhaps it was coincidence, or Craig had requested it due to its physical closeness to Dili, or maybe Australia wanted to make a point after the April massacre. Either way, she was glad to be returning. A vindication of sorts.

It was already late morning and the delegation had scrutinised several booths in Dili by the time they arrived at a clearing with a grey Besser block structure at the rear. A little cooler than Dili, a mild sea breeze tempered the heat of the clear, dry season day. As they got out of the car, Ava could smell the ocean. The bleak emotion of her last visit to Liquica came rushing back, but today was about courage and light, and she forced herself to return into the present.

'Can anyone see the *Sixty Minutes* team?' one of the delegation asked.

'Why?' Ava asked.

'Because Wayne agreed they could follow him for their story.'

'Who instigated that?' Ava hoped the media attention wouldn't distract him from his formal duties. Perhaps it was proving hard for him to let go of the spotlight. Only two weeks ago he'd resigned as deputy prime minster to spend more time with his young family.

'I think it was mutually beneficial,' Maggie said, raising her eyebrows.

Ava surveyed the polling booth. A bunch of scraggly-looking militia watched from the edge and the people queuing to vote appeared tense. She looked for the Indonesian police, who were supposed to be providing security, but couldn't find any.

Instead she found a UNAMET staff member and asked her how the day was going.

'Pretty good, considering,' the young Canadian woman replied. 'There were some shots fired up in the Redato area earlier today, and we received reports of nearby roadblocks. We sent some people to sort it out and they've been taken down now. One of the militia leaders tried to jump the queue here, but we told him go to the end of the line. He left in a huff and returned wearing different clothes and tried to jump the queue again. Apparently he thought we'd refused him because he was wearing a pro-Indonesia jacket. We explained the situation again and he eventually agreed to wait his turn like everyone else.'

'And the militia over there?'

'We're watching them. They know they're not supposed to be here. We'll try to get them to leave again soo—'

They were interrupted by one of the militia revving his truck engine loudly before speeding off, its tyres churning clumps of grass behind him.

Ava walked to the back of the building where she found ten Indonesian police sitting and smoking cigarettes. In their spare hands they gripped long-barrelled weapons pointed at the sky. They went silent when they saw Ava and she stopped in her tracks. She'd hoped to ask them some questions, but instead nodded and said *Selamat siang*, good day, before turning back. Were the Indonesian authorities shirking their responsibilities again?

Back in the voting area, the *Sixty Minutes* team had arrived. Wayne was being interviewed by lead journalist, Robert Cross, a tall, slightly portly man. He was renowned in the journalistic community for fabricating stories in hotspots, and always travelling with gourmet food and wine. But ironically, the Australian public saw him as the man who told it how it was. Ava had dealt with him before in East Timor, had even shared a flight with him, although he'd refused to acknowledge her, most likely because she was too junior.

'Let's get going everyone,' she said to the delegation, and soon they were off to the next polling booth.

60

LIQUICA, 30 AUGUST 1999

Standing in the queue at polling booth 42/43 was Isabel. She avoided looking directly at the militia off to the side, but from the corner of her eye she could see they were agitated. They paced, chain-smoked and talked too loudly, except for one who stood with his feet planted firmly on the ground and his arms folded, staring at her. She had a right to vote for whoever she wanted, she reassured herself his eyes bored into her.

Several vehicles pulled up behind her and a group of foreigners carrying notebooks got out. How big they were and how different their skin and hair colours. One woman was wider and shorter than the others with brown skin and black hair, there was a giant man with speckled skin wearing a strange hat and a tall, pale woman with hair the colour of rust. She looked familiar. Was she the one she'd met at the nun's place after the massacre?

Gabriel's boys left in a huff, but now a red van driven by a Timorese pulled up and more foreigners got out carrying strange objects. One had a portable box with what seemed to be a camera at one end while the other had a long metal stick with a fuzzy oval-shaped object at one end. They shoved these things into the face of the strange-hatted man. Isabel expected him to be upset, but he immediately began smiling and talking to a third, even taller man.

'*Televizaun*,' she heard someone say and she realised the box must be a special camera. She would have been in awe had she not been so anxious.

After a while the first lot of foreigners left, but the television people stayed and Isabel put her head back down.

One of the TV men began speaking to people in the queue, asking them a question as the camera looked on. One woman shook her head and a man turned away, but others answered. Would they ask her the question? She gulped, taking her umbrella from her bag and opening it before pulling it down so she could hide her head in its metal ribs.

A commotion nearby made her peer from underneath it. The tall foreign man hovered over her and the camera stared as the furry, oblong object hung above her head.

'*Independensia? Integrasi?*' the tall foreigner asked her in a mix of Tetum and Indonesian as he looked her directly in the eyes.

The camera loomed above her, almost demanding an answer, and she didn't know what to do. The ballot was supposed to be secret and yet the people in blue hats were allowing this man to ask this question. Could she really ignore someone so important?

'*Independensia*,' she blurted.

As soon as she heard herself she gasped, placing her free hand over her mouth. One of Gabriel's militiamen stepped between Isabel and the tall foreigner and began ranting at him. The militiaman tried to manoeuvre the tall foreigner away from the queue, but he was too sturdy. Now the camera and oblong object turned towards the militiaman.

'Why won't you let these people express their opinions freely?' Isabel heard the foreigner's translator ask in Indonesian. 'What are you afraid of?'

Isabel took the opportunity to retreat back under her umbrella, but she knew this was would not make her safe. She grabbed her bag from between her feet and ran, ditching her umbrella and clutching her sizeable belly. She'd spoken too much, and yet hadn't had a say at all.

61

LIQUICA, 30 AUGUST 1999

Father Ribeiro's yard looked exactly the same to Ava as it had four months ago. She sat under a tree next to a small outhouse with the rest of the delegation, sheltering from the midday sun. It was a strangely peaceful spot to eat her lunch of canned fish, rice cakes and sugar bananas, yet only four months ago it had been the scene of a massacre. She stopped chewing to remember the disorienting emptiness that had paralysed her, checking herself for similar sensations but feeling nothing. Today was too practical for such otherworldly contemplations.

Her phone rang and she swallowed her food.

'Everybody,' she said after hanging up. 'Over ninety-eight per cent of people who registered have already voted. What's more, there have been no reports of interference or violence.'

The delegation clapped and cheered. But Ava's merriment was soon tempered by a realisation. By ensuring the ballot was safe and secure, *TNI* had confirmed to the world they were in complete command of their soldiers as well as the militias, and that there never were any rogue elements. The question now was, what did *TNI* intend for the coming days? The Jasman plan for widespread destruction niggled at her again.

'We have ten minutes before we need to leave,' she told the group. 'We're going to a voting station in the hills back there. It's been a trouble spot in the past and earlier today there was a roadblock there.'

They packed up and Ava peered around the building to see if their police escorts had returned from lunch.

'Where's our security contingent?' she asked before looking at Wayne. 'And weren't the *Sixty Minutes* crew meant to be here by now?'

Wayne shrugged and Ava began dialling the lieutenant when a vehicle pulled up. Within moments he came rushing around the corner. '*Milisi.* Journalist,' he gasped.

'*Di mana*?' she asked looking him in the eyes to calm him. Where?

'*Milisi* hit big journalist. Kidnap him from voting place. I get in kidnap van with milisi, make them go to *polisi*. Very, very angry. Come quick before…'

The delegation jumped into their cars, Wayne and Ava together.

'What on earth were *Sixty Minutes* doing following us around anyway?' Ava asked him.

Wayne cleared his throat. 'I told them they could.'

She'd had made her point.

The lieutenant took them to the police station at the edge of town. Ava jumped out and Wayne followed. She saw no sign of a red van or militia. Hopefully they still had time.

Inside the sparse, white-tiled room they found Robert Cross and his *Sixty Minutes* team seated on old sunken couches and lounge chairs. They looked both terrified and sheepish, shrinking as they caught a glimpse of Wayne. A militiaman paced in front of them, spitting angry words and gesticulating wildly. Ava recognised him as one of Gabriel's *Aitarak* boys. At the back of the room, a dozen Indonesian police stood near the counter. With their hands on their hips and sneers on their faces they looked almost as agitated as the militiaman. Ava nodded at them. Given they weren't doing anything, she decided to try and placate the situation herself.

'*Selamat siang, bapak*,' she said respectfully to the militiaman, bowing down to his height and speaking loudly enough for the police to hear. 'My name is Ava Vuyk and I'm from Jakarta. We know these people here. Can I ask you, *pak*, what's happening?'

'I'm Marco Pesqueira,' he said turning to face her. '*Aitarak* commander.'

Ava nodded, noting he didn't appear to be on drugs and had no visible weapons. But if he got violent, would the police protect her and the journalists? Her instinct said they wouldn't want an international incident today. Then again, if more militia arrived the situation could change. This was Liquica, after all, and the police here—if they were police and not *Kopassus*—would have been involved in the April massacre.

'These crazy foreigners have been asking people if they're going to vote for integration or independence,' Marco said breathlessly. 'Are they stupid? Everyone knows voting is secret. This is not some money-making media thing. This is a UN process. This is our life!'

Cross shrank even further into the couch at the tone of Marco's voice.

Ava privately shared his disgust. Cross had jeopardised the safety of locals by asking them a loaded question in front of militia at a known trouble spot. Were those who'd responded *independence* still alive? Yet the irony of Pesqueira's statement—a militia leader defending a democratic UN process—hadn't escaped her either.

She turned to the *Sixty Minutes* team and translated, hoping Cross would apologise. But he sat silent and white-faced, staring at the floor. She glanced outside again. No militia reinforcements yet.

'What's your name?' Marco said to Cross.

Silence.

'I want your name!' he yelled and Cross and his team jumped.

Marco was behaving erratically, whipping himself up.

'*Bapak*,' Ava said bowing to him again, but also peering in the direction of the most senior police officer. 'Perhaps this is something we should let the police handle.'

At last the senior officer stepped forward. 'Where are you from?' he asked Cross in English.

Cross looked up. 'Sydney, Australia.'

'Typical,' the officer said under his breath and Ava cringed. 'Where are your UNAMET press cards?' He paused. 'You don't have any, do you? If you did, you'd have been told by UNAMET that for your own safety, you should report to the police in every town you travel to. Do you even have proper working visas?'

Cross looked at Ava and she gave him a look of encouragement.

'I apologise for causing you offence and for breaking the rules,' Cross said, looking at the officer and militiaman. 'It wasn't my intention to create problems. We've travelled to other areas today and haven't had any issues.'

'Just go home,' Marco screamed at Cross. 'And if you ever return, I'll cut you up into little pieces.'

Ava pretended she hadn't heard properly and asked Marco to repeat what he'd said. She hoped he'd retract his threat, or that the police would step in.

'Never come back. Or I'll cut you to bits!' he screamed.

Cross and his colleagues turned an even more ghostly white when Ava translated. But the police officer approached Ava and Wayne and told them the group could leave. Ava breathed a sigh of relief.

'Thank you, *bapak*,' she said to the police officer. 'I sincerely apologise for the behaviour of this journalist and his team, which the Australian government doesn't endorse in any way. We have great respect for the peaceful way the ballot is being run today, and once again would like to thank you for your assistance.'

The officer looked somewhat placated. 'We'll provide you with a police escort back to Dili. The immigration police will deport them from there. It's best we get them out as soon as possible.'

They moved outside and as they got into their cars. Cross turned to Ava and Wayne and asked, 'Do you have to take me to the Dili police station?'

'Yes,' Wayne snapped.

'We don't have much choice,' Ava added, pointing to three large trucks filled with heavily armed police about to escort them back to Dili.

Cross sunk his head down and looked away. As they drove they passed the missing red van on the side of the road. A militia wearing a maroon *TNI* beret sat in the driver's seat smoking, and Ava wondered what had happened to the Timorese driver and owner. She doubted the vehicle would ever be returned to him, or that it would even occur to Cross to compensate him for it.

———

By the time Ava returned to the Turismo Hotel it was nearly midnight. She walked into the hotel garden brimming with foreigners celebrating the peaceful day. While the peace in East Timor was likely transient, today was a day worth savouring. No matter what happened in the future, the vote could never be taken back.

Ava made her way through the crowd to find the delegation, passing a large table of journalists. On seeing her they began cheering and clapping. Ava looked around to check it was her they were acknowledging.

'Well done on deporting Cross,' one of them said. 'Can I buy you a drink?

'When will he be leaving?' another asked.

'What happened?'

'Did he bring out the gourmet food and wine?

Ava laughed. 'Yes, he brought out deli meats and pâté , exotic cheeses, water biscuits and white wine from an esky, which he shared with his team. You didn't hear that from me, though.'

'Did he offer you any?'

'Just privately, two biscuits with salami and that was it.' She excused herself to join the delegation. Maggie beckoned her over.

'Aleixo wants to talk to you.'

Ava took the phone from her. 'Congratulations, on such a wondrous day, Aleixo, and for everything you did to get here. I hope the Indonesians release you from house arrest soon.'

'You are very kind,' Aleixo replied in heavily accented English. 'We have very long way to go, but we're on the right path. We cannot be stopped now.' She heard him light a cigarette and take a long drag. 'I wanted to say also, a big thank you for your work. You are an angel, Ava.'

She smiled, placing her hand on her heart. It was a small reckoning, but it meant a lot to her.

She returned the senator's phone and joined in the revelry, pushing the reality of the coming days from her mind. The threat of conflict that would surely descend on East Timor rumbled in the background like a building storm following the sunny tranquility of the ballot day.

62

DILI, EAST TIMOR, SEPTEMBER 1999

Two buffed-up Indonesian police officers stood guard at either side of a front door that Ava and Quentin approached. The door opened and one of Ava's contacts, Rolando from the *CNRT*, greeted them. In 1975 he was the leader of a pro-Indonesia political party, but had since switched allegiances. Being a mix of Timorese and Portuguese blood like many of the elite here, he was taller and lankier than most Timorese, but Ava thought he looked gaunt today.

'*Bondia. Bondia,*' Rolanda said beckoning them in, a smouldering *kretek* hanging from his mouth.

He seated them in his lounge room and left to get drinks. The house was typical upper class, busy with ornately tiled floors, traditional carved Portuguese furniture, floral rugs, elaborately-painted porcelain and Catholic memorabilia. For Ava it was like going back in time.

He returned with a tray of espresso cups filled with steaming Timorese coffee. She wasn't normally a coffee drinker as it kept her from sleeping, but the smell was too inviting and she was too tired.

Quentin leaned in towards Rolando. 'The ballot result is being announced tomorrow. I'm interested in your thoughts on the coming days, and also about the *CNRT's* ideas on reconciliation with the pro-Indonesia Timorese.'

Rolando nodded as Ava translated and mentally noted that not even Quentin bothered to pretend autonomy might win.

'Since the ballot four days ago, my fellow pro-independence supporters across East Timor have been murdered, terrorised and intimidated at the hands of *TNI* and their militia. East Timorese UNAMET staff have been killed, UNAMET hasn't been able to get ballot boxes out of some areas, many houses have been burnt, and in some towns the police and *TNI* have left and the militia are running wild.' He took a deep drag of his cigarette.

'But we've instructed our people not to be provoked at any cost. They can run and hide, save themselves, but there must be no violence on their part. This will not only prevent conflict, but prove to the world that the violence is completely one-sided and being instigated by *TNI.*'

'What do you think *TNI's* strategy is?' Quentin asked. 'I don't understand what they hope to achieve.'

Rolando rubbed his hands together and looked Quentin in the eyes.

'Their strategy is to create total chaos so that all foreigners—UNAMET, the media, you too even—are forced to leave. That way East Timor will become like it was in 1975, with no outsiders knowing what's going on so they can wreak any havoc they want.'

Quentin's brow creased.

'That's why they beat up that *BBC* journalist. And it worked,' Rolando added. 'The *BBC* and seventy other journalists are leaving today. The Indonesian media left yesterday, ordered out apparently and put on a military flight.'

Quentin looked to Ava for confirmation and she nodded. She'd reported it in a cable.

'You might also be interested to know,' Rolando continued, 'that I was at a meeting last week with *TNI* intelligence and UNAMET. *TNI* told us there will be *great chaos* in East Timor if independence wins, just as that leaked document promised.'

So the Jasman document *was* real. Ava mentally cursed Nev.

Rolando leaned back and lit a new cigarette off his old one. Swirls of smoke spiralled through the humidity and surrounded them in clouds of clove.

'I understand that theory,' Quentin said. 'But how is it in Indonesia's national interest to force the international community out and create chaos here?'

'*TNI* plans to make it look as though the violence is intra-Timorese— like another civil war has broken out. Without neutral witnesses, who'd know any better?'

Quentin frowned. 'While this might fulfil some radical general's wishes to hold on to the place, how does supporting a civil war benefit the government and people of Indonesia?'

'Ah,' Rolando said, his face lighting up. 'It didn't benefit Indonesia to use the militia past the point when it became clear that traumatising the population wasn't going to force a vote for autonomy either, yet they continued to do so. Why? Because they think that if there's chaos here the international community will throw their hands in the air and tell Indonesia, *Here you are, you can have East Timor back. It's too difficult.*'

At last. Rolando had got to the core of things. Ava hoped Quentin—and Canberra—would acknowledge now that the violence was being orchestrated from high up in the Indonesian government. Not that they couldn't already know.

'But why do they want to hold on to East Timor so badly?' Quentin persisted.

'Pride.' Rolando smiled. 'It's about rejection and betrayal, fear and anger.'

'Whose pride?'

'*TNI's* pride and that of their nationalist political counterparts. At a higher level, it's a power struggle between the old guard—*TNI* and their nationalist supporters who don't want to lose their grip on power—and the new guard—Hidayat and his Muslim fellows who want democratisation, modernisation and change. What's happening on the ground here is really a proxy struggle over who will rule in the new political era.'

At last! Ava thought. The struggle over East Timor made no sense and yet perfect sense—the battle for power between Jakarta's old and new guards being played out in an irrelevant corner of their sprawling archipelago where local lives mattered little. If it weren't for the Dili massacre the world probably wouldn't have cared, but from the moment the video footage of the brutal killings was smuggled out and the world got to see what was really happening in East Timor, Indonesia's hold over the place was doomed. It was just a matter of time.

'It's probably also a warning to other parts of the archipelago with aspirations for independence that Jakarta will not cede Indonesian territory easily,' Rolando added.

Quentin sat back, giving nothing away.

'The ballot was a miracle,' Rolando said, his eyes beckoning. 'But we Timorese continue to die every day. We need a peacekeeping force. If we ask you, Australia—who know and understand Indonesia so well—to come and guarantee the security of the Timorese, we hope with all our hearts that you will listen and help us.'

Chills ran down Ava's spine. She noticed that Quentin went strangely quiet, despite having received this request many times. Was it the looming mass violence that made Rolando's plea more poignant this time?

Quentin took a sip of water and cleared his throat. 'As you know we've raised the issue of peacekeepers many times with the Indonesians, but it was never something they considered, not even for a moment. The issue now is how to go ahead with the process under the current conditions.' He leaned in again towards Rolando and lowered his voice. 'Or should we not go ahead with independence? Should history stop here?'

Rolando shook his head. 'No. We want peace within the existing process. But for that process to succeed—for all our investments of time and money and lives to be worthwhile—we need support from you so that

Indonesia doesn't fail, so it keeps its part of the bargain and provides proper security.'

'Let me say this,' Quentin said. 'There's a lot of goodwill behind you. The international community is tired of the way this situation has been mishandled by Indones—'

One of Rolando' colleagues tapped Rolando on the shoulder and whispered something to him.

'Ambassador. The suburb of Becora is burning as we speak. Ten houses have gone already, and my home and family are there.' He stood. 'Now is the time for the international community to use the statements made by several Indonesian ministers that if the security situation requires it, a peacekeeping force will be allowed into East Timor. You can leverage this to get a peacekeeping force here as soon as possible.'

Quentin stood and shook Rolando's hand. 'Thank you for your time. I hope your family is safe.'

Rolando kissed Ava hurriedly on both cheeks and rushed out.

As Quentin walked out ahead of her, he seemed different than when he'd arrived. There was determination in his stride and wrath in his narrowed eyes. She put her notebook in her bag and followed, wondering if she'd ever see Rolando, or any of her pro-independence contacts, again.

63

DILI, SEPTEMBER 1999

That afternoon, Ava sat in the car with Dave driving back from an outer Dili suburb. A group of young Australian activists had called the consulate after being repeatedly threatened by the militia. She and Dave went to see them, imploring them to leave East Timor, or at least to move to the inner city where they'd be less isolated, but they'd refused. Ava respected idealists, but their naivety would surely mean trouble for the consulate.

'I'm certain that's a decision they're gonna regret very soon,' Dave said.

'And us too when we have to rescue them,' Ava replied.

Her phone rang. It was Aaron, the shy one-night-stand journo. 'We were just attacked by the militia,' he almost yelled at her. 'You guys told us to go to the Indonesians if we got in trouble, but they refused to help us.'

'Where are you?'

'At the Mahkota.'

'We'll be there in five.'

Tension had been building throughout East Timor as the vote announcement approached. The nearby town of Ermera had come under siege with the militia refusing to allow ballot boxes to be collected, local

UNAMET staff were being targeted and killed for their role in the vote, and militia harassment of internationals was on the rise. The threat of grand-scale upheaval hung over Dili like a wet season about to break. Things appeared quiet, but behind the scenes everyone was preparing for turmoil.

Ava and Dave found a large group of media gathered in the foyer of the Mahkota, a run-down concrete box of a hotel where they lived alongside international UN staff.

'What happened? Dave asked.

'The militia shot at us,' Aaron said pointing at a bullet hole in a window. 'Then they charged at us through the front doors, a dozen of them waving machetes and guns at us. It was fucking crazy!'

An Australian photojournalist stepped forward, his hands planted on his hips. '*TNI* stood over there watching the entire charade. In fact, they had a little conference with the militia out the back a couple of hours ago, probably planning the entire thing.'

'They're trying to keep us boxed in here so we won't report what's happening out there,' Aaron said.

'They're trying to scare you into leaving,' Ava retorted. 'They don't want any foreign journalists left here to report whatever's going to happen after the vote result is announced. We hope—the world hopes—you all stay.'

The journalists avoided eye contact with Ava. A *Reuters* reporter stepped forward. 'We're pulling out in the next couple of days. Orders from HQ.'

'Yeah. It's too dangerous,' the *CNN* reporter crowed. 'Liability issues.'

'We'll talk to the authorities again,' Ava said.

'We'd better get going. I'll just use the boy's room first,' Dave said.

Ava walked out to the car before realising Dave had the keys. He insisted on driving, which Ava found tiresome but had so far indulged. She happened to be a good driver with a no-accident record, which was more than Dave could boast. She rested against the passenger door.

Suddenly a Timorese man dressed like a militia pinned her against the car, planting a hand on each arm and leaning in so close his face was just centimetres away from hers. Adrenalin surged through her as thoughts of kidnap and rape raced through her mind. But then a calm voice interjected. *Surely he knows who I am. He wouldn't dare, would he?*

'You're the one from Jakarta,' he spat accusingly in Indonesian.

She longed to turn her face away from his cigarette and alcohol breath and wipe his saliva from her face, but even if she could, she wouldn't give him the satisfaction. Whatever was going on here, it was planned, just like the stunt they'd pulled on the journalists.

'Yes I am, *mas*,' she said, using a brotherly term of address and smiling at him.

Should she scream? Knee him in the balls? Run and find something heavy to fight him with? Where the hell was Dave? As for those useless, bloody journalists…

The militia reached behind him. He drew something from his jeans and put it to her temple. A pistol.

Ava stopped breathing. The whole world stopped as sweat broke out on her forehead. She had to take in air. Force herself to breathe. Was the gun cocked? Should she talk to him, or would that agitate him?

'You Australians,' he said, spraying more spit across her face. 'You should get out while you can. The lot of you.'

Now Ava was annoyed. She refused to flinch. 'What's your name? Which militia are you with?'

'Pfftt,' he huffed and moved his face close towards her. Ava narrowed her eyes.

The sound of the hotel door opening broke their stand-off. As suddenly as he'd appeared, the militia pulled his pistol away and disappeared around the corner.

Ava was motionless. She heard footsteps and the sound of the car being unlocked remotely. She glanced to where the militia had gone. Part of her wanting to follow him. But more of her eager to get away.

'You all right? You look a bit pale.'

Ava couldn't speak. Things felt dreamlike. Had she imagined the whole thing?

As they drove away, Ava tried to hide her shaking hands. She took a tissue from her bag and wiped her face. If she told Dave what had gone on, he'd tell Quentin and Craig and they wouldn't let her out of the consulate again. Worse still, they might send her back to Jakarta.

'I'm fine,' she mumbled, taking a cigarette from her bag and lighting it as she opened the car window.

'Craig'll have a fit if he knows you've been smoking in here.'

Ava ignored him, staring into the distance. If she looked him in the eyes, she risked spilling everything.

'Right then,' he said. 'How about giving me a drag?'

Ava handed Dave her cigarette and closed her eyes, distancing herself from him and the car and Dili until the world dropped away and she was hovering alone in her seat. She quickly found herself yearning to be comforted in the fold of someone's embrace. But whose? Not Pete. And Juliette was a child. A face materialised in front of her and she recognised him. Tom. He was where her solace lay.

———

It was nearly 11 pm before Ava and Tom finished work and made their way to his house. The ballot result was being announced the next morning and no one knew what came next. From tomorrow, Ava would also be staying at the consulate, which meant restricted independence. She swore Tom to secrecy before telling him about the gun being pulled on her.

'But you're all right,' he said aghast, unsure whether to grab her hand.

'I refuse to let them get to me that easily.'

Tom went quiet, frowning and chewing his lip. 'I don't know what I'd do if something happened to you. I…' He shook his head as though it was impossible to imagine.

'I just wish…' Ava began, but she wasn't ready to tell him.

They went on sitting under the Dili sky, once more on the precipice of something immense, knowing only that it would involve yet more struggle. Life suddenly felt fragile and transitory. Ava yearned for Tom to hold her before he took her inside and they spent their last night together.

'Me too,' Tom said moving closer, but still not touching her.

The universe contracted around them, and even though they respected proper physical boundaries, they made love in every other sense, their hearts fully submerged in adultery.

64

LIQUICA, EAST TIMOR SEPTEMBER 1999

Since her attempt to vote a few days ago, Isabel had awaited her fate at the kitchen table in the militia shack. Her hands clasped together in her lap, or her arms folded on the tabletop to support her head as she dozed or wept, she stirred only for the bare necessities.

At last she heard a car door and footsteps. She sat tall as Gabriel placed himself opposite her in a chair, his face filled with loathing.

'My deputy commander was killed this morning,' he sneered. 'His face was beaten so badly by those pro-independence bastards he was almost decapitated. I couldn't even recognise him.'Isabel grimaced. Always the pointless killing. Yet she no longer felt fearful for herself.

'Then I find out you've been disloyal to me—disloyal to East Timor. Do you know what you've done? You've voted for the people who did this to my deputy, who left him to rot in a shallow grave without a proper burial or any thought for his widow or children.'

Isabel wrapped her arms around her large belly and drew into herself.

'Christ, Isabel!' Gabriel screamed, banging his fist on the table.

She lifted her head and said, 'I didn't vote.'

'What?'

'I didn't vote, for anyone.'

'Is that so?'

Gabriel took a deep breath and looked up to the ceiling. When he looked back at her, his face had relaxed and his body was no longer rigid.

'Do you really think I don't know what you've been up to?'

She shook her head.

'I know you've been talking to the other side. I know what you told the whole world the other day. I know you don't want my baby. I know you want to escape.' He paused. 'I hear you singing those resistance songs. But now you have my baby, *my* baby. And now you must choose.'

Isabel gave him a questioning look.

'I'll forgive you if you come with me to west Timor.'She'd expected punishment, banishment, death even, not this. Then she thought about west Timor. Had East Timor's fate been determined before the ballot result was even announced?

'I'm asking you this,' he said struggling to get the words out, 'because I don't want you and the baby to die in the destruction that's coming. In west Timor we'll have a home, a future. We'll be safe.'

Isabel looked into Gabriel's bloodshot glassy eyes.

'If you stay here,' he continued, 'you'll be throwing everything to the wind. There will be no tomorrow for an East Timor without Indonesia—no food or homes or schools or jobs for our child, no animals or crops. Just civil war. Perhaps not at first, but it will happen soon enough.'

Who was he, this desperate stranger? She should have felt stronger, but she didn't. The choices he offered her were not her own. West Timor, go or stay, the baby, all these things belonged to him.

'I'm telling you this, Isabel, because I—'

The room closed in around her and her chest tightened. Her breaths came too frequently and yet not frequently enough. The more air she attempted to take in, the more she felt herself suffocating.

'Dizzy…' she gasped.

Gabriel lay her down on the floor and stroked her head. She stared up at the tin roof, her breathing gradually slowing. But no matter his newfound kindness, she knew she would never love him back.

65

DILI, EAST TIMOR, 4 SEPTEMBER 1999

The town of Dili held its breath as Ava and Dave made their way in silence to the Mahkota. It was Saturday, a working day, but all the shops and offices were closed and the streets barren as East Timor waited.

'People seem to know the result already and what's going to happen,' Ava said.

A car passed them going in the opposite direction. An extended family filled the inside, while suitcases, furniture, a cane basket stuffed with chickens and a live goat either burst out of the boot or were piled on the roof. In other circumstances it might have looked humorous, but today it looked tragic.

'Heading to west Timor I s'pose,' Dave aid.

From around the corner a fast-travelling ute came towards them, its tray piled with militia clutching guns.

'Long barrelled weapons. Jesus,' Ava said, wondering if they were militia, or police or military.

Inside the hotel's plain concrete ballroom, people spoke in hushed tones. Only a handful of media remained in East Timor and they waited, notepads in hand. Sharon had left the day after the ballot for a holiday in

France, appointing Aaron to do her job, and Denise wasn't there either. Her posting had ended a month ago and her replacement, a seasoned middle-aged man who liked partying and local women, stood near the front. UN staff, an American diplomatic colleague and an Indonesian official were the only others there. Dili was a far cry from the bustle of the ballot just five days ago.

The head of UNAMET, Neil Johnston, along with Tom and a few other senior UN officials strode into the room. Ava nodded at them and they back at her.

Neil gazed at the clock. Nine am exactly.

'Good morning everyone,' he said. 'The announcement I'm about to read from the Secretary General of the United Nations is being made simultaneously in New York by him:

On 30 August, in a show of courage and determination, the people of East Timor turned out in massive numbers to vote in the Popular Consultation. I hereby announce that the result of the vote is 94,388, or 21.5 per cent in favour, and 344,580, or 78.5 per cent, against the proposed special autonomy.

Ava calculated the meaning of the numbers—nearly eighty per cent had voted for independence. That was a landslide. How were the Indonesians going to react?

The people of East Timor have thus rejected the proposed special autonomy and expressed their wish for independence. After twenty-four years of conflict, East Timor now stands on the threshold of what we all hope will be a process of orderly and peaceful transition towards independence. Let me assure the people of East Timor that the United Nations will not fail them in guiding East Timor towards independence. [7]

Ava felt the room turn into a mix of joy, righteousness and fear.

'Bloody hell. What a huge loss of face for the Indonesians,' Dave said.

'It worries me too.' Dread sat heavily in the pit of Ava's stomach.

Out of nowhere, a cry for joy erupted. An Australian freelance journalist working in the UNAMET press office was hugging and congratulating every Timorese person in the room. Many appeared uncomfortable and didn't respond, others cried quietly to themselves. Ava frowned. It wouldn't be the freelancer who'd suffer the consequences.

She checked the reaction of her Indonesian diplomatic colleague who stood at the back of the room. Humiliation and disgust were written across his face. He unclipped his phone from his belt and made a call as he stormed out. At the same time, Ava smelt smoke from what she knew must be burning buildings and steeled herself. It had begun.

Tom gathered his papers from the table and as Ava's eyes met his, the corners of their mouths lifted into faint smiles mixed with sadness. What they had between them might always go unrequited.

Ava wrenched herself away from him and ventured outside into the new world of Dili that was already frantic with the business of fight and flight.

66

DILI, 4 SEPTEMBER 1999

Ava got out of the car to the sound of a nail gun clacking ominously like gunfire. A local worker was fixing razor wire along the consulate's boundary wall—not the gentler kind with barbed wire with knots, but the unforgiving version with miniature razors welded on every few centimetres. Although the UN had banned it, they had also put it up around their compound.

'So, what do we know?' Quentin said to the group seated around the large office table inside.

Dave was first to respond. 'UN offices and residences were attacked in three outer districts this morning. A number of Timorese UNAMET staff were killed.'

They paused to take it in.

'In response, UNAMET's evacuating all international and some local staff to Dili, but just from those areas. For now.'

This was the first time the UN hadn't stood its ground. They all knew the death of a foreigner would jeopardise the ongoing commitment of contributing nations, but withdrawal seemed premature to Ava.

'Ava?' Quentin said.

'Three points. First, there's continuous automatic gunfire going off around the UNAMET compound as we speak. Second, *TNI* just warned the head of UNAMET that they are the target now and need to get international staff out, particularly Australians. Lastly, shots were fired at a UN vehicle carrying the electoral commissioners this morning as they crossed the bridge on their way to the airport.'

Craig, the Consul General, shook his head.

'Nev?' Quentin asked.

'We just received advice that *TNI* have formally taken over security from the police. They might be setting the stage for a state of emergency. Apparently the Indonesian foreign minister and chief of defence are on their way to take control.'

Many in the group raised their eyebrows.

It was Craig's turn. 'In terms getting out of East Timor, Merpati's stopping all flights at the end of today or early tomorrow. Given they're the only airline that flies here, if people want to get out after that some other arrangement will need to be put in place.'

Quentin cleared his throat. 'Clearly the situation's deteriorating. This is systematic violence and it's being perpetrated openly by the Indonesians to get foreigners out. The PM won't be happy about any of this, especially after his call to Hidayat yesterday.'

Quentin placed a hand on his chin. 'We should get all Australians out who want to leave. We need numbers so let's compile a list of who's here, where they're staying and who wants to go.'

'I'll manage that,' Craig said.

'At the same time, we have to be careful not to encourage the international community to leave. We don't want to be seen as assisting the Indonesians. Craig, Ava, Dave, we have conference call with UNAMET in half an hour. Then we'll update Canberra and advise them to be ready to evacuate people at short notice. Everyone else, let's meet again with all Australian-based staff at 1600 hours.'

Ava secretly relished the thought of a conference call with UNAMET in which Tom would likely be involved. She went outside to call Juliette and have a cigarette. She needed to tell her some things, she needed to hear her voice, before the situation deteriorated.

The air outside was heavy with black smoke and Ava heard sporadic gunfire. How long before they targeted the consulate to force them out too? She lit her cigarette and dialled home.

'Hello?' Juliette answered and Ava smiled, which she hoped her daughter would pick up from her voice.

'Hi darling, it's Mummy. How are you?'

'Good,' Juliette said, sounding like a disengaged teenager.

'I'm going to be very busy with work soon, so I thought I'd call you now.'

Juliette didn't respond.

'You know, even though I'm here and working all the time, I love you lots and lots.'

More silence.

'I know, Mummy,' Juliette said. Ava wondered if she'd picked up that she was saying goodbye to her, just in case. Perhaps Juliette thought it would be bad luck if she told her she loved her back.

A series of single gunshots rang out from behind the consulate wall and Ava jumped. They were so close by she could smell the gunpowder. She went back inside, mostly out of concern for what Juliette might think.

'Was that guns?' Juliette asked.

'No darling. Just some fence work being done here at the consulate with a pneumatic nail gun. Ask Daddy what that is.' It was half-true, although the worker had already left despite the job being incomplete.

'The Ambassador's calling me. I have to go,' Ava said because the gunfire continuing outside and she didn't want her to worry.

'Okay,' Juliette sighed.

'Do you remember the string that runs between my heart and yours?'

'Yes.'

'Well even though I have to work now, that string is there no matter what, and you can feel my love and hugs whenever you want, whenever you miss me.'

'Yes Mummy.' Ava thought she could hear a smile in her daughter's voice.

'I have to go now.'

'Bye bye, Mummy.'

'Bye Juliette. I miss you. And I love you so much.'

Ava's finger hovered over the red button and she forced herself to press it, her bottom lip wavering. She walked back outside to finish her cigarette, but it had burnt down. The ashtray overflowed with buts from her, Dave and Craig. 'Bloody job. Bloody place,' she muttered.

She lit a new cigarette, and as she inhaled a wave of nicotine calm and energy washed through her. The gunfire had stopped, but instead of feeling relief, she felt alarm, her thoughts running rampant in the ominous silence. What if they launched an assault on the consulate? What if she was hit by a bullet fired by some out-of-control militia or fanatical soldier. All it would take was one random act and she'd be dead. She began to shake.

Her phone rang. It was Pete.

'Why didn't you ask to speak to me? When are you coming home?' he asked.

'I sent you an email earlier saying I don't know. The situation's unpredictable.'

'You mean it's turning to shit?'

His tone cut deeply. She needed smiling Pete, the one who loved and knew her better than anyone to tell her she'd be all right, as though that would make it more believable.

'Tell me everything's going to be okay.' 'I don't know what you're even doing there. You should be here with us, with your family, your daughter. Not putting yourself in danger. You need to come home. Now.'

'But it's my jo—'

'You're a selfish idiot if you stay.'

Ava hung up. She should have known better than to hope for his support. Why did he refuse to understand how important her work was to her, just like his art was to him? Why couldn't he see she was trying to do her best, and not just for herself, but for those who were counting on her?

She dialled Tom's number, the terror that had immobilised her metamorphosing into anger.

'Do you think I'm being a selfish idiot by staying?' she asked him.

'You're doing your job. You're doing something important. You're doing what you need to do.'

'Thank you, Tom. I guess Pete's worried about my safety.'

'Probably. But Ava, I'm glad you're here. Really glad.'

She closed her eyes, certain she could feel him and he her, despite the mounting threat that separated them.

She took a final drag of her cigarette before putting it out. If my time's up, it's up. Not that she truly believed it. She and Tom had unfinished business. She was also an Australian diplomat, and they wouldn't dare touch her and her colleagues, would they?

67

LIQUICA, EAST TIMOR, 4 SEPTEMBER 1999

From behind a large tree trunk, Isabel peered onto the road adjoining the militia post. The ballot result had been announced earlier that day and the air was filling with smoke. Everything of value in Liquica was ablaze—public buildings, homes, cars and crops. Occasional bursts of gunfire startled her. But even more frightening was the sombre procession of people heading to the refugee camps in west Timor. Government organised truck after truck, luridly decorated public vans from west Timor and old local cars edged their way forward. A few weary families marched alongside them, parents carrying children and bits of luggage either on their backs or in wheelbarrows.

The people who'd stayed in Liquica after the massacre had left too. They'd either slipped into the hills or been herded up by the authorities. Gabriel had sent Isabel a message to pack her things and be ready to leave for west Timor later that afternoon too. But did she want to be a militia wife or...?

For the last few days, she'd agonised over her future, eating little, pacing for hours and sleeping fitfully. Even the baby had been restless. Her first option was to pack her bags and go with Gabriel, but that would mean enduring his brutality and never seeing her family again. What sort of a father would he be to their child, anyway? Her second option was to turn to Sebastiao, but would he help, and did she really want help from a man so lacking in courage? Finally, she thought about running away, but where to, and who would help her?

Unable to bear watching the morose travellers any longer, she headed into the bush. Aimless, she let her legs choose her direction. They took her up the road, her hips swinging with the weight of the baby as she climbed the steep hill towards her family home.

She reached the edge of the suburb, heaving and sweating. The burning buildings and smoking shells of homes didn't slow her down. For the first time in months she had purpose. Her breath quickened as she came to a lane, and at the other end, her family's house.

The trees in the front yard were dead, and behind them the house was just a charred shell. Weeds grew along the dirt floor and up the blackened brick remains indicating the destruction wasn't recent.

Isabel's legs gave way and she crumbled to the ground. Tears of disbelief fell onto her belly. She was more alone now than she'd ever been. Why had no one told her—the villagers, Father Ribeiro or Sebastiao? This was the biggest lie of all.

After some time, she picked herself up and dried her face, hoping her legs would transport her to someone who could tell her where her parents were.

She tried one house and no one was home, so she went to another and another until she spied a woman in her side garden hurriedly collecting washing.

'Excuse me, *Senora* Gomes.' Isabel smiled meekly at the neighbour she'd known her entire life. 'Do you know where my family are?'

Mrs Gomes looked at her, eyes wide. She scurried inside, dropping half her washing and slamming the door behind her. Isabel approached the house. 'Please. In the name of God. I need to find my family.'

There was no response so she knocked, quietly at first, then louder.

'Help me. Have mercy, please.'

She persisted until finally the husband opened the door.

'*Senor* Alves.' Isabel dropped to her knees and bent forward to kiss his feet, but he stepped back.

'*Milisi* whore. You'll only bring trouble.'

'Leave!' the wife screeched.

The husband shooed her away as though she was a stray dog. As she backed off Isabel glimpsed their children, who she'd taught at Sunday school. She smiled and the youngest boy smiled back until his mother hustled him away, confusion crossing his face.

Paralysed by her neighbours' cold-heartedness, Isabel looked up at hazy sun and rubbed her tired belly. Where to now?

Perhaps the nuns knew where her parents were. She headed towards the town centre. As she neared their residence, she saw the doors and windows had been barricaded. They were Indonesian and had probably returned home.

She would try Father Ribeiro. There was no response when she knocked on the back door of his new place, but on trying the door discovered it was unlocked. Inside she found Father Ribeiro packing a suitcase in his bedroom.

He looked up and scowled, not bothering to lift his hand for her to kiss his ring. She didn't attempt to prostrate herself either.

'My family are long gone. Please tell me where they are,' she said.

Father Ribeiro sighed loudly. 'I'm busy, girl.'

'Please Father. I have nowhere else to turn.'

'Your family are safe. We had to get them out of Timor Leste. They were a target because...'

She buckled, grabbing hold of a chair. Her family was safe. This was good news. But where?

'Can you help me get out of East Timor to be with my family?'

He closed his suitcase and looked at her. 'Our networks have been destroyed. It's anarchy. Even the lives of the bishops are under threat. I can't do anything for you.'

Father Ribeiro lifted his suitcase off the bed. 'I must go now. It's not safe.' Isabel fell to her knees, blocking his way.

'Father, I don't want to go to west Timor. I don't want to be Gabriel's wife. I beg of you, take me with you.'

'I can't help you. Now go. He mustn't find you here.'

Isabel erupted into gasping sobs. Father Ribeiro reached down, grabbed her arm and pulled her up. He led her to the back door, opened it wide and shoved her outside into the fiery oblivion.

68

LIQUICA, 4 SEPTEMBER 1999

Numb and weary, Isabel headed towards the stream. Now that Gabriel knew her spot, she went upstream and crawled under some bushes where she lay down on a bed of leaves. Craving some respite from the treachery of the outside world, she fell asleep, only to dream of her family, Gabriel, the baby and fire.

A man's voice woke her. '*Hei, menina* Isabel! Are you there?' She stayed silent.

'It's Sebastiao. Where are you?'

She crawled out from her hiding spot.He appeared both annoyed and relieved. 'I've been searching for you all afternoon.' 'I went…home. And then to see Father Ribeiro.' Sebastiao's head dropped. 'Perhaps I should ask you, *maun,* where have you been these last weeks?'

'Gabriel found out I was talking to you. His men beat me up, so I had to leave.' At last he looked up at her. 'But I've come back for you now.'

'Why didn't you tell me about my family?' Her brows knitted together. 'Father Ribeiro said they've been gone for months. Was it because you were afraid I wouldn't give you the information?'

'No *Menina.* It wouldn't have made any differen—'

'At least I'd have known they were safe. At least I'd have understood why they never...'

'That's why I couldn't tell you. I didn't want to take away your hope.'

Isabel cried out with grief. Sebastiao put a hand on her shoulder but she shook it off. When she finished, she straightened up. 'You have to help me find my family, Sebastiao. You have to tell me where they are.'

Sebastiao's face was filled with regret. 'All I know is they're not in East Timor.'

She shook her head, unsure whether to trust him. 'So where am I to go? What am I to do?'

'Gabriel's men will find you here and Dili won't be any better. We have to hide in the mountains. We'll find *Falintil* and they'll protect us til this is over.'

What was this *we* he talked of?

'Then we can get married. Yes, a fresh start for a new Timor Leste—you and me, together.'

'But—'

He grabbed her hand with both of his. 'I'm willing to take you as you are, Isabel.' He hesitated. 'Under one condition. You must give the baby up. The sisters can take care of it.'

Isabel gasped. She didn't want Gabriel's baby, but it was her baby too. Without it, part of her would be forever missing.

'I'm offering you a chance at a new life.'

Isabel's mind whirred. 'Gabriel says there'll be no future for East Timor without Indonesia. Everything will be destroyed and there'll be civil war.'

'He's wrong,' Sebastiao hissed. 'Once the Indonesians and the militia have gone, we'll rebuild East Timor—a new, free, peaceful Timor Leste.' 'But will the Indonesians ever leave us alone? Gabriel said if his side lose, *they'll* wage a guerrilla war here for twenty-four years until they win Timor back.' 'The world won't let that happen. The UN is with us this time.' 'The UN?' Isabel chided. 'They said they'd stand by us, but I don't see them now. All I see is *TNI*, *Kopassus* and the militia. Liquica is burning, and truck after truck is taking our people to west Timor.' 'The independence movement has waited twenty-four years. We have to be patient a little longer. That's what Aleixo says.'

'Aleixo. Where is he right now? And where's his *Falintil*? Where were any of them when I needed them?'

'Come with me Isabel. We need to hurry.'

In his eyes, Isabel saw certainty over his neat solution for her life. Since her kidnapping she'd felt invisible, except for those early meetings by the stream when she believed he cared for her. Now she understood she was no more than a mirror upon which he saw his own reflection, just like Gabriel. He didn't like her, but what he could turn her into. That didn't feel like a basis for a marriage. That didn't feel like love.

'You don't have to make up your mind now,' Sebastiao said. 'We'll get to the safety of the hills and talk some more. Wait here til I get my things back at our usual spot. I won't be long.'

'*Sin*, she said. But while her mouth said yes, her thoughts marched on.

When he was far enough away, she stood. The sun had just set and the bush around her looked eerie in the light of the flames and half-moon. She headed towards the hills, needing some quiet to silence the clamour of voices inside her head—Sebastiao and Gabriel with their ultimatums, her neighbours and their heartless insults, and the padre's cruel news.

In the darkness tall trees loomed, dry scrub scratched her legs and ghostly rocks impeded her way. She picked up her pace, trying not to stumble. But there was no peace in the hills behind Liquica at night. Noises and shadows propelled her forward faster and faster—breaking sticks, darting silhouettes, crying animals, screaming humans. Who was chasing her? An animal? Gabriel? His militia? Sebastiao?

Every tree, every obstacle and sound became a man with a weapon closing in on her until she tripped down the hill, tumbling over herself. And then...there was nothing.

69

DILI, EAST TIMOR, 4 SEPTEMBER 1999

Quentin hoisted himself into the front passenger seat of the four-wheel drive with some difficulty. Nev got in the driver's seat while Ava hopped in the back. Quentin looked ten years older than when Ava arrived in Jakarta. His hair had turned white, his middle had thickened and he hunched slightly as he walked. The stresses of evacuating thousands of Australians during the Jakarta riots, and this ever-deteriorating problem of East Timor seemed to have pushed him into infirmity. During one of their jaunts around Indonesia he'd told Ava that being able to keep up physically was his greatest challenge. For the first time, she felt sorry for the old man in front of her.

One of the *TNI* soldiers guarding the front of the consulate opened the door and got in next to Ava. He wound the window down and rested his large, automatic weapon on the edge. Ava grimaced at the gun, not having been warned they were getting personal protection. She tried to make eye contact with the soldier, but he ignored her. She shuffled as far away as she could, wondering how much protection he would provide if it came to it?

The main road was hectic with activity. *TNI* marched processions of people towards the police station, a succession of government trucks loaded with a hundred people each headed in the direction of west Timor, and groups of armed militia drove around in utes searching for trouble.

Phone calls from Ava's contacts and other Timorese had begun within minutes of the announcement. 'Can you help me and my family get out?' 'My neighbourhood's on fire and we don't know where to go.' 'We're surrounded by militia.' 'Can you get me to the airport? The militia aren't letting any Timorese leave.'

Ava had braced herself before speaking. 'I'm sorry. All I can do is report it to the authorities here and to my government back home who are monitoring the situation closely. The world knows what's going on.' But she knew these platitudes weren't much comfort for people needing urgent action, yet the callers were polite, telling her they understood.

As the day progressed reports of violence poured in, each more horrific than the last. Since Sujati's downfall and the early days of East Timor, Ava had trained herself to expect worsening depravity and was rarely wrong. It allowed her to get on with her work, which was of far greater use to the Timorese than outrage or distress, especially now that most of the media had left. Australia had bear witness to what was taking place here, and that was how she would get them, with her detailed reports providing fodder for Canberra to use in their representations to other nations and in the UN Security Council. Words were all she had.

For now she, Nev, Quentin and their guard were headed to Bishop Basso's house where two and a half thousand people, including three Red Cross international staff, were surrounded by armed militias preparing to attack.

They were only half a kilometre away when Ava received a call from a young Australian–Timorese. 'The militia are trying to kill me,' he whispered breathlessly in a panicked voice. 'Please help me.'

'Where are you?' He gave her a rendezvous point.

'Tell him we'll be there in five minutes,' Quentin said.

Being Australian gave the young man priority over the Timorese and Swiss nationals waiting at the bishop's house. Nev redirected their car but the man was nowhere to be found. Ava called him and he said he'd be there in two minutes. They waited but again he failed to turn up. This time her calls went to voicemail.

By the time they got to Bishop Basso's house it was too late. *TNI* militias were discharging weapons into the air as they herded captives with arms raised in the air onto the beachfront. Ava spotted the Red Cross staff in the melee. They looked terrified.

'SS1s and M16s,' Nev said.

'This is the same beachfront where Timorese were killed en masse in '75,' Ava said.

'Nev, come with me,' said Quentin. 'Ava, you're translating.'

They found a senior officer, a marine, who Ava hoped would help. The marines were better trained and more respected by the Indonesians than other parts of *TNI*.

'Don't go in there,' the marine warned. 'You'll only make things worse and get yourselves killed. I can't—I won't guarantee your safety.'

Quentin nodded. 'Sir,' he said. 'There are internationals in there. They're on official business, protected by your government under an international agreement.'

The marine took some convincing, but he agreed to talk to the militias about freeing the Red Cross staff.

Forty minutes later, the three pale-faced men were brought out and directed to the consulate car. As Nev drove them all away, the three men sighed quietly with relief but remained silent, possibly sharing Ava's fears for the Timorese they'd left behind. The independence war had begun on that beachfront and might end there for some too.

Back at the consulate, Nev checked the car's roof. 'Jeez. We've been shot. It's gone straight through.' He inspected the holes. 'The bullet entered here and exited in that corner…where Quentin sat.'

Quentin's eyes flickered. 'Did anyone notice anything?'

'No,' Ava and Nev said.

'A simple stray then.'

Did Quentin believe this, did she? Surely no one would dare assassinate the Australian Ambassador. Whatever the truth, Quentin had spoken and that was the line they'd use with Canberra. One of them might have been hit, killed even, but through luck, destiny or happenstance, it hadn't happened.

Ava checked herself. She felt no fear but wondered, was it wrong not to worry about what might have happened, or indeed what could happen at any moment? No. In conflict the present moment was all you had, and you held on to it tight.

70

DILI, 4 SEPTEMBER 1999

At 4 pm Ava joined the other consulate staff at the large table on the second floor. Quentin looked to his right. 'Dave. Key points only.'

'There's been a lot of gunfire across Dili, and both Dili and Liquica are on fire. *TNI* are planning a formal evacuation of locals tomorrow and the deputy commander told Nev and I that we should *leave while we can*. Also, the East Timorese *TNI* battalion has split, and the disloyal half are AWOL with weapons.'

Quentin raised his eyebrows, then said, 'Ava.'

'Ten thousand Timorese are holed up at the Dili police station. They, along with government vehicles—ambulances, fire engines, etcetera—will be evacuated tomorrow on Indonesian warships. UNAMET has been under heavy fire for an hour now as has the Portuguese delegation, including their ambassador. According to UNAMET, the Indonesian foreign minister and defence forces chief won't be arriving until tomorrow now.'

Quentin looked surprised by her news, but at which part? Probably the shooting of diplomats, another significant upping of the ante. The Indonesians were deadly serious about getting all foreigners out. It was only a matter of time before they targeted their consulate.

'Also,' Ava continued, '*TNI* and the militias are trying to draw *Falintil* out from their cantonment sites, possibly so they can claim civil war's breaking out. Aleixo's been put back into prison, then placed back into house arrest. Lastly, the bishop is reportedly on his way to Baucau, but numerous Timorese from the beachfront are being shipped to west Timor. Some people were reportedly shot and killed on the beach, but I don't have numbers.'

The room became still, everyone breathing in then exhaling together. Ava hadn't even mentioned the unconfirmed reports of heads on sticks along roadsides, the credible claims of houses burning with bodies inside or the many attacks on church buildings and NGOs. East Timor was in a state of carefully orchestrated mayhem. The place was in the strange netherworld of the Indonesian destruction plan. But how far would they go? The answer flashed through her mind. *Bumihangus*—scorched earth.

'Nev,' Quentin said.

'We have strong indications that *TNI's* plan to control the situation will be effective. I'll be going directly to *TNI* headquarters after this to get more details.'

Nev was more of a fool than Ava had thought. Despite the overflowing cache of evidence, he still chose to believe what *TNI* said because it was impossible for him to imagine that a military charged with defending its own citizens could intentionally target them. Yet they'd been doing so for years, and especially here.

'Craig. You have an update on Canberra's preparations for an evacuation.'

'Yes. I spoke with our illustrious boss in Canberra this morning and she said, 'I suppose I'll have to go into the office then even thought it's the weekend.' Go into the office!'

Ava knew this was strong condemnation coming from Craig, who was usually reserved.

'You need to hear this,' interrupted Jody, a junior army office from

Jakarta. She held up a CB radio with a shaky hand. 'A UN police officer's been shot in Liquica. Deliberately.'

They listened as UN staff in Liquica described to UNAMET headquarters the victim's high velocity gunshot wounds and their efforts to stem the bleeding. He had three in total—one in his belly, another in his chest and one through an arm. The UN staff requested a helicopter rescue, warning they were surrounded by armed and hostile elements. They mentioned the injured cop's name and blood type, and his nationality: American.

'This changes everything,' Quentin said. 'We need to move from wait and see to a full-scale immediate evacuation. Craig, Ava, Dave, let's meet downstairs in five.'

Ava nodded. 'I'll call Greg from the US embassy in case he doesn't know.'

'There might be a positive side. If you can call it that,' Dave said to Ava as she waited for Greg to answer her call. 'Perhaps the Americans will get involved now.'

'They certainly won't like one of their unarmed citizens being shot like this,' she agreed.

After she informed Greg, she took the stairs to the ground floor. The surrounding empty blocks of land were muted by the smoky haze, confirming that large areas of Dili were on fire. Armageddon-scented incense, Dave had termed it earlier that day. An appalling joke, but Ava had laughed heartily because it was sickeningly true.

A loud burst of automatic gunfire rang out nearby. There'd been sporadic shooting earlier, but this went on longer and was even closer. She checked the area below and saw six men dressed as militia creeping towards the consulate walls. They looked professionally trained. She hurried downstairs and found Quentin and the others.

'Did you hear that gunfire?' she asked. 'We did.'

'There are half a dozen men dressed like militia sneaking up on the consulate from the back. There could be more elsewhere.'

'Are there indeed?' Quentin said, not appearing alarmed. Perhaps, like her, he'd been expecting this.

'They're ramping up the intimidation another notch,' Craig said.

'We should black out the windows,' Nev grumped before making his way across the hall to his staff. Within moments they came out with garbage bags and tape.

While garbage bags and tape would make them less visible to those outside after dark, it would also make it impossible for them to see any lurking danger. They'd be an easy mark, Ava thought, like ostriches with their heads stuck in the sand.

71

LIQUICA, EAST TIMOR, 4 SEPTEMBER 1999

When Isabel woke it was still dark. She was wrapped awkwardly around a tree trunk with her spine twisted and one leg caught under the other. The ground underneath her was cold and sticks jabbed at her back. Her skin stung all over, her head thudded and her mouth was dry.

She tried to lift her torso but her belly seized with severe cramps. Turning her head to one side, she vomited. As she lay her head back down on the earth, she saw above through the canopy of trees to where the half-moon hung next to some stars. She trembled as pain wracked her body. Was God looking down on her?

She must have been lying there for a while because her body was damp with moisture from the night. But it was more than that—she was wet. She reached to the inside of her thighs and felt a warm, sticky liquid. Holding her hand under the dappled moonlight, all she could tell was that it was dark in colour. Blood. She rubbed her belly and there was no movement from the baby.

The stinging all over her body intensified. She knew it must be ants. She wiped wherever she could reach, but they were too small and there were too many of them. It was as though she was prey, a wounded animal being eaten alive.

'Off. Off,' she cried frantically at the jungle. 'Off!'

But nobody heeded her distress in the secluded night, least of all the hungry insects. The aching in her head worsened and her belly cramps grew stronger and more frequent, making it even harder for her to focus.

Where were Gabriel and Sebastiao now, who'd each laid claim to her with their different terms. But were their claims born of love? It didn't feel like it. Neither of them had asked her what she wanted.

She rubbed her belly again. Where she'd earlier felt an intrusive presence, there was now an absence—a dead lump. Tears trickled down the side of her face. It had been the only thing keeping her company these last wretched months.

In the roaring stillness Isabel felt her heart labouring. Her breath grew shallow and her body heavy like a great bag of dried rice. She knew she should get up and find help before it was too late, but this didn't translate into action.

'*Mama*,' she called out. 'Help me.'

She gazed up again at the speckled moon. Soon she was dizzy and there was no more waiting for her mother or pain, or wondering about God.

Isabel woke to the sound of Sebastiao's voice and felt his arms cradling her.

'I've been searching for you all night. I thought you... You're so cold.'

Insects buzzed around them and he attempted to shoo them away. Taking out his worn plastic water bottle, he lifted her head. 'Drink,' he whispered, but Isabel couldn't move. He dribbled a little into her mouth.

Placing an arm under her neck and another under her knees he gathered her up.

'Ants,' she said, as she hung limply in his arms.

She lapsed in and out of awareness as he carried her through the jungle, waking again when he lay her down on the bank at their spot by the stream. He ran a wet cloth over her to wipe away what insects he could and then over himself.

'I'm going to get help. I'll be back soon.'

When Sebastiao returned, he hoisted her in his arms again. 'It took me a while, but a coffee truck agreed to take us to Dili.'

The next time she woke, Isabel could feel them hurtling along a road. 'Don't worry my *ipa*,' my sweetheart, he murmured as he cradled her tight. 'We're nearly at the hospital.' But Isabel could feel the warm flow of blood coming from between her legs. She wanted to tell him something, but her thoughts would not make it into words. My baby, she wanted to cry, but the world shut down around her.

72

DILI, EAST TIMOR, 5 SEPTEMBER 1999

As Ava and Dave turned a corner in their SUV, they were hit by the sight of four giant Indonesian warships looming in Dili's small, antiquated harbour. At more than five stories high, they cast shadows over them and at least half a block of houses. Through a side opening, Ava noticed the ship's belly devouring trucks, ambulances, goods and people, many people.

'Fuckin' hell,' Dave said.

'Christ,' Ava gasped at the same time. 'Look at the lines of people and vehicles. This is a massive evacuation.'

'Would have taken months of organisation. The Jasman plan unfolding in front of our very eyes.'

Dave slowed the car as the militia brazenly herded people into the ship's gaping mouth using motorbikes like a drover would dogs with his sheep. Soldiers with automatic weapons observed. What would happen to any independence supporters who boarded? Ava wondered, imagining them being pushed off the deck into the notorious currents of the Ombai Strait.

Her heart raced. Last night she'd slept only five hours, yet today she felt hyper-alert. She'd been ordered to move from the Turismo to the consulate, gladly taking the supply room as her bedroom because it had no windows, making it harder for anyone to shoot her. She'd set up an army cot between rows of metal shelves filled with photocopy toner and reams of paper, and collapsed into a deep, dreamless slumber until the gunfire started. Every half hour it sounded off for five minutes, none of it aimed at the consulate building, but close and regular enough to prevent them from getting proper rest. Every day the Indonesians were upping the pressure on them to leave.

Tom had woken her first thing with a phone call. 'Sorry. Were you asleep?'

'It's okay,' she said.

'I wanted to see how you are.' He sounded tireder than she'd ever heard him.

'I'm fine. How about you?'

'The gunfire and grenades didn't stop all night. We're lucky no one was killed. We're sitting ducks here at the bottom of the hill.'

'Grenades. Shit. Now I know why they housed you in that old school. To have the strategic advantage.'

Tom went quiet.

'Is everything else all right?'

He gulped. 'A big group of locals came over the wall last night—women, kids, babies, old people, the lot. *TNI* spooked them and they thought they were about to be shot.'

Ava pictured the wall. She closed her eyes, knowing what was coming.

'They came over the razor wire. We tried to help them but this girl, only ten years old, got caught. She was cut to shreds.'

Ava imagined the scene. The panic as everyone scrambled over the high wall, the girl becoming ensnared, her screams as she thrashed about in an attempt to free herself, but only entangling and cutting herself deeper.

'I'm so sorry, Tom.'

She heard a loud bang over his phone.

'Are you all right?'

'That was a grenade going off outside the periphery. Been happening all night.'

'Arseholes.' She tried to mask her fear for Tom's safety.

'I have one piece of good news,' he said. 'A baby was born last night. The parents called him UNAMET.'

Ava chuckled. 'There's always a baby born in a crisis here. The same thing happened at the Liquica massacre.'

They laughed and Ava heard automatic gunfire from his end.

'I need a favour,' Tom said. 'The situation here is untenable. We've hardly got any water or food or medical supp—'

'What do you need most?' She wondered why they weren't better prepared. They had military officers acting as advisors.

'Medical supplies—bandages, antiseptic, antibiotics, anything you can get your hands on. We've been out collecting what we can, but I thought with your contacts.'

'I know someone who can help.' She paused. 'Promise you'll be careful, Tom.'

'I will,' he said softly. 'I have unfinished business.'

Ava smiled. Observing the usual proprieties would have been ludicrous against the mounting threats.

She showered and grabbed some coffee before the distress calls began.

Tom called again. 'We just met the Indonesian foreign minister and defence forces chief. Wayudi told us TNI had *taken care of things.*'

Ava's body stiffened. 'How did you respond?'

'Neil detailed the incidents of *TNI* and police complicity in the carnage here, including in the attack on UNAMET in Liquica.'

'I wish I could have seen that.'

'Irawati shouted, 'Those are very serious allegations,' to which Neil said, 'Yes they are. So what are you going to do about it?''

'Did they answer?'

'Of course not.'

'How much longer can they get away with this? How many more people have to die? How many more children need to starve and women get raped?'

'I just wish…' Tom said.

Ava paused. 'Me too.'

73

DILI, 5 SEPTEMBER 1999

The Turismo Hotel looked quiet as Ava and Nev made their way to room two rented by Ian, the foreign correspondent from *The Australian*.

He'd called her ten minutes ago and whispered, 'I'm lying in my bath. The militia are searching my room. Come and get me. Now!'

'We're on our way,' she'd said before informing Craig and grabbing Nev.

They knocked on the door and Ian answered.

'They left a few minutes ago,' he said, shoving clothes and other items into his suitcase. 'Can you take me to the airport? The media gets no protection here. We have absolutely zero rights.'

'I understand,' Ava said.

On their way back from dropping Ian off, Ava asked Nev if he'd mind stopping by the Motael clinic.

'What for?'

'I need to check something. It's pertinent.'

She knocked on the clinic door while he waited in the car. No one answered. She knocked louder and more insistently.

Eventually a nun opened a window and poked her face out. 'Try across the road,' she said.

A French-sounding doctor peered out the door. 'What do you want?'

'Is Dan, the American doctor here?'

'No.'

Ava explained that him she knew him and needed medical supplies.

'I'll get you what I can. But perhaps you can do me a favour too.'

Ava looked at him, her eyebrows raised.

'What blood type are you?'

'A negative.'

'Perfect. Would you donate some blood? I have a patient who urgently needs a transfusion and none of us here are negative.'

'Who's it for?' Ava asked.

'A young Timorese woman. She's a militia...'

'Captive?'

He nodded.

Ava had sent a cable about young women being taken against their will by militia and taken to observation posts where they were forced to cook, dance and become wives of sorts. One day justice might be served, but when was it ever for the women?

'What happened to her?' Ava asked.

'She was escaping into the hills when she rolled down an embankment. She was pregnant. Lost a lot of blood.'

'Who found her?'

'A young man brought her in, but...'

Ava waited.

'I'm not sure whether the girl couldn't have done more.'

Was he questioning her will to live? 'Will she be all right?' Ava asked.

'With hypovolemic and septic shock, she's not just fighting organ damage but a serious infection, and we had to perform a hysterectomy to stem the blood loss.'

'Oh.' Ava was uncertain her blood would do her any good, but it was worth a try.

The doctor showed her to a room and began the process. After a while Nev found her.

'What's going on?' he asked, hands on hips.

Ava explained and he made a show of looking at his watch.

'It won't take much longer.' He left in a huff.

The surgeon returned with some water for her and removed the needle from her arm.

'I took quite a bit from you, so make sure you eat something soon.'

'I'm quite lightheaded. What about the baby?'

The doctor shook his head.

'Do you know which group took her?'

'The leader, I believe. The one with the hair.' He traced his long hair with his hand.

'Gabriel Martinez?'

He nodded and Ava felt herself turn white. Was this the same girl she'd met with the nuns during the massacre investigation?

'I think I know her. Can I see her?'

The surgeon hesitated. 'Just for a minute. She's in the second room on the left.'

Ava found the young woman she'd met with the nuns in Liquica. She looked grey and shrunken. The chart at the end of the bed gave her name as Isabel. A young East Timorese nurse came in and began the transfusion, then left.

'Isabel's my middle name,' Ava whispered to her. 'I'm so sorry you're here. I can only imagine…'

In the privacy of Isabel's infirmary, Ava allowed tears to collect in her eyes, not just for the young woman in front of her, but for all the travesties being endured by the East Timorese. She wouldn't let herself cry. She wouldn't give those bastard Indonesians the satisfaction.

After a few minutes she got up to leave.

'*Selamat jalan, nak.*' Goodbye, my child, she said, reaching her hand out to touch the young woman's. It was clammy and cold like death, and Ava quickly drew hers back.

On her way out, she told the surgeon if he or any of the others wanted to leave, they should do so as soon as possible. 'Merpati isn't putting on any flights after today and it's pretty chaotic out there.' The doctor looked surprised and thanked her.

As she walked down the corridor with the medical supplies for Tom, the nurse who'd given Isabel the transfusion followed her.

'*Missus,*' she said. 'You speak Indonesian?'

'Yes,' Ava nodded.

'I heard what you said to the doctor, *bu*. Can you tell me, are UNAMET leaving?'

'UN staff from the regions have been evacuated to Dili. I'm not sure how many will stay here.'

The nurse looked dismayed. 'Please, can you tell them from me—from all of us. If UNAMET leaves, we will die.'

Ava inhaled, held her gaze and nodded. She opened the door and the smoke overwhelmed her, forcing her to cough. Dili was burning, East Timor was burning. A scorched earth.

———

That night after another evacuation coordination meeting, Quentin called Ava to one side and said, 'You and I will be leaving on the last evacuation plane tomorrow.'

Ava struggled to keep her surprise from her face.

'This is not your post. Your post is Jakarta.'

Her stomach wrenched. *Not her post.* Perhaps she ought to remind him that last year he'd given her no choice but to drop Indonesian politics and take over the East Timor portfolio. Her workload hadn't reduced an iota since the consulate had opened two months ago, and she'd spent much of that time here. While he was technically correct, what else was her job if it wasn't East Timor?

'Look,' Quentin added. 'It's clear this issue matters to you. But Jakarta is our territory and we both have work to do there.'

There was no point arguing. Ava went to her room and closed the door. She called Tom insead.

'But…' His disbelief rendered him silent. 'You can't go. You have the best contacts. You know the place better than anyone. They need you here.'

Despite his protestations, Ava felt a sudden distance grow between them, as though she'd already left.

'Apparently not. I'm so sorry, but I've been ordered onto the last plane out tomorrow. I have no choice.'

Tom went silent and hung up. Ava dangled at the end of the line feeling like a coward, and worse, a traitor.

74

DILI, 6 SEPTEMBER 1999

In the middle of the night, Tom called Ava. Neither of them had been able to sleep, Ava because of the quarter-hourly bursts of automatic gunfire at the consulate's boundary and Tom due to the continuous tracer fire—brightly burning bullets you can see as they head towards their target, he explained—over the UNAMET compound.

Given her imminent departure they avoided discussing the future. Instead they talked about their childhoods. Tom was one of two boys who grew up in a privileged white neighbourhood in Boston where he never felt he belonged, but neither did he feel at home in the black community. She told him how her parents sent her to an alternative school before forcing her into the government system. Yet they refused to let her wear a school uniform for fear of militarism, which made her feel like she didn't belong either. In fact, not long after she arrived, she stood up to a bully of a teacher called Mr Larvis after he beat a boy in front of the class for the offence of frequent whingeing. She paid dearly—had to stay back and do a project instead of going to school camp, and he dropped her marks from straight As to Cs. Yet he failed to break her. His punishments simply confirmed to Ava that she did not belong.

Later that day the two spoke again.

'The UNAMET mission's close to collapse.' Tom's distress was clear in his voice.

The next time they spoke he sounded despondent. 'What's wrong?' she asked.

'I've been chosen to tell the Timorese who climbed the wall that they're not going to be evacuated to Australia. Your government's refusing to accept them.'

Ava gasped. 'I'm so ashamed. No, disgusted.' Their fear of boat people was trumping their humanity. A stupid political decision that didn't reflect the sympathy Australians held towards the Timorese.

'Also,' Tom added, 'without mentioning any names, I found a senior Australian police officer who works for UNAMET shredding documents, including critical reports detailing Indonesia's involvement in the carnage.'

'What the fuck?' she gasped. Had the policeman acted under instruction or of his own volition?

'Don't worry. I've secured the rest.'

The most sinister moment came in the middle of that afternoon. Every hour for three days, three thousand Timorese had crossed the land border into west Timor, many others had escaped to the hills and the consulate's phones had rung off the hook with pleas for help. But at 3pm the phones, streets and harbour—the whole of Dili—went dead. Ava stood by her desk, waiting expectantly for the next call, but it didn't come. Outside the buzz of traffic ceased and there was only silence and smoke. It felt far scarier than all the recent bedlam put together.

By dusk it was time for her and Quentin to leave. They climbed into two vehicles, Ava in the back of one, with Nev driving and Dave in the passenger seat. As they passed the police station set back off the road with its large front turning circle, Ava noticed thousands of people camping in the foreground. Not everyone had left Dili yet. The militia were there too, discharging their guns into the air from their motorbikes as they circled groups of children playing soccer. The children went on playing as though nothing odd was going on. Their homes were burning, people were being evacuated and murdered, but no one watched any more. This was normal— this was East Timor. Ava grimaced.

They approached the long, wide metal bridge where UN vehicles had been shot over the last few days. Ava expected that Nev, who was already speeding, would slow down as civilians walked along either side. Instead he accelerated.

He lost control. Their car veered to the left and hit something. Ava watched in slow motion as a Timorese boy, a teenager, tumbled over the bonnet and hit the ground. Nev quickly regained control and drove on.

Ava drew in air. 'Shouldn't we—'

'No!' came the chorus. She bit her clenched fist and looked into the distance. They spent the rest of the trip in silence.

As they got out of the car, Dave handed Ava a narrow strip of photos printed on fax paper. They were a series of date and time-stamped images of her alone in the office standing by the printer, picking up a document and then reading it.

'What's this?' she asked.

'A keepsake,' Dave smiled.

Ava took them from him, but not for a moment did she believe they were intended as happy memories. They were more like a reminder that everything she did and said was recorded, and that if she felt tempted to talk to the media she should restrain herself. Who the hell did he think he was?

Inside the terminal she called Tom again. 'I'm leaving soon.'

There was a pause.

'Yes.'

'Stay safe.'

'Of course… You too.'

An Australian Special Forces officer signalled to Ava and Quentin it was time to board and she hung up. A group of Australians, the young ones Ava and Dave had warned to leave days ago, were last to board. The militia had surrounded them and Quentin had been forced to ask the police chief himself to directly intervene. Startled and sheepish, the kids refused to have any eye contact with Ava.

The door closed and the plane lifted off. East Timor was now behind Ava.

75

ON A PLANE BETWEEN DILI, EAST TIMOR, AND DARWIN, AUSTRALIA

Darwin was only two hours south of Dili by plane, yet for Ava it might as well have existed in another time or dimension for the stark difference between them. As she sat in the back of a RAAF Hercules mid-air between these two realities, she thought how strange these matters of place, time and history were, and the luck, or misfortune, of one's birth. She had the option of getting on a plane to safety, even if unwillingly, while others didn't.

To her right, rows of people faced each other strapped into seats made of orange webbing. Most were UNAMET staff, and all were police in uniform—multi-coloured thick cotton pants with matching shirts emblazoned with their countries' flags, topped with now-redundant blue UN berets. After the deliberate shooting of the American cop in Liquica, they'd been ordered out of East Timor. Whether this directive came from foreign governments, the UN bureaucracy or both, Ava wasn't sure. These were the last UN police in Timor, and by leaving, UNAMET had broken its promise to protect the people no matter what.

The looks on the faces of the cops around her reflected Ava's thoughts. Male and female, large and small, black, white and Asian, some buried their faces in their hands while others looked blankly ahead, too ashamed to make eye contact. Many had tears leaking down their cheeks and a few sobbed openly. Several shook their heads repeatedly in what appeared to be a mix of disgust and disbelief, but no one spoke. It would have been difficult over the roaring of the plane engines and through their earplugs, but they didn't even try. Ava would have preferred to be in the cockpit with Quentin than endure this guilty dismay.

She, on the other hand, hadn't accepted it was over. East Timor tugged at her. The second the back door had been pulled shut and the tarmac disappeared, part of her had been excised. All she could think about were the helpless people she'd left behind—the sickly child with the stoma and his diligent mother, Abel from the human rights commission, her other *CNRT* and guerrilla contacts, the women who'd told her about being raped and the two hundred thousand people who'd been deported to internment camps in west Timor. Then there was the young woman, Isabel, to whom she'd given blood. Was she still alive? She recalled the words the East Timorese nurse at the clinic had said to her yesterday, *If you leave us here, we will die.*

She wished she could do something other than sit back and reflect, aware that this transition from one place to another gave her too much opportunity to look back. Here on the plane without a role or purpose, who was she?

Tom nudged his way into her thoughts. Would she see him again, would they ever get together? Until now she'd been so certain they were meant to be, but it was his wife who had rights.

As the kilometres grew between her and East Timor, Ava resolved to return. *I will go back,* she said out loud, hoping that by pushing the words past her vocal chords and out of her mouth they would become concrete. Though nothing—not this declaration, not the droning of the plane or the sobs of the police around her—could drown out the collective cry into the abandoned silence of the East Timorese people that rang in her head. The cry of the forsaken.

76

DARWIN, AUSTRALIA, 7 SEPTEMBER 1999

The next morning Ava woke lying on a floor. In the dark, she wasn't sure where she was. Her heart raced as possibilities fired in her head. Was she in the Turismo, her consulate bedroom, in a transit hotel in Bali, back home in Jakarta or…?

Of course. Her heart dropped into her stomach as she felt the carpet beneath her and remembered she was in Darwin. Ergh. Australia.

The faint green light of the alarm clock that read 4.36 am lit up an uneaten pizza, an ashtray full of cigarette butts and a half drunk glass of red wine. Wasting food made her feel ungrateful at the best of times, let alone now when many Timorese were starving. But a quarter of a pizza was all she'd managed last night before exhaustion had gripped her.

As she stood to go to the toilet, a wave of dizziness and nausea hit. She grabbed onto the nearby TV table and stumbled into the bathroom. Kneeling down over the toilet seat, she clutched its rim to steady herself. Every time she thought she'd throw up all she could do was dry retch leaving her with a lingering queasiness. No way was she pregnant, so this could only be, what—pain, exhaustion?

Back in the bedroom, she opened her suitcase to get her bathroom bag.

The stench of smoke from the burning buildings took her back to the chaos of Dili and she coughed, her chest wheezing. She placed all her clothes in the hotel laundry bag, except for a few items that she hung over a chair, and returned to the bathroom, this time putting the light on. How luxurious it was, all marble and unnaturally white towels. She turned the shower on and revelled in the strong hot water. That too reminded her of East Timor because most people there didn't have hot water.

When she'd finished, she lay back down on the bed and stared at the ceiling. What now? She'd called Pete late last night, but Juliette was in bed and it was too early to speak to her now. She pressed Tom's number and waited for several minutes. Finally, she heard a disconnected signal. That couldn't be good. Panic grabbed her chest.

She took a breath and switched back into professional mode and called the DFAT emergency centre. A young sounding man Ava didn't know answered. She told him who she was, hoping she wouldn't have to fight him to get information.

'Can you tell me what's going on?' she asked.

'The Ambassador's heading back to Jakarta this morning.'

'And everyone at the consulate. When are they coming out?'

'We don't know. The Minister wants them to stay.'

Ava gritted her teeth. How much longer was Stretton going to keep them there? They didn't even have guns, although they had a supply of just about everything else.

'Don't worry. They're doing fine,' he said.

Ava rolled her eyes. 'What's the situation in Dili? The phones don't seem to be working.'

'Correct. Power, phones and water have been cut off at the consulate as well as the UNAMET compound, but they're well prepared.'

It was clear the Indonesians were upping the fear campaign another notch. But how far would they go?

'The consulate was shot at from dusk until dawn,' he added. 'But on the plus side, the streets in Dili are much quieter now, except for a bit of looting.' Shooting all night long was a serious escalation. Psywar, psychological warfare, Dave had called it. The Indonesians were trying to wear them down into leaving.

'Just let us know when you want to go back to Jakarta, Ava, and we'll organise everything. Stay in Darwin as long as you need.'

She was touched by the department's uncharacteristic show of consideration. Her annoyance at her junior colleague faded. 'Thanks for the update. I'll let you know about flights.'

Dawn light peaked through the cracks in the curtains. Ava put her shoes on and went outside. She was taken aback by the eerie tranquillity. There was no heavy smoke, just fresh air was and clear blue sky. No people either —no militia, no fleeing Timorese and no *TNI*, no one. The streets were almost empty of vehicles too, just a few parked cars scattered here and there. And the harbour was empty, no daunting warships. But most striking of all was the absence of gunfire. All she could hear was birds tweeting. She'd become so accustomed to the sounds of war that peace felt wrong. She no longer belonged in her home country.

Ava wandered the vacant streets, something she hadn't been able to do for years. In Dili and Jakarta the footpaths were too narrow, broken or crowded, and it wasn't safe to walk alone. She picked up her pace, invigorated by the lack of restraint. Soon, despite her exhaustion and flimsy sandals, she began running. She was alive when so many weren't. She was safe when Tom and Dave weren't.

Faster and faster she went, until her lungs were burning and her feet throbbed. But she continued because others couldn't. The faster she went, the freer she felt—for her and for them—yet she'd give almost anything to be back in Timor to escape this solitary confinement of her liberty.

77

DARWIN, 7 SEPTEMBER 1999

The lunchtime crowd meandered through Darwin's open mall as Ava waited for a UN colleague, a fellow Australian called Ruth, by the fountain. Jets of water spurted through the air reaching high until they fell back down to its mosaic floor. UNAMET staff wandered the mall taking advantage of the UN discounts many shops were offering. All around, lampposts were pasted with bills advertising East Timor rallies. Darwin was in solidarity with the East Timorese, which made Ava feel more at home.

Ruth approached. A welcome familiar face. They hugged.

'Where do you want to eat?' Ruth asked.

'This is my first time in here, so I've no idea.'

'I went to an Italian place around the corner last night?'

Ava shrugged. 'Sounds fine.'

The poorly lit restaurant decorated in dark colours was empty except for a group sitting off to one side in a large circular booth.

'Where shall we sit?' Ava asked.

Ruth looked around the room. 'I know those people. They were based in Liquica. Want to say hello?'

'The ones who were shot at? Sure.'

Ruth introduced Ava to the ten or so members of the Liquica group who insisted they join them. Ava suspected they'd be intruding on their close circle, but Ruth happily sat down. Someone poured them a glass of red wine even though it wasn't yet midday, and they ordered coffee. Ava sat back as they continued their conversations.

Opposite her, an Austrian police officer beseeched several others, tears running down her face. 'But we said we'd stay. We said we'd look after them.'

A Malaysian woman, who Ava recognised as an electoral officer, comforted her. 'It wasn't our decision.'

Another conversation focused on the latest developments on East Timor. 'Surely someone will step in soon?' a UN volunteer said.

'It can't go on like this. It just can't,' agreed another police officer.

The coffee mixed with wine made Ava lightheaded again. She wished she and Ruth had sat by themselves. Dealing with the group's anguish on top of her own was too much. She was thinking of returning to the shelter of her hotel room when a large man with a goatee leant forward and stuck his hand out.

'Hello, I'm Rick,' he said with a booming American accent. 'A cop from Liquica.'

'I'm Ava,' she said shaking his hand. 'I'm an Australian diplomat based in Jakarta. I flew in from Dili last night.'

'Right,' Rick nodded. 'You'll have to excuse us, Ava, but this is the first time we've met up since the attack.'

She nodded.

'So tell me. I've always wanted to know what diplomats do,' Rick smiled. Ava was in no mood for small talk and felt particularly jaded by his loaded question. Yet this was also an opportunity.

'Among other things, we gather information and pass it to our government so they can make informed decisions.'

'Like a spy,' Rick said as though testing her.

'For example, I'd be interested to know your thoughts on how an unarmed American was shot in East Timor and yet there have been no repercussions from your government? I thought you guys looked after your own. I thought by now you'd have sent in the marines.'

Rick drew breath, swapping his insincere smile for indignation. 'It's been covered up so's no one much knows about it back home. *Apparently* none of you dippo types wants to *embarrass* the Indonesians.' Apparently Rick was one of those emphatic, expressive sorts who liked to make a show of things.

Ava turned to Ruth for a second opinion. 'Did you know about this?' 'No,' Ruth frowned. 'What makes you say it's being hushed up?' Ava asked. 'Only that the partial announcement the UN made about the attack happened in a tiny press briefing in Dili nearly twenty-four hours after the fact and to a small group of mainly Australian journos. There were no announcements in New York or elsewhere in the US. There was no condemnation by the UN, or by anyone anywhere for that matter. Nix, nada, nothin'.'

He was right. Ava hadn't seen anything in the media about the incident, which had struck her as being odd. But she'd suspected it was because most journalists had already left Dili.

'So, what actually happened that day?' she asked.

Rick leant in close towards her and Ruth.

'We'd heard rumours about an attack for days. When I look back now I can see the locals knew. They tried to warn us, but you know the Timorese and rumours. You never know what to believe.'

Ava nodded.

'It's ballot day and just in case they're right, we put a lookout up on the roof and line the sides of our cars with bags as, you know, armour. Then the ballot results are announced and the next thing we know our lookout is shouting, 'They're comin'. They're comin'!"

'We're not sure what's happening, but we have a plan and we start making our way to the cars so's to escape. But before we're in, they're on top of us and there's shootin' coming at us from everywhere.'

'I had no idea you were attacked at your post,' Ava said, and she looked at Ruth whose eyebrows were raised.

'Anyways, it was so damn quick that me and Ivana over there got left behind at the house. So I tell her, *Run. Zig zag,* but she doesn't know what that means, so I do a snake motion with my hand and she goes for it. She makes it to one of the cars and I'm not far behind.'

'Who was shooting at you?' Ava asked. 'Did you get a good look at them?'

'Oh, I got a good look at 'em all right.' He sat back and folded his arms. 'It was *TNI*. The Indonesian military.'

'In uniform?'

'Abso-fuckin-lutely. Recognised their faces from the *TNI* post up the road.'

Why had the UN deliberately kept this from Australia and America, from everyone? She narrowed her eyes, resolving there and then to reveal the truth to the world.

'So we're in the cars and we take off. We're driving as fast as we can to get out of there, but those arseholes are close behind, shootin' at us non-stop. So far, the bag lining is doing its job. Then before we know it, we come across an ambush.'

'Where exactly?' Ava asked.

'On the way out towards Dili, just past the *TNI* post.' Rick's hands were shaking. Beads of sweat were collecting on his forehead. '*TNI* was on both sides of the road. And now they begin shooting at us while the other lot's still behind. Somehow, we just keep on driving and make it through and now the ones behind are gone. So we think maybe we're gonna make it, maybe we're gonna get to Dili in one piece.'

Rick looked momentarily off into the distance and back again.

'But now there's another group of soldiers standing on the side of the road. At first we thought, they're some of the good guys—they do exist, you know. Then one of 'em raises his gun and locks and loads. I'm right behind the passenger seat and he looks in my direction, but not at me, at Ed sitting in the front passenger seat. He aims and fires and hits him.' Rick gulped. 'Hits him three times, lookin' him straight in the eye.'

'God,' she and Ruth said simultaneously.

'We're thinking we gotta stop, Ed mightn't make it to Dili. *We* mightn't make it to Dili. Maybe we can call for a heli to come get us. So we have no choice. We go to the police station up the road and ask for help. But the head guy there looks hellish scared. Tries to turn us away but we insist. We tell him he has to help us, he's bound by the UN security agreement. So we carry Ed in on an old door and I seal his lung with a pressure bandage and wrap his arm up tight and all this time we're radioing Dili.'

'I heard some of it,' Ava said.

Rick looked at her. 'Live?'

'The consulate has UN radios, to keep in touch.'

'Right,' he paused, his face briefly softening. 'So then, this militia guy comes in all smug like—runt of a guy, real uptight. He sees Ed and the American flag sewn on his shirt and I swear he turns white as a ghost and begins making calls on his mobile, like real frantic.'

'Damiano da Silva, the head of *Besi Merah Putih*—talks a hundred miles an hour, usually on speed?' Ava said.

'You've had the pleasure,' Rick nodded. 'Anyways, the heli finally arrives and we clamber in. The pilot looks us over and begins doing calculations on a bit of paper and tells us someone has to stay behind. By now *TNI* have arrived at the police station. I volunteer and one of the Africans says he'll stay back with me. But I won't let him. I insist he goes in the heli.

'Now *TNI* begins shootin' at us and me staying behind is looking like a *real* bad option. The pilot asks us all our exact weight and he does another calculation and says he thinks we can get away with all of us.'

Ava heard Ruth breathing easier.

'So we take off, and *TNI* are all lined up in front of the heli waitin' to take us out. But the pilots do this manoeuvre. Instead of taking off in a forward direction like usual, they rear and turn the thing so it twists and goes sideways and up, almost stalling. But it works. It FUCKING WORKS. Those pilots from Lloyds, I swear, they went above and beyond. So we get to Dili and here we are.'

'Wow,' Ava said. 'Neil Johnston told our consul the cars were riddled with bullets, gave us photos even. But he didn't mention the attack on the post or the two ambushes. And he certainly never mentioned *TNI* in uniform.'

Why hadn't Tom told her about this? Did he know? Had he forgotten in all the chaos? Or was something more underhand going on?

'Do you have proof?' Ava asked. 'Photos, videos, bullet casings?'

'Sure do. Ed has the bullets taken from him—two 7.62 by 39 millimetre cartridges, Indonesian special forces issue. You can tell by their batch number. They're the same batch as others we recovered from them before.'

'Do you think he'd be willing to tell his story, on camera I mean?'

'Hell yeah,' Rick almost yelled. 'He's just sittin' in hospital bustin' to get his story out. He's rankled as all hell.'

'Leave it to us,' Ava said, exchanging a conspiratorial look with Ruth before taking Rick and Ed's contact details.

They stood to leave.

'You know,' Rick said, reaching out his hand and grabbing Ava's arm. 'Ed was only in Liquica a couple of days before he was shot, but it was the darndest thing.' He paused. 'He kept saying to me 'You'll look after me if I get hurt, won't you?' It was like he sensed something was gonna to happen to him.'

Ava didn't know what Rick expected of her. Was he making his story feel more personal to pressure her? Diplomacy was often best done on the quiet. Besides, she'd given him his word. She freed her arm and put some money down on the table for their drinks.

Once outside, Ava sighed. 'Phew.'

'You can say that again. And after all that, we didn't end up eating.'

'I know some journos here I can give the story to. They'll get it out. And I'll let Canberra know.'

'And Stephen's still in Darwin. I'm sure he'll do some interviews. He's pretty pissed off at the Indonesians for those death threats against him, so he won't care about New York. He just won't tell them.'

'Great,' Ava said. 'If we get this into the US media and their pollies find out, it'll hopefully result in greater pressure on Indonesia to let peace-keepers in.'

Ruth smiled. 'It has to.'

78

DARWIN, 7 SEPTEMBER 1999

Sitting on her hotel bed, Ava stared at her phone. She was nervous about talking to the media, even if everyone from The Minister and Quentin down used the press when it suited them. She wasn't leaking information, revealing state secrets, or benefitting personally. She was simply directing them towards public information that had been buried. Yet it felt like manipulation and she worried about unforeseen consequences.

Her heart raced as she dialled the *ABC TV* newsroom and asked to speak to a journalist she knew who'd been back and forth to East Timor many times.

'He's on leave,' said the young man. 'He won't be back for a few days.'

She tensed. Her information couldn't wait. Every day that passed, more atrocities were being committed.

'Can I help you with anything?'

'Yes. My name is Ava Vuyk. I'm a diplomat based in Jakarta, and I was evacuated out of Dili last night. I'd like to tell you something—off the record.'

'Okay,' he said casually. 'Let me get a pen.'

'I wonder if you're aware of what really happened in the shooting of the American cop in Liquica?'

She gave him the details, expecting an excited reaction, but he gave nothing away. She was concerned he might not understand the implications and that the story wouldn't make the news.

'The police officer who was shot is in hospital. He's expecting a visit from you,' she added. 'He'll tell you it was *TNI* who shot him. He has the evidence—a bullet taken from his belly that's marked *TNI*.'

She gave him Ed's details and hung up. It was done. The information was in others' hands.

Lying her head down on the bed, the room began to spin. Suddenly Ava understood what it meant to be worried sick. No matter whether she ever went back to East Timor, her posting had altered her. These Timor days would be her reference point for everything to come. They'd be the days against which she'd compare good and bad, and what was important and trivial. They'd be the days against which she'd judge herself and what she did with the rest of her life. She'd seen the violence and horror and courage and splendour of people. She'd watched their struggle for life and truth amid death and evil, yes evil. She'd seen things she could never unsee, knew things she could never un-know, and she would never be the same.

Ava rushed to the toilet, hung her head over the bowl and threw up. With that her queasiness finally left her, yet she didn't feel purged. She lay back down her bed and eventually dozed off, only not to the peaceful sounds of Darwin, but to the remembered sound of shooting. The only way she could sleep was with her gunfire lullabies.

79

DILI, EAST TIMOR, SEPTEMBER 1999

Isabel lay unconscious in a white room. White walls, white tiles, white curtains and white sheets on the stainless steel-framed bed, just like in a hospital. Only this was no hospital. It was a room in an orphanage run by the Silesian nuns in the foothills of Dili. Isabel had been moved here after things became too dangerous at the Dili clinic.

Thin and wasted, her grey skin hung loose, a tube of saline drip feeding into her arm. Her chest rose quickly then fell, pausing a time before rising and falling again. Isabel clung on.

Sebastiao sat by her side, holding her hand and gazing into her still face. She barely looked like Isabel any more. Rather she seemed younger, retreating into childhood, her origins perhaps. Her face showed no more pain or joy or betrayal or hope. It was a face at its most pure and peaceful level—the face of Isabel's soul.

Sebastiao spoke in the hope she'd hear him. 'I'm sorry Isabel,' he said, crying. He moved closer towards her, holding her hand with both of this now. 'I should never have asked you to… If I'd accepted the baby, you wouldn't have run…'

He swallowed, stopping himself from crying. He lay his head down on one side on the bed and closed his eyes.

'Come back to me,' he begged. 'I love you.'

80

DARWIN, AUSTRALIA, SEPTEMBER 1999

The queue to board the plane to Singapore moved slowly.

'Look who it is!' a steward screeched to the man a few places in front of Ava, flapping his hands with glee. 'Well fancy meeting *you* here, Bishop Basso, Sir. A Nobel Laureate!'

The bishop appeared uncomfortable, averting his eyes and shifting from foot to foot. Ava cringed. The man was no film star seeking recognition. He was a creature of misfortune, and right now, as he fled his homeland, it was probably the worst time to be lauding him.

When it was her turn, Ava showed the same steward her boarding pass.

'Thank you Ms Vuyk. Take the business class corridor on the left.'

'Business class?'

'This way,' he indicated.

Ava found her seat on the other side of the aisle from Bishop Basso.

'Botardi, Your Eminence,' she said.

'Botardi, Ava,' he half nodded. It was the first time he'd used her name.

'How are you?' she asked.

'I'm fine, thank you.'

'Where are you flying to?'

'Rome, then Portugal.' He looked away.

So it was true. She'd heard the Pope was furious with him for abandoning his people in their time of greatest need, ordering him to Rome for a reprimand. Yet she had little doubt that had he stayed, he would have been murdered. As it was, she'd learned that getting him out had been an ordeal. When he and other Timorese in danger had attempted to board an Australian evacuation plane in Baucau, they'd been pinned to the ground by rapid gunfire for over four hours.

'And where are you going?' he asked.

'Home to Jakarta,' she said, the word home sticking in her throat. 'Unfortunately there are no direct flights.'

Bishop Basso looked her in the eyes. 'Perhaps you can tell me. Is it true the US has halted military relations with Indonesia?'

'Yes. Pressure is building behind the scenes. Everyone's hopeful a peacekeeping force will be allowed in soon.'

'We can only pray,' he nodded.

Ava buckled herself in, feeling as though she was leaving the Timorese and her colleagues yet further behind. Earlier that day, she and Tom had finally talked by satellite phone. He'd sounded excited. 'Your government's finally agreed to accept the Timorese refugees from the UNAMET compound. That means I'm coming out in a few days.'

'I'm so glad Tom,' she'd laughed. 'I have news too. You probably already know that Dave and the others came out yesterday.'

'Uh huh.'

'Now that they're safe, I'm returning to Jakarta. I'm leaving tonight. There's nothing more for me to do here.'

Tom hesitated, their fate dangling in the silence. 'Of course you must go home. You have important work to do.'

Ava swallowed back tears. 'Before you leave, can you do me a favour?'

'Name it.'

'I donated blood to a young Timorese woman, Isabel, in the rooms opposite the Motael Clinic. I'd really like to know what happened to her. On one of your recces, maybe?'

'I'll do my best.'

Up in the air dinner was served. Ava had barely eaten for days. The food placed in front of her, served on white crockery with a starched napkin and polished cutlery, looked and smelt exquisite. Against her will, her stomach rumbled. If she ate, she'd no longer be in sympathy with the Timorese. She picked up her cutlery and cut her steak. She tried a piece and it was tender, tasting better than anything she'd ever eaten.

After her meal, she settled down in a light alcoholic haze to watch a movie, something feel-good and safe. But an hour in, the hero—a child—died suddenly and unjustly. Ava put her tea down as her eyes threatened tears. Was everything good in life doomed to end in tragedy? Grief welled inside her.

She peeked up and saw the steward pointing out the bishop and her to a female staff member, who threw them a sympathetic smile. Ava abhorred what she saw as pity and leaned forward, pulling her serviette over her face and breaking into sobs. Guttural sounds rose up her throat and her chest heaved. She wasn't only weeping for the genocide being committed in East Timor, but for all the injustices of the world along with the inexcusable way people watched on in silence. She wept too at being forced to leave Dili. What could she possibly achieve in Jakarta? Then there was her return to home life, to Juliette, for whom the ache was so strong she'd pushed her far away, but also to Pete and their impasse.

But more than anything, Ava cried for her loss of faith in humanity and the feeling of defeat that consumed her. Life no longer had order or meaning. Things didn't happen for a reason. Chaos was the only certainty, and above all, life was cruel, with moments of magnificence being gifted only to be stolen away.

She escaped into the bathroom, splashing her face with cold water before searching her carry-on for her makeup. Her hand came across a package. A book she'd bought at the airport for Juliette on Australian spiders. She had a terror of them and Ava hoped that by demystifying them Juliette would feel less scared. But when would she be able to give it to her? Not tonight. She wasn't even in Singapore yet and wouldn't arrive home til after 1 am. The next morning she was unlikely to catch her before school because Juliette left so early, and tomorrow night she was sure to be working late. In all likelihood, she wouldn't get to see Juliette until the weekend, yet she badly needed to see her now. In an uncertain world where people murdered one another, Pete and she slung hurtful words back and forth, and Tom pursued her yet remained catholic in his marriage, Juliette was the only constant. Her complicated daughter was the only thing that felt solid.

Ava remembered her old promise to herself. Despite Juliette's predictable grumpiness, she'd wake her when she got home, give her a cuddle and leave the book on her bedside table with a note filled with hugs and kisses.

For the first time in a long while, Ava smiled.

81

JAKARTA, INDONESIA, SEPTEMBER 1999

In the rear of his new armour-plated, bulletproof BMW, Ava sat beside Quentin. Threats of violence against Australia over East Timor had risen, and she was thankful the vehicle had finally arrived. Just yesterday, she'd returned from a meeting to discover a bomb threat on her answerphone hours after it was meant to go off. But the Australian School hadn't been so lucky. A bomb had exploded one lunchtime, remarkably causing no injuries.

Quentin's driver pushed through the small crowd of activists to get to the British embassy where Aleixo had been staying since his release a couple of days ago. Was the gaggle of young male protesters genuine, or had they been paid to be there by someone powerful with deep pockets and an agenda as per usual?

Inside, a team of Australian immigration officials processed visas for Aleixo's entourage to enter Australia where they'd wait until it was safe to return to East Timor. It had been a week since the ballot announcement, and while the pressure on Indonesia to allow peacekeepers in had mounted, they hadn't yet succumbed.

Ava and Quentin were ushered into the ambassador's office, a plain functional room similar to Quentin's, only a little more homely with its handmade tapestry of an English countryside scene and a few pieces of antique furniture. Julian Bird, the British Ambassador, an unaffected, well-spoken man, sat behind his desk with Aleixo directly opposite. They stood to shake hands with Quentin and Ava.

'I'll leave you to it then,' Julian smiled.

One of Aleixo's advisory staff, an Australian woman called Petra entered and made tea, which she served in Her Majesty's crockery with Arnott's biscuits. The mood was more informal than usual and Petra stayed to translate into Portuguese.

Aleixo looked at Quentin, shrugged his shoulders and raised his palms to the ceiling. He looked tired and worried, but also strangely invigorated, perhaps from his newfound freedom.

'According to the United Nations, East Timor is seventy per cent destroyed,' Aleixo began. 'Nearly thirty per cent of the population has been moved across the border. Over a hundred thousand of them are being forced to stay in camps surrounded by barbed wire and patrolled by men with guns. Another hundred and fifty thousand displaced people remain inside Timor.' Quentin cleared his throat. 'There comes a time when something morally unacceptable and outright wrong happens, and one must act accordingly. That time has come for Australia regarding Indonesia's behaviour in East Timor.'

Ava had never heard such frank talk from Quentin or any other Australian official. The barriers between him and Aleixo, Australia and East Timor, fell before her eyes. It was liberating. She took notes for the usual cable she'd have to write later that day.

'The real problem now is how to save the people who remain in East Timor,' Aleixo said. 'One of my *Falintil* commanders told me that over three hundred children died in his area this week. It's the same all over Timor—much worse than 1976.'

Quentin sipped his tea. 'But what do you think Indonesia's strategy is?' The same old question. Surely he was done playing devil's advocate.

'*TNI* doesn't want to let go of East Timor,' Aleixo said. 'I guaranteed the militias their lives as well as their political and economic interests, but it wasn't enough. *TNI* and the militias want nothing less than to hold on to East Timor—to hold back the tide of change. They tried intimidating the people, but that didn't work. They leaked the evacuation document to force me into agreeing to autonomy without a vote, but it failed. Just now they tried to make it look like the Timorese people rejected the ballot outcome and that's why they fled to west Timor, which is a lie. At the same time, they attempted to draw *Falintil* out of cantonment to make it appear like civil war was causing the problems rather than *TNI*, but *Falintil* wouldn't leave. No one's buying their ploys. Not any more.'

Ava recalled her earlier conversation with Petra. She reported that over satellite phone the senior commander in East Timor had pleaded with Aleixo to allow his starving men, their few remaining weapons and sparse ammunition to defend the people. He and Aleixo had screamed at each other, then finally cried together, each understanding that they mustn't do anything to jeopardise the support of the international community because it was their last and only chance of rescue. Afterwards Aleixo, who was still under house arrest, had smashed up every piece of furniture in the room.

'Can you make your case to the political opposition here in Indonesia?' Quentin asked.

Aleixo shook his head. 'Political parties and the democratic process are new and weak here. But through a business friend I did ask Wayudi to consider allowing a *TNI* contingent to work with a UN peacekeeping force, to avoid a loss of face. Wayudi's the lynch pin in this political game. Everyone needs him and his twenty-eight *TNI* seats in the parliament, and he knows it.'Quentin's interest piqued as did Ava's. This was a real possibility. Aleixo could have been crippled with anger. Instead he'd devised a generous and face-saving way out.

'The *TNI* contingent would include *Falintil* and the militia, real Timorese ones,' Aleixo added. 'I think the militia would go for it too. It's a good opportunity for them. The general could then withdraw *TNI* and we'd soon see how many rogue elements there are as opposed to Indonesian special forces who've infiltrated regular *TNI* and the militia. The police would also be moved out and the Indonesian marines would go in.'

'*Dum vita est, spes est,*' Quentin replied. 'While there is life, there is hope.'

82

JAKARTA, SEPTEMBER 1999

The closer Ava got to actual separation from Pete, the more she also felt drawn back to the safety of their marriage. One night, after eating dinner alone on the back balcony, Ava moved into the lounge where Pete was watching TV.

'Pete,' she said in the kindest voice she could muster.

He looked at her.

'Do you think… Is there any hope?'

Pete had claimed many times he wanted to be with her. But did he really? Was he willing to scrutinise their marriage and himself? He'd always been adamant there was nothing wrong.

Ava gulped her wine down, moved next to him and took his hand. After studying the back of it, something she hadn't done for a long time, she looked him in the eyes, which were enthusiastic, moved her lips up to his and kissed him before they walked, hand in hand, to her bedroom. She tried to put her heart into making love, but it had been so long. She said things to him she wanted to believe, attempting to lay herself open, but none of it felt real. No matter how hard she reached out for him, there was nothing to grasp onto.

Pete pulled away from her and lay in her bed looking at the ceiling. Ava calculated the litany of turning point moments like tonight where he'd withdrawn into himself. She had a sudden suspicion this is what he'd intended all along, to be the one to reject her.

'You could stay,' she said. 'We could try again.'

'Do you remember that old friend of mine Pat, who used to boast about his drug dealing days when we lived in Amsterdam?'

'Sure. He sold…was it cocaine?'

'Yeah, Pat was small time. He used to brag about it non-stop, but I was the one who was dealing for real.

'What?'

'Remember how I used to help deliver sailing boats around the world, moving them from one place to another? I'd bring kilos of coke back. In those days, no one checked small yachts.'

Ava stared at him, her mouth agape. Pete, her husband, the father of her child, had been a drug dealer. Not some desperate, small time user or peddler, but a player. Her world shifted on its axis. A sickening feeling of betrayal hit her. What other secrets was he hiding? Had she ever truly known him? Why was he telling her this now?

Tears seeped from the corners of her eyes and ran down her cheeks. Theirs was a marriage based on lies. But at least she knew what the end of the road felt like and that there was only one clear pathway for her to go down. Perhaps that's what he'd always intended.

83

JAKARTA, SEPTEMBER 1999

The birdlike trill of Ava's mobile phone woke her. It was dark and the clock on her bedside table read 2.30 am. Who'd be calling her at this time?

'Yes,' she answered, seeing an Australian mobile number.

'Hellooo,' a male voice bellowed on the other end of the line. Ava moved her phone away from her ear. 'It's Rick, the Liquica cop. We met in Darwin the other day, talked about Ed. You know, the cop what got shot.' 'I remember.' She hoped he had a good reason for waking her.

'I just had drinks with this American diplomat guy. Matter of fact, he was drowning his sorrows. Said a couple of days ago he sent off a report to Washington that would either, I quote, 'make or break his career'. Said he felt 'compelled to tell the truth' about what happened in Liquica with the shooting and all.'

Ava sat up in bed, searching for pen and paper in her bedside drawer. 'Really?' His information implied that the American diplomat was instructed to hide the truth. Had Australia requested the US be silent on *TNI* and the Indonesian leadership's destructive role in East Timor for fear of threatening Indonesia's fragile transition to democracy? It was very possible. Yet in her opinion, calling out *TNI* in particular on East Timor would weaken their power, paving the way so elected civilians could take control as was normally the case in a democracy. Even Sujati knew *TNI* had become inordinately powerful and had created the modernist Muslim movement *ICMI* as a counter balance.

'Apparently this guy's report, along with some intel material and satellite photos showing the destruction in Timor, ended up in the hands of US President Allen,' Rick continued. 'But listen to this. The guy said that on his way to that APEC meeting in New Zealand, Allen became 'more engaged on East Timor the closer his plane got'. Cool, huh?' 'Wow,' Ava said, unsure what to think. 'That may be why the President made such a strong statement on East Timor today.'

'There's more. Apparently Allen gets to New Zealand and asks his people who his first meeting's with. He cancels it and demands to see the Indonesian representative. The guy, that foreign minister apparently, walks in and Allen bangs his fist on the table and says, 'Nobody shoots Americans, especially unarmed ones. You WILL let peacekeepers in, NOW!'' Ava was uncertain whether Rick's interpretations were accurate, yet they sounded plausible. 'You don't get it, do you?' Rick said. 'This dippo guy, he said the State Department was forced into doing the inquiry 'cause of public pressure. And where d'ya think that came from?' He waited. 'The media attention Ed's shooting got in the US. And that's cause of you! You tipped off, what was it, *ABC TV*, didn't you? It was their report with Ed holding up the bullets taken from him sayin' 'I was shot three times with these bullets by an Indonesian soldier who looked me in my eyes as he pulled the trigger' what ended up all over the American media.'

Until now Ava had wondered if the story simply disappeared. 'I don't know what to say. Except that's the reaction I expected from the US all along. I hope it means peacekeepers go in soon.'

'I knew you meant what you said. I knew you'd get the story out.'

'Thanks for letting me know, Rick. It means a lot.'

'No. Thank you,' he said.

She lay back down on the bed, grinning at the faintly lit ceiling. What a wondrous world it was where a one-minute Australian news story could snowball into something greater. East Timor had been in mayhem for ten continuous days now, but that might end soon, possibly encouraged by the story she'd given to the media.

She closed her eyes and felt more hope for Timor—for humanity—than she had for a long time.

————

Ava sat next to Juliette on their lounge room settee, waiting expectantly for a press conference to begin on the TV. President Hidayat had assembled the world's media in his palace to make an important announcement on East Timor.

'We're watching history being made here,' she said to Juliette, who nodded earnestly.

Hidayat moved up to the podium, clearing his throat. The TV cameras began rolling and flashes lit the hall. Ava had her pen at the ready:

I have taken the decision to inform the United Nations Secretary-General to invite international peacekeeping forces, together with the Indonesian military, to restore security to East Timor, and peace and safety to the population, and to enact the ballot result. [8]

'Yes!' Ava hooted, jumping off the couch into the air before grabbing Juliette's hands and leading her in a quick dance around the room. Juliette looked confused, then amused as she joined in, throwing her head back and laughing.

'You were there a lot, weren't you Mummy? You helped people.'

Ava smiled. 'I did what I could, darling. I tried to help people, even though there were...challenges.'

They sat down and Ava listened to the rest of the speech as Juliette resumed colouring in, snacking on her almonds and sultanas. What did

Hidayat mean by peacekeepers restoring order together with *TNI*? From the cable traffic, it was clear *TNI* wouldn't be staying behind to work with UN forces. In fact, they'd be made to leave immediately. Perhaps Indonesia was face saving again. Inviting international troops into East Timor was a public admission of their failure to bring about order, even though the world understood that Indonesia itself was the behind the disorder.

It would be days before the Australian-led UN forces entered East Timor. But today's announcement was something to hold on to. If only *TNI* and their militia henchmen could restrain themselves in the meantime, although it was more likely they'd indulge in one more revenge-seeking binge before they finally let go of what was left of East Timor.

———

That night Tom called Ava. They'd spoken every day since he'd left Dili, often more than once, yet neither of them had broached the topic of the future.

'I have news,' he said. 'I'm coming to Jakarta to be the UN's representative for East Timor. I'll stay until the peacekeeping mission settles in, maybe longer.'

Ava read between the lines and smiled, noting that until now he hadn't mentioned this possibility. 'That's amazing. Congratulations.'

'I'll be there in two days. I'm arriving in the afternoon, so how about dinner?'

'Okay. I'll book something. There's a new restaurant in one of the big hotels. Do you like French food?'

'I do,' he laughed. 'But anywhere is fine if it's with you.'

Ava bit her bottom lip to stem the ridiculous smile that threatened to turn her back into a teenager. But then the doubts. Should she? What about the wife? Would she anyway?

84

JAKARTA, SEPTEMBER 1999

So much had transpired in the two weeks since Ava had seen Tom on the eve of the ballot when they'd consumed wine and oysters under an unknown sky, that it felt to Ava more like two months. She walked through the marble hotel lobby into the modern-looking French restaurant where Tom was seated. On seeing her, he stood and smiled like a coy adolescent. Ava smiled back, equally bashful. The dance had begun.

'How are you?' she asked as they kissed each other's cheeks before sitting down.

Tom leaned forward with his elbows on the table and clasped his hands together, tilting his head slightly and looking her into her eyes. 'I'm glad to be here.' 'I'm glad you're here.'

They were content, for now, to take each other in. 'We missed each other in Darwin,' Tom said. 'By two days.'

'A pity.'

'Good news about the peacekeepers though.'

'At last.'

They ordered some wine and Ava asked the waiter if snails were on the menu.

'You like snails?' Tom asked.

'I do. And you?'

'I love them.'

Ava added snails to her long list of things they had in common.

'Let's share some,' he said.

When they returned to the topic of East Timor, Tom shifted in his seat.

'Is something on your mind?' Ava asked.

He looked down and sighed. 'Did you know there are questions being asked about the UN's decision to hold the vote given the poor security environment?' 'No,' she said, frowning.

'Even Aleixo's saying he relied on the UN to determine whether it should go ahead or not.'

'He's only trying to deflect the blame away from himself. You and I both know that whenever the UN or Australia—and I'm betting Portugal too—asked him whether he wanted the ballot to go ahead, he said, 'It's better to do so than not.' I know he wanted peacekeepers, we all did, but that just wasn't possible—not until the Indonesians shot a cop and the US put its foot down.' Tom grimaced. 'But I drafted the UN security annex. I thought it would be enough to make the Indonesians behave, but it wasn't. Not by a long shot.' He seemed diminished.

Ava felt for him, but was equally proud he had a conscience. She moved her hand closer towards his in the middle of the table. 'Anyone who knows Indonesia could have told you no UN document was going to be sufficient. It's not your fault they didn't live up to their part of the agreement. They never intended to. East Timor got caught up in the post-Sujati power struggle—it's as simple and complex as that. Most Timorese said they wanted the ballot to go ahead despite what they *knew* was going to happen.'

Restraining herself from grabbing Tom's had was proving difficult.

'Maybe, but I still can't help but feel responsible.' He half smiled at her. 'It's good you're here. I don't know what I'd do if I didn't have you to talk to.'

Tom moved his hand so it touched hers. A current travelled up her arm into her chest and she broke out in goose bumps.

'There's something else,' Tom said, looking into the distance. 'Did you hear about Simao?'

'Petra told me the militia captured him on one of those Indonesian warships going to Kupang and tortured him to death.'

Ava recalled a night last year when she'd bumped into Simao in the Turismo's beer garden. He'd told her over a drink about the murder of the Balibo five, claiming the militia's figurehead still had one of their cameras in his cellar as a keepsake he loved to boast about. Once a guerrilla, Simao seemed a gentle man now, and proved to be one of her best contacts.

'They cut his legs off,' Tom said, drawing his hand away from hers.

'Petra told me that too.'

'But what you may not know is that he came to me for advice.' Tom swallowed hard. 'He asked me where I thought he should go, and I told him to get on one of those warships.'

Ava closed her eyes. She could think of nothing to say to salve Tom's guilt. She would never have advised a high-profile independence target to get on an Indonesian vehicle, especially a ship where there was nowhere to hide. Obviously Tom still didn't understand the Indonesians.

She opened her eyes again. 'You weren't to know what they'd do, Tom. And anything could have happened to him if he'd stayed back.'

Tom nodded into the serviette he gripped with his hands.

'Did you know Father Albrecht?' she asked.

He shook his head, appearing distant.

'He was a Jesuit priest. A real intellectual and a nice man. He was walking down the street a few nights ago when *TNI* ordered him to stop. But he's mostly deaf so he didn't hear them and kept walking. They believed he'd failed to stop so one of the soldiers shot him in the back. Just like that. So the point is, it's crazy in Timor, and you're not to blame for that.'

Tom attempted a smile of gratitude.

'Did you find anything out about Isabel?' she asked.

'I tried but there was no one at the clinic. Dili's pretty much empty now.'

A waiter placed their snails and a basket of warmed, crusty French bread on the table. The small snails were slathered in butter and garlic. It was so different to Indonesian food that Ava relished the change.

'Enough of all that. Let's eat,' Tom said.

When they'd finished, he looked up at her. 'How are things with you and Pete?'

Ava sat back. 'We need to separate. The irony is that after five years of me trying to get him to couples counselling, he suddenly wants to go. But it's too late for me.' She looked away to hide her sorrow at Pete's revelation, his final betrayal.

Tom put his hand under her chin, gently pulled her face around, and for a moment she thought he was going to kiss her on the lips. Instead he kissed her on the cheek and she blushed.

'How's Nancy going?'

'She's glad I'm out of Dili. But I have to admit, I feel distant from her. We don't have much to talk about any more, apart from buying our apartment and practical things like that. This is where my life is now.'

'You're buying an apartment?'

'It's part of our plan,' he said.

'That's a big commitment. How long are you staying in Jakarta then?' 'I'm not sure. Our parents are pressuring us. They want a grandchild.'

Once again, Ava was at a loss to understand how he allowed his life to move ahead without him. She was more confused than ever at his mixed yet increasingly strong signals towards her. Part of her wondered if she should run a mile before things got more complicated. She knew she wouldn't.

'You'd be a good father,' she said. 'Children are the most difficult, self-less and rewarding thing you can do. They make you grow up, but give you an excuse to behave like a kid again.' 'Things have always come easily for me,' Tom said with what looked like regret. 'I've never had to struggle for anything. Nancy's the same. But I'm beginning to realise, I don't feel the things I want to feel for her. Perhaps I want to fight for something.' Ava stared at him, attempting to grasp the meaning beneath his words.

'There's no passion between her and me. And to be honest, I don't think I even knew what that was until… I'm just now becoming aware of greater possibilities.'

Their mains arrived and they ate slowly, sharing their plates. Food was now a privilege for Ava, and she didn't take a single mouthful for granted.

'Shall we go?' Tom said after they had some tea.

In the taxi, Tom held her hand and squeezed it, which Ava took as a promise of things to come. He unlocked the front door of his apartment and stepped inside. Turning to face her, he took her hands and gently pulled her inside over a threshold. There he held her face and kissed her on the lips, long and deep. Like him, Ava kept her eyes open, savouring every moment. They began pulling at each other's clothes.

Tom faltered. 'I need a moment. I've only been with one person for a long time.' He turned and went into the bathroom. 'I'll be in the bedroom,' Ava said, mentally preparing for him to change his mind. It wasn't too late for her to change hers either. He was buying a house and talking about having children, yet her heart trusted what she felt between them.

Tom walked into the room. He'd already taken off his shirt and pants and now stepped out of his boxer shorts.

Ava drew in breath, not at his beautiful body or what was about to happen, rather at how exposed he'd made himself as she lay fully clothed. He got onto the bed next to her, kissed her on the mouth and began undressing her.

'You and I have been unfaithful for some time now,' he said. 'Perhaps since that first day. I wanted to take you out the back and do things to you there and then.'

'At the bishop's house?' she giggled.

He nodded and in a moment they were immersed in each other's skin. Like a ballet, they fit together with the grace and flow of a couple who'd danced with one another for most of their lives. Coming together and pulling apart, lifting and falling, letting go and catching, reluctance and willingness, sweat and tenderness, and an almost unbearable rawness. As agonising and nightmarish as these last months had been, tonight was exquisite and otherworldly.

'I love you, Ava,' Tom said. 'I have since that first day.'

'I know,' she said, almost choking on tears. 'I love you too. I always have.'

85

JAKARTA, SEPTEMBER 1999

These are the things Ava held on to. Love would triumph, and she and Tom would end up together because it was inevitable. Why else would everything have led them to this point? Why else would their extraordinary love exist? As for Pete and Nancy, she and Tom had been too young when they committed, too lacking in themselves to realise greater possibilities existed.

Also, good would triumph in East Timor. The peacekeepers would go in, calm would be restored and, with the help of the international community, the people would rebuild their lives. Order always won out in the end. Yes there had been pain and dying, but new life would emerge. Of course there would be in-fighting in the new country, but things would settle. All of Ava's work, the way she'd pushed herself hour after day after month, but most of all, the truths she'd told—her gift to others—would be justified. In the new world, such values would occupy a place of importance.

She turned off the tap in Tom's ensuite shower, dried herself and picked up something of Tom's to put on. His apartment was sparsely furnished but always messy. His bed was never made, their clothes were permanently strewn across the floor and dirty crockery inhabited the free surfaces. But neither of them held any concern for such things now. When they weren't at work they only had time to make love, or occasionally, like this after-noon, to cook. Tom was making tomato sauce for pasta. Ava pulled herself up onto the kitchen bench dressed only in his shorts.

'I don't do this with my wife,' he smiled. 'We've never walked around naked or had sex in every room of the house six times a day. We're all elbows and knees in bed, which only happened once every—'

'I suspect you've led a somewhat protected life,' Ava said, not wishing for more detail.

'I didn't realise *this* was even possible.' He looked at her longingly. 'I imagined it was, but not that I'd meet the right person.'

Tom was about to say something further when his mobile rang. Both of them saw who it was, and he looked her in the eyes. She picked it up, he nodded, and she pressed answer.

'Hello, Tom Quayle's phone.'

Ava heard breathing, a woman's, and then she hung up. A few minutes later his phone rang again and this time Tom answered. He left the room for a few minutes.

'You wanted her to know about me,' Ava said.

'I'm not ashamed about us and I never will be. She wanted to talk about the house purchase.'

'Did she ask who I was?'

'No,' he said stirring the sauce. 'She also said she's going on hormones.'

'So you're going back soon?'

'I don't know what I'm doing.'

Normally Ava would have fumed at being strung along like this. But after everything she and Tom had been through, the present felt all impor-tant. Or perhaps she simply loved him so much that any time they spent together meant more to her than all her years of marriage. Was she a fool?

Tom looked at her. 'I only know I love you.'

86

JAKARTA, SEPTEMBER 1999

Today was the twentieth of September, the day the Australian-led peace-keeping force, INTERFET, short for International Force for East Timor, was being inserted into East Timor. Ava believed it deserved a worldwide fanfare, a visible swelling of the force field, or at least a private celebration as the contingent of nearly six thousand soldiers from twenty-two countries went in. The wait had been excruciating, and even though the troops' arrival would initially be into Dili only, she wanted to share with someone her surging relief and satisfaction. She checked the cable system and found nothing—she was no longer part of the main effort. There was nothing about it yet in open sources either. She'd have to wait for the Australian TV news that night like everyone else.

At around six a colleague from the economic section poked his head into her office.

'Ava,' Oliver said, appearing embarrassed. 'I went to the toilet just now, and when I got back to my office I found...' He swallowed and opened his hand to show her a bullet. 'This was on the floor. My window's cracked too.'

It took a few moments to register what had happened. Ava wasn't shocked that *TNI* would try something like this, the petulant child that it was. If it wasn't so calculated, she might have been scared.

'Let's check your room,' she said.

She ran her fingers across the hole in his window and the web of shattered glass radiating outwards. She followed the line of fire and saw a pedestrian bridge and sneered.

'It definitely entered here. It was probably fired from that bridge over there.'

She picked up Oliver's landline and dialled the defence section. Nev was still in East Timor and the navy attaché answered, quickly arriving in the room.

'It's a *TNI* issued sniper's bullet,' he said. 'Probably fired from that overpass there.'

'I suspect they did this because INTERFET went into East Timor today,' Ava said. 'I'll let Quentin know. This needs to be formally recorded and investigated.' She already knew that nothing would come of it.

Oliver's face turned white, the reality of it hitting him.

'If they wanted to hurt you, or any of us, they would have,' Ava said. 'We all have window offices and they waited until you were out of the room.'

Oliver nodded. 'Yes, of course.'

'Maybe it's time to go home?' she suggested and he nodded.

As she walked back to her office, Ava considered how commonplace it felt to be shot at and harried by protesters. Yet something about this incident got to her. Under the UN convention, and this being an embassy equivalent to Australian soil, *TNI* was supposed to protect them. Indignation rose. She'd considered herself immune to the Indonesians, but now their impervious childishness and flagrant debauchery caused her suppressed emotions to bubble to the surface. She wanted to run out and hunt down the pathetic sniper, and scream at him like the incensed savage she was inside.

She inhaled deeply. No, she wouldn't let them ruin today. She wouldn't *become* them. She pictured peacekeepers in East Timor capturing militia, shooing wayward *TNI* away like the pretend soldiers they were, and her body gradually relaxed.

After driving to Tom's apartment, they sat together on his couch as the Australian news came on. East Timor was the only story that night. Wave after wave of heavily armed Australian, New Zealand and Ghurkha soldiers poured out of landing craft onto the beaches holding large rifles and machine guns, and began taking Dili. Building by building and street by street they surrounded the largely destroyed structures before clearing them of hostile elements and moving onto the next.

'That's *TNI*'s barracks,' Tom said with wide eyes.

'There's the governor's office,' Ava added from the edge of the couch as they watched Australian peacekeepers disarm militia and handcuff them with cable ties. 'They don't look so brave now, do they? And look how puny they are compared to real soldiers.'

Next they saw Australian soldiers persuade *TNI* to put their weapons down and retreat. Shots rang out in the background, but there were no accompanying visuals.

'*TNI* resistance?' Ava said. 'Nev's over there trying to smooth the waters so there's no INTERFET–*TNI* contact.'

'It wouldn't surprise me if there was. You can see by *TNI's* faces how unhappy they are.'

'They look humiliated. And I'm ashamed to say—or perhaps not—how completely gratified that makes me feel.'

They watched the entire half hour bulletin.

'I still can't get the pictures out of my head of what must be going on in the districts,' Ava said. 'It'll be weeks before INTERFET get out there.'

'At least they're in,' Tom said.

'Did I tell you what Aleixo said to Quentin at our last meeting?'

'No.'

'Have you heard about the Indonesians cancelling our mutual security treaty?'

'Yes.'

'Aleixo told Quentin not to worry about our relationship with Indonesia. He said, 'You used to be great friends, but they thought they could walk all over you. You're no longer friends, but now they know they can't get away with anything.''

'Ha.'

'Then Aleixo said, and I love this comment, 'I think it's better to be respected than liked by the Indonesians, don't you?''

———

Two days later on her way to a meeting Ava got a call from Sakti, Denise's former assistant who now worked for the new *SMH* correspondent.

'Sakti?' Ava said. 'How are you?'

'Oh, God.' Sakti was breathless. 'They found him, his body. He went missing, and we were worried, and we prayed and prayed but INTERFET found him this morning.'

'Found who?' Ava asked, closing her eyes to prepare herself. She must know who it was or Sakti wouldn't have rung.

'Hugo. Hugo Vossen.'

'Oh no. No.' Ava lowered her head.

Hugo was a close friend of Denise and Sharon's, a financial journalist who knew little about East Timor or conflict journalism. Only a few weeks ago, Quentin had asked her to brief him on East Timor.

'What happened?'

'INTERFET told us not to leave the barracks, but he went anyway. He was checking things out on the back of a motorbike taxi when they came across a roadblock. Two *TNI* soldiers attacked and shot him as he tried to get away. The driver, a local, escaped, but saw the whole thing. They injured Hugo first, then shot him at close range. In the back.'

'In cold blood,' Ava said, her jaws tightening. 'Cowards.'

'There's more,' Sakti said, breathing heavily. Ava steeled herself.

'One of his ears is missing. We don't know if a dog…you know, but INTERFET think it was…'

'Trophied,' Ava said, attempting to push the image of soldiers hacking it off from her mind.

'When will this end?'

'Surely soon.'

The part of Ava that needed to take back some control and do something stepped in.

'Sorry to ask, but which ear? And do you have the name of the taxi driver?'

Sakti filled her in.

'Does the Dutch Embassy know?'

'I haven't told them.'

'I'm going call them and let the Australian government know. Ok? But before I do, are you all right, Sakti? Are you safe?'

'Yes. We're doing exactly what INTERFET says. God bless you, Ava.'

'You too. Just promise me you won't take any unnecessary risks.'

Ava looked out of her window at the protesters below who were preparing to burn another Australian flag. 'Cold blooded butchers,' she murmured, picking up her phone.

'Wim. I have some bad news.' She gave her Dutch colleague the details of Hugo's murder.

'No, I wasn't,' Wim replied with no emotion.

Ava asked her driver to return to the embassy and postponed her meeting. In her notebook she began penning a cable:

We received a call from … who informed us that local East Timorese driver, Fransisco da Rosa, witnessed two TNI soldiers attack and shoot an unarmed foreign national, Dutch journalist … The two were riding on a motorbike taxi through Becora when they hit a TNI roadblock.

The soldiers reportedly shot Vossen, injuring him. As he attempted to escape, they shot him in the back, killing him. It was possible they also desecrated his body as his left ear was missing and his face was cut. We have informed the Dutch embassy.

Back in her office, Ava made some calls and wrote it up, adding that the Australian forces were reportedly assisting with the repatriation of Hugo's body and that so far there'd been no public reaction from Indonesia, including whether they intended to investigate the matter. Even if they did, Ava already knew they'd never prosecute. It would become one of those issues raised at every bilateral meeting to no avail.

She sat back in her chair, numb with suppressed exasperation. Soon she would need to vent, but in a controlled way—she would scream into her pillow at bedtime or in her car as she drove through the empty streets late at night, or sob in the shower before bed, or frantically pedal her exercise bike to a place faraway from this godforsaken hellhole.

87

DILI, EAST TIMOR, SEPTEMBER 1999

Just before the dawn, Sebastiao sat slumped in a chair in the corner of Isabel's orphanage room. He slept as she lay between the clean sheets on a bed. Despite the destruction of the local water system and shortage of supplies, the nuns had kept Isabel alive. But she looked even thinner and greyer than before, like a wizened old person whose life had all but left her. She hadn't regained consciousness, but Sebastiao refused to leave her side.

He woke in fright to a sudden commotion outside. Trucks were pulling up and people were decamping. He heard men's voices and then the nun's. Was this *TNI* and the militias on one last homicidal rampage ahead of the peacekeeping forces? He checked Isabel, saw that she hadn't moved and stepped out of the room.

Sebastiao joined a group of nuns and orphans at a window at the front of the building. The soldiers outside weren't *TNI*. They were foreigners, mostly white men, but some dark-skinned, Chinese-looking ones, and some women soldiers too. They'd surrounded the orphanage.

The head sister cleared her throat and moved to the front door while a few nuns ushered the children to a middle room. Clutching a piece of white cloth, she pulled the front door open and waved her fragment of fabric high in the air.

Through a local translator, one of the soldiers ordered her to approach. She stepped forward and stopped where they told her. A soldier approached and the two spoke until the head sister turned back towards the house and ordered everyone to come out. The nuns slowly brought the children out who were sobbing with fear. The soldiers grouped them together and a translator attempted to reassure them they were safe.

Sebastiao didn't join them. He rushed back to Isabel's room, got down on his knees and began praying aloud. He held one of Isabel's hands, hoping she might sense his urgency and wake up.

But something in her changed. She stopped breathing. Sebastiao lifted his head and held his breath as he listened for her to draw in air.

'Breathe *mana*. Breathe.'

The door to Isabel's room burst open. Two soldiers pointed their rifles at him.

'On the floor,' they yelled.

'No *milisi*,' Sebastiao said, shaking his head as he lowered himself down.

'Hands on your head. Spread your legs,' they shouted.

'Isabel. Isabel. She's dying!' he said in his language.

The soldiers would not be distracted. They searched him and escorted him out of the room. As he left, Sebastiao heard Isabel gasp.

'*Deskulpa*, Isabel,' he said behind him. Sorry.

Inside her sick room, Isabel lay alone as a soldier stood guard at the door. A captain wearing a bright safety vest with MEDICAL written on it and a red cross on her arm entered. She put her bag down beside Isabel's bed.

'She's breathing,' she said to the guard. 'But only just.' The paramedic checked her over, feeling her pulse and palpating her swollen belly.

By now the gaps between Isabel's breaths were longer. The paramedic stood over her as Isabel took a breath and quickly let it out. There was a pause and the paramedic checked her pulse again. Isabel took another deep breath in and out, and this time there was an even longer pause. Finally, Isabel took an even deeper breath in then out, her face tightened and contorted and then went slack.

The paramedic tried her best to revive Isabel, but it was a short and rudimentary attempt.

'Too late. She was too ill,' she said to the guard as she packed up her bag.

The paramedic left the room, closing the door behind her. At last Isabel was liberated.

88

JAKARTA, INDONESIA, OCTOBER 1999

Tom and Ava drank herbal tea in his fourteenth-floor apartment overlooking Jakarta's lights, their bare feet wrapping around each other's on the floor. It was late and they'd just finished work. They'd known each for five months and been together for a few weeks, yet Ava's feelings ran deep.

Was this due to the intensity of their time together—living days in hours, weeks in days and years in months? Were their feelings a repudiation of the bloodshed that had coloured their time together—an affirmation of life as dissent? Or was she being perverse, attracted only to the wrong types of men—the non-committed inventors and married ones?

No, Ava thought, filtering out the noise of other's opinions and her own doubt. Their bond was greater than that. They were binary—deficient when separate, complete when together. They would have found and loved each other no matter the time, place or context.

'I have news,' Tom said.

'Oh?' she said dreamily.

'You're not going to like it.'

He stood up, looking nervous, which snapped her back to attention.

'Aleixo's coming to Jakarta in six weeks' time on an official visit,' he paused. 'And I'm organising it.'

'That's amazing. Only a couple of months ago he was a political prisoner here and now he's returning on a state visit.'

'What I'm saying is—'

'You'll be even busier than you are now.'

Tom sighed, running both hands through his hair and Ava looked at him with pained resignation.

'Right now, I hate Aleixo for stealing my time away from you.' He sat next to her, holding her hand in both of his. 'Move in with me so we can spend as much time together as possible.'

Ava opened her mouth to say something, but stopped short. What exactly did he mean? And what about Juliette?

'There's another reason I want you to move in.' Tom looked away and down. Ava liked the look of this even less.

'After Aleixo's visit, I'm going back to New York.'

She closed her eyes to take in his words, but perhaps she wanted to shut him out too. In that moment he'd transformed from being her redemption to raining pain down on her. Her sensible mind wasn't surprised that Tom needed to be sure about his marriage before ending it. But her heart, which he'd coaxed out and demanded she give to him fully, felt like he'd struck her hard.

'My family, my beliefs. They're telling me I need to go back and try. But the way I feel about you, it's…'

Ava's eyes bored into his, seeking a more believable explanation. How could he go back to his wife given what they had?

'Why did you pursue me Tom—and you did pursue me hard—if you were happy with your marriage? Why, when you were always going to return to your wife?' She spat the words at him in a raised voice, inciting an argument so she could hate him. Hatred held at bay the pain that threatened to overwhelm her.

'I couldn't not pursue you, Ava,' he answered, looking at her with such tender sorrow that her resentment fell away. Bitterness wasn't what they were about. They were about love. It was as simple and honest as that. Compared to their love, his marriage and work were inconsequential. Had they not each declared that no matter what happened, it would be a comfort as they lay on their deathbeds to have experienced such love once in their lifetimes? Pity rose in her for the way Tom was allowing his family to prevent him from realising his other, truer self.

She walked to the window, her back to him. 'Well I have news too.' She turned to face him. 'I've been envious of Dave telling me how gratifying it is to watch INTERFET restore order in Dili. I don't have that kind of closure on East Timor.'

Tom nodded.

'What would you think if I told you I wanted to join the new UN mission there? Would I have a chance?'

Tom hesitated, his brow furrowed. Was he surprised that she too could make plans for a life without him?

'I think you'd have a strong chance,' he said, his face breaking into a smile. 'They need good people like you.'

'I'm not sure I want to go—if I want to be away from Juliette—but I'm fed up with DFAT. The culture's unhealthy—misogynistic, exploitative, sycophantic. Plus, I don't think I want to be a government lackey any more. This is a good opportunity, a springboard perhaps.'

The room fell quiet, each of them absorbing the implications of their decisions. Would Tom come back to her? Would she even wait?

'What about my question? Will you move in with me?'

'I have Juliette to think of. Not just myself.' While she spoke these words, others whispered guiltily of her desire to be with him to prove their love worthy of his divorce. 'During the week isn't a problem I guess, given I hardly see her. But on the weekends, I'll need to spend time with her. Time without you.'

'Of course.' He wrapped his arms around her waist. 'I'll take whatever time I can get.'

Tom was beaming as though she'd agreed to marry him. She tried to stop herself, but grinned back. Six weeks was a long time in their relationship, even if the moments were sandwiched between their hectic work schedules and Juliette. They kissed and flopped down on the couch. Whatever time they had would no doubt be naked, sleepless, punishing and blissful.

89

JAKARTA, OCTOBER 1999

They sat side by side in the back of a car, yet Ava and Tom were unable to hold hands. His gossipy UN driver might see them, and he'd let the embassy drivers know, who'd let her driver know, who'd spill the beans to Pete. Instead they allowed the edges of their little fingers resting on the seat to touch as they looked out their respective windows and pretended they wouldn't rather be staring into each other's eyes.

They'd just finished lunch at a nearby hotel café and Tom was dropping Ava off at the embassy. As they neared the gates, the usual large congregation of Indonesian protesters waved red and white flags and placards saying, *'Fuck off Aussies'* and *'Die Prime Minister Beaumont'*. The Indonesian police stood at the edges, smoking and chatting amicably with the demonstrators.

'Is it like this every day?' Tom asked her as his driver pulled up some distance away.

'Yes.'

He shook his head from side to side and turned white. 'No. No. This is too much like Dili.'

Ava took his hand in hers and squeezed hard. It was clammy and his breath was rapid. Suddenly there was a sound of smashing glass followed by a loud whoosh. They both jumped.

'Molotov cocktails,' Ava said, her hand reaching to reassure her racing heart. 'One reached my office yesterday, all the way up to the fourth floor.'

'I don't know how you cope with it,' Tom exhaled loudly.

'We're not quite back to normal yet, I mean stress wise.'

'I know. I get spooked at every sudden noise.'

'Me too.'

'They're setting something alight now that's wrapped in your flag.'

'That'll be an effigy of the PM. It happens a couple of times a day. Yet a few days ago, when an Australian protester burnt an Indonesian flag outside their embassy in Canberra, the Indonesians demanded we make flag burning illegal and jail the person responsible.'

'Now you know—Australia knows—what it feels like to be America,' Tom said, recoiling as the effigy went up in flames.

Ava supposed he was right. On the matter of East Timor, Australia was the global cop. They'd put up most of the money for the peacekeeping operation, and staked the lives of their troops as well as their international reputation on its success. She understood now why they must tolerate Indonesia's attacks and complaints about the flag burning no matter how duplicitous it felt.

'We're hoping it dies down once the Indonesian parliament formally annexes East Timor and hands it over to the UN, and the new president is elected,' she said.

'Are you sure you don't want me to drop you somewhere else? It doesn't feel safe here.'

'I'll be fine. I'll wait in the café next door til it dies down a bit.'

An hour later, she sat opposite Quentin at his desk. How tired he looked. Timor had taken its toll on them all.

'You have something you wanted to discuss?' he said.

'Yes.' She cleared her throat. 'I'd like to request an early departure from this post. My husband and I need to separate, properly I mean, and divorce. As you know, we've been living in the same house for months so he could take care of our daughter while I worked.'

Quentin pursed his lips and scrutinised her. 'When were you thinking?'

'Around Christmas, about seven weeks away. That would make my departure six months early.'

'I'll see what Canberra says.'

'Thank you.'

'I don't think you need worry though. You're nearing the end of your posting anyway. No one should hold a grudge against you.'

Ava found his reassurance unsettling. It hadn't occurred to her that despite all the things she'd done—changed jobs, worked ridiculous hours, risked her health and life, foregone leave, lived in the same house with Pete, sacrificed time with Juliette—her leaving early could reflect badly on her. Did the department not know what she'd given up? Or was she being the precious one? *No one's irreplaceable*, was the public service mantra.

She took a slow breath in and out. 'Also, I wanted to let you know that I've applied for a position in the new UN administration in East Timor. I know the government's looking for volunteers to join them and I was hoping DFAT would support a six-to-twelve-month secondment.'

Quentin raised his eyebrows then scowled. 'The two aren't tied are they. Your divorce and working for the UN?'

'No. As you know, I separated from my husband over eighteen months ago. Living in the same house has become untenable.'

'I guess I could relay the news separately so Canberra doesn't get the wrong idea.'

Ava was surprised he'd do this for her. Was it a form of acknowledgement?

'You do realise though, a secondment is unlikely to do much for your career. As much as I dislike the place myself, Canberra is where you want to be to get ahead.'

Ava was again warmed by his benevolence. On the other hand, where was the promotion he'd practically promised her when he'd betrothed East

Timor to her? She'd go nowhere without his patronage, yet he'd already forestalled her prospects by pulling back her performance appraisals, so much so that Donald had argued with him over it on at least two occasions, and apparently with raised voices and slamming doors.

'All right then. *Alea isacta est.* The die has been cast. I'll let you know.'

Ava smiled.

'One last thing. Are you having an affair with that Afro-American in the UN?'

Ava hesitated. 'No, I'm not,' she lied and exited the room.

90

JAKARTA, OCTOBER – NOVEMBER 1999

With only weeks left in Jakarta, Ava began wrapping up her life. Along with practical dispensations, she wrote thought pieces—deeper cables that pondered East Timor's future. Despite weeks of threats by nationalist politicians to block the move, the Indonesian parliament had just annexed the province and the UN was now temporarily responsible for its administration. East Timor was free at last. Ava was in the parliament when the vote happened, taking all of two minutes—two minutes after twenty-four years of struggle and immeasurable loss of life on all sides. She knew that international pressure was behind this. No annexation meant no international loans to prop up Indonesia's failed economy. Yet the way such an historic moment almost slipped by didn't seem fitting. Indonesia's last insult perhaps?

She made a list of outstanding matters that warranted attention and began a series of meetings with contacts, old and new. The issue that stood out for her was justice for human rights abuses in East Timor. She'd seen nothing on this topic from Canberra, the Australian mission to the UN, or from the UN itself, which felt like an invitation.

She stood next to Grant, the new Political Section head who'd replaced

Donald. He seemed agreeable enough, but knew little about East Timor, nor was he interested in learning. Indonesian politics was the main game for him and he largely left Ava to her own devices. He read her cable title and summary out loud:

East Timor – Human Rights Justice?

> *According to a wide range of embassy sources in Jakarta and Dili, justice for human rights abuses committed in East Timor in the lead up to and after the 1999 independence ballot is unlikely to ever be realised.*

'You can't say that,' he said.

'I'm only reporting the views of my contacts,' Ava said. 'The rest of the summary explains why.'

Grant continued reading aloud:

> *First, the Indonesians human rights commission's investigation is being severely restricted by political forces, meaning few cases will reach their courts.*

'Who told you that?' he asked.

'The head of the Indonesian Human Rights Commission.'

Grant looked surprised.

> *Second, the UN inquiry is being white-anted by the appointment of allegedly corrupt, low-profile and insignificant members and is thus not expected to deliver substantive outcomes.*

'A senior UN official advised me about that,' Ava pre-empted him.

> *Third, the mooted East Timorese–Indonesian–UN tribunal to try*

such cases does not enjoy the support of any of these parties and is unlikely to get off the ground.

He looked at her sceptically.

Finally, East Timorese leaders are not interested in fuelling more tension with their close neighbour by initiating their own justice process.

He sighed loudly as Ava bit her inside lip.

'Show it to the Ambassador.'

Ava walked the cable over to Quentin's office and told him that Grant was reluctant to let her send it. He read her summary.

'Is this accurate?' His eyes were penetrating.

'It's what my contacts told me. You can read my notes if you like, or you can check with them directly.'

'No need.' He handed her back the document. 'Send it if you wish. But Ava…'

She waited.

'Whether you get leave from the department to work for the UN or not, just remember that at some stage you'll need to go back and work on a desk in Canberra. You might want to consider that during your final weeks here.'

'Thank you,' she nodded.

After reading her cable through one last time, she pressed send. She wouldn't succumb to self-censorship, second-guessing The Minister's views or lying by omission. She aspired to be the frank and fearless public servant as was supposedly her job, despite her experience telling her that Canberra preferred to hear anything but the truth.

91

JAKARTA, DECEMBER 1999

Tom paced the edges of his lounge room floor while Ava sat on the couch resting her head in her hands. He was dressed to go out. She wore casual day clothes.

'Do you really want to spend your last night in Jakarta with the Portuguese Ambassador and not me?' she asked.

Tom stopped pacing to look at her. 'We'll see each other later tonight and tomorrow. I don't have to be at the airport till three.'

Ava stood, her body tensing. She'd tolerated, understood even, his going back to New York to sort himself out. But this, no, she didn't understand this. He should have refused the woman when she'd called a couple of hours ago.

'You're scaring me, Ava. I'm not used to such strong emotion.'

'Oh,' she cried in a mix of indignation and pain that had a throaty edge to it. 'Do you expect me to just sit here and wait for you because you'd rather go out to dinner with someone who's not even going to further your career, than with me?' She paused. 'Do you know how that makes me feel, Tom? It makes me feel cheap and unimportant. It makes me feel like a fool.'

Her patient waiting, her selfless understanding and hidden anguish welled up. The futility of it. Drowning in realisation she doubled over, breaking into sobs. What had she done?

Tom stayed on the other side of the room. He looked poised to walk over to her, but his feet remained steadfast. 'You are important to me, Ava. Surely you know that by now? But that doesn't mean this dinner isn't important to me too. There are lots of things I could have done instead of spending time with you. For example, I wanted to buy furniture and take it home, but I didn't. I chose to spend that time with you.'

Ava still couldn't stop sobbing. The depth of her pain scared her too. Willing herself to stop crying, she blew her nose and wiped her face.

'Furniture. Really?' Tom looked away. 'Did you think about inviting me to dinner?'

'How could I?'

'You could have said you already had a loose arrangement with me. We could've gone together.'

'It would have been obvious.'

'So what, Tom? People have probably worked it out anyway.'

He appeared surprised.

'I didn't tell you. Quentin asked me if we were having an affair. I told him no, but I should have told him to mind his own business. I think someone saw us together at a hotel.'

'Oh.' Tom frowned.

'Do you truly want love, Tom? Real love? Because real love isn't always safe and steady. It's crazy and scary and risky, and it takes guts. Do you have the guts for it, Tom? Do you have the courage for me and my love?'

'I don't know.'

Ava sat down, deflated.

'What really went wrong with your marriage, Ava?'

This again. It was as though he was accusing her, the puritan in him breaking through.

'I've told you already. I want a man who has the courage to love me wholly the way I love him. Pete never gave himself to me and he certainly never challenged me. Either he didn't care enough, or he was too scared. Perhaps he just didn't run that deep, or I didn't bring it out in him. In any case, he never got me. Over time I saw him as weak and lost respect for him. You can't have love without respect.'

Tom's face showed a mix of emotions. Ava saw recognition, then sadness. 'I always thought,' he hung his head low, 'that would be the speech my wife would make to me one day.'

Ava was again taken aback. To her Tom was everything her husband wasn't. Or was he? Why was he forcing her to see him through his wife's eyes? Was he attempting to push her away and destroy their love to make it easier for him to leave? Or was he also weak like Pete? Had she hoodwinked herself?

At last Tom walked up to her and wrapped his arms around her. She nestled into his shoulder, her tears once more flowing.

'You scare me, Ava. This whole situation scares me. You're the opposite of everything I've ever known, of what's been normal in my life. You challenge me, and make me better and greater and more than I am. But in so many ways you're unfathomable. It's as though you have enough to carry both of us. But would that be good for us? Is that what you need? Is that what I need? I worry I won't be enough for you either.'

Tom released her and checked his watch. 'If you're not here when I get back I'll understa—'

'I'll be here,' she said without hiding the dejection from her face.

He opened the door, turning and glancing at her before closing it behind him. Perhaps he believed it was the last time he'd see her.

Ava went into the bedroom where her things were strewn across the furniture and floor. She slowly gathered them up, folded them and placed them in her suitcase. Tomorrow Tom would vacate the apartment and she'd return home. Home, she laughed and shook her head. Her life felt like one great transition.

92

———————————————————

JAKARTA, DECEMBER 1999

At the top of the corridor leading to the plane, Ava and Tom stood facing each other. They'd spent the night and morning making love, his scent embedded under her skin. Ava felt dazed and bewildered. Surely Tom wouldn't—no couldn't go through with this.

He hugged then kissed her gently. 'I'll always love you,' he whispered.

'Will you?'

'Oh yes. You're inside me. A part of me, forever.'

Ava didn't doubt he meant it now, but was unconvinced about his future self.

Everyone boarded and the hostess signalled it was time for Tom to join them.

'I have to go.'

Her heart fluttered. Surely it would be impossible for him to separate himself from her.

He placed something small in her hand. A flat brown stone, oval and polished smooth except for a symbol carved in relief on one side. A mandala.

'It represents the twists and turns of life.'

Ava looked at him, the depth of her distress on her face. A half final plea.

'Think of me whenever you hold it,' he said. 'It helped me get through a lot. I kept it in my pocket and squeezed it whenever I had difficult meetings with *TNI* or Gabriel.'

Ava nodded. Words had abandoned her. There was nothing she hadn't already told him.

Tom marched into the tunnel, reached the end and waved. She gave him a modest half wave back, which seemed an inadequate ending. Or perhaps it was fitting, after all.

She stood alone, her suitcase by her side, waiting a little longer in case Tom changed his mind but the plane soon taxied away. She swallowed her hurt and humiliation and anger, picked up her suitcase and sauntered off. She'd return to her house, to Pete and Juliette. Her life a tangled, infuriating mess.

———

Ava had some time before she had to attend a meeting. She checked her private email account on the unsecured network and saw one from Tom. Her heart beat loudly as she opened it but a colleague entered. Instead she printed it and went into her office, closing the door behind her:

Dear Ava

I can't believe how much I miss you. I feel numb being back here in New York. I have no idea what I'm doing here or how I can live here to the full extent I want to live. Nancy is very sweet, but we have so much work to do if this marriage is to survive. Do I want it to survive? You and our time together seem more real to me than does life here, but do I have the necessary courage? I love you.

Tom

If only she could be with him. Being together again would answer his questions. Although she'd believed that before and yet... She made her way to the embassy car and was near her meeting when she got a call.

'Where are you?' Judy asked.

'Near the parliament.'

'Quentin wants you to take his place at a briefing with the new head of the UN mission to East Timor. It's in half an hour. Can you make it?'

'Sure.' It was unusual she hadn't been asked to attend in the first place. Such meetings were usually delegated to the expert, yet Quentin hadn't even informed her about it.

Inside the seventies-looking UN office, many floors up in a high-rise block, Ava sat alongside representatives from twenty embassies in a room featuring claustrophobically low ceilings. Paulo Vasconcelos, the Brazilian UN diplomat who'd been chosen to head the new East Timor mission, briefed them about the UN's plans. When the time came for questions Ava wanted to size Paulo up, but also get him to notice her. At the end of the meeting she hoped to introduce herself and enquire about her application to join his mission.

She let others ask their questions before putting up her hand. 'Thank you for your most interesting briefing.' Paulo nodded graciously. 'A consistent theme of your briefing has been reconciliation, especially with a view to repatriating East Timorese from west Timor. One barrier to reconciling with the militias is fear of prosecution, particularly since Bishop Basso and others made statements threatening prosecution. What's the UN's position on this? Should perpetrators of human rights abuses there be held to account or not?'

'A good question. Thank you for asking it,' Paulo said, which Ava took to mean it was difficult and he wasn't pleased. 'Currently the new UN mission doesn't have the capacity to investigate crimes, nor is there a judiciary to hear cases...'

He was going to bamboozle her with details, she thought, as he gave the group specifics about the creation of an independent judiciary.

'That said,' Paulo concluded, 'I'm not too concerned about how human rights abuses are dealt with in the longer term. Although they've been serious, many can be dealt with locally through community service. This is, after all, the way Aleixo is talking about things.'

After the meeting ended, Ava walked over to Paulo.

'I'm pleased to meet you in person,' she said shaking his hand. 'I've sent an application to join your mission and was wondering if you might know anything about its progress?'

'What? Why haven't I heard about this?' he said to his assistant standing nearby. 'We need good people like you. We'll take down your name and speed up the process.'

Ava smiled as she waited for the lift. It seemed fate had at last dealt her a helping hand. Order was trumping chaos. Joining the UN was meant to be.

93

SYDNEY, AUSTRALIA, DECEMBER 1999 – JANUARY 2000

The long narrow tube from their plane into Sydney's international airport ushered Ava, Juliette and Pete towards their new lives. Ava held Juliette's hand as Pete followed behind. Soon their family would be no more.

At the other end of customs and immigration, Denise's smiling face greeted them. Ava was exhausted after packing up the house, attending farewell parties and creating progressively bolder wrap-up cables. She was relieved to have a friend for support as she and Pete went their separate ways.

Denise hugged and kissed her and Juliette first, and then Pete.

'How does it feel to be home?' Denise asked.

Ava thought how fresh the air was without the penetrating stench of clove cigarettes and how easy it felt to no longer be the white-skinned outsider. But they'd been away for years, so how could she know yet?

'Good. I think.' She smiled.

'Weird, isn't it?' said Denise.

Ava nodded, her insides a tangle of emotions. Today was the end of her marriage and a confusion of sadness, liberation and worry for Juliette stuck in her throat. Her future with DFAT and the UN was unknown too, although she felt optimistic about her prospects. Then there was Tom. She still believed he'd join her, although their time apart was accruing. Her life was all endings and beginnings, and navigating her way day-by-day was her only way forward.

Denise turned her attention towards Pete. 'You look terrible. Are you all right?' She gave Pete a motherly hug.

Ava saw tears in Pete's eyes, but he blinked them back. She was happy Denise showed concern for him in a way she no longer could. She swallowed and forced herself to look away.

Grabbing their bags, Ava and Juliette said their goodbyes to Pete, and followed Denise. They planned to stay with her in Sydney for a while before joining Pete in Canberra, albeit in separate accommodation.

Ava looked down at Juliette and squeezed her hand. 'Are you all right?'

'Yes Mummy,' Juliette said, wrapped safely away inside herself.

––––––––

For the millennium New Year's Eve, an extravagant fireworks ceremony was planned around the Harbour Bridge. One of Ava and Denise's former friends from Jakarta was hosting a party. She claimed to have a view from her balcony, but when they got to her tiny flat it turned out to be a sliver of an outlook if you stood in a certain spot and peered through the buildings in front.

Ava sat inside playing games with the children.

'Are you coming out to the balcony?' Denise asked.

Ava shrugged. 'I'm not really in the mood for socialising.'

As the new millennium drew nearer, Ava reflected on her sense of achievement, but also on her grief. There was the loss of her expat diplomatic life, the tragedy of East Timor, the death of her and Pete's marriage, and her most recent realisation, that she'd never be a full-time mother again given she and Pete would share custody. Then there was Tom who continued to dangle her from a rope.

'I feel like a bit of a failure over my botched marriage,' she said to Denise.

'That's normal. It'll get better.'

Ava nodded as people began to countdown to midnight and the fireworks exploded across the sky up and down the harbour. Ava bristled at the noise that sounded too similar to gunfire. The people around them hugged and kissed and wished each other a happy millennium.

Juliette stood, unsure of what to do.

Ava hugged her hard. 'Happy New Year, darling! Everything will be better soon. You'll see.'

Juliette smiled at her mother as though she wanted to believe her, but couldn't quite.

Ava also hugged the twins and last of all Denise. Their embrace was long and hard, perhaps embodying the extraordinary trials and tribulations they'd shared.

'Let's hope 2000 is a better year than the last,' Denise said.

They ushered the kids onto the balcony, leading them through the adults to view the fireworks.

'This might cheer you up,' Denise said. 'I overheard the kids talking about their mum's jobs. Juliette called you a hero for what you did in East Timor.'

'A hero?' Ava welled with gratitude. 'Sometimes that girl is wise beyond her years. She has a beautiful heart, even if she tries to hide it.'

Amid the merriment, Ava heard her mobile phone ringing. The number was international, American.

'Ava speaking,' she said, both hoping and dreading it would be Tom.

'It's Tom.'

'It's good to hear your voice. It just turned midnight here. Happy New Year!'

'Happy New Year to you. It's really great to hear your voice too.'

Ava thought she heard distance and sympathy in his voice. She escaped the party into the stairwell.

'I ah…' he began. 'As you know, Nancy and I saw our families in Boston over Christmas, and I've been doing some thinking.'

Ava stiffened at the formal tone of his voice. It was almost as though he was reading from a statement.

'I need to try to work out my marriage because of all the good between Nancy and me. I have to be sure. I can't just walk away.'

Everything around Ava stopped—the fireworks, the noise of the party, her thoughts, the planet.

'I'm not courageous like you, Ava. But I'll always want to see you—I'll always want to stay in touch with you.'

Ava stood in an emotional vacuum. Slowly the meaning of his words penetrated her mind. He was actually tossing aside what they had. But they were soul mates. And what did he mean by always wanting to see her. Did he want an ongoing affair?

'Thanks for being honest. I'm not sure how I feel about staying in touch. I'm a bit of an all or nothing person.'

'I'm sad to hear that.'

Sad? Ava held back her rising anger. 'I'm at a party. I have to go.'

'I'll write you.'

'Good-bye, Tom,' she said, pressing the red button for no.

94

SYDNEY, JANUARY 2000

Tom called a few times over the next few days. Ava didn't answer, feeling a mix of betrayal, foolishness and confusion. But today she was ready to communicate. She wanted them to go out with dignity, not the fear or weakness he'd demonstrated, or the hatred and anger that had been plaguing her of late.

After two hours of drafting, and another of cutting out sentiments that were too raw, she came up with what she hoped was a dignified letter.

Dear Tom

It was good to hear your voice the other night. I only wish I could have touched your face, kissed your lips and run my fingers over your body. I miss you so very much. You are still fresh in my mind and I wonder if I am to you? Since meeting you, I discovered beauty. Everything is more—I see, feel and understand more; the colours, sky and music are more. The world will never be the same after you, which is glorious but at the same time cruel and unfair because you're no longer in mine. I don't want a world without you and yet I feel lucky to have experienced it at all.

I've been in turmoil and pain since you left Jakarta. You told me you want to work out your marriage because of all the good in it. You also said you have to be certain and you're not courageous like me. At the same time, you always want to hear from me.

This doesn't make sense. You've made your choice and it's not fair to either me or Nancy to have a former lover hovering in the wings. Besides, I want the pain, the uncertainty, to stop. The only way I know to do that is to say goodbye to you, for good. You've made your decision, Tom. Now let me go.

I wish you only happiness and that you make your choice work. I will always love you, but please do not contact me again.

Ava

She sent the email, wishing she'd told him he'd destroyed love for her because how could she possibly find what they'd had again? But that would have demeaned her. Besides, after months of waiting, it felt good to take back control. Ha!

This was the first time she'd been single in years. Who was she without a man to reflect against? Which direction would she take? Her head spun with choice and uncertainty, but a least she wouldn't need to justify her decisions to anyone. Suddenly it felt to Ava like… Like freedom.

———

As well as applying to join the UN, Ava hoped to be promoted in DFAT. She had no guarantee the UN posting would come through and wanted to keep her options open. To be promoted she needed the support of someone senior, a patron, which in her case had to be Quentin. He was on holiday, but she'd got his private email address and messaged him a couple of weeks ago asking for his endorsement. Today she got a response.

Dear Ava

While last year was without doubt annus mirabilis, *the year of horrors,*

I think there are more competitive people who I know will be applying for promotion in the forthcoming round. My advice to you would be to wait. You will get there.

Sincerely

Quentin

Ava reeled with astonishment. She'd got top performance ratings, three division heads had offered her sought-after positions in Canberra, and she'd received multiple congratulatory emails from colleagues on her achievements during her posting. Yet for Quentin, she wasn't sufficiently competitive. She thought of Denise and Sharon, and how he'd failed to invite them to embassy media briefings. If only she had the threat of a newspaper headline to dangle over his head.

She deleted his email, wiping him from her life, although perhaps that was going a little too far. So much for a millennium of progress. She closed her eyes, tilted her head upwards and begged for the UN posting to come through.

Her mobile rang. It wasn't the UN but DFAT's head of staffing. Until recently he'd headed up the East Timor section in Canberra, so they knew each other well.

'You'll be coming back to the EU trade desk,' Paul told her.

'EU trade?' she said checking she'd heard him correctly.

'Yes. EU trade.'

EU trade was a non-career position and would normally be given to a non-graduate officer. Taking it would be career death if she didn't die first of boredom. What was she being punished for? Were they trying to get rid of her?

'But I've had offers from three division heads for career positions, and I was told by your staff I was free to accept any of them.'

'The EU division has been pushing for someone good for a long time,' Simon said. 'You've had a decent run. It's time to do something for the department.'

She was speechless. It was she who was due a reward and he knew it. 'What about my possible secondment to the UN mission in East Timor?'

'We can't guarantee you'll be given leave. All secondments are subject to operational requirements.'

'I understand the Australian government is encouraging people to volunteer for a secondment there and you haven't got enough applications. Am I not a logical candidate?'

'Nothing is guaranteed. We'll let you know.'

'Thanks very much.'

Ava hung up and threw her mobile down onto the couch. Not only were Quentin and DFAT denying her the promotion she'd been promised and deserved, but they were dismissing her work in extraordinary circumstances as insignificant. But why was her former East Timor colleague doing this? Was he under instruction from that narky deputy secretary who'd complained about her coming home early? He'd always disliked her, probably because she'd refused to be reverential towards him. Maybe the fact that her colleague happily toed the line was what made him a successful public servant and her not so much.

95

KUPANG, WEST TIMOR, JANUARY 2000

In a refugee internment camp across the border in west Timor, Gabriel sat at a table in a demountable building. His face was puffy and red, and he had dark rings under his eyes. In his hands was a document, which he read half-heartedly, turning his head at a knock on the door.

'What is it?' he barked.

The door opened slowly. A short militiaman poked his head through and said, 'I have news, *bapak*.'

Gabriel waved him in.

The militiaman stooped to ingratiate himself. 'It's not good *pak*.'

'*Maksudnya?*' Meaning?

The militiaman took a deep breath. 'I found a grave, *pak*. At the orphanage in the foothills of Dili.'

'And?'

'The grave was for…'

'For?' he said loudly.

'For Isabel, *pak*.'

Gabriel gasped, the document falling from his hands onto the ground.

'She got lost in the hills behind Liquica and fell. She wasn't found until the next day and by the time she got to the clinic in Dili she'd lost a lot of blood.' The militiaman hesitated. 'She died on the same day INTERFET—'

'And the baby?' he asked, his eyes wide with hope.

The militiaman hung his head low and shook his head. Gabriel's body stiffened and he turned away.

'There was an inscription, *pak*, on a wooden cross at Isabel's grave. It said, *Isabel Cardoso. May you find peace with God. Begging your forgiveness, Sebastiao.*'

Gabriel slammed his fists down on the table, his drink spilling. 'Get out!' he screamed.

The militiaman crept backwards out the door, closing it firmly behind him. The night air around him was filled with the hum of generators and the sound of a crying child.

Unexpectedly, a loud crack pierced the night air. The militiaman froze for a near eternity, then turned and raced back into Gabriel's office. Lying on an upturned chair on the ground he found Gabriel, a hole in his head, his blood and brains spewed across the walls and floor.

96

SYDNEY, AUSTRALIA, JANUARY 2000

It was a sunny day, not too hot, on the harbour side of Manly Beach. To the north of the ferry wharf Ava and Denise relaxed on towels on the pristine white sand, a row of Norfolk Pines neatly separating the beach from the street behind them. The women watched their children skim stones across the top of the calm sea.

'They're not very good at it,' Denise said.

'They need help.' Ava walked over to them. 'You have to hold the stone between your thumb and forefinger like this,' she said, showing them. 'Then as you bring your arm back, make sure your thumb is up. Now, as it comes forward, you flick your wrist and let the stone go.'

The kids got the hang of it and Ava returned to Denise. Putting her hand in her dress pocket, she felt the smooth side of Tom's stone, and then its rough carved surface reminding her of her crushed hopes for their future together. With a sigh, she took two documents from her bag. One was an acceptance letter to join the UN mission in East Timor with today's date as a deadline, the other was a resignation letter to DFAT. Staffing hadn't agreed to give her leave for the UN secondment, insisting she return to the dead-end job they'd offered her.

'What are you going to do?' Denise asked.

Ava turned to look at her. 'I'm torn.'

'About Juliette?'

Ava nodded, drawing in her lips to mute her anguish at the thought of leaving Juliette behind. At the same time, refusing the UN's offer and staying with DFAT felt untenable.

'Would I be a bad mother if I accepted the UN job? Pete says I'm selfish to even consider it.'

'Pfft,' Denise jeered. 'All mothers do the best they can in the circumstances. As for Pete, does he have a job yet?'

'No. He wants me to stay in DFAT in Canberra.'

Ava smiled at the kids' joy with their stones.

'Ask yourself this. How important is the UN job to you?'

'It's my dream,' Ava said without hesitation.

'Well then, if it's what you need to do…'

Was joining the UN what she needed, or what she wanted to do? If she worked for the UN, she'd spend six to twelve months away from Juliette, although she'd see her one week out of every eight, which wasn't bad considering it would be one-on-one time. It would also be a stepping stone to a better life for Juliette—postings in places like New York and Geneva where she'd get the best education. Then there was the fact that the UN offered her resolution on East Timor, something DFAT was blocking. Becoming part of the East Timor solution felt like an imperative.

But Juliette was her anchor, and despite her daughter's resistance, she knew she was probably Juliette's. Her heart ached. 'It's impossible. Being the mother and the breadwinner.'

Denise nodded. 'But that's our lot.'

'If I were a man, I doubt I'd feel this silent judge sitting on my shoulder.'

Her phone rang. 'Ava?' the male voice said. 'It's Dave.'

'Dave,' she grinned and moved away. 'How are things?'

'Pretty decent,' he said.

'And how's East Timor?'

'I can't describe how satisfying it is to see Australian Black Hawks flying through the skies. No more *TNI* and militias.'

'I'm jealous,' Ava said, feeling the pull to return stronger than ever.

'Listen. That Timorese girl you asked me about.'

'Isabel?'

'I got some answers.' Dave sighed. 'I'm sorry to say, but I found her grave at that Silesian orphanage. The one at the foothills in Dili.'

Ava sat down on a nearby low wall, closing her eyes and blinking back tears. She was being ridiculous. She barely knew the girl. They'd only met a couple of times during the massacre investigation and then when she'd given her blood—blood that would forever remain in East Timor.

'Dammit.' She'd hoped for a miracle, one piece of good news from that dim time.

'Someone made a makeshift cross to mark the spot where she's buried.' He read the inscription out to her.

'Who's Sebastiao? And why does he want her forgiveness?'

'The nuns said he dug her grave himself.'

'Thanks for looking into it, Dave.'

'Thought you'd also like to know, a cable went out from Jakarta this week on restoring relations with Indonesia. It was called *Mending Fences*.'

'Wow. Already.'

'You looking forward to working back in Canberra?'

'Actually Dave, I'm thinking of leaving.'

'Oh. Hmm. All the things you possess—passion, morals, a conscience —they're the things that've been missing from Australian foreign policy the last twenty-four years. Don't chuck it in. We need you.'

'Unfortunately, that's not the message I'm getting.'

'I put a word in for you when I was there over Christmas.'

'Really?'

'I told them to be nice to you, that you'd been through a really tough time—in Timor I mean and with your divorce. Told them they should treat you gently.'

'You said what?' Ava felt as though he'd put her on a pedestal, which he'd then jerked from under her. She knew this tactic of Dave's. He'd maligned another female colleague slated to be in Timor before him as being over reactive, ensuring he got to go instead. But she was no threat to him. DFAT's recent behaviour started to make more sense.

'Gotta go, mate. Talk soon.'

'We may well,' she said with an edge to her voice.

SYDNEY, JANUARY 2000

Seated on the same low wall, Ava weighed up her options one last time. The UN, DFAT or neither? Australia, East Timor or somewhere else? Voices in her head quarrelled as Juliette approached.

'Mum,' Juliette said. 'I can't find any more stones.'

'Here.' Ava pulled the shiny stone Tom gave her from her pocket and placed the carved surface on her palm. 'This is a good one. Nice and flat.'

'Thanks,' Juliette said, looking it over. 'Are you sure I can use this one? It looks kind of…special.'

For a moment Ava wasn't sure. She felt herself withdrawing from Juliette and her surroundings. The past washed over her and she felt overcome by a wave of malaise—the long hours she'd worked in Jakarta, having to prove herself repeatedly to those in power, waiting for overdue acknowledgement, her protracted separation from Pete and her tireless patience with Tom. Why had she worked so hard and given up so much? What or who had it been for? The Timorese?

She smiled. Who did she think she was, placing herself in the middle of others' genuine woes when her troubles were comparatively insignificant? All she'd been was history's scribe, and right now she questioned how good she'd been at that. It had felt so important at the time, so life and death to tell the unsavoury truths she hoped would persuade those in power to prevent a war and save lives. With hindsight, it was clear their agendas were decided long before. The way Australia had backed the ballot, reassuring *TNI* and other senior Indonesians the vote could go their way; how Beaumont and Stretton had downplayed human rights violations, minimising the predictions of a scorched earth strategy while assuring the world *TNI* would provide adequate security when this was always doubtful. The Australian government had played with the lives of the Timorese to put the problem of East Timor to bed once and for all. The Indonesians were always going to lose the ballot and destroy the place, the Timorese girl Isabel was always going to die and, in the end, UN peacekeepers were always going to go in. In the grander scheme of things, Ava saw she'd probably made little difference. It was naive and grandiose of her to have thought otherwise. Yet, in the name of truth she'd put her job ahead of everything else, setting herself apart, risking her livelihood and life too. Perhaps Pete had a point after all. But what should she have done? Remained silent, been compliant like Quentin had demanded, reported what the government wanted to hear and won a promotion? Should she have betrayed herself?

Juliette stood in front of her wanting an answer on the stone. Ava forced herself back into the moment, struck by her daughter's unashamed eagerness. If only she could find her own innocence again, but she'd experienced too much darkness and oppression.

Then suddenly, for just a brief sprawling moment, the weight of the last few years fell away, and she became like Juliette. Perhaps it was the warm sun on her back, the cleansing air in her lungs and the sounds of peace interrupted only by the calm waves lapping and joyful children squealing. But for now it was plenty, no, it was everything to be here with Juliette on this white sandy beach. She was free and with that freedom she'd chosen to stand up for what she believed was true. She could have lied in her East Timor reports, or omitted things to advance her career, but she hadn't, and perhaps that was something. It had been life and death in East Timor, and she'd helped some people, saved a few lives perhaps, which was better than nothing. And if that media report on the Liquica cop's shooting really did influence the US president, well that really would be something.

She understood now she would never be recognised for what she'd done. But in this moment, sitting under the midday sun with Juliette for whom her love would always be necessary and enduring no matter the circumstances, it was plenty. In the end it did triumph—love. For Juliette, for her choices, for this day.

Ava smiled because she was no longer the restless woman who awaited the next day, next promotion, next job or next relationship—*the* one. All those promises had slipped through her fingers like the sand between her toes. Perhaps her expectation that jobs or lovers would bring her completion were always an illusion. But she recognised now as she inhaled her daughter's guilelessness, that she was no longer the uncertain young woman who'd got on that plane to Jakarta a few years ago.

She wrapped her hands around Juliette's. 'Yes my love. I'm absolutely sure you can use the stone. But only if you give me the biggest hug and hugest kiss first.'

A naughty smile crept over Juliette's face before she wrapped her arms around her mother and squeezed her, placing a firm kiss on her cheek. Juliette turned and ran to the water where she carefully positioned herself. She practised her wrist action a few times and when she finally let go, Tom's stone jumped along the surface of the water five times before sinking into obscurity.

'That's my best one yet!' Juliette shouted, jumping into the air and looking back at her mother.

'Well done,' Ava hooted, clapping proudly.

Ava dropped her sarong onto the sand and sprinted towards the sea. She grabbed Juliette's hand and together they ran laughing into the water, into the vast expanse of the world that lay waiting for them.

ACKNOWLEDGMENTS

I wish to thank the following people: Phillip Haddad for his support; my children for being there; editor Andrea Barton for her structural editing advice and editor Marcia Batton for her copy editing and proofreading work; Arts Law Australia for providing affordable legal advice; and beta reader Bronwyn Kelly for her constructive comments and encouragement.

BIBLIOGRAPHY
SHORTENED URL LINKS PROVIDED

1. Chapter 3.

Inspired by the official resignation speech given by former President Suharto on 21 May 1998. English text as quoted in *The New York Times,* May 21 1998 https://tinyurl.com/pmewzcms

(longer URL https://archive.nytimes.com/www.nytimes.com/library/world/asia/052198indonesia-suharto-text.html)

Bahasa Indonesia text as provided by Yusril Ihza Mahendra, the President's formal speech writer, to *Merdeka* 'Ini pidato terakhir Soeharto sebelum lengser,' Kamis, 21 Mei 2015 by Yulistyo Pratomo.

https://tinyurl.com/np82z9vw

2. Chapter 23.

Don Greenlees and Robert Garran,

Deliverance: The inside story of East Timor's fight for freedom, Crow's Nest, NSW, Allen & Unwin, 2002, pp 76-7.

3. Jonathon Head, "East Timor Breakthrough", BBC News (United Kingdom), 28 January 1999, available at https://tinyurl.com/45bpwz49

(http://news.bbc.co.uk/1/hi/events/indonesia/latest_news/263828.stm), accessed 20 April 2009, quoting Information Minister Yunus Yosfiah's announcement on 27 January

4. https://tinyurl.com/e6me9s Quoting Information Minister Yunus Yosfiah's announcement on 27 January 1999

"East Timor: incident at Liquica - Report of Embassy Visit 9-13 April 1999 (DFAT)" in *East Timor in Transition 1998–2000: An Australian Policy Challenge,* Department of Foreign Affairs and Trade, Commonwealth of Australia, Canberra, 2001, p 189

5. Inspired by a report allegedly signed by Major General H R Ganardi, a retired Major General and member of the Indonesian Government's East Timor Task Force, written in his official capacity as Assistant to the Minister, Lt Gen (ret) Feisal Tanjung, with responsibility for Internal Politics and as a member of the joint ministerial body on East Timor (P4-OKTT) over which Tanjung presided. See Garnadi, "Gambaran umum apabila Opsi I gagal," July 3 1999 (Yayasan HAK Collection, Doc #35)

https://tinyurl.com/cd4besen (https://history.ucla.edu/sites/default/files/u184/robinson/robinson_east_timor_1999_english.pdf)

Also see https://tinyurl.com/4emf673y

(https://etan.org/et2000a/january/22-31/31iscor.htm)

6. Speech of press release broadcast over the radio in East Timor by Ian Martin, Special Representative for the Secretary General on East Timor, on 29 August 1999, as mentioned briefly on p 13 in *Appendix C, The United Nations and East Timor: A Chronology* of an APH House of Representatives Committee Report https://tinyurl.com/yf89zd64

https://www.aph.gov.au/Parliamentary_Business/Committees/Joint/Completed_Inquiries/jfadt/army/ETrptinx referencing http://www.un.org/peace/etimor/etimor.htm (no longer live)

7. Statement made simultaneously by Ian Martin, Special Representative for the Secretary General on East Timor, and UN Secretary General, Kofi Annan, on 4 September 1999 www.un.org

8. *AFP* report from televised speech by President Habibie as reported by ETAN https://tinyurl.com/m25beurs (http://etan.org/et99b/1tmp.htm)

GLOSSARY

(t) – denotes Tetun (language)

The rest is in Bahasa Indonesia (Indonesian language)

ABRI, Angkatan Bersenjata Republik Indonesia – The Indonesian Armed
Forces, so named until November 1998

ada apa – what's up?

adat – local customs

Aitarak – Thorn, militia group based in Dili

alin-feto – younger sister (t)

apa namanya, kesepakatan itu? – what's the name of that agreement?

arak – alcoholic spirit distilled from coconut palm trees

ayo – come on

bakso – meatball soup

bapak / pak – sir, Mr, father

Batak – Northern Sumatran, Batak-speaking ethnic group in Indonesia

belum – not yet

becak – rickshaw

Besi Merah Putih – Red and White Iron, militia group based in Liquica bodoh – stupid

bondia – good morning (t)

bonoite – good evening, good night (t)

botardi – good afternoon (t)

bu / ibu – madam, Mrs, mother

bumihangus – scorched earth

cinta monyet – puppy love (direct translation, monkey love)

CNRT, Conselho Nasionale Republik Timor – National Council of Timorese Resistance

deskulpa – sorry (t)

DFAT – Department of Foreign Affairs and Trade

di mana – where

diam – silence

dwifungsi – dual function

Falintil, Forças Armadas da Libertação Nacional de Timor-Leste – The Armed Forces for the National Liberation of East Timor, the military wing of political party FRETILIN that opposed integration with Indonesia (t)

FPDK – United Front for East Timorese Unity and Autonomy

Gardapaksi – Upholders of Integration Guard militia group that later evolved into other groups

halus – refined, soft, smooth

hei – hey

ICMI, Ikatan Cendekiawan Muslim Indonesia – The Indonesian Association of Muslim Intellectuals

iha o-nia liafuan – have your say (t)

ini – this

ibu / bu – madam, Mrs, mother

independencia – independence (t)

integrasi – integration (t)

ipa – sweetheart (t)

Intel – Intelligence forces

kampung – village

Kijang – SUV-looking Indonesian car

KKN, acronym for Korupsi Kolusi Nepotisme – corruption collusion nepotism

Kopassus – Indonesian Special Forces

Krakendang – sweet caffeine drink

kretek – clove cigarette

krismon, krisis moneter – monetary crisis

losmen – basic lodging

maaf – sorry, pardon me

macet – stuck, traffic jam

makanan busuk – bad (off) food

maksudnya – meaning, intention

mana – older sister, older female cousin, woman older or of similar age (t)

mas – brother, sir, sibling

masuk angin – catch a cold

maun – older brother, older male cousin (t)

menina – miss, young single lady (t)

merekayasa – to engineer

milisi – militia

na'i maromak – Lord God (t)

nak – child, colloquial

ne'e asun-hein – guard dog (t)

nggak – no, colloquial

oan-feto – daughter, niece (t)

oan-mane – son, nephew (t)

obrigada – thank you (t)

padi – rice (seeds)

Padre – Father, Catholic priest

pak / bapak – sir, Mr, father

pao – bread roll (t)

pergilah – go away

permisi – excuse me

persona non grata – a diplomat whose status of diplomatic immunity is
withdrawn

polisi – police

preman – criminal, hoodlum, thug

pulang – go home

sambal – chilli paste

selamat jalan – goodbye

selamat pagi – good morning

selamat siang – good afternoon

selamat sore – good evening

senor – sir, Mr (t)

senora – madam, Mrs (t)

siapa namanya – what's your name

sin – yes (t)

sop ayam – chicken soup

televizaun – TV (t)

Timor Leste – East Timor (t)

Timor Timur – East Timor

TNI, Tentara National Indonesia – The Indonesian Armed Forces, so
named from November 1998

to'o loron seluk – until we meet again (t)

UN – United Nations

viva merdeka – long live freedom

west Timor – Timor is the name of an island. The term west Timor is not a
proper noun (name) but a description of the western part of Timor, so it is
not capitalised. The western part of Timor is part of the province Nusa
Tengarra Timor

ya – yes

www.ingramcontent.com/pod-product-compliance
Lightning Source LLC
Chambersburg PA
CBHW020007120726
47903CB00004B/1170